Deep
Delta T

Deep Delta T

A journey into the universe and into the Spirit.
(Second Edition)

Dan Lemaire

Deep Delta T is a planet that is so far from Earth that the potential for human survival there cannot be fully assured. Two travelers make the journey, believing that God will make a way for them. What they discover there is completely unexpected, and it changes everything for them and their 'Close Team' on Earth. It eclipses their prior concerns about survival, impressing them instead to reevaluate the real purposes for which they have been brought here.

Deep Delta T, Second Edition

© 2021 by Dan Lemaire

Endorsements:

"...explore a startling idea that I have never seen before anywhere. When the book came to an end, my eyes were tired, but I had a happy heart. I felt like one feels after reading The Narnia Chronicles.
Pastor David Johnson

"beautiful imagery and incredible concepts ...these concepts drew me into the world, and left me wanting more.
Sean Moss, author of 'Anhedonia and the Orion Sound'

Are you one of those who tap deep into their imagination and ask "what if?" I'm sure most of us do. This book will answer one of those "what ifs" for sure!! I couldn't put this book down and when I did I couldn't stop thinking about what was going to happen next! Mr. Lemaire has written an out of this world story. Dare I say sequel?   Sean E

...a deeper journey of who we are and who we could be. Thought provoking, leading you to a desire for more. I highly recommend it.
Victor Tremblay

"It was a wonderful read. Had it not been for my work schedule and needed hours of sleep that made me put the book down, I would have read it in a day. It definitely is a trip into deep spirituality. There were several times when I sensed very strongly the presence of the Almighty."
Alex Vargas, Missionary Pastor

"The story line is absolutely brilliant!...very significant simple truth."
John Trentalange, PhD, LPC

"Just reading about [certain incident], like Anj, I almost fell over (internally). Your book is making me 'dizzy.' That's a good thing!"
Miss Missionary

Dan Lemaire takes you on an exciting space journey where the two main characters find themselves wanting to escape from the troubles of this world to start a new life...and is a must read." Josh Skroch

"The author drew me in and made me want to root for the characters right away. I was pleasantly surprised by Deep Delta T.
Pastor CJ Ellis

Acknowledgments:

Georgann, my bride of forty-two years brought me to tears when she read my rough draft.
She was the first to have a peek at the work for which God had been holding me at the computer for weeks and months. Thank you, hon, for your profound encouragement.

Thanks go to Gil and Todd of the Restoration Place, which was the peaceful context for writing most of this story. Your personal, heartfelt encouragement was meaningful, probably more than I, or you, fully recognize.
Many thanks to Victor and Heather of Grace Manor, where the final revisions of the narrative took place. It is a lovely place to work.

All of my other rough draft readers, John, David, Nate, Jill, Mark, Tim, and Aug, your feedback is what moved this from a rough draft to a finished work, to the best of my ability. Let me assure you, your input was crucial, so helpful and encouraging.

To all those who have prayed for me and for this whole venture, thank you so much.

I think the Lord wanted this story written because He kept feeding it to me, sometimes line by line, and it was an exciting adventure to be involved in such a project.
May it bring glory to You, Father.

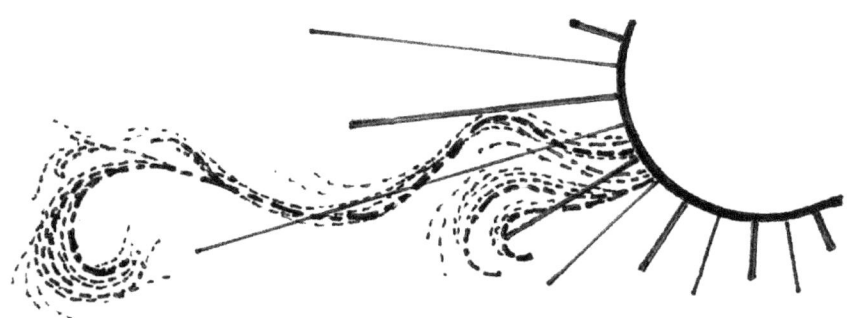

Chapter One

Soundlessly gliding through space, a titanium-clad vessel rotated ever-so-slowly on the axis of its direction, and the light of three nearby stars shone through the round portholes, projecting bright discs that glided across the interior bulkheads of the cabin, like streetlights through a bedroom window. Snug in her hyper-sleep capsule, the young astronaut was unaware of it, but at that moment the lights blinked on in the ship, a predetermined electronic contribution to her programmed awakening. LED illumination flooded the ship's interior with synthetic brilliance that washed out the starlight projected on the walls. The light revealed two hyper-sleep capsules. The one which held her displayed a tiny blinking green light, indicating that her reanimation sequence had been initiated.

The first of her five senses to register since the prep-room at Launch Central was her hearing, as she became aware of the gentle swishing sound of oxygen-rich gas being added to the hyper-sleep enclosure. Her first halting attempts to inhale after six years of a below-hibernation breathing rate felt at first like something she was dreaming, but this could not be a dream; she was actually breathing.

So far out in space that only starlight and gamma-rays crisscross carelessly, this ship was an alien visitor, bearing the fingerprints of man. Inside her capsule, there was the flutter of an eyelash. Her eyes were tracking back and forth slowly under her eyelids. She was coming to. Gradually, bits of consciousness began to come online in her prefrontal cortex, although her eyes were still closed. Into her conscious thought came, "Alpha Centauri." It was uncomplicated. It emerged as her first working thought in six years, and still only a rather dreamy recollection.

Like one waking up in an unfamiliar room, she began to mentally search through what she knew and put it together. She was not yet capable of recalling all of the training, programming, and equipment that had to have worked flawlessly to bring two people alive to Alpha Centauri, but that name and location in the universe was her starting point in recalling where she was, and why.

She was rationally collecting all the information she was going to need in the next thirty minutes. Intruding upon all of that, came her gathering realization that she *really was* waking up. She recalled how often it had been discussed, on the basis of how many different things could go wrong, that the two astronauts might never survive to awaken. Everyone knew the risks. Her first emotion blossomed within her mind without invitation; it was surprise, simple happy surprise, and an easy smile lit up her face that had been an inert mask for years. Her eyes opened. She could dimly see that the cabin lights were on through the translucent lid of her capsule. More joy emerged, and thankfulness swept up from within her. "I am awake! I am alive!" Everything seemed to be in order as far as she could tell so far. "Oh thank God," her thoughts responded, her heart celebrating for this moment about which her colleagues had been so openly skeptical. 'Would they awake and live?' Science said 'Yes,' according to the numbers, but there were so many computerized mechanical operations that could have failed.

Faith also said 'Yes,' which was why she had voluntarily offered herself for this mission. She had set aside every concern based on that faith. Many times she had told her Launch Central Close Team, "God's fingerprints are all over this whole expedition. The manner in which this came together, the people who have been brought together to work on it, the newest revelations of scientific minds - everything about it bears the marks of God's sovereign touch." So when it came down to whether to make this mission a 'go' or not, she was assured that it was 'go.' When they were at the final point of decision, she said again, "I know that I am not going to die in a cold machine trillions of miles from home. I am going, but it is not for the purpose of dying out there. It is for the purpose of living out there."

Being 'out there' she knew was her calling from God. He had given her a premonition about it when she was only ten years old - a child's elemental knowing that she was destined to be a leading figure in space exploration. She had ceaselessly set herself in that direction ever since. Now in her capsule, awakening and becoming aware of the subtle Presence that imparted to her the original vision and the confidence for this expedition, she spoke to Him in her spirit, "Yes, I'm here; I'm here; we've made it; I thank You; I praise You with all my heart."

Gradually coming to consciousness in that capsule, she was also feeling the beginnings of a penetrating headache and hearing a soft pillow-pounding sound of her heartbeat in her inner ear that came with it. Aside from that, the only sound in the capsule at that moment was the whisper of oxygen.

Her thoughts began to crystallize around the programmed plans for which she had repeatedly trained; the actions she must execute next. Her first scheduled and practiced task was to squeeze the activation switch already cradled in her right hand, placed there by her handler well after she was deeply unconscious. She could now feel it there, a little heavy and solid, reminding her about all of the drills that had prepared her for this moment.

Her Launch Control Close-Team, in attempted humor, referred to the white plastic-encased capsule inside of which she was awakening as the 'coffin,' and the reality was that she and March, the pilot in the other capsule, could very well perish out there, for a dizzying variety of reasons, in those oh-so-sophisticated boxes in this oh-so-sophisticated vehicle.

The sophisticated box now began an audible four-minute countdown. There it was, a familiar, friendly, recorded voice coaching her as she prepared her body for action. "Alright Anj, you know the drill; count off three seconds to breathe in, and three seconds to breathe out, very regular and easy," Carla's friendly recorded voice said. "Remain still but allow yourself to become aware of your body. Tune your awareness to your muscles and limbs now, for they will begin to function soon, after a long stillness. Begin to feel a sensation of warmth move from the top of your head, slowly down over your face, your neck, warming your shoulders...."

By the end of that count-down, Anj had wiggled her fingers, flexed her arms and legs, and turned her head right and left. She was now to begin moving out. At the tone, she squeezed the activation switch and watched the curved Lexan lid to her coffin slide to her right with a reassuring hum and a soft thump when it was fully opened.

Because of months of rehearsing in the simulator, much that was coming into her view and awareness was quite familiar except for the starkly unfamiliar position of her present location in the cosmos, almost four-and-a-half light-years from home. Being aware that she was the first human being to awaken to that reality was both thrilling and terrifying. Part of her training had included psychological preparation for what she would be facing upon coming out of hyper-sleep so unbelievably distant from Earth. For the moment, she successfully bracketed and set aside thrilling and terrifying emotions by directing her mind to the immediate agenda that required calm reason. As a former fighter pilot, experienced in staying rational in situations that could get the untrained person killed, she knew how to do that, but knew that she would also eventually need to face her own emotional state that was aroused by being in this place. Right now, it was essential to allow the familiar agenda to press in and take precedence.

From her prone position on her back in the coffin, the lid now open, she gradually and cautiously pulled herself to a sitting position. Five-foot-eight and slight, her straight dark brown hair unfolded and relaxed down around her shoulders, for it had been growing slowly all this time. Focused, she did not look around yet. In weightlessness, sitting up was not at all strenuous, but flexing after six years without movement revealed significant stiffness that she noted would have to be worked out. Bending to that position helped her circulation open up, and her muscles came to full alert. It was actually a pleasant awareness of her body's function, the first she had experienced since going to sleep. It ignited a cascade of motivations warming up to the agenda for which she had trained and programmed her entire being. From this moment on, it would be pay-off for all the study, the drills, and the endless simulator sessions.

That sharp headache was beginning to subside now, as Browning had said it would. As Consortium for Space Exploration (CSE) Launch Control Leader, he sometimes gave reassurance that was psychologically encouraging even if not entirely backed up by data. This headache, data had predicted, but the rate at which it would subside was mostly Browning's guess. At this moment she loved him for predicting its swift abatement. She thought maybe the act of coming to a sitting position triggered the capillaries in her brain to open, allowing improved blood-flow up into her head.

Now she looked around the cabin. Everything was familiar. This place had practically been her home for the last few months that she could remember. Every component, every toggle, button, or dial was a familiar tool that would assist her and March to survive. The cylindrical walls were packed with equipment, instruments, and controls. Opposite her was the flight deck with two reclining pilot chairs and the navigation monitors awaiting live pilots.

Volunteers willing to risk their lives for the advance of science and space exploration had gone into extended hyper-sleep and had been awakened in the same coffin that she was using. Their trial runs however could only be carried out in a weighted environment. No one was certain how well a body would function after six years of *weightless* hyper-sleep.

It only took a slight push of her arms to the sidewalls of the capsule for her body to drift up and out, floating like a dandelion seed in the stillness of the cabin. She began to feel the blood vessels in her feet open up with a tingling sensation. It was familiar and reassuring. She moved her athletic body down to a standing position on what would become the floor of the cabin when they came under gravity's pull again. In the simulator, this was the position from which she was oriented to work in this space. She could begin to feel the non-slip irregularities of the carefully designed floor through her thin soles.

Finally standing in a position that she was accustomed to in this place, she pushed the button on her lapel microphone and spoke her first message to Earth, "Proxima One to Launch Central, this is Anj, awake and well." She felt assured that her Close Team will have been eagerly attentive to the continuous feed from the instrumentation, informing them of the most recent sequences that had taken place, but she knew also that they would be anxious to hear from her personally.

This was all so surreal. Her message to Earth was short, not to be stingy, but because she had not collected her thoughts enough to compose a complete paragraph yet. She knew she would get around to a longer monologue soon, but for now, that brief greeting was all she had.

Having the sensation of the deck at her feet now, and holding herself there was the catalyst to help her gather final wakefulness. She was fully alert to her surroundings. The ship's cabin was all well-known territory, but, with some excitement, she became curious about what she would be able to see outside. The exterior wall of the vehicle was less than a meter from the coffin's side. Moving forward from her position by the empty coffin, and placing one hand on each side of the ship's near portal, she looked out.

Familiar blackness of deep space and myriads of stars greeted her, but unfamiliar, very large, and new, was Alpha Centauri, a binary star, a bright pair of stars that orbit one another around a common center. They were at the edge of her view, still one-tenth of a light-year beyond her present position. Also new was Proxima Centauri, the red dwarf, Earth's nearest star, very close now in Anj's view, just a little smaller, redder, and less bright than the sun from Earth. She could also pick out Deep ΔT, their destination planet, as yet, little more than a bright speck, like Venus from Earth, orbiting the reddish star. She was seeing it all first-hand from a closer vantage point than even astronomers on the European Extremely Large Telescope had ever seen it, and not one other human was there to see it with her. Even though millions of voices were crying out to hear some word from her, and wanting to know how she was doing and what she was experiencing, she could not have an actual conversation with anyone about this view from her window.

A profound awareness of being alone swept over her. It felt life-threatening, an oppressive, all-enveloping solitude and isolation. She was shattered by how lonely she felt. She became momentarily dizzy and struggled to ground herself. She directed her thoughts to recall that she had survived previous occasions in which she had been alarmed at being totally on her own. One occasion she remembered was a cold sunless day on a climb halfway up El Capitan when she had lost line-of-sight contact with her climbing partner for several hours. One thousand feet from the ground, with two thousand more in the ascent, she had to fight off a similar panicky desperation and will herself to keep climbing. Alone, peering out of the spacecraft, looking at Alpha Centauri felt much the same, and she had to 'keep climbing.'

It was about being out of touch. It was about distance. It was also about the elemental dangers of the situation. Hanging from a rope a thousand feet from level ground was allegorical to this circumstance she realized. Here, everything was hanging on a few yards of tubing, wires, carbon fiber, and titanium riveted together, and the dangers ahead were real, no matter how well trained she was. The possibility of death out here however was not the haunting menace. It was just being so alone that gripped at her heart. She forced herself to take solace that all she had to do was press the call button on her lapel mic, and her words would be formed into text and radioed back to Earth. But then she had to nullify her logical protest that no one would get her message until more than four years from now, when the radio signal finally, at the speed of light, reached Earth.

An ache in her heart and unpleasant generalized anxiety threatened to nullify all the determination she knew was crucial to her success and survival in this moment. Success and survival being the priority, she shoved that aloneness aside like a warrior must shove aside the possibility of flight from battle. This desperate emotion must not take dominion today for what she had ahead of her.

Still peering out at her new solar system and her new sun, she was aware of the numbers. This ship had brought her more than twenty-five trillion miles from Earth. There was no turning back. She forced herself to remember that her life's goal was to be right here. "I don't know what you expected as a little girl," she said aloud to herself, "but its being a little intimidating should not take you by surprise, girlfriend."

She pushed herself away from the portal and looked at the other hyper-sleep capsule. March was not scheduled to arouse yet; he was still inert in his coffin. She had been scheduled to awaken sixty-four hours before him to ensure that all the life-sustaining systems were up and running by the time he came to, but it left her without human companionship for the interim.

She had felt the familiar invisible Presence of her Heavenly Father in the first moments of her consciousness. She turned back to the portal, scanning the expanse of that side of the universe and her new home. Directing her awareness to God and still peering out the window, she spoke in her spirit a rhetorical question, not actually looking for an answer, "Did You really make all of this?"

Almost startling her, that familiar Voice was right there, and it caught her by surprise in this extreme context. The Voice of her Heavenly Father was as near as it had always been on Earth. "I know you don't doubt that," was His reply. That familiar Voice was near, closer than her own thoughts as always, in fact, even more starkly apparent than usual. Then He added, "I am with you," four words that have calmed the hearts and minds of people in crisis from the time of Abraham and Moses. There was no impatience in that Presence, but a Fatherly smile, having a moment with His daughter and even amused by the idea that she would be surprised to find Him 'out there' with her. She found herself immediately immersed in the unmistakable Presence of the God of the universe, appropriately, in a place that could be called 'the edge of the universe.'

Consolation replaced panic and anxiety. She was relieved of the task of battling those troubling and threatening emotions. Her heart and mind became peaceful. The tension that had been building in her body dissipated. Sweat that had begun to form a little rivulet down the center of her back now became just a damp spot. It was time to get to work.

First check: the temperature in the cabin of the ship. The large enclosure in which she was now free to move was comfortable, perhaps a little too warm. She could address that. Only an hour ago she knew it had been well below freezing in there, but Artificial Intelligence (AI) had been successfully programmed to bring the temperature up to human standards in time for her awakening.

Next on her checklist was to measure and establish a stable oxygen level in the cabin air. CSE and Launch Central had decided that even some of the simpler tasks should be manually initiated rather than automating everything. Anything left up to a machine is subject to failure. Anything left up to a human is also subject to failure. CSE Team philosophy had emerged to create a balance between what they had to depend upon the machines to do and what they counted on the crew to carry out manually.

Oxygen level then was her responsibility, with the aid of what was still loosely called Artificial Intelligence. AI had been programmed to measure the volume of the gas that had, just minutes ago, been released into the compartment to achieve the appropriate levels, and it began a slow bleed anticipating the rate at which the oxygen would be used up, but Anj's responsibility would ultimately be to adjust the levels to ensure peak performance from the crew. She had been given the assignment partly because she was particularly sensitive in her cerebral function whenever there was slightly below optimum oxygen level.

As she began to switch over the systems that now were her responsibility to manual control, her thoughts returned to all those people who were light-years away and waiting for word about her arrival. Proxima Mission had attracted a popular following worldwide, and anticipation of this historic first in space exploration, astronauts landing on another planet, captured the hearts and minds of millions. She had already been out of touch, in transit, for more than six years. They would not know for an additional four-and-a-half years whether she had even awakened, and she would not receive a reply to her report of arriving and awakening for almost nine years from this point. She was startled by a sudden realization that human beings were not designed for this. Stepping out of one's comfort zone was one thing, but this was altogether beyond comprehension. She again felt deeply the need for some company and began banking very heavily on March's waking up. The digital read-out on his coffin said she still had sixty-three hours and twenty-three minutes to busy herself before he joined her.

"Browning would be both amused and concerned right now if he could see into my head," she thought, "in fact probably downright worried about me."

"It's okay, Frank," she said out loud to him, "Your training will carry me, just like you always said it would. It is going to work."

"We are a long way from home," she said only to herself, half amused at the observation, well aware of the unimaginable distance, speed, and travel time involved. Being here was the ultimate end of six years of college, four years of training, and untold numbers of youthful dreams as far back as she remembered. Space, distant stars, light years, rocket engine developments, and new sources of energy production, all these considerations had been in the background thinking of her growing-up years. As the puzzle pieces and scientific developments began to fit together, they clearly interlocked with her own notions of what she believed she was made for: travel to distant planets. When finally selected for this mission, she was not surprised. She knew it was her destiny. Browning seemed to understand that about her too, and worked with her both from a personal level, building her strength of character, and from a performance perspective, drilling and training to get her to be as much like a machine as possible, all about function and performance.

Frank Browning was bigger than life right now, her only tether to...what...reality? "*This* is reality," she reminded herself, "I am not on Earth anymore," even though to her memory it seemed only hours ago she had been greeted with genuine smiles, handshakes, and pats on the back from the staff of the launch-preparation unit. Frank had been there too. He was a large African American man with close-cropped hair who preferred to speak of his ethnicity, when it was needful, as simply 'Black.' He was legendary around Launch Central for his guidance of the department and his personal engagement with everyone. Plus he had been there almost two decades.

She was glad she could think of what he would be saying right now and how helpful his guidance and vision had always been, including in this moment. They had talked late many evenings, long past all reasonable time to go home, about how this experience would be when they awakened trillions of miles from home. He was the 'Old man and the Sea' around Launch Central taking time with the young astronauts, she and March. He always assured her she would be able to rise above it, above the fear, the newness, the loneliness, and operate as a very well adjusted human being in an environment that, from Earth, could only be imagined.

Had anyone been able to accurately imagine what she and March would be facing? Certainly not in the stark reality that she was experiencing in the present, but trying to picture it and hearing his confidence in them had been helpful then, and it was helpful now.

She turned her attention to the oxygen level in the cabin which had been initially established by AI from liquid-oxygen tanks only an hour ago, but could now be augmented from the cold-fusion engine. She soon had the output stabilized to meet her needs, which would of course change whenever she slept and when she exercised in this small space. She allowed her mind to run ahead and remember that the exact percentage of oxygen on Deep ΔT was not a number that could be determined accurately from Earth, but that there *was* oxygen had been established. This was a crucially important unknown on the planet. Was there enough oxygen for human life? Was there too much? Either eventuality had the potential of fatality in the long term. She caught herself gaining momentum for an over-thinking session on the whole situation without enough data to reach a conclusion, so she shut it down. They would have good data by the time they landed and before stepping out of the vehicle.

Next was to set some parameters for navigation. AI had brought them thus far, but skilled human piloting would be indispensable in getting them into the correct orbit of the planet to set them up for entry into the atmosphere and landing.

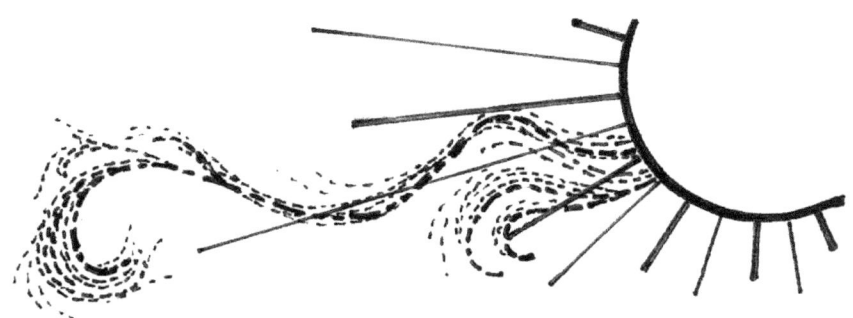

Chapter Two

"Two hours and forty-one minutes to get this fine-tuned before the man wakes up," she said to herself. Anj was her own best friend by now, and she was trying to become better friends with the unit that would be producing the energy she and March would be needing for the foreseeable future. Twelve years ago, when the cold-fusion breakthrough had been made, she was just entering her post-grad program, and she knew that this development would make the difference in realizing her up-till-then only imagined travel to other stars. No other energy production system could provide the power needed for such a voyage and for the needs of a vehicle that was to function for a decade or two. Carrying enough conventional fuel was out of the question.

This cold-fusion engine had, with only a few gallons of fuel (water) propelled them into the cosmos for the last six years. It had accelerated until reaching a final speed eighty-five percent of the speed of light, 158,000 miles per *second*. Before reaching their target system, the need was to decelerate. That would take as much energy as acceleration had. AI had accomplished most of that, executing the slow-down while they were still sleeping. Such a slow-down had been one of the key responsibilities of AI because it took 28 days of deceleration generating 4 G's constantly. Such forces would have been unsustainable for an awake and alert human being, but in hyper-sleep, the effect was minimized.

Still, they would have to engage the thrust of the engines for further slowing in the approach. Establishing an orbit around Deep ΔT was going to be complicated by the need to meet up with their landing module, which they affectionately called LEM. That was the acronym for Lunar Exploration Module. That name was used because of its basic similarity to the module that had taken man to his first extra-terrestrial destination, the Earth's moon, so long ago. Of course this unit was not for lunar exploration, but it brought a comforting little piece of history of man-in-space with them. The Mars team had started the tradition, calling their landing vehicle LEM, even though it bore even less similarity to the original than this one did.

Anj noted that their LEM had already established contact with the ship, even before she awakened. Anj had whispered a "thank You Jesus" when her data read-out confirmed that LEM had established a stable orbit around ΔT. This was where there was a great risk of failure. It was crucial that AI get that engine to ΔT and stabilized in orbit ahead of them. It had been launched ten days before them, unmanned. Its only cargo was the conventional retro rockets and the jet engine needed for a vertical landing in completely unknown terrain. The plan was for them to dock with LEM, and it would carry them to the planet's surface. Their ship was to be the living quarters on the planet, and it carried provisions for feeding them and keeping them warm or cool until they could establish a self-sustaining system of their own, but LEM had to get them there. Proxima One's landing on ΔT was scheduled five days away, by Earth's measurement.

The cold fusion engine now had to be engaged to implement further deceleration. It was to be gradually stepped up as they neared their target. Anj powered up the thrust, and she felt the slight press, towards the floor like weak gravity, from deceleration. It was gentle now but would be increasing to several

G's as they stepped through the procedure. She and March would be strapped into their seats during that part of the trip.

Cold fusion also had to provide for the ship's survival systems of heating, cooling, oxygen supply, and power for radio transmissions. After landing, it would be the only source of energy to carry them through the long cold nights and scorching days that were anticipated on ΔT. She had a basic understanding and familiarity with the inverters that transferred the intense heat of fusion into usable levels of electricity so essential to their survival. In her indoctrination with the unit, she had been faced with simulated emergencies of all sorts including the potential of a nuclear explosion in the eventuality of certain malfunctions. She was thankful that nothing that extreme had occurred in the last day-and-a-half. It was functioning well, but it seemed to have a tendency, with the new settings since she had taken it off of the flight program, to creep into decreasing levels of output, which could be dangerous, because it was essential that it not ever shut down; there was no way to re-start it here. She did not want to have to constantly adjust it, and she knew there was a way to get it balanced. Feeling like she was missing something, she referred to the on-screen tutorial to find the key.

March would have had this figured out, she knew, yet a stubbornly entrenched fear of being judged as a woman if she couldn't get it right now drove her to solve this problem before he was awake to help her with it. March was very patient, and she knew he wouldn't make fun of her or judge her, but some residual fear of how males regarded her present role, and her need to prove herself, drove her on.

As she stared at the screen, she was having trouble focusing on the complex operations suggested in the service manual. This was a very intricate unit with a multitude of factors that contributed to its operation; complicated layers of force fields and heat-drains tapped into the energy production. Balancing the rates of those cooperative forces was the key to a safe and sustainable power supply for the entire operation. Most of the system was run by AI, but an alarm had alerted her three times now that the balance was out, promoting a slow-down that needed to be interrupted. She had gotten it back into balance twice, and now was working on a solution that would be more than a stop-gap.

"Jesus, what am I missing here?" she said out loud.

Coming into her mind's eye immediately was a picture of Frank Browning stepping up to stand beside her and placing his big dark brown hands folded together by the keyboard, just as he would have helped her back home in the simulator. In her mental picture of the moment, he looked at the screen for what seemed to be a long time, studying. Then it came to her. It was right there on line 32; "By-product oxygen use influences the conductivity of the magnetic field...." There it was. Turning on the cabin oxygen had changed the back-pressure in the oxygen generation aspect of the unit, creating the imbalance.

"Frank, you're a doll," and she tapped in the new settings with a few keystrokes. "Jesus, thank You for Frank Browning, my friend." Turning to face March, she really would not have minded getting his help, but part of her felt pretty happy that she would have the cold fusion dialed-in perfectly. Her face gave in to a subtle contented smile.

As she began to expectantly look to March's awakening, she began to turn her conversation more toward him. She missed him even though it seemed like only a few hours, a good night's sleep, since they had talked. The reality was that they had been 'out' for years while they traveled trillions of miles from Earth.

March had come into the earliest stages of planning for the Proxima Mission, at first just one of the several astronauts who were interested in being included on the mission. Like most of them, an ex-air force pilot. He also held an MS in astronomy and had a passion to 'get out there.' Instead of just having head-knowledge, he wanted to *go*, and not just to Mars, but beyond the solar system.

Anj was mildly interested in his potential as one who might go with her. She knew in her heart that she was going to be chosen to go. Alpha Centauri was hers. And March was far and away the hardest worker and the most diligent contributor in every brainstorming session, with a lot of sound thinking. He liked her ideas, maybe a little too much, and she had wondered if he was trying to impress her.

Needing to talk to March now, she told him, "Our sun is only a faint distant star now. You have to know where to look to even spot it. And Earth? Unless we build a huge telescope, we will never see it again if this all works out the way we hope it will." Her voice trailed off too quiet to be heard. "Never see it again," she repeated in a whisper. Turning to the Eternal who had assured her He was with her, she asked, "Why was I so willing to propose that? Is this all about me? About my fame? About my willingness to sacrifice myself? About my need to escape? Is there something wrong with me?" She knew she was not perfect in all her motivation to be a Proxima astronaut. She had an adversarial relationship with her mother, and her Dad had passed away with a brain tumor just four years ago, so there was not a lot to stay around for. Plus her frustration with the human race had become a mounting problem the closer she got to being able to leave it all for good. She thought there was probably something unhealthy about an attitude leaning toward escape.

She felt a tangible tug on her body just like from the belaying rope that her grandfather used to hook her up with when she was on the climbing-wall as a girl. He would tug it lightly when he saw her register fear of falling, to remind her that she could not fall, but that the harness would catch her and she would be lowered easily to solid ground. God seemed to be coaching her, "Come on back to what you know to be true. You are in Christ. You need not try to get it perfect by yourself." With that, all questioning of her motives dissolved. Wonderful Counselor Spirit reminded her of the character traits that He had forged in her. She knew His right hand was on her shoulder. "Where can I go from Your Spirit? Or where can I flee from Your presence?"

The assurances of that Psalm had been upon her when this expedition had taken shape.

In the earliest planning stages of a manned expedition to Alpha Centauri, she was the one that put forth the idea that she was willing to go without a plan to return. Logistically, that would make a huge difference. What looked almost impossible if a return voyage was integral to the plan became a realistic possibility if the ones who traveled there planned to stay. But the team sat in stunned silence when she proposed the idea.

"What are you thinking?" someone asked from this erudite crowd of very cerebral-driven people.

"A colony," she said. "Maybe sometime in the future a way to travel back to Earth could be achieved, but we don't have to include that if we commit to establishing a colony, a permanent settlement."

Her idea instantly tugged at the imaginations of even the most logical thinkers. "We establish a colony, a New World," she repeated.

It was Browning who finally broke the uncomfortable silence, saying, "Ahem, well, let's take a look at what kind of difference that would make; I know Anj is serious; I, for one, am willing to take a realistic look at it."

March was the next to agree that her concept had real merit. "It makes a lot of sense after all; what is it that says we have to come back?"

"We?" someone quipped.

"Sure, 'we.' I'm willing to leave it all behind just to go see something out that far."

"That means," the quipper continued, "You and Anj would have to have children."

March's eyebrows went up ever-so-slightly. "That's not a problem," he said, so matter-of-factly that no one even chuckled. And he did not mean it in any way to be humorous. This was a space expeditionary brainstorming session, and he stayed completely in character. He admitted to her much later, after they were married, that he had seen himself as her partner in travel and husband from the time he first saw her, and she admitted that she knew too, from the moment he said, "That's not a problem." Something began to crystallize between them from that moment.

This guy, in whose heart were the highways to the galaxies, met her right where she was. She knew now, thinking of March, that being here was not mostly out of a need to escape, but about fulfilling what God had put in their hearts at a young age. His passion to touch other solar systems, to take incredible risks to do so, set him apart in her mind, from anyone she had ever come across. And beyond their shared passion for what was just the night sky for most people, he cherished and cared for her in a way she had never before experienced. He infused life to a longstanding dead place in her heart and brought out aspects of Anj that surprised and delighted her co-workers at Launch Central. Browning had given her a big hug when she told him of their engagement, and said, "He's a gem alright; no doubt the one for you."

She was herself joyfully fascinated by the love that emerged from within some hidden place in her. To trust so implicitly and to feel so safe was like the mending of broken bones. The resulting transformation in her heart was stronger than anything she had known before, and it only kept on getting stronger. Love at the human level gave her a new sense of connection with God in prayer and worship.

As Proxima One began to take real shape, March and Anj owned it like a kid who wants to buy a bike he has seen in the store; in his mind he already owns it. They planned together, felt it together, and talked about it endlessly. The possibility that their New World would turn out to be hostile to human life, and that it might not be an ideal place to establish a colony, intruded upon the considerations of everyone but her and March. She knew by faith it could work, there was only the occasional shadow of doubt. That kind of faith towards a goal with so many unknowns was not ordinary to her, it was not something from within her, rather it was emerging out of the relationship with her Father who had created her for His purpose. Father had spoken to her. He had even given her a husband to partner closely with her. She knew better than to ask the next question like a three-year-old, "Why?" She did not actually care why this grand plan was hatching right before her eyes, apparently just for her. She was just overjoyed that she got to be the one to propose the idea of a colony with no return and to be the first volunteer to go. Sometimes she did wonder why, but she knew that ultimately it was so that the Creator would be glorified on the Earth, and perhaps in the greater universe.

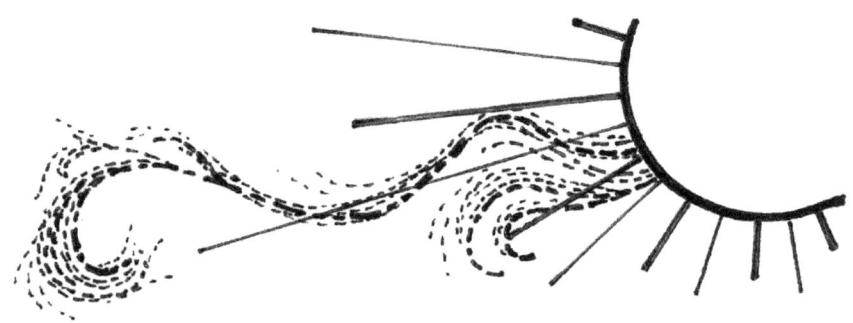

Chapter Three

Anj peered down through the Lexan cover at March's inert face. The Lexan was translucent from his side but transparent from hers. "We are up and running darlin'. I'm just waiting for you to wake up so we can get the rest of this program on stage." They had rehearsed this so many times it sometimes reminded her of the plays she had done in high school. Finally, it was time for them to step onto the stage and play their part in this incredibly complicated and ambitious expedition. This time it was not a rehearsal. The curtain had actually been up for some time already. So far, it had been mostly automated as the action was carried out by programmed mechanical devices. She and March were safely tucked into their coffins hours before liftoff. Every procedure since then had been either automated or initiated from Launch Central. The data recordings she had reviewed in the hours since she had awakened revealed the flawless performance of all the systems that had been designed to carry them far beyond the solar system and on course for Alpha Centauri.

For her, this complicated mission began as a little girl's dream about being an explorer in outer space. She had known since sixth grade the name of this star system of three stars, the closest to Earth, a mere four light-years away. When she was in high school, it had been verified that Proxima Centauri, the one separated from the other two stars, had planets, one of which was in the habitable zone, not too far from, nor too near to the star.

Spectrography had revealed the presence of oxygen and water on the planet. Widespread interest in a manned expedition seemed to catch fire worldwide, tantalizing the imaginations of both armchair astronauts and realistic scientific astronomers. By that time, Hyper-sleep had been extensively tested and proven as a means of long-term travel that greatly reduced the necessity for carrying food and oxygen. Then the cold-fusion breakthrough tipped the scale. Travel to distant stars could now be realistically considered and the little girl's dream was becoming a career trajectory.

An early cold-fusion engine had been employed to send a probe to do a fly-by of Alpha Centauri. Data from it had revealed that the planet circling Proxima Centauri rotated so slowly that it had fifty-six hour days. Its orbit around its star was so small in comparison to Earth's, that it circled its sun every four-and-a-half of its days. This was their target, not far from here now.

"We are gonna do this my sweet. We are here. Just wait 'til you get a look around from this vantage point. The Binary is unreal from here. I can't wait to see the night sky from ΔT. Thank God we get to land when the Binary is up at night. You are going to want to stay up all night getting used to a new sky. What a crazy thing to get used to; four-day years, no winter, spring, summer, or fall."

She was chattering like a schoolgirl. All her work was caught up and she was feeling a little desperate for conversation. They had talked about all these subjects so many times, trying to prepare themselves for life on a new planet with every day and every night almost twenty-eight hours long. That was the reason that they had decided to name the planet Deep ΔT. Engineers use that language to talk about the temperature differential between the inside and outside of a building. The temperature differential between day and night on the new planet was going to be deep. It was going to be extreme, and perhaps life-threatening without some adaptations that they would have to make up as they went along. In twenty-eight hours of daylight, the heat would continue to build all day. They were hoping it would stay below 45° C (115° F). And similarly, the night chill could be below what anyone on Earth routinely experienced below the Arctic Circle.

More wondering out loud to herself, she mused, "You think we'll stick to our twenty-four-hour system there? How locked-in is the human bio-system to the twenty-four-hour cycle? I remember reading about those cave-exploring spelunkers who spend weeks underground and never see the sun. They completely lose track of day and night eventually, and they tend to adopt a pattern of longer and longer days, like twenty-six or twenty-eight hours. But those twenty-eight hours still included eight hours of sleep, and the rest of the time working, cooking, and doing daily chores. I wonder what we will eventually do with twenty-eight hours of daylight followed by twenty-eight hours of night."

These musings had been much-discussed between them and with Browning and the rest of the Close Team on many occasions both formal and informal. She just needed to be talking to someone for the moment. And in the face of it, these questions were unanswerable until they had fully inserted themselves into this new planet.

March was not a super conversationalist at his best, and now he was as still and pale as he would have been in a real coffin. "Why did we think that was so amusing back in the simulator?" Anj wondered out loud with a shudder. A thought, "What if he doesn't make it?" re-visited her. More than once in preparation for all contingencies, she had been forced to look at the possibility.

"You're right," she spoke encouragingly to herself now, "Anj, you can run anything on this ship; you could even land this rig all by yourself. You've done it plenty of times in the simulator, even with the sim-room techs throwing sandstorms and engine-failures at you. You are well trained in every aspect of this operation, and you can complete every sequence of it all the way to touchdown."

Returning to her sober worried mind, she said, "Well, I won't get very far alone on this venture," more to March now. Swimming before her mind's eyes were all the dreams that had gone into this. It was what they had put their lives on the line to do. She saw her future children, she saw March, being the daddy he wanted to be, and willing to do it on ΔT with her. She saw it in the best-case scenario, which was what her imagination always came up with; she saw a nice home well adapted to the rigors of this new world, and a new life in a world unstained by the discord, avarice, and injustice that was so typical of humanity on Earth. Her greatest hope was for a new start. Her heart beat strong in her chest just to think about it again, this time from within an intergalactic stone's throw of its reality.

Escape from all that is disappointing about life on Earth had been an aspect in the background of her being willing to commit to a one-way trip, with no return. Dismay over the daily news, both local and international, had begun to eat away at her like a horrible infection. She could not fix the world, and becoming a mother, which was a major goal of hers despite her career path, looked less and less appealing with every reported corruption, murder, or new war. Now all of her dismay over the world stood a chance of being put behind her, forgotten forever.

Since waking three 'days' ago, she had gone through the entire systems-checklist twice because all operations had proceeded so smoothly. She had been allowed three days to work out the bugs, but there had been relatively few. She had taken time for three exercise workouts on the inertia equipment, per the agenda prescribed by the Medical team. She could feel the effects of significant atrophy in her muscles and looked forward to the effect of full gravity again, although she would not be quite as heavy as on Earth. Weight loss was something neither she nor March needed at all in their excellent physique, but it was a common joke among the Team that this was the most expensive weight-loss program ever since they would only be at about eighty percent of their Earth weight.

She had slept three eight-hour 'nights,' somewhat fitfully, because turning the lights off, even with a face mask, did not nullify the 'sun,' Proxima Centauri, shining in the portals. There were also too many things on her mind for her brain to slow down enough to sleep well. Part of her was as excited as a child going on a train ride for the first time tomorrow, and not able to come to rest. She was also constantly rehearsing all that had to be accomplished before this flight came to its end with a touchdown on ΔT, taking into account all the contingencies if things went wrong. Courageous and steady as she was, both by nature and by training, all that was ahead generated an undercurrent of anxiety she could not deny.

Carla Peretti at Launch control had taught her how to calm herself through simple breath-control meditation. Carla had helped her find her optimum breathing rate at four breaths a minute. Breathing deeply at that rate, she could bring her brainwaves down to a peaceful frequency pattern with just a few breaths. Looking out the portal before lying down to sleep and breathing slowly, she found that she could ground herself significantly in her new reality.

She had begun eating lightly, hoping to go easy on her digestion system which had not passed anything through for an unconscionably long time, but also aware of her physical energy needs. In tests carried out in gravity, the prescribed eating schedule worked well on the human volunteers who were recovering from years of hyper-sleep. Anj felt good. She was just two hours into her fourth workday. March's waking in a couple of hours would set off a domino effect on all the levels she had established so far for the functionality of the ship, but she looked forward to the inconvenience.

Almost immediately they would have to begin their itinerary for the slow-down, establishing an orbit, and docking with LEM. She was so glad he would be there to help carry the load, to say nothing of the joy of being able to share things with him. He would be able to look out the window too, and say things like, 'Alpha Centauri is the weirdest thing I ever saw in the heavens!' and she could say something like, 'Yeah, it's phenomenal, surely not a part of the old solar system,' and she could already tell how good that was going to feel to be able to share these once-in-a-lifetime moments with him. Missing having someone to talk to had been one of the most difficult things about the last three days, contributing to the anxiety that was not an integral part of her normal life function.

March's coffin displayed a digital count-down to awakening. As it proceeded, she found herself checking and re-checking the scant few other read-outs that the coffin offered. But there were no adjustments she could make, so it was a meaningless exercise. It was all AI; just like on her own capsule, everything would go according to technological prediction. She busied herself checking to store all loose gear properly like a yachtsman preparing for a storm. The 'storm,' so to speak, was going to take place when a significant effect of inertia set in as the deceleration rate increased. That would multiply further when they made the first pass of the planet and came under its gravitational pull, the force of a new gravity, from a new 'Earth,' a new home planet.

Deep ΔT was not a complete unknown, but things like vegetation, other life forms, water, and food supply, so many things could not be assessed from Earth or by the probe that passed by here some eight years ago. They had brought seeds in hopes that soil would be similar enough to host crops, and that the hardy varieties they had brought could withstand the heat and cold extremes. Lost in thought about how all that was going to look, Anj heard a soft click from March's machine, and that soft hissing sound of oxygen flow was now just audible from behind his Lexan cover. She took a deep breath and went over to look. That pale countenance that was so grim to look at an hour ago had already begun to pink up a little.

A sigh of relief escaping her lips reminded her that, although she had trained for every logistical and psychological possibility, and was technically prepared for it, there was a very real terror within her that March somehow would not make it. True enough, she could navigate, she could pilot, she could land the craft, she could probably survive in the new environment, but she desperately did not want to have to do it all alone. Everything she had imagined about future life on a new planet had March in it and included children in the future. She had spent absolutely zero time imagining life on ΔT by herself, yet here she found herself somewhat forced to think about and maybe prepare herself for how that might look. She knew, even just from the last three days' experience, how much of the richness of life was derived from loving others, being social, talking, and sharing. "Maybe all that hyper-sleep changed me. I don't remember ever being that hung up on the importance of having someone to talk to," she murmured to herself. Desperate loneliness was an unfamiliar companion and she certainly did not look forward to being a castaway in a different solar system.

Recovery from hyper-sleep carried the highest physiological risk the astronauts faced. It was the factor most subject to failure. In spite of the science and the trials and the immense successes so far, there were still so many variables, and the balance between life and death at that level was so precarious; everyone involved got nervous around the capsule when a subject was awakening. Anj rationalized that at this moment it was why she was feeling so jumpy. "God I give you my heart, thank You for Your ever-available peace. I apprehend peace right now." She knew her professional performance could not be compromised by emotional turmoil and pointless worry. She spoke to herself, "It is useless to worry, I came out fine; he'll be good." Gnawing fear remained. She went to her default calming skill, breathing very slowly and welcoming the Presence.

Purposefully stepping away from March, she went to the seat she would soon be strapped into to withstand the G-forces of deceleration and looked over the auto-pilot parameters she had set when she initiated the engine to thrust for slowing. The program included a step-up procedure that gradually brought the vehicle into slower speeds that allowed the pull of gravity from the planet to increase its influence on the trajectory. It was a very basic program based on a theoretical estimate of the gravitational pull of ΔT. The actual influence of its gravity would only be ascertained as the trajectory it generated was analyzed. She noted that thus far the course was well within limits of the program and did not show an alarming degree of deviation from what was anticipated.

She knew she was just occupying her mind to keep from obsessing on March waking up. He continued to look better, and eventually, she could hear Carla's familiar recorded voice speaking to him to prepare to open the cover. She went over and looked into his now-opened eyes and thought she noted some fear there. He could not see her because a one-way reflective coating prohibited the subject from receiving any input other than the tested and proven programmed regimen. Even though muffled, she was able to follow the count-down to the point at which he was to squeeze the activator switch. He did, right on cue, and the cover slid to the side.

Her face was right over his, and his features noted recognition, but she saw now that fear in his eyes was really there, and it seemed to become more accentuated as he saw her.

"First officer reporting to the captain, all is in order, sir!" she said, pretending and hoping that everything with him was in order. As a couple, they tended to work through trying circumstances with humor, trying to keep the mood positive.

"Hey partner," he replied, wincing. "Did you have a headache when you came out?"

"Oh yeah," she said, relieved if that was all he was worried about. "But it goes away pretty quickly."

"This one's a doozey, sorry, can't even think yet. Too painful." He bent to a sitting position slowly and held his head in his hands. "Oooo my head, my head! This is no fun. Isn't this supposed to be the fun part?" He also was attempting a little levity.

"Take your time March, we are cruising along fine, no immediate needs."

He made no further move to exit the coffin. He lay back down and pulled his knees up in a fetal position, still holding his head. His breath was hissing in and out through his clenched teeth, and she knew he was hurting badly. She had never seen him like this and was getting genuinely alarmed.

"Take your time," she said again, moving in close and putting her arm over his shoulders. He was trembling slightly. "Maybe cold," she thought and stepped away to get one of the Mylar blankets. Spreading it over his now shuddering frame, she began to pray desperately.

"Help me, God, what can I do? I speak life to March in Jesus' name, not fear and not pain, but health and strength. You did not bring him out here to die right at the door! No, Lord, You are our help, God; be here, God; come and be King; help me, God, touch March with your loving-kindness. Oh, God!" Now whispering, "March, baby, come on, you will be okay. Browning says it will go away quickly. It did for me. It will go away soon, just hang on."

March had gone very still, his eyes closed, mouth slackened, and he was breathing very heavily. Alarmed, she began to recognize what she was seeing. When she was seventeen, she was with her grandfather one afternoon when he had complained of having the daddy of all headaches, and he had lain down hoping to nap it off, but it got worse. Finally, he had assumed a fetal position, holding his head, and quickly slipped into a coma before the paramedics arrived in response to her 911 call. Later the word came that he had passed away in the hospital from an aneurysm. All of the symptoms March was exhibiting looked the same. "No! Please God, NO!" She pulled close to March's strong, healthy body and held him, just held him. He was still breathing heavily, seeming to be sound asleep.

Her thoughts collected around what would happen if he died. It would put an end to everything that she was sure God had promised her about the family they were to have, their home, and all the hope that He had given them in the face of huge unknowing. So much was not known about this planet, but they had been given, like a package, great peace and hope for what was in store for them. It was all from God. Right now, all of that hung in a balance and seemed to be tipping towards disaster. Then he stopped breathing.

Fear gripped her at first, but then from deep within her there rose up a cry; "March, come back! In the name of Jesus, come back! You are not finished with your life! You have things to do! You have not had your children; you have not led our colony. You have not done what God called you to do. You must come back! Jesus, bring him back!"

She believed she could command the heavens at that moment; she believed she could wrest March from the jaws of death. She *knew* it was God's will for him to live, and she spoke it, *willing* it to be by the authority of the name of Jesus.

She opened her eyes and blazed into his face, still yelling, having not yet exhausted the faith that was pouring out of her deepest hidden places. As she placed one hand on each side of his face, gripping his jaws to command him to return, she was startled to find him staring back at her. The fear was gone from his eyes. There was a sparkle there instead. He was breathing easily again.

"March! March! Can you hear me?" His hand came up and gently grasped her wrist where it was, by his cheek.

"I'm here, Anj, I'm here, I'm good." His limp body recovered its firmness, and he straightened out his legs.

Anj was relaxing her grip on his face, her hands now tenderly embracing, to hold his face before her in amazement at what had just happened. "I was afraid, March. I thought you were going to die; oh, thank You, Jesus, Thank You!"

"I think I just saw Him. He sent me back and He canceled out that headache. Whatever it was, it's gone. I'm fine. I know I'm going to be fine."

"Jesus? You just saw Jesus?"

"Yeah, I think so, maybe it was the Father, hard to tell. He was God; such a Monarch, such brilliance I could hardly look at Him, and oh, the love that I felt! No headache could stick around with such love coming at me! All the troubles of this life were worth it to just be looked at once with that kind of love. Anj, you should have seen Him, Anj; those eyes, it was beyond explanation."

"What did He look like?" She couldn't help but ask.

"Look like? Like no one you could ever imagine, like no one you could ever describe, and with beauty that has never been seen in the realm of humanity." March was so deeply at peace. His demeanor was now totally relaxed, like someone who has just awakened from a Sunday afternoon nap on the couch, kind of gradually coming back to reality, and enjoying talking softly with his lover.

She said again in a relieved whisper, "I thought you were going to die."

"I was dying. I think I did die. I was conscious that I lifted right out of my body and the pain in my head went completely away. Suddenly all was peaceful, even though I could still see you here yelling over my body lying there crumpled up in the capsule. I heard you crying out to God. I was amazed: I didn't know you had that in you for me.

"Then He came to me from some very nearby place. I could feel His arm around my shoulders, and He directed me to go back. He said I was not done with what I am called to do. You were praying and yelling that too. I couldn't tell whether He was agreeing with you or you were agreeing with Him; both statements were like parts of a strong river that was carrying me irresistibly in that direction."

March and Anj's eyes were locked together, each trying to grasp what they had just seen in themselves and what they had just seen in one another. "Nothing will ever be the same," they were both thinking at that moment. "We have just been laid hold of by the right hand of God. He has saved us. He has saved the mission. And He has preserved everything that this has all been put together for. It is all for His purposes."

"Thank You, God; thank You, God; thank You," they said over and over, not in unison, but each directing appreciation simultaneously to the One Whom they knew was to be thanked for intervening in what would otherwise have been a crushing disaster.

In the moments that they spent thanking God, they were also becoming aware of emerging new depths of understanding about this place in the universe to which they had traveled, and why they were here. Understanding was being birthed in them, affirmation that God had a plan far beyond the workings of science and the imagination of man. This was all somehow His idea, and He was making sure that nothing would interfere with it.

They were both receiving a new way of thinking about their position in the cosmos. "We had the notion that this expedition was mostly our idea, man's idea, but we have just seen evidence of God's overarching purposes." It was clear, in the Spirit at that moment; what God had done to save March and save the mission was because He was in it all. "He guides me in the paths of righteousness for His name's sake," was a tangible reality in their space-ship cabin several trillion miles from what they had called home. It was all for Him.

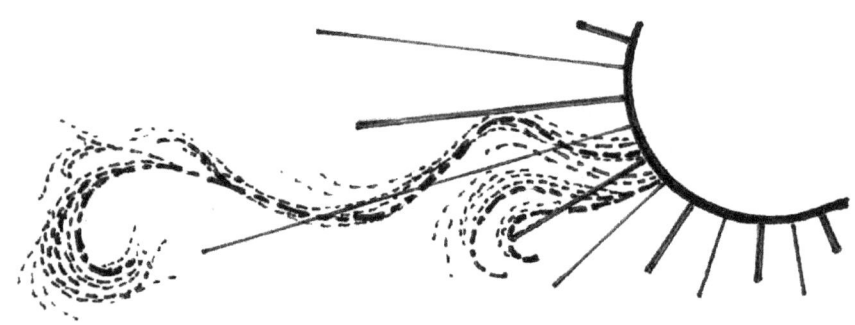

Chapter Four

Anj watched in amazement as March sat up, looking strong. He was a square-shouldered six-foot Air Force guy all the way, but his normal military-cut blond hair fell down over his ears, having grown while in transit, and a reddish beard made him look more like a mountain man than an astronaut. Anj couldn't contain her amusement. "Did we even bring hair-cutting scissors? Look at you. You look the part of the frontiersman, soon to lead a survival episode in the wilds of Deep ΔT!"

He smiled slightly, still gathering his perceptions around him. Sitting up for him was a little more difficult than it had been for her in complete weightlessness. At this point, they were at thirty percent of their body weight because of the deceleration. He seemed fine. Just minutes ago he was suffering a condition which would have been his mortal end apart from the Divine intervention that he had experienced. A few minutes later, as he put his feet on the floor, he had some tingling sensation there as the capillaries reopened. Finally standing, just as she had, the first thing he did was to put one hand on each side of the portal on his side of the vehicle, lean forward, and look out.

"Oh, man, can you believe that? What Browning would give to be able to be here!" By this time, the planet they were targeting loomed large in the window for March. The planet looked a little like the moon, lighted on one side, the dark side profiled against a sprinkling of stars far beyond it. "This is unbelievable, hon. I have imagined this moment many times, but this..." his eyes darted from ΔT to Proxima, to Alpha Centauri, then back, "This is beyond imagination. Browning ought to see this."

"We'll send pictures," Anj encouraged.

"Yeah, but he has to wait four years to get them. All I had to do was lean over and look out the window."

"And subject yourself to a science project of weightless hyper-sleep for six years that almost killed you."

"Yeah, well, that too," he said trying to be casual about his close call with death. He was not one to exhibit a lot of emotion, especially perhaps at times when more transparent emotion would be a usual response. Between his father's upbringing and his military training, he had developed rigid patterns of what was permitted in his definition of manhood. In times of crisis, one must focus on the task at hand and get it done. Conversely, when he was comfortable in a relationship, he could wear his heart on his sleeve.

She was still watching him, fearful that the headache would come back in force, and this was all an illusion, but turning his focus from the view outside, he was all business. "I can feel that we are slowing, how do the coordinates look for docking with LEM?" Ever the professional pilot, he was centered on the immediate assignment.

"Not too good, depending on the final effect of the planet's gravity in the fly-by. Best case scenario, we are going to be out of alignment with its orbit by about fifteen degrees."

"Hmm, that's significant. How is our placement at insertion?"

"Those coordinates look pretty good. We will be very close to the same longitude, but it is going to take a skillful pilot to achieve capture." With a challenging attempt at humor, she declared, "That's why I screamed at Jesus to bring you back. There is no way I was going to try that by myself, fly-boy!"

He stepped over close and pulled her to him, his brave little bundle. It was endearing to him that she was willing to express so transparently her genuine desire for his help. In turn, he was telling her in his enfolding arms that there was no one else in the world he would have wanted to be with in this unbelievable situation, no one else he knew who was as reliable, skillful, and generous with herself. They were so counting on one another and dependent upon the Eternal One in this place so completely devoid of any other human being.

Just then, they felt the engine step up its thrust and their weight eased higher, from thirty up to forty percent. It would not be long before they were experiencing multiple G's, weighing several times what they weighed on Earth. There was a lot to do to prepare for that transition.

For her part in navigation, she began to gather the data input from the nearing planet, gravitational influence, assessing for the magnetic field, altitude or distance from the surface, and its own trajectory around its sun. She breathed a quick thanks that ΔT did not have any moons to complicate the approach.

March set to work opening more specific communication from LEM; its present trajectory, altitude, orbital apogee and perigee, speed, and its systems overview. His face, only a few minutes ago contorted in agony, was now enraptured with the stuff of piloting a spacecraft that he knew he was born for.

Nevertheless, both of them were subconsciously processing the astounding events of the last half an hour. When miracles happen, they had learned to make a comprehensive review of what really happened. Consciously and accurately adjusting one's view of the world and how it is that God has intervened is necessary. The easier route is to rationalize it away. It would have been possible for them to conclude, "Well, it must not have been an aneurysm after all, just a worse headache than Anj had when she woke up," ignoring the possibility of God's intervention.

Recognizing God's role in what happened, however, would inscribe permanently on their minds those strong first impressions that they had immediately realized: "God has a purpose in bringing us this far, in protecting us for the completion of the mission. God has brought us here. We are instruments in His hands for something He has not shown us yet, for something glorious. God *does* want us to be here! We yield to You Holy Spirit, let us be as clay in Your hands."

This was not their first experience of Divine intervention. A little boy in their church had been healed of leukemia. March had been delivered from periodic migraines. Several times, early in their marriage, financial 'mailbox miracles' had fully convinced them that God is the provider, plus nothing. In virtually every instance of a miracle they had seen, the natural path of events had taken a distinct turn because they recognized and prayed into the Divine hand that had been displayed. What were they to expect from God in this venture from now on? They would be watching for Him and remain open-handed about their Earth-based agenda.

Still in a contemplative place, at one point before the G-forces set in and prohibited easily moving about, they both intuitively went to one of the portals and stood temple to temple at the tiny window, visually assessing the approaching planet. March asked, "Mars is known as the 'Red Planet,' and Earth is called 'The Blue Marble.' What do you think this planet is going to be called?"

Anj countered "Or will it ever be visited by another human being who would want a name for it?"

All future projections of missions to Deep ΔT were contingent upon that happened to March and Anj. It would probably be a couple of years before they could report with any assurance the likelihood of their survival and how favorable the conditions were there. And it would be another four years before that report was received on Earth, and four more years before the colonizers knew if anyone else was coming. The first pioneers were mentally preparing for the long run.

Staring out at the planet, large enough to mostly fill the window now, they could see one of the poles, clearly covered with ice. Swirls of cloud-cover obscured a few large areas.

March noted with immediate interest, "It looks like tiger stripes going diagonally across the whole surface, see, kind of parallel, weird misshapen stripes."

"I think those are bodies of water. I can't imagine what else would make stripes like that. And if it is water, it looks like close to a third of the surface is covered. Intriguing."

They discussed this for a few minutes, assuming it was water, was it salty? How deep? How accessible was fresh water going to be? Would it need to be purified? All were questions discussed many times in the round table sessions, where they tried to corporately think through all the possible questions that would arise in this unknown place.

March was not usually impulsive, but staring fixedly out that portal at their new home, he said, "I can't wait to get down there, run down the beach, and take a flying leap into one of those lakes, or oceans, whatever they are."

Anj turned an inquisitive look towards him. "What has come over my husband? Hey, I'll be right behind you once you assure me there are no biting creatures in the water."

"I'll tell you what has overcome your husband; this has been the journey of a lifetime, and I know that when it is completed, nothing will ever be the same. I am basking in the favor of God's having just spared my life. I am looking forward to the experience of getting to land this craft on our new world of choice. And when that is done, I will no longer be a pilot, but a pioneer in an empty planet, carving an existence out of the dirt. I will swim in the lakes, drink water from the rivers, and build a log cabin for my family. I am anticipating becoming a very different sort of man; a father, a builder, and an explorer," and his face broke open with the most liberated grin she had ever seen.

This of course was not the first time they had talked about life on a new planet, but standing here looking at it, some things were crystallizing for March. Two large silent teardrops overflowed from his eyes and ran rapidly down his still-smiling face. "Back on Earth, when we faced the eventualities of what could happen here, I put on a brave face, but to prepare myself for the worst, I also steeled myself for the possibility of an environment that was so inhospitable that we would eventually, in the long term or the short term, despite our agricultural preparedness and best-laid plans, slowly starve to death, or die of heatstroke, or freeze to death in the harsh climate. Seeing this is such a relief. I think these are tears of joy, maybe tears of hope, but then there is still so much we don't know yet."

Anj leaned herself against his chest listening to his heart, one of her favorite pastimes, and squeezed him with her arms. She held him still for a while even though she sensed that he was winding down from this moment of free expression and his attention was turning back to the work at hand.

"Lots to do," said the man who was still a pilot. He gave his wife's shoulders a little embrace, kissed the top of her head, and stepped away from the window back to his computer screen displaying a steady stream of navigation data.

Within two hours, they were experiencing two G's, twice their Earth-bound body weight. The ship was slowing despite being also pulled forward by ΔT's gravity. Reverse thrust from the engine kept stepping up, continuing to slow them from the phenomenal speeds that brought them this great distance. 'Warp-speed' was still just the fiction of those sci-fi episodes popular near the turn of the century, but travel at eighty-five percent of the speed of light was what made the idea of travel here even an idea to think about.

Soon after they passed the planet, they would come under the pull of its gravity slowing them dramatically to within a speed that would allow them to navigate into an orbit roughly parallel to that of the LEM, and begin to line up for the essential capture of that entry-rocket.

Again, no one knew how well their bodies would adapt this quickly to several G's after six years of weightless hyper-sleep, which was basically hibernation in the extreme: low body temperature, super-slow heartbeat, and breathing that was hardly more than a draft. The human volunteers in trials had provided data that had brought them thus far, but those subjects had not been weightless for six years. Volunteering experimenters were subjected to up to 4 G's within an hour of their waking and were able to function and think and perform through it, so the medical minds, taking all they had learned about long-term weightlessness thus far had deemed this progression of events to be a safe venture for Proxima One.

As March and Anj passed through maximum G's during the long sweeping turn on the outskirts of ΔT's gravitational pull, March passed out briefly from low blood flow to his brain. In their banter, trying to keep up the humor in spite of the situation, she told him she was going to be able to tell their children about this someday, and he mock-pleaded with her not to do that. She had had three days to exercise and move around in preparation for this, but he went into it almost immediately, which put his body at a disadvantage, especially his heart, struggling to keep up blood supply to the brain. As the G's eased off, they were both pleased to have passed through that phase of the deceleration with no significant problems, although Anj had somewhat anxiously watched the read-out of his vitals throughout the whole episode.

It was time for Anj to sleep. Captain March would take the con and pilot the craft into an orbit designed to intersect with LEM at the exact point for capture. She put a mask over her eyes and put in earplugs, but he also turned the lights off and turned down his screen monitor, just to help with her sleep mode. Strapped into her seat, on her way to relaxation and sleep, she murmured, "You doin' okay?"

"I never felt better in my life," which was his standard reply to a casual "How'r you?" "I can't wait to get down to the numbers here." He was rising to the challenge before him - how to get the vehicle lined up to capture LEM. It was tricky, but it was nothing beyond what he had done dozens of times in the simulator, and with a much better longitudinal position than the sim techs usually gave him. He would come in not far behind the LEM and able to intersect with its trajectory, creating the opportunity for docking, thus marrying the engine module to their vehicle, ready for entry into the atmosphere of Deep ΔT.

He was soon lost in calculations, and he could hear Anj's breathing become deep and regular. He knew from experience that she could sleep curled up on a bench in a busy airport. He looked over at her with a little envy and a lot of appreciation. He loved that girl, and his newly-reawakened soul was awash in excitement and assurance about their future together, even though how that was going to look was still full of unknowns. All his worries were put to rest, replaced by a deep peace that it was going to happen. "God is in this; I know it for sure now."

His revived attitude spilled over into his work as he mapped out the speeds and the vectors in three dimensions. This was incredible fun for him. He targeted a rendezvous with the LEM at its apogee, the highest point in its orbit, in order to get the widest view of the planet for the reconnaissance pictures they would be taking as they orbited in a stable state preparing for entry. From those shots and their own observations, they would choose a landing zone (LZ). Later on, the pictures would serve as the only map they would have of their world. Any meaningful exploration down there would be dependent on those pictures. 'A planet completely unexplored by human beings;' the thought fascinated him in a fresh way in this moment. "God help us to choose a good starting place."

Hours later, after maneuvering into position, a retro thrust was initiated to slow the ship down to close to LEM's speed; Anj came alert, in her unbelievable ability to translate from deep sleep into sharp attention. March always marveled at her capability for that. He had tried it, just out of admiration for her, thinking he could learn how to do that too, but after suffering just a few groggy mornings trying to pretend he was awake, he realized his brain chemistry was different from hers, and he was not going to change it. He made peace with himself as a slow-awakening person, and that had to be okay. One little additional snooze usually put him in a good place to truly awaken. He just had to plan that time into his awakening schedule. But there Anj was, eyes wide open at the jolt from the retrofire. She sat up, and said, "That was a big one. I didn't know we still had that much speed!"

"I did the numbers twice, officer," he said, teasing. "We've got some speed on that LEM, no doubt about it. I'm just glad AI got her to where she is; hats off to those aerospace nerds back home. They'll be sweating bullets right about now, and won't be able to know how good they did for a long time."

"I pray God gives them peace about us. We are in a good place, large thanks to them," Anj said.

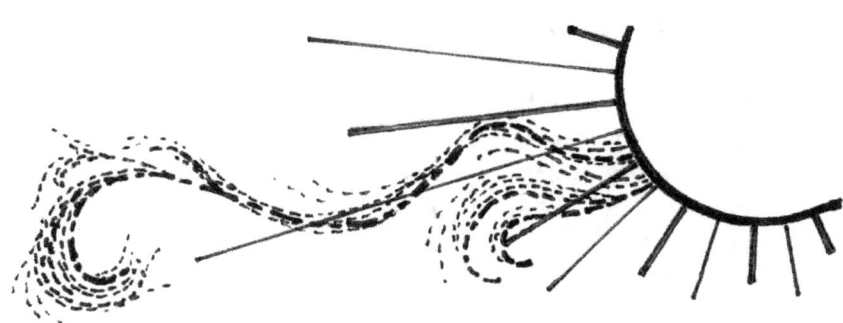

Chapter Five: Launch Central

At the same moment that March was making his final adjustments on his approach to the LEM, the annual staff convention of the Consortium for Space Exploration was in progress back at Launch Central. Usually, the vision of the Board of Directors was the focal point, and break-out sessions presented by the various departments were offered to anyone interested, even from other departments, to foster an interdepartmental comprehensive understanding of all the levels and specialties of all the arms of the greater CSE organization. Part of the philosophy of CSE was that unity between all the departments and between all ten countries involved would improve the overall performance of the entire effort.

CSE was formed to create a globally supported and internationally staffed organization dedicated to space exploration. It had emerged out of an almost frantic worldwide interest in what was 'out there.' Fervor to investigate our galaxy was so high that it seemed like a living breathing entity on the Earth. Sociologists attributed the high cultural interest in outer space to two phenomena. The first influence was all of the new pictures and information about what is happening in the universe that seemed to bring nebula and other solar systems to our back door. The second was the development of pervasive fantasies of escape from all of the frightening scenarios of Earth popularized by recent movies and other media releases. People seemed to have a hope that there was a feasible alternative 'out there.'

CSE's convention this year happened to coincide with the estimated date on which Proxima One would be approaching Deep ΔT, about which there was understandable excitement, some would even say, obsession. Frank Browning was chosen by the convention planners to deliver the keynote address on the first night. He led the huge branch of CSE known as Launch Central, which did a lot more than launch rockets. Launch Central both trained the astronauts and developed the spacecraft and technology which those astronauts would be using. Launch Central maintained those two tracks simultaneously so that the astronauts had input into the designing of their units and were therefore intimately familiar with their operation.

The team that developed the LEM also worked hand-in-hand with Launch Central, matching the capabilities of the LEM to the ship, and matching the docking systems for combining the two vehicles into one. In addition, the development of the hyper-sleep technology had fallen to Launch Central and the astronauts who would ultimately depend upon those systems. Furthermore, all communication to and from the missions that were in progress were, understandably, directed through this department, making Frank Browning the most knowledgeable on any recently received transmissions.

Browning spoke that first night about what was happening within sight of Deep ΔT, "at this very moment, where March and Anj, our pioneers, are most certainly, if everything is proceeding as programmed, entering a critical phase of the journey, which involves docking with LEM and ultimately landing on the surface of the planet." He commiserated with the audience, "I am certainly with you, somewhat anxiously awaiting actual word from March and Anj about their well-being, but, as you know, even though the events we are talking about are happening as we speak, we will not receive messages broadcast from Proxima One for over four years because the distance is so great, and the speed of light (and of radio waves) is so frustratingly slow." He got a little chuckle from the audience.

Browning was the picture-perfect chief executive. Calm, confident, every bit the professional, he was the scientist, and the leader who had been so essential to the establishment of a base on Mars, through launching multiple sets of astronauts and equipment to that experimental station. Then Proxima One had caught everyone's interest, including his, from its inception, and he could not have been more pleased with the vision as it had been developed by his team along with March and Anj. He went on to say, at the close of his speech, "Tomorrow afternoon, Launch Central is offering three extra breakout sessions beyond the usual offering, which may be of interest because of their relevance to the present position of our astronauts drawing near to Proxima Centauri.

"Slade Zaminski from the hyper-sleep lab will be talking about the design and essential function of the form-fitting beds which hold the astronauts for the entire journey, and he will explain what March and Anj will have experienced for the last six years since they left our launch-preparation unit, quite soundly asleep. In another session, Carla Peretti has been the personal coach for each astronaut who has been launched from our department for the last twelve years. She knows both March and Anj personally and can tell you a little about what they will experience physiologically and psychologically as they awaken. And thirdly, we will let Cooper Smith bore you for an hour about their bodily sensors and the information we get from those gadgets placed on their bodies," he laughed his characteristic engaging laugh and looked at Cooper in the front row, who threw his head back and slapped his knee, and said something back to Browning, pointing back at him, but no one heard it because of the affirming laughter from the audience.

No one who was involved in planning the convention anticipated that those three break-out sessions would be the choice of ninety-five percent of the attendees that afternoon, and all three had to be moved to larger venues at the last minute. Carla, after her presentation, fielded a lot of questions about the psychological state of the astronauts after such a long time in hibernation. She was the inveterate optimist, and she knew these two people very well and admired them. Consequently, she was seen by some as presenting an overly rosy picture of how the awakening would work out. She handled the unkind questions like, "What if one of them does not awaken?" diplomatically with the knowledge of a scientist. One worker from the visitor's reception area asked, "What is the likelihood that the mental strain will be too much and they will fall apart facing the reality they awaken to?"

Carla smiled as one who knows the subject thoroughly, "You are absolutely correct that they will face an unbelievable challenge when they awaken twenty-five *trillion* miles from Earth, a challenge that would crack many a person, I am sure. But these two are cut from some pretty unusual cloth, so to speak, not the run-of-the-mill human being. Smart, resilient, strong, determined, and capable, on a scale of one-to-ten for any of those qualities, they are a fifteen. Going crazy because they are facing something never before experienced by a human being will not happen with them. That is the least of my concerns. They are trained, prepared, and more than adequate to the challenge." Carla leaned over onto the podium to express a little more intimacy with the one who asked the question, "What might even be working out at this very moment, is that they know they have a job to do and they know they can get it done. That is all that is on their minds right now. Furthermore, as most of you are aware, both of them have a serious faith that God will bring them safely to their destination, so if you are a person of prayer, I encourage you to partner with the heavens in agreement with March and Anj for the very best conclusion to their journey."

Slade Zaminski was not a public speaker and was more than a little intimidated by the hundreds of people who had come to hear his little talk about what would ordinarily be of little interest to anyone but him and the astronauts blessed by his craft. He stuck to his printed presentation and the accompanying power-point, carefully trying to avoid being a bore. As he closed, much to his dismay, several hands went up. "How do you make sure they don't get bed sores?" was the first question. Zam found to his surprise that he sailed easily into his answer because he knew this science, and he had engineered those capsules to the point that volunteers had subjected themselves to six years of hyper-sleep and successfully recovered. Less nervous now, he took the next question. "Have you ever lost anyone during recovery, either in your experiments or on an actual mission?" Zam, the scientist and engineer, found it easier than most people would have, to tell about the one volunteer who had died in an early hyper-sleep trial, emphasizing that much had been gained and learned from that tragic outcome. He emphasized that March and Anj's safety could be fairly well assured because of that one lost life, a volunteer who knew very well both the risks and the potential gains from subjecting himself to the experiment. Zam's calm and deliberate delivery of that answer seemed to take the wind out of any other questions that were waiting in the crowd, and soft applause began from somewhere near the back of the room and spread over all present with a message of appreciation for both the volunteer he had spoken of and for Zam's stellar work. Everyone present left with a more positive expectation of what they would hear about in just over four years.

Cooper Smith was the only one who could provide any hard data about the well-being of the astronaut-pioneers. Those sensors that technicians had carefully placed on the astronauts in deep sleep to monitor heart rate, blood pressure, body temperature, rate of breathing, blood-oxygen level, and nervous states had been sending back those readings for six years. The difficulty was that the further out they traveled, the longer transmissions took to reach Cooper. Their speed was so incredible that by now the information he was getting was four years old, but what he had received to date indicated nothing but good information about their overall health in that precarious state of hyper-sleep. In the course of his talk, he reviewed, in great detail, the various vital-signs and their relevance to one another, and how each astronaut's capsule monitored and adjusted its settings to maintain life, just barely, year after year. "I see some of you looking at your watches, so I think I have sufficiently bored you, as Browning predicted. In defense of doing that, I know there is a percentage of you out there for whom knowing these numbers is important, and I salute you. We should have coffee sometime. I will open it up now to questions for the last few minutes of the session."

He pointed to one of the young women in the front row who had been checking her watch, and she asked, "Are you worried about how the awakening sequence will go in the next few days without you to be there personally watching over it?"

"Always. I have the illusion that it is part of my job to worry about them, and that it does some good if I lose sleep over them." There was a little polite laughter in the room. "At this point, I am not losing any sleep, because it is really out of my hands. I think I did all my sleep-losing while we designed and tested these capsules, and I am satisfied we have a reliable system. I don't mind telling you, I do pray for them all the time, especially this week, and I am not under any illusion whether that does any good or not. I know it does. March and Anj walk with God. Whether those are ideas that you agree with or not, I know that they have a lot of confidence in where their true well-being rests. It is in the hands of the Almighty. Four years from now, as we begin to receive the radio signals that are being sent this week, you can pray for them and also pray for me. I may be losing some sleep in those days."

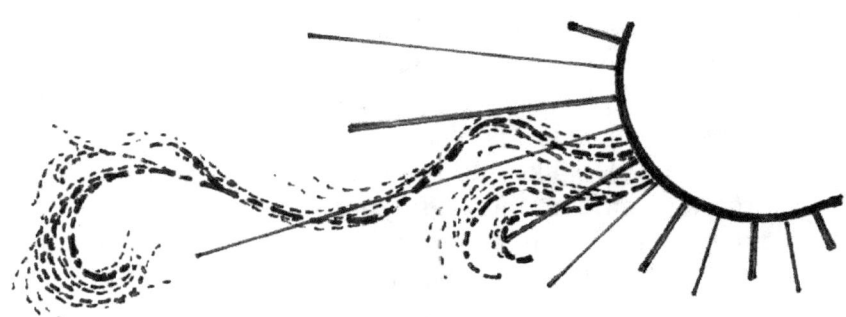

Chapter Six

"I'll be feeling a lot better when we dock with that contraption up ahead." March was looking at the screen on which radar was showing an object ahead of them that was slowly drawing closer. As LEM took shape on the screen, something was wrong. "That's puzzling," March said, typically calmly understating the situation. "Is it going backwards?"

Anj put her face closer to the image, squinting, her teeth bared in concentration. "Not backwards. But, look at that! The shroud over the docking port didn't blow off."

"Extra-vehicular anyone?" His humorous offering did not have an accompanying grin. He knew that the possibility of working outside of the vehicle was something they were not equipped to do. The decision to strike the extra-vehicular jet packs, suits, and umbilicals was not a difficult decision, considering how slim the likelihood they would need them was, and considering the weight. However, there was more than a shade of concern in his voice. Anj settled back in her seat and folded her arms, thinking.

"They never did this to us in the sim," she said, "but I did have to dock once when the LEM was stuck forty-five degrees out of alignment. I had to take over its controls manually to turn it to the correct orientation. Since we can do that, we should also be able to manually blow that shroud off. That contingency should be listed in the LEM's manual controls tab somewhere."

"Unless the wiring..." he began, but caught himself. "Hold on, not going there in my imagination. Let's just work the problem, one step at a time." He knew he was talking to himself more than to Anj. Yes, she could over-think a problem as well as he, but was less likely to go to all the negative possibilities in the process. Concentrating on staying hopeful, he accessed the fine print descriptions of contingency operations. His lips were moving over the screen, but no sound was coming out as he clicked through pages of instructions one after the other.

Anj went to her default, which was prayer. "God, thank You that You know exactly what went wrong here and we are grateful that You are going to reveal the solution to Captain March. It is available to us; someone thought of this and put it in the instructions and the software, so we can get that shroud out of the way. Open a way for us. Give us creative ideas, yeah, we thank You, we thank You in advance for the solution to this problem. We know You've got it."

March was shaking his head slowly. "I see the procedure for the manual takeover for attitude correction you were talking about, but nothing is showing how to blow that shroud. It is supposed to take place as a part of the disengagement from the engine. As the propulsion engine blows clear, the shroud is supposed to go with it automatically."

By this time LEM was just visible through the window, approaching slowly, about fifty meters away. Anj had her cheek pressed against the quartz-glass to try to see it better. "March, yaw to starboard about fifteen degrees so I can get a good look at this."

"I'm going to slow a bit so we have more time to look. We only have a couple minutes max to get this or we'll have to start over and reconfigure the whole approach. But I can give you the view. Hold on." The craft felt a small soft thump, like an elevator coming to a halt on the ground floor, followed by a slow silent rotation bringing LEM into full view from her window.

Anj peered, wishing she were closer, but seeing something. "Captain, come look at this. I think it is actually loose and drifting along behind LEM like a dry leaf, but way too close."

March took her place at the portal and brought a small monocular. He settled the seven power glass on the LEM's back end, gazed for too long, Anj thought, waiting, before he spoke. "Good eye, Anj, I believe you are right. But it is still in the way. Any ideas?"

"Sure, take over manual control on the LEM, pitch it down and I think LEM will bump the shroud so it will jettison towards the planet, then bring her back around to align with us, all clear."

"You are an intrepid rocket-scientist young lady. I believe that will work."

He went right to the keyboard and soon had the cryptography he needed. "Okay, hard pitch downwards, then stop; ready, initiate." Anj, back at the window watched LEM tip like a dump truck, and it did hit the shroud. It floated downwards, soon to be a major meteor in the ΔT sky.

"All clear, Captain, you may restore LEM to proper orientation," as LEM continued without interruption to close the space between them.

"Just another day in the life of an astronaut," his lungs released audible relief in a long slow exhale through pursed lips as he righted LEM again.

Rotating the ship back fifteen degrees, the LEM was so close now that it was only partially visible through the window. Anj took her seat and strapped in again, turning on the video of the docking area. LEM was gratifyingly close now, but drifting to the left more quickly than they were comfortable with because of the fifteen-degree dissimilarity of their orbits. March brought the nose of the ship around to alignment, adjusted for some drift to the left, waited for the painfully slow closing of the gap, again adjusted for alignment, waiting, trusting all that practice in the sim. The camera and a solid grinding clunk both registered that there was contact. A green light at the top of the console came on, under which was the single word, "CAPTURE."

Now it was Anj's turn to exhale long and slow. "That was not the smoothest docking ever," March apologized, "but, my dove, but we are now 'go' for entry into the atmosphere of a heretofore unexplored planet. Are you ready for this?"

Both were feeling more than a sigh of relief. And everything else could now move forward. The rest of life can now proceed on the basis of this one accomplishment. They had just achieved success in docking with the LEM, which was, in the whole journey, the one crucial element, the greatest single potential for failure.

She gave March a big smile from her seat and said, loud and clear, "Thank You, Jesus! Thank You! Yeah, we're smart, and March is a good pilot, but You showed us the way. Thank You." They both got real quiet, aware in their spirits of a real brush with disaster and the grace received to carry them unintimidated through it.

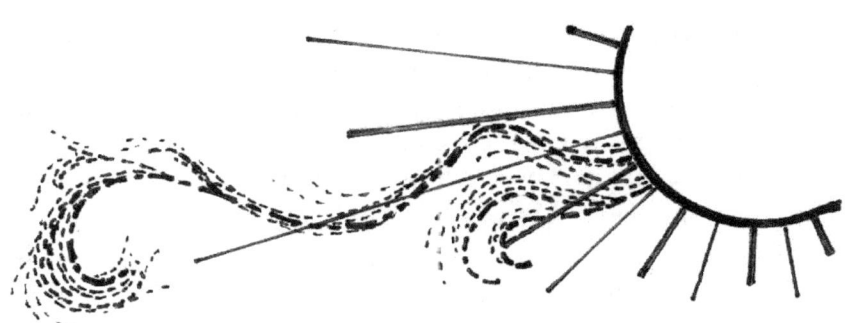

Chapter Seven

To the pilot sensibility in both of them, the ship now felt bulky and hard to maneuver, for, in fact, it was a very different craft, twice its original weight, and more than twice its length. Its primary function now was to execute a huge rocket thrust, slowing the craft to enter the atmosphere, after which the rockets would be jettisoned, leaving the heat-shield to withstand the heat of the air screaming past at almost twenty-thousand miles an hour for several minutes. After slowing enough, a triple parachute would deploy, carrying them gently down close to the landing zone (LZ), at which time the auxiliary jet engine would thrust downwards, providing some maneuvering ability in the final moments to enable the pilot to acquire the most favorable landing.

Anj set to work taking pictures of the planet they now orbited, and putting them together into a database which she could zoom in on to assess for any likely looking landing spots. March was re-figuring the apogee and perigee and the final course of the orbit in preparation for retrofire that would be appropriate for targeting the LZ they were soon to choose.

Below, Anj could see a few huge areas on the surface that looked like desert, not dissimilar to what she had seen of the Sahara and the Gobi from an orbit above the Earth. Tan expanses filled the spaces between some of the bodies of water. Those huge lakes she could see were now more easily qualified as seas.

Smaller lakes could be seen dotting some areas between the seas. High mountain ranges separated the larger seas, and rivers coursed down both sides of the ranges into the seas. Towards the poles, huge areas were ice-covered, and cloudy areas elsewhere indicated perhaps weather fronts similar to what is seen on Earth.

A sudden thought interrupted her fascinated study of the geography below. "I have about three hours to choose where we will be living for the rest of our lives. Why am I not at least a little bit anxious about choosing the right spot? I know we can't land just anywhere, and do well." She could not put her finger on why she felt so calm about finding an ideal place for their log cabin. They had in their minds for a long time now the idea of a log cabin, not even knowing if there would be trees, or suitable trees for such a structure. She envisioned them as pioneers in an untamed land. Some kind of permanent home would have to be built. Despite all those factors vying for attention in her mind, she found herself feeling an unusual peace. "God, I trust You, I only want to hear from You, follow You. I know You are with us; I know You have prepared a place for us. Thank You for invading me with peace about where we will be on this planet You have made. I rest in Your guidance. I yield to Your thoughts." Peace intruded upon her every consideration of the surface of the planet as if she already was familiar with the location of their landing zone and had but to enter the coordinates.

Ferocious creatures roaming this planet, or, even more scary, intelligent and hostile beings had been discussed, of course, as a possibility. These visuals were in the minds of the whole team. However, it had been the consensus of the group not to take firearms. The thinking was that becoming dependent upon such means might be dangerous when the ammunition ran out, either in dealing with hostiles or in using the gun for hunting. March and Anj agreed that they would rather find their way in the new world without the guns.

Anj turned her attention to the screen again with the pictures sequentially appearing before her as they were taken by the reconnaissance camera. "Fascinating place, March you really must take a look at these pictures. Look, there appear to be forests and mountains and lakes and rivers. There are even huge deserts."

"Just pick out a lake, with a river running into it, with a forest nearby. That sounds good to me." He was torn between complete absorption in his navigation and Anj's enthusiasm. He turned his head from his screen full of coordinates and navigation diagrams to her monitor and leaned in towards the images going past, slideshow-fashion. "Wow," he said staring at the many lakes, rivers, and what looked like forests. "God is so good. How are you going to decide where to land?"

Seeing those pictures, again his eyes filled with tears of joy, but his primary focus at that moment was piloting the vehicle to the surface, and he could not give in to the sweeping waves of relief triggered by the favorable possibilities that the planet seemed to be offering their adventure. He smiled at his wife through his tears and said, "I trust you. Go for it, dove." He turned back to his numbers and refocused. Before retrofire, he had a long checklist to go through. There were many sequences incorporated in the entry and landing, and a glitch in any one of them could be disastrous. To these, he turned his attention completely.

Anj was thinking, 'Lake, river, forest, sure, that's reasonable,' and resumed her perusal of the scene below, seeing high thin clouds, now. 'What was that? A snow-covered peak stabbing through the clouds? That would be a high one! Volcanic maybe, hard to tell from this high. Mars had a volcanic history. Earth certainly did, why not ΔT?' "March, here is a landmark you might be able to use to establish your prime meridian. This peak should be visible most of the time."

One of March's tasks was to create a basic latitude and longitude grid over the planet that could be used for navigation. A program had been created back at Launch Central into which he could put the values that he discovered as they orbited, primarily the circumference at the equator and the location of the prime meridian for ΔT. The program would then generate a coordinate system just like that used by GPS on Earth but specific to ΔT. Creating this grid was essential to determine the point at which to fire the retro-engine in order to land at the site Anj chose for the LZ.

He turned his attention momentarily to the high peak. "Good one, but it's a little early to pick the prime meridian just yet. Note any other features you see that would work for that, and next time around we'll be ready to establish Greenwich on ΔT. Thank you, good spotting. I think you are having too much fun over there!"

She turned a big smile towards him, knowing that he was having just as much fun in his own way.

After two more orbits, at a little more than an hour each, they were ready. Anj had been able to get good pictures of the entire equatorial region of the planet as they circled it, including what was in 'night' because of the light from the Binary stars Alpha Centauri on the night side. March selected a site that would be the prime meridian, the equivalent of Greenwich on Earth. On ΔT it was to be the sharp southern point of a sea that was surrounded by desert and close to the equator. It would be an easily recognizable feature, should there be any future missions here. Plus the team would want to be able to map out the planet in detail back home, just for the sake of research, and they had to have a reference point.

Anj settled on an LZ where there appeared to be a level surface above the beach of one of the seas, near a river flowing into the sea, but not too near, given that rivers may flood. What seemed to be thick vegetation, hopefully forest, appeared to begin not far above the targeted landing point. March had given his approval of the spot, based on her report of it and his complete trust in her discernment and wisdom, plus he knew she was praying about it and would be well guided.

"T-minus eight minutes and twenty-seven seconds on my mark..." the exact time of the retro-fire was determined. The captain said, "Mark." The digital count-down began, just for a visual of where they were at on the timeline. Anj finished stowing the instruments and any loose equipment. Entry can be a rough ride, and there was a lot they did not know about hurtling into this planet's atmosphere at this speed.

Retro-fire put the brakes on in a major way, pressing them deep into their G-force assisting seats. As the vehicle slowed and dropped closer to ΔT, the atmospheric drag began to add to the braking effect of the retro-fire until the burn was complete and the rocket package was jettisoned, blown off to four sides, clear of the ship, to become four burning lights in the sky if there were any eyes to observe them from below. The heat-shield then took the brunt of the insult from the air as they slammed into it. Engineers say that air can cut concrete passing at that speed. All astronauts can do is sit tight and pray during entry into the atmosphere. March and Anj were each thanking God for His marvelous hand upon the entire journey thus far, believing He had safe landing ahead for them.

When the big 'chutes deployed they felt a final jerk, then a slow swinging feeling as the craft swung at the end of the long lines high above the surface of the planet but still descending. March switched on the video designed to guide them into their landing. His screen remained black. He tried another approach, maybe the camera did not extend out from the side of the craft as it was designed to, but to no avail, he had only a black unresponsive screen. "We're going to have to back this rig in manually Anj. I need you at that window, please."

"Oh Jesus, we need Your favor," she prayed. "Okay, captain, I can only see one side of the view; I need you to rotate slowly so I can get a perspective of the whole LZ"

"You got it chief," he said beginning a slow rotation which allowed Anj to see that they were right over their sea and the target beach area near the mouth of a big river. As they got lower, she told March that there was a sharp embankment between the LZ and the beach, and on the other side, there were what appeared to be tall trees that they definitely had to avoid. They had to hit that narrow area between the embankment and the forest.

Captain March was all business; "Since we are rotating, use hand signals to show me the direction we have to drift when I start the landing jets. I don't trust my inner ear to be able to tell me which side is the beach and which side is the forest as we spin. I am going to go entirely by your hands. So, how are we looking?"

"Right, we are still too high for maneuvering, but we are close to bullseye; we shouldn't need much adjustment." Silence ensued as they dropped for another minute, the swinging motion had stopped, and March kept up a slow spin on the ship so Anj could get an update on the whole perimeter every fifteen seconds. Finally, she said, "Ignite thrust on my mark... five, four, three, two, one, mark!"

With a significant roar of jet engines, it felt like the whole ship settled onto a huge soft cushion as the vehicle basically became a hover-craft. March released the parachutes to drift free. Anj, intent on the scene below, had both hands pointing straight up, as if in prayer position, where March could see them. Descending still, but very slowly, they were approaching the level spot, but Anj did not want to be too close to that embankment, a sharp drop-off down to the beach. She dropped both hands to point away from the beach, and March skillfully started a drift as indicated while maintaining the rotation, so Anj could see towards the forest now. Her hands were pointing straight up again, the descent looking good, but as they rotated further around towards the view of the river, she could see a rocky dry gulch, apparently left over from past floods, so she tilted both hands pointing down the beach, away from the gully, and March slid the dropping ship down the beach, completely trusting those hand motions, having no visual reference for his piloting. The shrieking engines rendered useless any voice communication.

Rotating around now, Anj had seen the entire LZ and felt assured that safe landing was in the bag, away from the gully and the embankment and the forest. Still slowly dropping vertically, they were close now; she held up ten fingers for ten meters to the surface, and March slowed further as her fingers disappeared one at a time. Three, two, one... a solid crunch and a jolt let them know, that this trillion mile journey had ended. Stillness. Silence took over as the jets whined down to a stop.

Euphoria; relief; paradigm shift; no longer astronauts, but pioneer/survivors in the wilderness of ΔT. The next sound was the click of releasing seat belts as they slid out of their chairs to stand once again held solidly by the mysterious pull of gravity.

A wide range of thoughts and emotions were vying for attention in Anj's mind and heart. March, more the linear thinker, had been preparing for this moment, and virtually had the ax in his hand, ready to start building that log cabin. For all he could see ahead, he would probably never fly anything again; he had settled that in his mind and heart and released it.

Both of them were noticing a clear and distinct new idea intruding gently into their spirits that seemed to emanate from this place at the moment they landed. It was a fully developed idea, and more than an idea, it came to them like a finished painting, and all they had to do was to hang it on the wall. It represented a new reality, a new mentality, something firmly established. It was a picture of a war that was over; over, having ended well. Later, when they talked about it, they wondered what great conflict it was that they were sensing had ended? March told Anj, "I felt it too as the end of some ongoing battle, and ending it enables us to hear clearly for a peaceful future. It was relief, but I could not define what it was I was relieved of." There was nothing rational about the impression, but they simultaneously received it. Since there was no place to fit it immediately into the matrix of thoughts and plans for life in this place, it got shelved along with 'random thoughts that don't add up.' But the peace that attends the end of a terrible conflict, that peace, that relief, remained with them, and subconsciously altered their manner of approaching the next steps onto this new planet.

Released from the confines of their seats, they immediately began to check the instrumentation for environmental data, as the new tranquility remained. Temperature, 31° C (89° F), and rising. They were well into the morning of the twenty-eight hours of daylight, and it promised to get much warmer. March turned his attention to powering up the air conditioning. They thanked God for electricity from the cold fusion unit. The ship included a portable air conditioner that could cool a space twice the size of the cabin so that they would be able to transfer it into the shelter they would eventually have to build. It would serve them at least as long as they had electricity from the cold fusion unit, several years at least.

So many things had to be figured out. Was the soil any good for crops? How would they plow and plant, and how much area would be needed to harvest enough to survive? Was there any food growing here naturally? How was the water? Would they need to irrigate? How would they be able to get water from the river for irrigation? What kind of weather conditions were they going to encounter? Would crops survive the extreme temperature differentials? How well would they function in the extreme heat and the extreme cold? What kinds of building materials were available? All of this had been prepared for, as best they could. Every possibility they could think of was considered in planning their approach to living on a new planet. They had dehydrated food stowed on board for nine Earth months, which they counted on giving them enough time to figure out a growing season and how to raise food.

All of these future considerations were set aside for now, immediate needs coming first; is survival possible outside of this ship?

Atmospheric analysis came up with 15.2% oxygen, significantly lower than at sea level on Earth, perhaps like high altitude living, eight-thousand feet plus. Nothing toxic was detected in the air, thank God; they really did not want to have to wear helmets all the time. There was a light breeze coming to them from the sea to their west, blowing towards what would be the sunrise. The blue sky out the portal would have looked like home to the casual observer, though it was a shade darker blue. Motion detectors did not sense any movement of creatures, and a visual check also revealed no visitors. It was time to open the hatch and step outside.

Anj turned on the lapel mic so that someday, Earth would find out what happened here today. She had been sending home a few meditations and comments so far, but this was the climax of all they had all worked for. "Greetings from Deep ΔT. We are opening the hatch onto a warm day..."

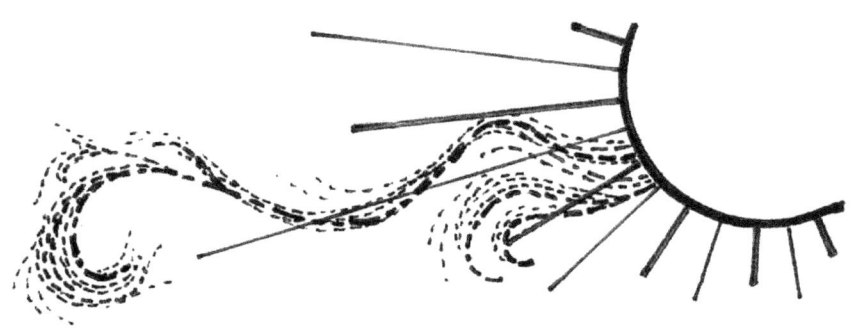

Chapter Eight: Launch Central

- some four years later

Browning opened his terminal first thing in the morning as he had for the last three months. Because the time of his astronauts was earlier than Earth's time, due to the speeds they had sustained, he had begun expecting to hear of their arrival at ΔT significantly before a straight calendar would have predicted. He had been tracking every shred of information he was getting fed from Proxima One. He had observed the month of slowing down. They had achieved a greatly reduced velocity of thirty thousand miles an hour. All of the survival systems appeared to be working, but he had not heard from a human being yet. Others on the Close Team had taken to gathering around him each morning, as he sat at his monitor because word had gotten out that the time was approaching when cabin heat would be turned up and the air in the ship would be oxygenated. Excitement and anticipation were rising.

This morning they were all transfixed, as AI fed line upon line of data onto the screen from four-and-a-half light-years away. They were not interested in what the power supply wattage was, how much radiation the ship was exposed to from the nearby stars, or the exact course variation being caused by ΔT's gravity. They wanted a word from Anj. They hungered to hear from life out there, from their two friends who had been gone for six silent years already.

Lines of data streaming onto the screen stopped. Everyone involuntarily stopped breathing. The last few words from AI read, "Lexan cover open." A collective yell went up from the group because they knew the cover would not open unless Anj had squeezed that activation switch. It was a short celebration because tension and anxiety surged back into the mood of the room. Carla was openly crying. Cooper's arms folded, his fingers drummed silently on his other forearm. They waited, trying to imagine what was happening, actually what had already happened four years ago, an impossible concept.

Lines of text started up again, and all eyes hungrily took it in: "Proxima One to Launch Central, this is Anj, I am awake and well." Applause exploded again.

Untold man-hours of work, turning ideas into hardware and equipment, designing, testing, revising, discussing, scrapping things that would not be strong enough or safe enough, starting over, redesigning, testing, and proving every aspect of this mission to preserve the lives of two human beings for so long and so far out there that it was really beyond imagining. At least for this moment, it looked like it had all worked. The celebration this time lasted all morning. Nobody got any work done. Word spread through the entire facility and extended 'family' began to pour into Browning's office for a look at the monitor and the print-outs as data kept coming and occasionally a note from Anj. She had stated next, "Ship is looking good. You ought to see the view from up here. Hope all is well on Earth." Always the professional pilot, she also understood they would want more than a cryptic line or two from her, and she knew that AI would give all the mechanical and navigational data without any additional input from her.

They selected out her comments from between the dozens of other lines of information coming from AI. "March looks good, well not really; he looks dead, but the vitals displayed on the hyper-sleep module indicate that he is alive and well. I am believing for the best in a couple days when he wakes up. I know you are not all persuaded that God had anything to do with this, but He is here. He talked to me not long after I woke up. He says He is here with me. I would not have wanted to take on this adventure without all of you; you made this happen; you got me here; it's going to work; and God helped us all; God helped us all. None of this works without Him. I am very thankful to all of you and to God."

"ΔT is drawing closer, no longer just a bright speck. It looks like a tiny soccer ball from this far away. Black and white; I believe I see large green areas too, and I'm praying for chlorophyll. Would that not be astounding? What else could be that green? Copper deposits? Copper would not be very helpful for this pioneer family yet, but chlorophyll, that would mean plants, growing plants, maybe food-bearing plants. This is not wishful thinking; it is well within my imagination that God would do a similar thing with vegetation in other parts of His universe, as He has done on Earth."

"Let me give you just a little visual here, since there is no one else to talk to. Alpha Centauri is hanging out there in space, two huge stars within spitting distance of each other, nothing to compare to it in the night sky where you are. Somewhere between a star and a sun, they are dancing an astronomical whirling dervish around one another every seventy-nine years. I can practically see between them the tension of the gravitational pull against the centrifugal force. Right now I see them about as far apart as they ever get. In another thirty-seven years, trusting we are still here, God willing, they will be very close, or one behind the other. What kind of difference that makes to us on the surface of the planet as far as light and heat, remains to be seen.

"Needless to say we are excited; well March is still out, but I know he will be excited. The astronomer in him will be, and the man I know who loves to explore and find out new things will be over the top with the thrill of seeing this new solar system. This is something I have dreamed about since I was ten, but no amount of imagining ever got me to this place, or to this vision. Nevertheless, here we are, and it is my brand-new reality.

"On one hand it is a strange thing to put so much trust in a machine made of titanium and wires and tubes to get us from here to that soccer ball over there, but I know that my trust is actually in God's gracious choosing of each of you to join this effort, and my trust is in all of your good work designing and building it. I can tell you it has been a thrilling thing to look back on the last six years of travel in this machine and see that everything operated perfectly. I hope you feel appropriately good about that. I also want to let the LEM team know how great it was to find out that it is in the right place at the right time, just waiting for us to come along and hook up with it. Well done, team! Feel my embrace and our huge thanks.

"I'm going to work now. I will keep you posted. So weird to know you won't hear from me until after the next presidential election. Praying for continued funding for Proxima Mission! Haha!"

Several pages of information about every possible aspect of the ship's operations followed, and several hours of celebratory talk as groups of specialists clustered around several of the desks. A giddy rejoicing mood set the tone, especially among those to whom Anj had directed her praise, the research and development teams that had designed and built Proxima One and the LEM from the ground up. Their celebration was tempered also with multitudes of unanswered questions which could only be answered on the same time-line that Anj and March were walking through. It was like reading an exciting story while being restricted to seeing only a page a day.

Browning, who stayed at the monitor and was able to most easily glance over to it, finally said "Here's something."

Anj had posted, "LEM is here, got here ahead of us, but you already know that. It is a little insane, from my perspective here, that we bet our lives on an electronically controlled piece of equipment managing to precede us here and be orbiting ΔT like a good puppy. You cannot possibly identify with the lonesome place I have woken up to. I'm talking into this little microphone because it offers a shred of hope that indeed my words will be heard, all the while knowing that I will not hear any reply from you for over eight years. I go over sometimes and talk to March too because, even though he can't hear me, I will be able to hear him in a couple days. You can only imagine how much I am counting on his awakening. It is frightening, because if he did not make it… Well, change of subject. We are slowing again, down to entry velocity, but you know that. ΔT is looking better and better. Power supply has been a little sketchy; I'm not sure what is going on. You could probably help me figure it out, Browning, but you will be a little late. I'm going to do my exercise routine now and get my first good night's sleep in six years! Haha. See you tomorrow."

Well, it was past time to go home anyway. Browning entertained the thought of sleeping in the back room on the cot he used when they were up against a deadline, and he'd catch a nap. But he knew there would be nothing from Anj for nine or ten hours. Everything from Proxima One was being backed up in the cloud anyway for future review and analysis. He could always go back on the timeline and catch up. So he gathered his coat and umbrella and stepped out into the rain to get into his very ordinary four-wheeled vehicle, while his head was still back in a space vehicle hurtling towards ΔT.

Two days later, he did take the option of the cot because March was scheduled to awaken about midnight and he did not want to catch that on a replay. Everyone went home but he, Carla, Slade Zaminski (Zam), and Cooper, all of whom had been anxiously anticipating the awakening of the second astronaut. Their intense involvement in the hyper-sleep project left them hungry to know the well-being of both pioneers.

Carla Peretti, as the personal coach for each astronaut, had prepared them mentally and had overseen their physical readiness for the arduous prospect of six years in the coffin. It was her voice Anj heard talking her through the wake-up, and she felt responsible for March's waking tonight as well.

Zam couldn't keep his fingers from drumming on his desk, or the desk of whoever he was talking to. He knew he would not sleep until he knew March was alive and well, so he might as well lose sleep in his office chair instead of at home. His design of the inflatable memory foam pressure pads that held the sleeping pilots was a particularly critical factor during the twenty-eight days of 4G's they had just experienced while asleep.

Cooper Smith - some of the others called him C.S, like C.S. Lewis, because of his intellect and his fantastic imagination - had been monitoring the data from all the astronauts' vital signs for the last nine-plus years, watching the essential input that sustained the delicate balance of keeping them barely alive. He had recently seen some inconsistencies that worried him in the telemetry that no one else paid attention to. He was not giving voice to what worried him yet.

They all napped or drank coffee, awaiting anything streaming to them that indicated the necessary changes in March's status. Cooper, of course, was the first to notice warming in Zam's mattress and alerted Carla and Zam sleeping in their chairs, and Carla went to wake Browning.

Anj broke in with a line or two, "I am preoccupying myself by staying busy so that I don't get nervous about March. I'm really looking forward to having someone to talk to."

In that office, every face illuminated by the computer screen's blue-white glow registered identification with her, knowing what a ridiculous understatement that was. She and March were inseparable, almost telepathic the way they read one another and worked together. This had to be a rough couple of days for her in that state of inhumane isolation.

For a nervous half hour, most of them watched the data scroll down the screen looking for something familiar and counting on C.S. or Zam to call attention to anything that was important. C.S. finally was muttering something, "...not sure I like everything I'm seeing." He pointed out heart rate and blood pressure higher than would be normal, and other factors in the brain waves that were out of sync with what the human experimenters had typically experienced.

Anj's words came again, "Okay, I hear the oxygen coming in to him now, and he is turning pinker, thank God. I did not like seeing that gray face. I know it's normal, but grim nonetheless."

Carla chimed in, trying to be more cheery, "My recording has started; he's getting his in-module warm up now." But the suspense around the monitor was solid and not letting up, because of Cooper's expressed concern.

Four minutes of Carla's forced smile of optimism, four minutes of finger tapping (both Zam and Browning), four minutes of intermittent throat clearing, and four minutes of unblinking staring by Cooper were broken when Cooper said, "Come on March, calm down man, give yourself some time." Then "Oooo not good, not good. I don't know what is happening but it's not good," more to himself than to the others in the room as he watched the numbers keep on refreshing dispassionately.

Silence took over while they all tried to make sense of the vital statistics coming fast, line upon line. Cooper was turning even paler in the minimal light, and it was Zam who finally said, with unbelief in his tone, "Is that a flat-line, C.S.?"

Cooper, straightened a little, still glaring at the screen. Trying to remain very professional, he said, "I did not want to say something too early, but Zam, you are right. He didn't make it. I can't tell what happened, but there is no heartbeat and no breathing." Cooper was being a scientist on whom the truth about his friend had not yet penetrated.

A sob escaped from deep down in Browning's big chest, and he turned away, moving to put his face in his hands, but then he reversed himself and took a stance against the facts of that screen, and said loudly, "No! I don't accept that this is happening." Then much more calmly, "NO; no; no; absolutely not; this is not happening to Anj and March." It was not the desperate cry associated with denial of the facts which often accompanies that kind of bad news. It was as a mathematician, knowing there must be some kind of mistake, "No, that cannot be the answer. Anj and March *knew* God was going to get both of them all the way to Deep ΔT. They knew it. They convinced all of us."

With that statement taking up residence in the office, they all continued to stare at the monitor for a full five soundless minutes, and the screen was matter-of-factly stating heartbeat zero, and respiration zero. Zam finally walked away, unable to look at those numbers any longer. Carla was not far behind him, her head and heart flooded with disbelief in the face of all she had believed for them.

Cooper, ever the statistics man, insisted on staring, willing the screen to say something else. Even so, when it did, at first he questioned what he was seeing, but finally offered, "Hey, this just started to show some respiration. He's breathing again."

Like iron filings to a magnet, they flew back to the screen, transfixed. Now it was showing heartbeat and breathing normal, everything normal. Browning said, "I *knew* it had to be some kind of mistake, it just could not happen to them; just could not."

Now they wanted desperately to hear from humanity on that machine; what happened? Definitely relieved, the vital signs remaining steady, they waited an unbelievable twenty minutes before Anj finally came on.

"Oh, sorry team. That must have been scary for you. It was scary for us. March died. It looked like an aneurysm. He was gone, but my Jesus, my Jesus!" They could practically hear her voice in the text on the screen, even though it had been years since they were in the same room, that strident voice of confidence in her God which they had heard so often whenever team members began to waver about the wisdom of this expedition. Over time, during training, Browning, the only unbeliever in this little group, had come close to acquiring a vicarious faith as unbending Anj's, and he was in this moment joyfully drinking in her words. "My Jesus, He met March and sent him back to me, to us, here in this humanly contrived contraption, so that we can finish what He told us to do. My Jesus, oh thank You, God. He is with us right here. I can feel Him." Everyone in the room could feel Him.

A pall of incomprehension remained in the group, the remainder of having had incredibly bad news juxtaposed with equally good news. As it was all gradually absorbed, eventually Cooper went home; Carla went home; Zaminski went home; Browning went back to his cot, exhausted, but nobody was able to sleep, not for a long while, still making sure they were remembering and believing the right thing. By the time they gave it up, Anj was reporting that March was engaged in calculations for intercepting LEM.

Life went on; the mission went on, and Anj's posts became less frequent as the pilots engaged increasingly with the planet. A few pictures of Deep ΔT began to come through and immediately went to the front pages of world news posts.

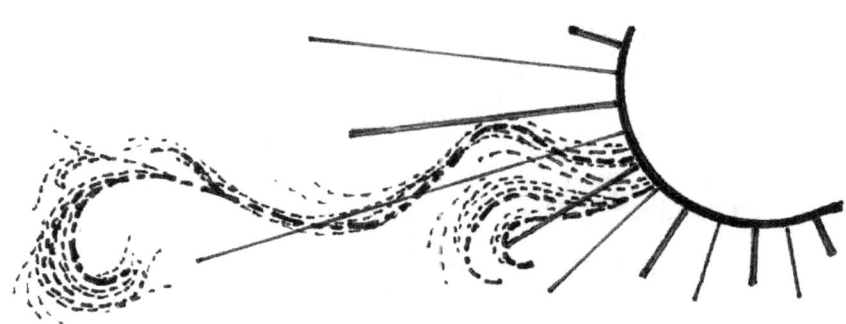

Chapter Nine

Minutes after landing and stepping down to the ground, March and Anj walked cautiously up the gradual slope above the ship's resting place to the edge of the trees, where what could only be described as a forest began. They were drawn irresistibly, after the briefest reconnoiter of their immediate surroundings, to those living organisms growing out of the ground. Fascinated, they looked them up and down, almost wondering who had imported trees here from Earth. They were not the same as the scrub oaks with which March was familiar in Northern California. The trunks in shape were very similar, but the bark was much thicker, and the leaves were brighter green with a waxy sheen like the Modrone, also common in California. March placed his hand on a trunk and leaned into it a little, feeling its strength, and suddenly felt something from it that was so unexpected that he pulled back as if shocked. "It's alive!" he said, startled by the sensation of its response to his touch.

Puzzled and looking at him, Anj's eyebrows posed a question. March tried to explain, "I felt something unmistakable from that tree. It's like when I would pet my cat, and she would begin to purr. That tree felt me and responded as if it were alive. Of course, it is alive, but you know what I mean, really like it was appreciating my hand resting on the bark. I could not deny it, and it startled me." He put his hand gingerly on the trunk again, looked at Anj, and nodded, "Yeah it's there alright. Go ahead, try it."

When she put her hand there beside his, she waited, looked at March with the same startled eyes, but did not draw her hand back in alarm. "What is that?" the scientist in her wanted to know, "Whatever it is, it feels nice, friendly even, very calming. I don't feel it in my hand, but in here," and she placed her hand on her abdomen, " Deeply. Quietly."

Both of them continued leaning against the tree. Actually, they were tapping into that calming influence, in harmony with the 'end of war' impression from a little earlier, and it helped them review their surroundings with the most at-ease attitude, like they were merely discovering a new campground on the Pacific Crest Trail instead of being on an unexplored planet. Looking around slowly, March commented, "It looks like you have picked a beautiful campsite. Wow, did you ever imagine this in your wildest dreams?"

Anj was speechless. Indeed, she had dreamed of verdant planets to explore when she was a child, before Mars was well known and the first rovers discovered that there was not even a germ there, let alone trees. After that, she had become a little more realistic. She remained hopeful but subdued, based on what had been gradually discovered about every moon, planet, and large asteroid within the reach of astronomers' analysis. All were desolate and/or had incredibly hostile environments, like Europa, Jupiter's moon, for example. It was much the subject of speculation about human habitation because it had water, but it was deep-frozen and the atmosphere was almost entirely oxygen, plus it was bombarded by radiation from Jupiter. Unrealistic measures would have to be taken to make human life feasible there. Looking around here, and taking in a deep breath of warm sea air, this was intoxicating. She continued to lean into the tree, stabilizing the euphoria sweeping through her mind.

Eventually, they left the trees and strolled leisurely back to the ship feeling the soft soil underfoot. Small grasses sparsely covered the clearing that was their landing zone. Standing back beside the ship, March stared at the new darker-blue sky so long that his neck hurt. He was looking for stars that would be visible during the day. The Binary stars were barely above the eastern horizon and clearly visible, but he hoped to discover others.

Anj sat down cross-legged in the shade of the ship, gently stroking the short grasses like they were newborn kittens, and thinking freely now beyond the constrictive images of inhospitable environments that she had considered so much more likely than this almost familiar place into which they had stepped moments before. After nearly an hour of soaking in the pleasant surprise of ΔT's first impressions, March commented that it was getting too hot and he proposed going inside and getting some work done in the air-conditioned interior. Converting the ship into a home of sorts required collapsing and stowing the hyper-sleep coffins and unpacking the 'kitchen.'

Other first-day activities included air, soil, and water analysis. They also began a basic log, regularly recording temperatures, barometric pressure, wind speed, humidity, gathering all the weather data they could, in hopes to be able to eventually predict the weather, essential to any future planting and harvesting. They knew that years and seasons did not exist on this planet because it only took four and a half ΔT days to circle the Proxima Sun. Any sort of weather cycles generated by the planet's spin or by its orbit were yet to be discovered. In appearance, their new sun was a little larger than Earth's sun and noticeably redder. Its rays felt warm but not as intense as at home.

After the long day, with only a couple of brief naps, evening promised to bring out some of those early stars that March wanted to see. Cooler now, they sat out under the sky, and stars appeared with the same irresistible invitation to think beyond them into that inky blackness. "How far does that go?" is the automatic question in response to a gaze into the night sky. Infinity apparently looked the same from anywhere in the universe.

Adjustment to the new planet would take months, they anticipated. Every night they would look out into a different quadrant of the universe and different constellations. This was indeed a very different world, a new reality that was going to take time to take root. Daylight for twenty-eight hours was impossible, and the interminable nights. Most basically, for the first few days, they felt their entire bio-systems attempting to adjust to a very different day-night cycle.

Not long into that first day, Anj had begun to feel a cerebral edema headache coming on, which she had anticipated as soon as they observed the low oxygen level outside of the ship. In her undergrad years, she had participated in an anthropological summer semester in Tibet, in the foothills on the north side of Mount Everest at about sixteen thousand feet. There she had experienced these symptoms the first time, and could not do the work that the others were able to do, hiking from village to village, observing the herders, the craftsmen, and the home-lives of the children. She did what mountain climbers must do at the Everest base camps. They have to take time to acclimatize. About the fifth day, she began to be able to exert herself and was gradually able to keep up with the rest of her classmates. So she knew that on ΔT she would have to do the same thing, let her body adjust, and she counted it a blessing since it did give her time to contemplate, mentally and emotionally reorienting to so much newness.

Most impactful that first day was the heat of the day. The day wore on and on, their new sun barely creeping across the sky, the temperature climbing steadily for hours and hours longer than was even conceivable, and topping out at a merciful forty-six degrees Celsius, (115° F) before it finally began to cool as the sun approached the western horizon. They dozed during much of the heat of the day, unable to sleep deeply with all the excitement of the new place. As the sun set in the west, the Alpha Centauri Twin Stars were directly overhead, bright enough to help maintain the latent warmth of the day well into the long night, but when the Twins sunk below the western horizon twelve hours later, the temperature began to drop more quickly. After another fourteen hours of darkness, the thermometer showed a low of negative seven degrees Celsius, well below freezing, before the sun broke free on the eastern horizon to rewarm the frosty landscape.

With twenty-eight hours of night, they were awake for much of it. Although they were exhausted from having missed a lot of sleep during the long day, one can only sleep so much, and one can only be awake so much. They discussed, during the endless black of that first night, how they could set up a sleep cycle that they could live with. Unable to come up with anything that seemed good, and in the rather frantic attempts to make this planet's days and nights work, they started out just sleeping when they were overcome with exhaustion, but over the next two fifty-six hour days it was wearing on them, especially March since he was exerting himself more exploring the surroundings.

On the second morning, Anj was lying in the shade of a tree, gazing at her new sky, a different darker blue than Earth's, with a few distant clouds retreating to the east. The clouds had brought a little rain to the land during the night and were following the surface of the planet, remaining mostly in darkness. Weather here was going to be interesting to figure out. With the radical temperature shifts, it stood to reason that some big storms could be generated. She was hoping blowing gales would hold off until they had their temporary house securely anchored against such an onslaught.

As she pondered that clear sky, to her amazement she saw what appeared to be a high, gliding eagle-like bird. Her stomach knotted momentarily because her pilot's instinct identified it as a fixed-wing aircraft at first glance. The prospect of finding a population of intelligent beings here was a huge question on her mind. That knot in her gut disclosed that, hidden in her, a real fear resided. Perhaps because it was such a big question, and the possibilities were terrifying, she had hidden it away unresolved. As Anj was still watching, the flying thing made a couple of slow flaps of its wings and then glided, just like a hawk or raven at home. Anj reassured herself it was a bird. The proliferation of fiction about extra-terrestrials had been feeding speculation for decades to the point it was an accepted fact that they existed, and would show up on Earth someday. That knot in Anj's stomach when she saw a flying object let her know just how deeply she was hoping *they*, if *they* existed, were not here.

The big question on everyone's mind at Launch Central was whether there was Life of any kind on Deep ΔT. Of course, that question was basically answered with a single look out of the portal when they unbuckled the safety belts after touchdown. Those trees, with thick trunks and branches, with leaves and bark, stood not far from the LZ. What had looked like a forest from high altitude was indeed forest. Mars had proven to be entirely devoid of even the most basic bacteria, and yet the question lingered, "Is there life on any other planets?" Proxima One was the next great leap of exploration, in part fueled by something of Earth's life in a search of itself.

Immediately following her stomach knotting in fear, came genuine excitement over the evidence of a flying life form, graceful and free. It was the first creature they had seen. She could hardly wait to tell March. He would be coming back soon from a tour of the shallow dry gulch that they had avoided upon landing. He wanted to find out if it could be made into a channel from the river for their water supply. It would be very inconvenient to have to hike to the river daily for water, and if they were to eventually irrigate crops, flowing water would be essential. He came back carrying what looked like some kind of fruit. So they both had big news to share.

His pear-sized yellow fruit had seeds in it like an apple when he cut it in half, and it dripped juice. It was very tempting to taste it immediately, but, ever the scientists; they put a sample in the auto-lab for analysis. While it cooked, analyzing the sliver of fruity material, Anj put her hand on March's arm, and said dramatically, "Guess what I saw?" He looked expectant, knowing she wasn't playing a game. "I think it was some kind of hawk or eagle; very high, and I saw it flap its wings twice." Looking to his expression, "I thought at first it was an aircraft," she said. There, she saw deep concern momentarily flash across his face, letting her know that his reaction was similar to hers.

He tried to laugh it off, and said, "*That* would be a game-changer," and as the forced laughter evaporated from his face, that concern settled there and remained, thoughtful. "Yeah, I have thought about it too. The existence of extra-terrestrials always seemed like such a long shot, especially after Mars and the moon came up with no life at all. But this place, who knows what is over the next mountain or across that sea from here? It is rather sobering." That was on day two.

A beep from the auto lab indicated the analysis was complete. The fruit was negative on toxins, positive on sugars, carbohydrates, and included some minimal proteins. With shining eyes fixed on March, Anj took a small bite of the section he handed to her. He was waiting for a grimace of distaste to register quickly, but she rolled it around on her tongue carefully, thoughtfully, and finally bit down, slowly crushing the bite so that its juices were released on unsuspecting taste buds. She was tasting something never tasted on Earth, and it was beyond comparison to any other fruit that had ever crossed her lips. Superlative flavor and delight beamed from her face, much to his surprise. A long soft drawn-out "Wow," escaped her lips. "I hope this doesn't make me sick because I'm going to eat the whole piece. What kind of place is this?" March ate the other half, with identical surprise and pleasure, and made a mental note to visit that tree again.

Anticipating the need for marking time, they had brought clock software that they could adapt to ΔT. Much debate had gone into whether they would completely start over with new units: new seconds, minutes hours, and days, or use some of the Earth units. That issue seemed like an important thing to settle. To March and Anj's scientific, logical approach to adaptation to the new environment, it seemed to be essential. Time measurement was a centerpiece to the life they were used to.

On the second long evening, as the day cooled, and the sunset lingered lazily, March spoke up from his comfortable position sitting on the ground leaning against a friendly tree trunk, enjoying a bag of peanuts with the new fruit and a drink of river water. "You know, I am getting the distinct impression that ultimately, this new planet will supply all the time reference we need, just like the pioneers of old who watched the sun and stars. Forget the clock problem.

Surprised, Anj thought about that, unaccustomed to the laid-back attitude that her on-time and punctual husband was displaying. She said, "But surely some kind of conversion to Earth-time will eventually be important if there are to be future missions here. Let's begin with simple measurements of the length of a day here, using Earth units. That will give us the conversion factors needed to convert to Earth time if necessary."

"Sounds good to me. Can you take that on as a pet project? It's all yours if you want it."

"Roger, captain, glad to."

They also kept a calendar from Earth even though they could not accurately follow it. Because their speed in transit had approached the speed of light, time had slowed down for them. Their travel time, measured from Earth, was to be six years, but their chronometer revealed that for them, only a little over five years had elapsed. Anj had given up a long time ago trying to make sense of Relativity.

On the third morning on ΔT, Anj woke up as dawn was first bringing sunlight to the treetops. Her mind was trying to get a grip on the day, but she found her thoughts hovering here and there, unable to land anywhere. There were too many questions on her mind. The last few days had been intense. In fact, she thought they were probably the most all-consuming three days of her life in terms of being able to meaningfully consider everything that was assaulting her. A six-year journey through outer space had been brought to its conclusion. That was huge, but that, and even the tension of actually landing the ship on Deep

ΔT, was a simple routine in comparison to the last three days. The landing had been rehearsed, practiced to the last detail, and prepared for, but she had no practice for how to adjust to her brand-new reality, to everything being different, even the color of the sky.

It was becoming overwhelming, and there was no way to take a day off from Deep ΔT. It was culture-shock, a little as if she and March had moved into a very different city in a foreign country with an unfamiliar climate. It reminded her of when her Dad and Mom had decided to move to a new city. It was a move from her small home town, practically a village, to a mega-city. Anj was 12, in the middle of seventh grade. At first, she was excited about a move to a big city. Nothing much was going on in Latrobe, where she had grown up. It was a moderately sized town with the Loyal Hanna River running through it, tucked into the foothills of the Appalachians. She had heard of San Francisco and seen snips of it in movies. It looked exciting. It was by the ocean and was reached by spectacular bridges.

As a twelve-year-old, new to city-living, some of her earliest discoveries were that it had more than one movie theater. It had crazy-fun hills to ride up and down in the back seat of the car, "Dad, can we do that again?" Lombard Street was her favorite. There were many new things to see, and for a budding space explorer, it was thrilling to be near the places where some of the new scientific developments were taking place. However, adjusting to the social, climatological, and educational changes had her head spinning for months. People were too friendly. The school had an uncomfortable hard-driving atmosphere. Fog obscured everything for a major part of every day. Cold dampness was unfamiliar. Nothing was the same in the grocery store. It was exciting, yes, but for a seventh-grader there were too many unknowns to get used to all at once.

Yes, that was it; she felt like a seventh-grader again, completely overshot by the demands of all these new conditions for which she had no context. When do I wake up? How do I survive this insufferable ever-increasing heat? And conversely, the endless, ruthlessly cold nights? Where can I go that is safe? How is life going to work out here? How can we provide for ourselves here? Very little of her previous life-experience was proving to be helpful. Unable to decide what to do first today, she finally landed on the thought of just going quietly down to the sea and sitting on the beach for a while before it began to get too hot outside. She would take a thirty-minute vacation, try to let her brain just be for a while. Asleep in the reclining pilot's seat right beside her, March too was exhausted from trying to adjust to these endless hours of day and night. He had finally hit a wall; sleep had taken over, mandating a reset in his internal clock. He had left her a note on the screen some time ago in the long night, "Babe, we need a new approach to these days. I am not adjusting to these hours. It's not working. I'm going to sleep; don't try to wake me. Just going to try to catch up and feel rested again."

She crept quietly outside, stepping into the new frontier, so unfamiliar in so many ways, only wearing her flight jacket, not sure how cold it was. She could see that the sun would be warm on her back shortly if she sat facing the sea. It was crisp but no longer freezing out, and the fascinatingly colored pebbles of the beach crunched underfoot in a conversational way as if welcoming her. Every sound she heard in this place struck her perception as not just new, but revealing something to her of the harmony of it all. Sounds she had never noticed before were catching her attention. Breeze, the rustling of leaves, the waves on the beach, had all distinguished themselves in the last two days as uniquely communicative. Now the sound of the gravel on the beach seemed to be trying to tell her something or draw her attention to something fresh and lovely. Taking a moment to scoop up a handful and look closely, she could see that each little rock had apparently come from a different type of bedrock and was a different color. They all had been polished together by the waves' action here for millennia. A handful of them was the subject of her interest for several minutes.

As she seated herself cross-legged on the fine multi-colored gravel, she noticed it was there again, that tangible sense of peace they had experienced upon touchdown. It was moving in and taking over all her thoughts and feelings; this time she could define that peace a little better. It felt like the peace the world must have felt at the end of the great wars when entire continents were suddenly relieved of the constant specter of millions of men fighting and dying in the madness of worldwide armed conflict. All is well; "The world is whole again. You can let go of that background of fear and worry. It is over. It is over. Done, no more."

She felt the relief profoundly, but the magnitude of relief was greater than what she would have anticipated, even from the obvious ordeal they had recently concluded. Deciding to stick to her plan and give herself a thirty-minute vacation, she abandoned an over-thinking episode about the reason for the prevalence of such delightful peace, and simply settled into it. She let it move in and take over her quiet place there on the dry gravel, above the reach of the regular, smooth swells rolling onto the shore. The sound of those small breakers ministered to her also. They were saying the same thing, "Here it is, simply receive it; peace," with each wave.

Whatever it was, it came rolling softly over her like an atmosphere of blue presence. She had an impression of blue this time, a blue haze, although she could not see it. Enveloping her, it grew to be an awareness not only of the cessation of hostilities, but also an uncomplicated absence of even the possibility of hatred, let alone war; the absence of malice of any kind. A voice without words began, "Complete absence of all that gives birth to fear; not here on ΔT; never has been; does not exist; receive it." She did not hear audible sounds, but she felt silent words with a calming discernible vibration within, something like a massage chair, but the source was inside, not outside of her.

She was sure she was hearing from God. It seemed crystal clear to her that fear of attack and fear of wickedness were life-expectations entirely from previous Earth-based experiences, and were not present here. 'Not here,' she heard again somewhere internally. "It's not here," she spoke out loud. Then in her heart, she began to meditate on what was being impressed upon her, namely that the fear of coming to a terrifying end or being attacked in any way whatsoever was not something she needed to waste any emotional energy on here. It felt easy to let it go, that ever-present background of caution and vigilance that she had automatically imported to this entirely new world. She began to understand that it did not fit here.

She continued to sit, actually mostly incapable of moving. She was so captivated by this new tranquility. It was a tantalizing prospect that this could be a planet of peace, and at the same time her analytical side was suspicious. Was it revelation or was it just euphoria from having finally landed, finally having achieved a lifelong goal, a response within her core to the relief of the journey and its dangers being finished. Was that all it was? She did not know, but did not want to spoil it in any way because it was such a wonderful emotional place to remain for a while, here in this mindset, feeling becalmed, still, not even a ripple. She stayed motionless both in body and in spirit, with her eyes closed, allowing the freedom from all threat of danger to continue to be absorbed, to become clear to her flesh-and-bone existence. Gradually she began to feel loved. So loved. Child-like. Trusting. Safe. No place for any fear. "God is near," she said out loud to herself, "Father, You are here," over and over, recognizing His Presence in that wordless voice, warming her inner person with awareness of His attending goodness and speaking to her about an essential aspect of this place, something she had, by that time, a real need to know.

Warmth from the sun that felt good on her back at first finally became uncomfortable heat, and Anj eased out of her reverie, realizing she had been there some hours, not thirty minutes, and it was getting hot. Four hours into ΔT's twenty-eight hours of daylight, and she was thinking about going inside the ship to get out of the warm rays from Proxima. One of the contributors to this comprehensive disorientation she was feeling was that the sun looked different. "What is more basic than the sun? That's when you know you're in a different world, when the sun looks different, and you have to get used to it," she had commented wryly the day before. But right then she felt like a different person than she was yesterday, or even at dawn today. Her beach time had worked a subtle transformation.

An idea came to her as she tried to think about the rest of this day that was just beginning, and there was peace on the idea. Regarding a sleep cycle, it would make sense and closely approximate their Earthly cycle if she and March slept for about eight hours during the hottest part of the daylight, and woke up to do whatever they could with the rest of the hot afternoon and long evening. Then they would go to sleep again, about twenty hours later, during the coldest part of the night. They would wake again while it was still dark, but be ready by sun-up to make the best of the cool mornings at each dawn. Their daily cycle would be twenty-eight Earth-hours long instead of twenty-four, but they could adapt to that. They would alternate between a day that included the sunrise and the next day, one that included sunset. "Dawn days and Dusk days," she thought, and she liked the sound of it, and thanked God for the inspired idea, so simple, but out of the box for an Earthling used to both dawn and dusk each day. She would talk to March about it.

Standing up a little stiffly on the beach after sitting so still for so long was refreshingly easier than standing up on Earth because the gravity of ΔT was noticeably less than Earth's. That was an easy one to adapt to. High altitude living had been more difficult for her. The symptoms of cerebral edema were a headache, difficulty paying attention, and nausea after only a little exertion. She knew it was a condition that can become quite serious, so she had been taking it real easy, which was frustrating to her natural high-achieving lifestyle, but it was actually an opportunity to begin to feel at home in this place, rather than conquer it.

Like the crags on the moon and the ranges explored on Mars, there were prominent and striking mountains here, not quite like anything she had seen on Earth. Certainly the geology was different here. These peaks reminded her of pictures she had seen of the Tetons. Never having been to Wyoming in person, she could not say for sure, but she was delighted to have strong-looking mountains within sight. Unlike on the moon and Mars, living things abounded here, water was abundant, and on both of the long evenings they had experienced thus far, a soft rain had fallen for a couple of hours not long after it got dark. This nearby river was flowing down out of the mountains. That water must have been carried up there in a cycle similar to Earth's: evaporation, condensation into clouds, rain, and snow in the higher elevations, resulting in springs, streams, rivers, and lakes.

"Glorious! What a place You have brought us to!" she praised God for His favor as she pondered all the science fiction images of desolate planets like the fictional Dune with inhospitable eco-systems. March too had told her again how deeply relieved he was to discover that on ΔT there actually was the possibility of living by a river and a lake.

They had known so little, it was clearly a faith-based decision to volunteer for this mission. They simply believed it would be a life-sustaining habitat despite all the logical concerns. They trusted God, Who so clearly seemed to have His hand upon them for this. They knew it was what they were created to do. He would take them to a good place. At this point, any persistent worries were being removed one by one. March had brought back water from the river, which analyzed as potable, and it tasted more than amazing in comparison to the water stored in stainless steel canisters for six years. This river water seemed to speak life to them, from within them. Anj recalled that when she was little and would play outside too long in the heat, she would come inside for a drink of water. The delightful relief of drinking that marvelous cool essential for life was one of the great treats of summertime. This water straight out of the mountains of Deep ΔT was even better. 'Living water' was the idea that came to mind when they drank it. The seawater tested slightly salty, not like the Earth's oceans, but definitely not drinking water.

Up the bank from the sea about a hundred meters, the soil was black and soft, full of organic material apparently from the decomposed tree leaves. It appeared that these trees lost their leaves which eventually became part of the soil, not unlike the forest floors of Earth. This was encouraging to their plans for planting and growing food. Taking some of that soil in her hands, squeezing it and then letting it crumble and fall through her fingers, it seemed to be telling her - she was sure it was not just her imagination, but a real understanding that was transmitted to her from the soil itself - that the soil was capable of bringing forth a good harvest. It was good soil.

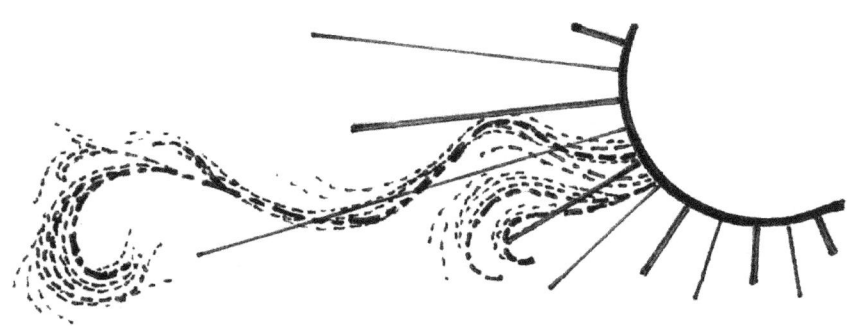

Chapter Ten: Launch Central

The whole team was present in the office for the actual entry and landing with a commensurate portion of nail-biting suspense and wild celebration not seen in Launch Central since the initial manned exploration landed on Mars. That resolute group of survivors was old news now, having established a relatively safe, sustainable station that was host to rotating personnel, for residential spans of four years.

What Anj had to report when she and March opened the hatch to step out onto the new planet was what everyone had been anticipating. "Greetings from Deep ΔT. We are opening the hatch onto a warm day, with a light wind from the northwest. We have four rungs of a ladder to climb down to the surface. I will, without shame, borrow the theme from Neil Armstrong's unforgettable words. It is a short climb for us, down to the surface here, but it is the conclusion of a great journey of mankind into new realms of space exploration. Our distance prohibits sending you live video, but pictures will be coming to you soon from our new home, which looks amazingly hospitable. We are seeing trees and oceans and mountains."

Evident excitement in her words was contagious. Admiration for the courage and faith it took to be there was the automatic secondary response to her report as it was sent around the world. For everyone, from Launch Central to the nomads watching on solar-powered televisions in West Africa, a mix of admiration and longing to join them welled up in answer to news of another habitable world, and a new frontier.

Days later, Browning and the Close Team were still hanging on every word that Anj sent them. They were even feeling a little irritated with Anj because they thought she was being a little stingy with her reports by about the fourth Earth day after they landed. Even the constant stream of information from the ship had dropped off dramatically after landing, so they could wait several minutes for any kind of update, and it could be hours to hear from Anj. A shout would go up from whoever was watching the monitor, "Words!" And the rest would cluster around to read. Sometimes the shout was, "Picture!" with a similar eager reaction, even though it seemed to take ages to gather the pixels into a cohesive image.

On that first day, upon touchdown, just after stepping out of the ship for the first time, Anj's descriptions had been of trees, oceans, and mountains, and she promised pictures. Anj was good to her word, and after she described their first stroll up the slope to the trees, a picture started to emerge, one line of pixels at a time, to the wide-eyed scientific community who had engineered the possibility of two human beings standing on another planet in another solar system. As trees began to appear, whistles of unbelief were heard.

"Could you have ever guessed?" Cooper was the first to try to speak.

"Coop, is this some kind of stunt?" someone questioned, knowing his propensity for high-tech tomfoolery.

"No, no, my friend, this is far too serious. I wouldn't try to trick you. Look; there is no tree you ever saw on Earth quite like that. It looks like a cross between a Modrone and a really old Cottonwood; look at that deeply fissured gray bark. I'll bet it is extra thick because of the extreme heat and cold it has to endure." Then smiling broadly, he teased Browning, "Did we send them with suitable clothing for those temperatures?"

Frank Browning rolled his eyes in pretended exasperation. "You guys still think we are a bunch of idiots in Central. Yeah, we just sent them out there with leotards so they can look like Captain Kirk."

Anj kept up a running description of what she was seeing for the first fifteen minutes, and the data stream portrayed environmental factors that were startling to the skeptic scientific minds looking on: mild temperature, favorable atmosphere, reasonable humidity, a slight breeze, and safe levels of solar radiation. Nobody had expected anything as hospitable as this. By the end of the first two hours, they had pictures of trees, the ocean, and distant sharp-peaked mountains. The sky was a deeper blue; the sunlight was as if from an incandescent bulb, towards the reds. Everything looked like it was sunset, but it was a brilliant morning on ΔT.

A thrill of excited fascination stayed with them, even though Anj's reports gradually became less frequent. She related the experience of the first long day's blazing heat at its peak. When the sun went down, she tried to describe Alpha Centauri, not a familiar-looking pair of stars, nor were they bright enough to be suns, more like mini-suns. They were not like a moon although visible during daylight sometimes like the moon, and illuminating portions of some nights. The pair appeared in different locations every day in the same fashion as Earth's moon, but much brighter, and gently warming, two far-distant suns.

On their first night on ΔT, everyone watched the thermometer on ΔT drop and keep on dropping all night and, unbelievably, sinking during all of Earth's next day, not reaching its low, -7°C, (19°F), until quitting time at Launch Central.

At the end of their second day, she filed this report: "I am going to try to describe some first impressions for you. We are feeling something interesting here. Simply put, it is peace. It is peace beyond what I would naturally expect to experience at the end of a long arduous journey, or at the culmination of a goal finally achieved. It is something that is here; it is not from inside of us. It is not a reaction to our circumstances; it is a perception of something in this place. We perceive peace here. Everything seems to talk to us in a way that I can only describe as friendly. Soil, trees, waves, ripples of a stream, even the rocks speak to me; I pick up a rock and it tells me how my appreciation of its beauty is a note of a sweet melody. It is not words, I don't hear voices, but it is unmistakably clear.

"It is not weird like an enchanted island, where we are waiting for the dragon to come down out of his cave and eat us. It is that everything here is in harmony. The waves rolling in from the sea don't just speak to me; they greet the gravel on the beach and the gravel answers. The trees talk to the breeze. Random blowing leaves huddle together and chat behind a rock and let the rock know how nice a place it has created for them. No words are necessary; I can feel it. It is as clear as what I have felt after a good creative meeting with all of you on our best day; friendship, harmony, agreement, joy. It is the joy of being able to work together well.

"This place is different in ways far beyond its size, rotation, orbit, and statistical factors. It is different on grounds of the communication-waves available here. Put simply, the creation here seems to have a good attitude. It's in a good mood. I know that is not very strong data-supported information about this place, but it seemed important for you to hear about it.

"I am exhausted and need to get some sleep. I just wanted to file a quick report that we are well and adjusting to this place. Good night."

Ten hours later, she reported, "Wide awake. The sunset is long gone. It is very dark out now. Alpha Centauri has set. Cold. Thermometer says 5°C, of course, you know that. I'm not the only one talking to you. Thanks, AI. These long days and nights are no joke. How are we supposed to adjust to this? This is our big job now, as pioneers in a strange land. Before we can have a life here, we feel like we have to adapt to sleeping longer, as in sixteen or eighteen hours. That leaves thirty-eight or forty hours not sleeping; who can do that? Or we need to come up with a creative solution for a new sleep schedule. Either option, you have to realize, from our perspective, is confounding to our previously stable bio-systems, every facet of which was programmed to a twenty-four-hour day.

"We are being reminded of how closely our thoughts and emotions are tied to our physical bodies. Emotionally, this has been incredibly distressing, a fight between depression, because this environment is not working for us, and euphoria because we have arrived after this incredible odyssey. In so many ways, the place in which we find ourselves is wonderful, but one never imagines that one's world is going to change, not in the dramatic ways we are experiencing. Can you identify with us? This dark night will last twenty-four more hours. Whatever time you are reading this report, it will almost be the same time in your next day before we see the sun again. Meanwhile, you got a sunset, a night's sleep, a sunrise, and a whole workday. It will be night here the whole time. Night, night, night. What are we ever going to do? Pardon me for dumping my discontent on you a little, just needed to share graphically what March and I are facing. You might be able to commiserate with us.

"Yours, from the New World, Anj."

Everyone went home that night, to a normal night, trying to imagine if it were to last twice as long. And it would still be dark on Deep ΔT by the time they were going home from work the following day.

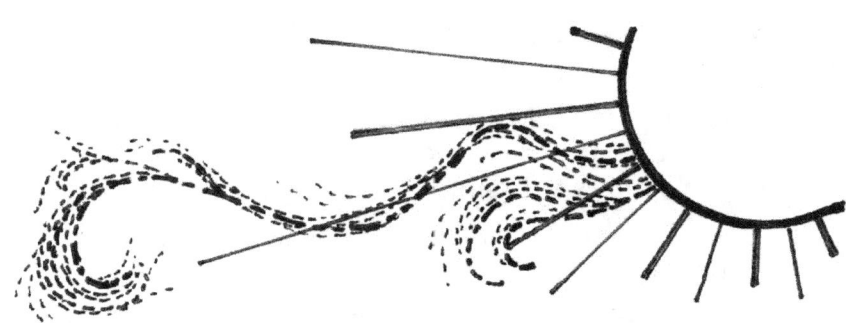

Chapter Eleven

Having heard, in her inner being on that third morning sitting on the beach, a message reassuring her that there was no threat, no attack being planned against her, no malice coming to her on ΔT, Anj's fear of extra-terrestrials was mostly dispelled. Concerns about who or what else was living on ΔT stopped gnawing on her stomach. That was before she saw lights across the sea. Just for just a few minutes, as the darkness closed in at the end of the third day, something shone out, a long way off, like someone turned on a porch light for a while then turned it off. It was far out across the sea. She wondered what natural phenomenon could possibly cause that? It was at that point she realized the ship had an exterior light turned on, and they decided to turn it off and curtain the portal, just in case. Just in case of what, they could not imagine.

In the following daylight, no land could be seen beyond the sea. Browning Sea, for that is what they decided to name it, from the beach appeared to be an ocean, extending out to the horizon until the curvature of the planet dropped the opposite coast below the horizon. Because they had seen it from high altitude, they knew that the sea was less than 80 km wide - fifty miles - even though it was maybe a thousand km long in that tiger-stripe shape typical of the seas on ΔT. There was a mountain range on that other side revealed by recon photos, as there was on this side, and they would be able to see the peaks if not for the sea haze, just enough humidity to obscure visibility at that distance. So, what were the possible sources of a bright light shining over on the distant mountains?

Anj asked, "Did you ever hear of the 'Lubbock Lights' phenomenon in Texas, where lights would appear in the sky seemingly unexplainably?"

March shook his head, looking up from his keyboard. "No, what is that?"

"People thought it was UFOs until someone figured out it had something to do with light bending where the summer's hot air interfaced with cooler air above it. In Texas, it was street lights of nearby communities that were appearing in the sky."

March turned to fully face his wife as he commented, "That makes sense. It must have really frightened some of the people in Texas. But here, where would the light come from? The only bright natural light was Alpha Centauri somewhere below the horizon. I can't figure out how it could appear low in the sky as if it was coming from those mountains."

"Or does it somehow reflect off of the mountains?" she posed, "some kind of geological feature that was reflective, maybe? Sheets of mica on a fault line can be very shiny." But she and March could both tell she was trying too hard to come up with an idea to ease her mind.

Not being able to figure out the source of that light was chafing at Anj. She said impulsively, "Let's find a way to go across and see where that light came from."

"I'll get out the speed-boat," he said facetiously. A short discussion followed in which she reluctantly agreed that more important tasks required immediate attention. First, they needed to decide if this LZ was where they would settle, or might they do better in the nearby foothills, or were there other options yet to be discovered? Where was the soil best? Would they have to plant and harvest? What other foods grew here naturally? And vestiges of old fear habits forced them to ask what safety concerns were still factors in choosing where to settle? Safety from storms?

From creatures which may be here? From intelligent beings who may be here? They had to factor that in, having seen those lights last night. Fear of the unknown is perhaps more plaguing than fear of a known enemy.

Anj would be able to hike and explore more energetically in a couple more days. Until then, March decided to keep his forays out into the forests and hills relatively short. It was tempting to go farther because of the extended daylight. He had at first stubbornly tried to get his body clock to adjust to twenty-eight hours of daylight, but then Anj got the idea of dawn days and dusk days. March was fully in favor of the new sleeping schedule that Anj had thought of. Consequently, on the fourth day, when Proxima was fully risen, he ventured out to the southeast, an unexplored direction. The previous day he had experienced that the heat of midday was not as severe up in the hills. This was to be a dawn-day, their first experiment with the new schedule. He set out to hike and explore for about five hours. At about what would have been noon on an Earth day, he sat cross-legged in the shade of a rock and tore open a lunch packet. He had also brought along two of what they were calling Δ Pears, the fruit they had tested and tried the previous day, and a flask of river water. Fresh fruit was incredibly welcome as they had only been able to look forward to nine months of MRE's (Meals Ready to Eat) an acronym that had been adopted from the military because it was familiar. All of their stored food was MRE's prepared by the CSE nutrition team using much of the military's technology for preparing nutritious food that would not spoil, ever. Nor, unfortunately, would it be very tasty.

He had checked in with Anj during the morning on portable radio whenever he had a relatively clear line of sight down to the sea. She was on a stroll down the beach to the southwest and reported that the beach was becoming sandier the farther she went south. After lunch, on his return, he took a little different route, just to see more territory. He got back to the ship at about dinner-time on the dawn day schedule, and Anj had some freeze-dried

Fettuccine reconstituted and hot. Even though it was approaching thirty-eight degrees Celsius (100°F) outside, they did their best to pretend it was evening, dinner time, and time to sleep soon. Over the meal he told her that from a high outcrop of rock at the farthest eastern point he had ventured, he had been able to see a distant valley nestled into the hills. It looked like a little paradise, so he noted its location on a rudimentary map he had begun to plot, until they could venture out that far together. He was getting restless to start on a permanent dwelling. The ship had all the comforts, but it was cramped quarters for two active adults.

She told him about some vines she had seen that looked like grapevines on the southeast coast of Browning Sea. There was grape-like fruit on them, but clearly, it was just beginning to form and was nowhere near being ripe. "I am puzzled that there were no ripe grapes. Unless there are factors we don't know about yet, it seems like there should be ripening fruit all the time since there are no seasons," she offered.

A clear diagonal crease that she called his 'worry wrinkle' appeared above his left eyebrow. It showed up whenever March had a menacing problem on his mind. He spoke; "My concern is the report of the probe about those 'brief but intense flares' on Proxima. What happens here then? Apparently, the forest doesn't all burn down; these trees are old enough I think, to have been here eight years ago when the probe came by and saw that flare. But rays like that might fry everything leafy green, and it would all have to start over from the root. What if that happens once or twice a year?"

Quietness settled in on their small space in the ship's cabin for a few minutes. It was a grave question. This was not their first discussion about it. Back at CSE Launch Control, they had stared long and intently together at a picture from the probe of a stellar flare. It was a grainy photo of a long tongue of flame curling out from the surface of the star to the planet. It looked just like the solar flares on Earth's sun, but ΔT was not ninety-three million miles from its sun like the Earth. It was only a fraction of that distance from Proxima. Depending on the timing of the flares, they could hit ΔT, realistically like a weed burner.

Predictions from astronomical analysts varied from, "No life could ever survive exposure to such heat on the surface of the planet," to, "Atmospheric conditions on the planet's surface will probably absorb the mostly infrared rays and will only result in some sudden and extreme warming, disturbing weather patterns for a time." In other words, "We don't know for sure." In praying about it, they felt that the flare did not signal a wholesale cancellation of the expedition. They had peace about it, and here they were, looking at a planet that bore no evidence of having been barbecued repeatedly, but it was still a concern. How had this verdant forest survived? How severe were the flares?

It was their new 'night-time', so they turned in to try to sleep on the comfy astronaut chairs that they had spent half their lives in, it seemed. Even though it was a very hot ΔT midday outside, with blindfolds over their eyes, and the AC quietly keeping them from experiencing being in a tin can left out in the sun, they both managed to sleep, if not deeply, at least without interruption for about eight hours.

Still a blazing hot day outside when they awoke, it was a mental exercise to try to think about it being 'morning' on this, their first dusk day. They did have about eight hours of daylight left before sundown as Proxima crept across the sky. Also, the evenings included many long hours of fading light, moderate temperatures, sometimes a sunset, and often gathering clouds and soft rain by dark, so there was plenty of time to have a full day. As different as this was going to be, it was encouraging to have been able to go to sleep before being completely exhausted.

Over breakfast MRE's and Δ Pears, "What are you going to do today?" they both asked at once. "You first," he prodded, knowing she was as eager as he was to get to work on the first necessary steps to establishing a permanent settlement.

She began, "As concerned as I have become about introducing plants into this eco-system that might be disastrous, I am going to try some seeds. I will use the larger MRE containers to hold soil samples and plant our wheat, oats, corn, and tomatoes in them. I won't plant anything in the open ground until I find out what possible staple crops grow naturally here, if there are any, but I should be able to learn a lot about how plants will do in this extreme daily cycle. I will do my seed-planting inside first to keep them cool until they get a start. I'm feeling pretty strong, so then I'll head northeast up the coast today, to see what I can see. If I get any sign of a headache, I will head back. How about you, where are you going; I assume you will explore?"

"I will stay in the hills above you to the east, just in case. If you need any help, I will be reasonably close. You know, maybe you will be carrying some huge watermelons home or something," he smiled. He secretly hoped she would want him to join her somewhere up the coast, just because it was more fun than exploring alone, but he did need to see as much land as he could before preparations to settle began in earnest.

He pulled both radios from the chargers and handed hers over to her. She fit it into the clip over her right collarbone. He stepped out of the ship and down to the ground. Her radio rasped out loudly, "Hello, are you the lady who came in on a space ship?"

Pushing the call button, she responded, "Yeah, the one with the handsome pilot husband."

Climbing back into the cabin grinning, he rummaged around to find a lunch that looked reasonably interesting, picked up his Nalgene flask, and announced, "There are two Δ Pears left which you can have. I'll stop at the trees on my way up into the hills and pick some to take with me, and I'll fill my water bottle at the river." He kissed her, squeezed her shoulder, and said, "Maybe next dawn day we can go look at that valley together. Tonight, let's check on how your blood oxygen levels did today."

"Don't fight any bears. Stay in touch. I love you."

"Love you too."

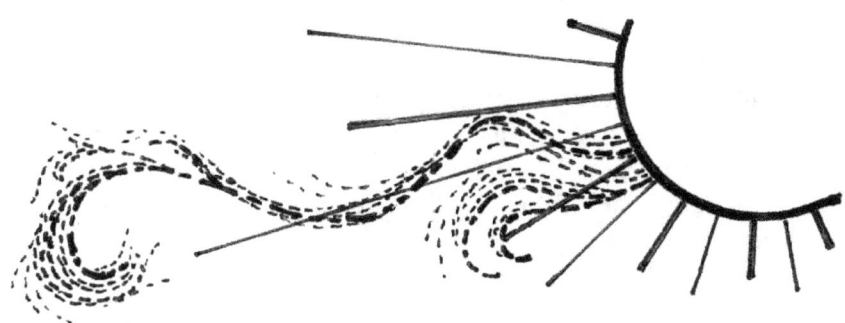

Chapter Twelve: Launch Central

"Big news. We have a plan on how to make these long days work for us. We are excited about it. We were thinking we had to fit into this planet's way of doing things, but these two human beings are not capable of it. Our new system will also give us the framework upon which to design a calendar for recording life here. I never thought about how much we depend on having a calendar until it was non-existent because nothing in this new reality correlates to the old calendar: no years, no months, and two-day-long days. Hours as we know them do not fit evenly into this place because the day is fifty-six hours and twenty minutes. So what o'clock is it, exactly? Haha.

"We started this new schedule at the beginning of our fourth ΔT day. We are going to sleep for about eight hours two times during a ΔT day. In the dark cold twenty-eight hour night, we will sleep through the very middle of it. The morning of our 'day' will start while it is dark, but we don't have to go to sleep again until ten hours after sunrise, so it is a practical workday. Then we sleep our second time during the hottest part of the daylight hours. Upon waking, we will have ten hours before sunset, followed by a long mellow evening of half-light. The bottom line is our workday will be four hours longer than Earth days, but we will get a full 'night's' sleep for each 'day.' How many of you would like to have an extra four hours each day to get things done?

"Yeah, I think we can adjust to that. This is going to work. Every other day will be a 'dawn day' or a 'dusk day.' I may be a little premature announcing this because today is our first dusk day and yesterday was our first dawn day. We slept today during the hottest part of the twenty-eight hours of sunlight, and now we are going exploring. March is already headed up into the hills as I am reporting to you, and I'll go up the coast as soon as I file this report, and after I plant some experimental seeds.

"Yesterday I went down the coast and found some fruit that was like grapes, but it was not ripe. That raised the question of what was 'spring' for that vine? Since theoretically there will be no seasons here, like living in the tropics. Is there a rainy season, or some cyclical variation that triggers these grapes to bloom and set fruit? And how often might that be? March is concerned that a stellar flare may have stopped the growth and now the grapes are starting over. But those pears we found are fully ripe, not bearing any evidence of having been burned out recently. I'm just thinking out loud. We obviously have a lot to learn, and you get to learn along with us. I will keep you posted with at least a daily report, daily, according to our new days, so roughly every twenty-eight hours.

"See you 'tomorrow,'

"Anj."

After reading this, Browning said quietly to no one in particular, "Four extra hours in the day; that might be a tough one to get used to. Hope it works for you, Anj." Zam and C.S. were the only ones who had also stayed late to catch the latest news from the astronauts.

C.S. said, "I'm just glad they came up with some kind of way to make sense of the daylight cycle there. That sounds like it will work for them. They will have a lot of work to do when they get to building a home, planting, and harvesting. They may need that extra four hours!"

"Maybe they will also start sleeping a little longer too, nine or ten hours," Zam commented. "I think that's what I would do, go for more sleep!"

Browning said, "We understand the numbers; how many hours here and there, but can we realistically imagine adapting to such a different world? Just being transparent here, I don't think I could. I'm not sure I would maintain my sanity if I had to do that. Good thing it's them and not me."

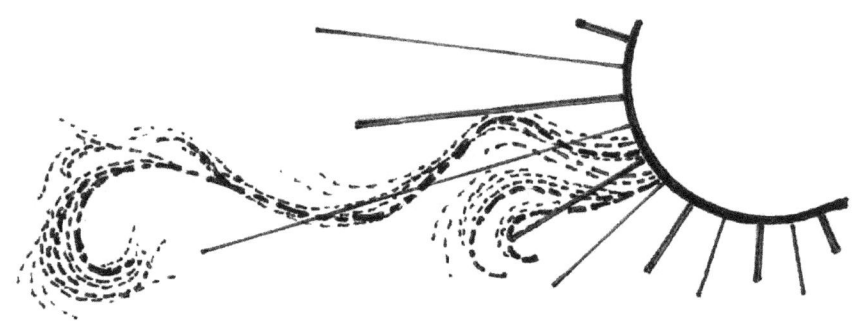

Chapter Thirteen

March's compass needle just wandered about aimlessly on ΔT. There was no magnetic north; no magnetic anything. He was thinking through the problems of navigation as he headed out into the foothills. "What if I decide to do some long-distance exploring here? How will I be able to find my way home?" Here, it would have to be done by the sun or the stars, all of which would be predictable in their courses, once March was able to observe and plot them. He remembered reading about Nathaniel Bowditch doing all the math for maritime navigation on Earth back in the 1700's so that with an accurate timepiece and sighting of the sun or stars, one's location in the vast oceans could be plotted accurately. "Maybe I get to be the Nathaniel Bowditch for ΔT," he laughed to himself as he stood on a high rock outcrop on a planet with a new sun, new days and nights, and with the stars in significantly different locations for navigation purposes.

As an astronomer, March could easily see in the night sky that most of the constellations were similar from here, a little out of shape and in the wrong places relative to the equator, but still recognizable. Canis Major, in the Earth's southern hemisphere, was the big exception, because Sirius was so close to Earth it now showed up in a different location, and of course, Centaurus because this three-star group itself had a significant placement in that constellation. Proxima was not that far from Earth in terms of the typical distance between stars in this galaxy. Orion, the Pleiades, and the Big Dipper appeared very much the same as

they did from Earth, but the North Star was not in the north for
ΔT. The north axis of this planet pointed in a very different
direction than Earth's.

The outcrop on which March stood, east of Browning Sea
had a good view of the ocean, and he could see short stretches of
the beach where there were breaks in the trees. He could also see
their space-ship, now parked in that clearing above the beach. It
surprised him how far he had already walked. Their little
temporary home looked so tiny and distant. He pushed the call
button on the radio, "Bravo One, Bravo One, this is Bravo Two,
do you read?"

"Loud and clear Bravo Two. What's your twenty?"

"On top of a bare outcrop probably directly east of you,
depending on how far up the coast you are by now."

"I just crossed the river; do you have a visual?"

"Roger, I think I can see you now. I'm a little northeast
from you."

"Copy, I see the rock, all white. Can't see you without the
glass."

"Oh let me take a peek." He took the monocular from his
vest pocket, reminded that he had it with him. Crunching up his
face to close one eye and peer through the glass, "Roger, I can see
you, cutie, waving at me even. Alright then, I haven't seen any
bears yet. You have anything to report?"

"It's a beautiful day in the neighborhood!"

"Indeed," he replied. "You take care. Over and out."

"Out."

Going northeast, she had crossed the river less than a
kilometer from the ship. It fanned out in a wide delta as it
emerged from the edge of the forest, breaking into a couple of
dozen streams meandering down to the waters of Browning Sea,
and Anj was able to dance from rock to rock and jump over the
narrow rivulets without even getting her boots wet as she

proceeded up the coast. She was waiting for a name for the River to come to her. 'Browning' had been an easy choice for the name of the Sea, just to honor their friend and leader, but she wanted names for the rest of the local features that would stand the test of time, 'for generations to come,' she thought, with a little thrill running through her. That was the plan, for future generations to continue here: children, and children's children.

Heavy humid heat along the shore was sapping her energy, and she was in direct sun, so she walked up from the beach and into the trees. Taking advantage of their shade, she thanked the trees for it. Sensing the unmistakable harmony she had with all of nature was becoming less surprising, more automatic, and certainly comforting. Anj became quite absorbed in picking her way through the trees, from shade to shade. The huge trunks of the forest in this area were amazing. Stepping around one particularly large tree, she saw, standing not far from her, still as a tree trunk himself, a boy.

In the first instant, not believing what her brain was interpreting from her eyes, she looked again, very carefully. Unmistakably it was a boy, about five meters away, and very still. She instinctively froze too, but knew it was too late to avoid being seen by him. She was amused at herself, that hiding was still her first instinct. Consciously she was not feeling fear, and he was looking at her in the manner that a boy looks at a museum display of something interesting but outside of his reality, maybe a never-seen-before creature, just openly curious and in no way fearful.

His hands hung at his sides, relaxed. In his left hand, he held a straight rod, less than a meter long, too thin to be a walking staff. He was wearing something gathered around his waist and covering his thighs. His torso was bare, brown, as were his exposed legs. He had a small bag slung like a purse over his right shoulder, the cord crossed his chest and suspended the bag close against his left hip, 'maybe large enough to hold his lunch,' she thought. A boy, about fourteen, in Earth years. 'Where there is a boy, there is probably a Dad or a Mom.' She wrested her gaze away from the boy and searched quickly among the trees. Seeing no one else, her attention went back to the boy. His eyes still registered incomprehension, as she knew hers did.

He turned his eyes away from her, apparently not sensing any threat from her, and looked slightly upward, tilting his head as if to listen to the large tree just a few feet to his left. Fascinated, she watched him. His eyes turned back to her, but his attention stayed on the tree as if he were listening to whispered coaching. From everything she had sensed from the trees thus far, she was hopeful that he was receiving affirmation that she was friendly. Something in his body language loosened, and his attention returned fully to the stranger in front of him.

He bent his right arm to hold his right hand in front of his bag on the left, palm up, and swung his hand across in a horizontal arc in front of him and all the way to his right, stopped, and held it there. Anj read it as a gesture of openness, maybe an invitation for her to speak. Anj copied his hand motion as carefully and slowly as he had, communicating to him the best she could, that she indeed meant him no harm.

He put his left forearm up across his chest, holding the rod parallel to his wrist, and began to speak. Soft and clear language came from this boy who was not from Earth. She strained to comprehend, forgetting that she could probably tell more from his intonation and posture than she could by trying to understand his language. After a couple of sentences, he stopped. Anj wanted to respond to him and she desperately also wanted to tell March about this, so she crossed her chest with her left arm as the boy had, and put her hand on the radio. She pressed the call button and began to speak in a conversational tone, thinking the boy would not understand anyway, and would think she was responding to him while she actually spoke to March. "Bravo two, I am standing face to face with a fourteen-year-old boy, not sensing any danger, just wanted you to know what is happening down here; please do not reply, out."

Everything changed in the boy's demeanor, but he registered neither fright nor anger, nor aggression. Anj couldn't tell what it was, but she knew instantly the mistake she had made. The boy had immediately sensed her deceit, and it apparently confused him more than her sudden appearance in the forest had. He turned his attention again to the tree to his left for a few moments, keeping his eyes on her, then he quickly turned and jogged off noiselessly towards the foothills, silently disappearing among the closely growing trunks.

"Oh Jesus, God, I fouled that up badly. What was that? I lied to that young boy; God, forgive me. That was foolish. Like he wouldn't get it? Like I could just trick him on this planet where everything is in harmony? What is this place? There is a boy here." She pressed the call button again, but still in shock, did not know what to say, so just released it without saying anything.

March was already running, trying not to break a leg, careening down the ridge towards where he thought Anj must be by now, when his radio beeped. He stopped and waited. She had pushed the call button but said nothing. Puzzled, he did not want to beep back. She did not want to have the radio going off right now, he thought. Twenty long seconds later, there was another beep, and this time her voice followed.

"March, he ran off. I messed up and frightened him by trying to talk to you on the radio. He is heading in your direction."

"Copy. I'll watch for him. You okay?"

"Kicking myself for being deceitful. He was not threatened and was trying to be friendly until I did that."

"What do you suggest if I see him?"

"I don't know; I'm still trying to get over the shock of seeing what is quite obviously a human being here. Be friendly."

"Copy. Out." He expected that he did not have much time to get a little further down the hill where he could hopefully encounter this boy.

March was on the lower end of a rocky ridge just above a copse of Δ Pear trees where the terrain eased to a more gradual slope. Grassy there, and cooler in the shade, March felt the prompting of the Spirit to sit and watch. He moved to a spot under a spreading tree. Pear tree branches with fruit hanging from them were less than a foot above his head where he chose to sit. Through the open space beneath the branches, he could see as far as fifty meters out between the trees in some places.

Anj, down the hill, asked God to guide that boy right to March, so he could see him too. She could still hardly believe her own experience of seeing a human being in another solar system. What would March think about this? She longed to be with him immediately, simply to be able to ask, "Did that really happen? Did we see what we think we saw?" She was also flooded with her own disappointment in her behavior in this place of unblemished harmony. He seemed like such an innocent and trusting young man, very much in the same sort of harmony with everything here, and she had tried to trick him.

She hoped that March would be able to connect with the boy in a more meaningful way than she had. "March will do well, I know he will." She began to wind her way up the hill cautiously, not knowing how far away March had been when she spoke to him on the radio. She did not want to interrupt March's encounter if indeed that could be happening. She made her way slowly uphill until maybe ten minutes elapsed. She was only able to guess the path the boy had taken but hoped for the best. She dared not use the radio, only searching carefully between the trees ahead. Beginning to doubt her chances of reconnoitering with either of them, she finally saw March, and then she saw the person who was apparently a native of this world walking away into the forest, and he turned and gave March a wave. Her hopes rose. March had succeeded in connecting with this boy somehow.

March heard Anj quietly approaching from down the hill. She spoke first, "Well done, it looks like you managed to win a friend." She said it with a hint of admiration as she came through the trees to him. They both stood speechless looking after the direction in which ΔT boy had disappeared, both still in shock. March turned to her and held her close, both of their minds full of questions about this development that had just turned their new world upside-down. Silently they turned to walk back down towards the beach, his arm around her shoulders and both deep in thought, somewhat in denial of the facts of what had just happened, not yet willing to believe in full, this incredible encounter, or face the changes it would inevitably bring to all their best-laid plans.

"Well, I guess that answers the question of the lights across the sea at night," March finally offered, trying to be light-hearted. But this was undoubtedly the most serious consideration they could ever have faced on a new planet. People were already here. Natives?

"We are intruders. We are aliens from another planet," she responded, with a short laugh, also trying to keep it from going too serious too fast, but knowing they had a lot to talk about.

In actuality, a complete re-design of the mission was what they had to talk about. Or maybe not. March started praying, "God You knew these people were here, and You did not deem it essential to tell us, or maybe we were not listening. Nevertheless, we thank You that You have a plan for what is going to happen here on ΔT, as we somehow interface with what may very well be a population of indigenous people. You have already told Anj there is no hostility here, so we thank You by faith that these people are going to continue to be friendly."

Anj continued the prayer, "God I pray that I have learned my lesson about being completely authentic with beings here because Your entire creation here seems to be able to see into the thoughts and intentions of my heart. God, we bless that young man with peace, and I ask You to speak to him about us. Make up the difference for my blunder. You have given us faith to come to Proxima, brought us here, made sure we would get here intact, even delivered March from the grip of death so that this interaction between the people of Earth and this person of ΔT could happen. Thank You for setting this up today, whatever it means. Thank You God; Thank You, God. We trust You."

Anj stopped, turned, and grasped both of his wrists, "March, there are people here! I still can't believe this experience. God, thank You. Only You will be able to adapt us to these new factors in the plan. March, isn't that boy every bit human? I did not sense anything alien about him, but I did not get as close or have as long a time with him as you did." Then with a start, looking up toward heaven with her hands outstretched, she asked the obvious and unanswerable question, "God! Why are there people here? We are trillions of miles from Earth!"

After pondering that for a moment, March said, "Yes, it is indeed a puzzle how this fits together with God bringing us here. And in answer to your question, Anj, yes, he seems to be every bit a homo sapiens boy child, and somehow exquisite in his features. Could you see the color of his eyes? Try not to let your jaw drop too far next time get a close look at those eyes, trusting that there will indeed be a next time. You never saw a kid quite like him on Earth."

The Red Dwarf's position in the evening sky told them it was about three hours until sunset. They checked the time on the Earth watches they still carried. March told her that the boy, through sign language, indicated that he expected to meet them in the same place, about the same time before the next sunset. It would be fifty-six Earth hours before the Proxima Mission's new and numerous mysteries could begin to be unraveled, or could they? "March, what if he comes back with an army of grown men? What if they take us captive? We could be walking into an ambush." Her voice registered shades of panic somewhat uncharacteristic to the Air Force pilot wife March knew so well.

"It will do us no good to approach this in fear, and God has already assured you that there is no malicious design prescribed against us here, so I am determined to agree with that and to believe God's promise that says, 'Do not fear, for I am with you;

Do not anxiously look about you, for I am your God. I will strengthen you, surely I will help you, Surely I will uphold you with My righteous right hand.' Walk us through this, God. We look to You for wisdom and for Your mind and emotion in response to this bewildering find on ΔT"

Under March's hand, Anj's shoulders released some of the tension that had moved in, uninvited. They walked in silence for the next few minutes. Anj was 'pushing her reset button,' as she called it when she caught herself fixing her eyes on things in the material world without including the perspective from her true position, seated in the heavenly places with Jesus. Collecting herself to start over, she asked again, "March, why do you think there are human beings here?" This time the question was anthropological instead of being loaded with frightened innuendos.

March began to think it through out loud. "He fits this place like a bird in a nest. I think he was born on this planet. So here's my best guess: God, who created us in His own image on our Earth, has done the same thing here, creating mankind here also in His image. Maybe that is too simplistic, but until proven otherwise, it is my theory, and it makes perfect sense to me. Why wouldn't He do it on more than one planet in the universe?"

They had descended back down to the sea and were walking up the beach further in the direction Anj had been going before she had decided to seek some shade in the woods and had encountered the boy. It was cooling now, and the sun's rays were coming in at a low angle, making the couple's long shadows reach across the beach and up to the trees, leaping over boulders and onto tree trunks as they strolled along in the gravel. Tranquility overruled fright; the peace of the place spoke up to them from the sound of their steps along the gravel beach and the slow rhythm of the breakers. Low waves collapsed softly onto the beach, soothing jangled nerves and declaring wordless wisdom about the order that was firmly established in this part of the universe.

For almost an hour, March and Anj proceeded on up the beach, listening and taking in what, by now, they were accepting as God's voice of rest to them. Finally, they reversed their steps back towards the ship. When the sun crept, so slowly as to be imperceptible, down behind the horizon on the west, they were halfway home, and it was nearly dark by the time they opened the hatch and stepped back into the ship, which somehow seemed to be a different sort of place than it was before they knew that other humans already lived here. Had anyone been here while they were gone? Had the ship been seen by them? They were no longer alone on this planet.

It was seven hours before time to sleep. There was time to prepare a meal and talk all this through some more. At times through the evening they found themselves laughing out loud at the preposterously unexpected discovery they had made today, so totally unanticipated. "Hostile aliens we had thought about, but human beings? Not once did I ever imagine." At other times they talked in soft tones, deep and serious, considering what manner of future there was here now, in light of the changes pressing in upon them, knowing they were sharing the land, no longer quite being pioneers in a new world. Much of their future would be determined by what sort of people these turned out to be. What would they find out in the meeting before the next sunset?

As the long evening deepened, and it began to grow frigid outside, Anj looked out the window to check for those lights again, since it was about the same time after the last sunset that she had seen them before. It was all darkness at first, then, distinctly, three lights came on again, far distant enough to shimmer and twinkle, and then were turned off one by one after a few minutes. It seemed as normal as lights seen across any body of water. Instead of stomach crunching fear this time, she experienced new curiosity, and rhetorically asked March, as he had come over to look, "What sort of lights are they? Why do you suppose they turn on those lights for such a short time?"

"Maybe someone is late getting home and it's like a lighthouse beacon, 'This way home,'" he offered, not trying to figure out a real answer, just whatever seemed to be the most natural possibility. "Or maybe they are signaling the neighbors, 'I'm going to bed now, good night.'" He was trying to keep it humorous, partly because it was beginning to strike him as hilarious that God would send them here to encounter, of all things, other people!

"I tell you," he continued, "I'm about to blink my light and signal 'bedtime.' I don't know if I can stay up until our agreed-upon end of the day; that's still four more hours. My body wants a twenty-four-hour day, but we are now living twenty-eight hour days, so naturally, I'm getting sleepy. I also anticipate sleeping like a rock tonight while it is cold and dark outside instead of bright and blazing hot like during our last sleep."

"So, this dawn day, dusk day thing you think is going to work?"

"Yeah, these last two days I have finally felt like I could function, and I know we are going to make it. It gave me hope. I never realized how much I depended on having a firm pattern, a schedule. I need that cycle and routine, but this is going to work. I just need to adapt to the longer days, which, as things settle down, I know I will be able to, and it will be good. This will enable us to set up a calendar too. Two days for every ΔT day. Have you given that any further thought?"

"Yes, in fact, I reported home that we could set up a calendar if this dawn day dusk day system works. A calendar as we know it needs days, weeks, months, and years. So we've got days now. What do you think about weeks? I'd like to have a day of rest, a Sabbath, once a week."

"You have obviously given this more thought than I have. You say you want weeks, but if we have a seven day week, then one Sunday will be a dusk day and the next Sunday will be a dawn day. That seems odd; it should be the same every week. What do you think?

"I agree with you that Sunday should be the same kind of day each week."

March asked, "So do we go to a six-day week or an eight-day week? And which type of day should our day of rest be, dawn day or dusk day? Hey, isn't this fun, creating our own little system of recording time? But then, maybe we should ask our new friend how he records time here," and he laughed heartily, still being struck by the hilarity of what this day had revealed to them.

Anj chose to remain all business. She was serious about this new calendar, "I have, in fact, given it some thought. Here's my reasoning: since each day is so much longer, in order to compensate, we should have six-day weeks. Days are longer, but weeks will be shorter, so the need for rest will be met when we have spent a week's worth of energy working, and are in need of it."

"Wow, you have thought about this pretty thoroughly. We can try it and re-write it if it doesn't work somehow. Or maybe our new friend's system will be superior and we will adopt it." He laughed again, wishing for a smile from her.

Not getting the smile, he continued, "What kind of day do you think Sunday should be, dawn day or dusk day?"

"No, you go first."

Pondering for a moment, March proposed, "A dawn day, because on Easter we can have a sunrise service. I would hate to have to miss out on celebrating that at least once a year. The day the Earth was redeemed and everything changed for us who believe."

"Oh, that's golden. I thought dawn day too, just because it seemed right, but had not thought of Easter. Are we going to put Christmas and Thanksgiving on the calendar too?"

"Of course, maybe even the Fourth of July!"

She rewarded March with a courtesy smile, but remained on-task, "This is making my brain hurt, but I think I will begin to put it on paper before we turn in tonight." While she searched for a ruler and some large paper, she was thinking out loud, "We have been here now for four full ΔT days." Counting off days of the week on her fingers, "Oops, with only six days, we have to skip one day of the week, which one do we drop?"

"Contrary to popular opinion, I never minded Mondays as back-to-work-day, so definitely keep that one. Let's skip Saturday; we don't need two-day weekends. Most of the world does not have a day off on Saturday. We will just have one day off a week. How does that sound?"

"It sounds like a workaholic," she then grinned openly, knowing she was a guilty as he. "Alright, we are carving it in stone; well, just on paper for now. We will say today was Monday." Head down, she went to work drawing out a six-day per week calendar.

While she worked, he wrote in his log for the day. He had thought it good to have a hand-written record of each day's work, activities, and discoveries, contrary to the usual digital ways in which things were usually recorded. Pen and paper constituted a soothing combination to him, and he had started it on their first day. He noted at the top of his entry, "Monday, 08-01-00." Today had been Monday, the Eighth day, of the first month, year Zero, not yet even one year. He pondered for a few moments what would be going on when he wrote the entry 08-01-01 after they had been here a year. In fact how long was a year going to be anyway? "It will have to be forty-eight weeks; twelve months, sure."

After writing for quite a while, having completed his account of meeting the boy, he lifted his head to find her looking at him over her new calendar page; looking as if she were seeing into him. He felt a little exposed under such a penetrating gaze, but he knew what was on her mind and simply asked her, "What are you going to tell them at home about the boy?"

"What did you write in your log about him?" He handed her the journal, and after he had gone to sleep, she filed the report which Browning and the CSE crew would eventually receive.

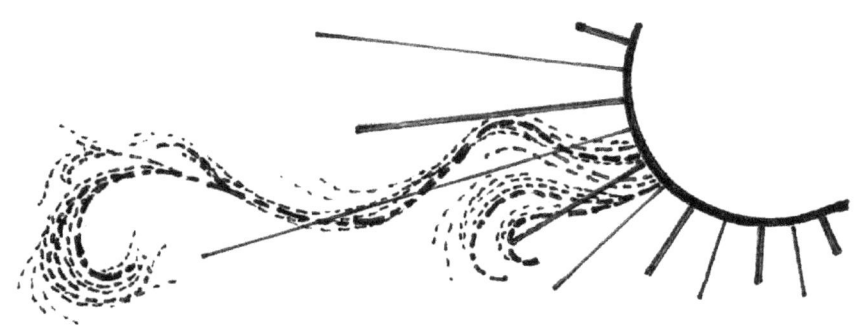

Chapter Fourteen: Launch Central

"Browning and team, greetings. Anj here; I am going to read you March's log entry for today, which was a dusk day, the second half of our fourth full ΔT day here. I am sending you his thoughts on the day because I was frankly at a loss of what to say, and he put it down accurately and with feeling.

'Monday, 08/01/00. Second half of our fourth day here: we are going to call it a dusk day, and on our new calendar it will have been Monday, the eighth day of our first month, during our first year. I am writing this in English because that is the language in which I am most fluent, but it occurs to me tonight as I write, that it might better have been written in a language of this planet, if that were possible, because we have discovered that there are other people here with their own distinct language. We encountered today what would be a teenage boy, maybe fourteen. From all appearances, he is entirely human; hair, eyelashes, ears, nose, and belly button. He wore no shirt, only some kind of loose wrap around his hips and thighs. He was not afraid. It was very striking how at ease he was with what must have been to him a confusing encounter. Picture us in our synthetic fabric clothes, our ankle-high boots, and in contrast, he had woven grass sandals and that cloth around his middle. He did not understand us; neither our language nor our behavior would have correlated with anything he had ever experienced.

'Anj met up with him first, (we were not together at the time she first saw him), but he ran away from her because she spoke to me on the radio and it confused him. But she called me and told me he was coming towards me, and to watch for him.

'I prayed, "I want to see this boy, Father, thank You for bringing him this way," and I had uncommon confidence that I would get to see the boy. At the same time, I had a complex set of questions in my head about what this meant. A boy here on ΔT? "Father, thank You for wisdom. I want to be the authentic human being that You need for this boy to experience."

'I found a shady spot under a fruit tree and sat down to watch and wait. My eye caught what certainly appeared to be a boy, angling towards me, jogging between a couple trees about thirty meters away. I felt it necessary to remain still. The figure was hidden among the trees, but he would come into the open soon only twenty meters away, and I waited. I thought of calling out, "Hello," but rejected that, and remained still, sitting cross-legged. I thought of standing to greet him, but felt that I should stay non-threatening as much as I could. Into the clearing, the boy appeared again, and he was walking carefully now, looking around, sensing something. He spotted me sitting still under the tree. An unexplainable thrill ran through me; you can only imagine how it felt to make such a discovery.

'He stopped, stood motionless, looking at me. He looked back towards where he had encountered the first stranger, then back to this one, clearly putting us together, and he just stared. Momentarily, I noticed a peculiar head-tilting mannerism. The boy seemed to be listening for something, and after half a minute, his attention returned completely to the strange person sitting under the tree.

'Without any additional body language, the boy lifted his right hand to waist height and swung it slowly, palm up, across his torso, stopping it on his right. It seemed to be a friendly gesture, opening the encounter to further communication. I instantly had the notion to reach up and pick one of the Pears above my head, which I could do without even standing, and offer it to the lad. Moving smoothly and slowly, I pulled a nice looking Δ Pear from its branch and held it straight out with both arms towards the boy and both hands open flat. At that, the youngster's demeanor brightened noticeably, even from twenty meters away. He stepped forward confidently like he was going to receive a blue ribbon, but he stopped three steps away from me and my offered Δ Pear, taking in the sight of this stranger from up close. I too, was rapt by the details of this young male teenager, apparently every bit human, not unlike a boy one would have seen in another country, from another culture on Earth.

'I noticed the boy held a rod in the left hand, had a pouch on a shoulder strap, and looked at me with steady eyes of a startling color between blue and deep green. I got uncomfortable staring at the youngster too long, and I nodded slightly towards the Pear, re-offering it. Deftly, the boy swung his long rod up into the tree above me and with a quick twist and a pull, brought it carefully down with a perfect looking Pear held at the end on some kind of a hook-tool. It was obviously a reciprocating gift, so I held out my left hand to receive it, still holding my offering out in my right hand. Gently the boy placed the fruit in my alarmingly large hand held out to him, and with a skillful motion, released it from the tool. He then took the last two steps forward to be able to reach out to my hand. The boy's finely featured hand and arm extend towards my hairy bare arm. Fascinated, I watched with the same concentration I would employ when doing a docking maneuver between two ships. As the boy's fingers closed on the Pear, I said, "Capture," almost in a whisper, not because I planned to, it just escaped from my lips.

'My eyes told me the boy did not understand, but that he heard the utterance and accepted it as friendly. He drew the pear back to his chest, looked upwards, and said something brief in his language. I was sure my blank expression registered non-understanding, but I couldn't help breaking into a big smile as the seriousness with which we had observed the last two minutes broke as we traded gifts. I tried to mimic the boy's words and said "Omeda latana, kamana," or something. The youngster's face showed me that he could tell how interested I was in connecting, and he responded, "Kapcha." My heart melted. My heart said, "I think I love this boy already."

'Simultaneously, we each took a bite, both now smiling with the discovery of the moment. In a rather ceremonial manner, youngster standing, and this adult stranger sitting straight-backed, we ate the pears. I was dripping juice into my lap, and the young teen wiped his chin with his open palm. My mind was searching, 'Where do we go from here?' Following the boy's lead when we finished, I tossed the pear core into the low bushes.

'Backing up three steps, from the shade into the full sun, the boy stabbed his rod into the ground and started talking, either not believing that his language was unintelligible, or not caring. With energetic expression, he began to explain, pointing at the sun, talking steadily, pointing at the course the sun would take to its setting. Then pointing in the opposite direction, where the sun would rise again, he looked at me, checking to see if I was following him. Apparently satisfied that I was paying attention, he continued to talk and indicated the track the sun would follow to its present position. He then drew a line in the soil with his finger right along the shadow cast by his rod and pointed at that mark. He then pointed to where he had met Anj; he pointed to me, and he pointed to himself. Still talking, he pointed at the shadow and the mark scribed in the soil. Not sure the stranger comprehended, he repeated the whole thing again, tracing the course of the sun and ending on the present location of the shadow line.

'By that time I was standing up and had stepped out into the sun, wanting to affirm that I understood that the boy wanted to meet again on the next full day at the same time. I said, "Very clever, I like your sun-dial." Then I repeated the gestures, talking through it, and said, even though I knew words were pointless, "Okay you want Anj and me to meet you here tomorrow at the same time," and I ended with both index fingers pointing to the ground. I said, "You want to meet here, in this same place?"

'The young boy, mimicking my gesture, also pointed to the ground with both hands and speaking out a couple more sentences, signaled agreement. Immediately I had to wonder who this youngster planned to bring with him. That was the first of several big questions that could not be asked or answered. With that, my new friend turned and walked away to the northeast, only looking back once. I waved to him. The boy held his rod up level with his eyes in reply. "Was that a standard wave? Where does he live? How many others are there? How will we ever be able to communicate? What is he doing here?" You can imagine the flood of questions in my mind at that point: such an interesting experience; such a surprising experience. We have thought of every possibility of what we would encounter on our new planet except this; perfectly normal human beings like us.

'Oh God, why did you bring us here now? What have You done placing other human beings on ΔT? Do we have a message for them? Do they have a message for us? What is the purpose in bringing us together?" This occupies my mind now. I think I now understand all the miraculous components of how we succeeded in arriving here. I think God brought us here by His own mighty hand for this. "God we need You. We count on Your promise that You will give us instruction in the way which we should go and that You will give counsel to us so we can see as You see. We will trust You with all our hearts. Your lovingkindness will surround us. Speak, Lord; we are listening attentively, and will seek Your face continually".'

"So that's March's log entry. It was plain and simple; that's what happened. As March said, I was the first to see the boy, but I unintentionally frightened him off, then March encountered him.

"Thank God March's calm manner and gentleness seemed to win the lad over, and now we hope we understand that he has invited us to see him again tomorrow. I say, 'we hope,' because we do want to find out more about him and his people, and yet part of us wants to be cautious. Might it be dangerous? The boy is apparently from a wild tribe of people; who knows how they will respond to very strange looking intruders? Even though we get the distinct impression of peace here on this planet, we can't seem to keep from exercising vigilance in the face of this unknown.

"So there you have it. You know as much as we do about this. We don't know much more than, 'this is shocking and amazing.' Tomorrow is Tuesday on our new calendar, a dawn day. I will get a good night's sleep now, and even so, we will awaken well before dawn. After breakfast and a little workout, it will begin to slowly brighten outside, barely light enough to hike without a headlamp, and it will be cold. March says he is going out to the hills again, to the southeast where he saw a pretty little valley day before yesterday. I am going with him, my first major hike. I think I have acclimatized to the lower oxygen content here, and if not, I can stop, and March can pick me up on his way back. I am curious about his valley. March was thinking it might be a good place to build a home, but now we are both wondering how that idea will have to be adjusted regarding the people who are already here. Will we meet more of them in that valley? There are too many unknowns for this simple pioneer.

"Out for now, Anj."

Browning turned from the monitor and to the incredulous faces of those around him. At first, everyone remained in stunned silence, then everyone began talking at once.

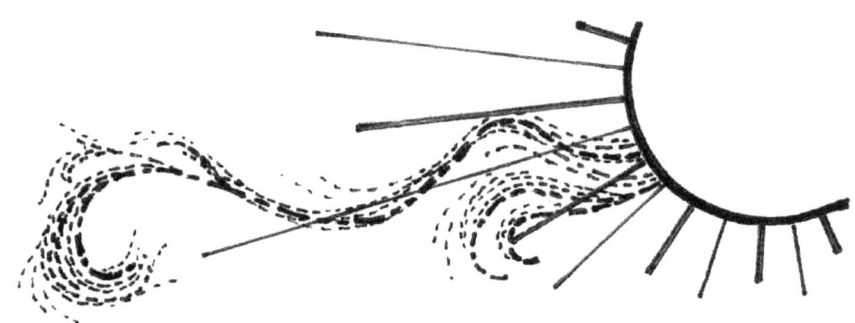

Chapter Fifteen

Crisp morning air froze the hair in March's nostrils, which he knew meant it was about fifteen degrees Fahrenheit. By the time they returned to the ship, it would be pushing a hundred. He chuckled to himself how, when they named Deep ΔT, it was on theory only. Now they were experiencing how well-named it was. He was also thankful that it was a livable temperature differential. A one-hundred-and-four-degree swing in one day was interesting to try to dress for, but not lethal.

March was a happy man, not only because he was going to get to explore that valley, but also that Anj was coming with him. He estimated that, even taking it easy, they would have time to look around the valley for a couple hours before they had to head back. Stepping out of the ship, they could see their breath in little puffs of vapor. Packs on, gear, food, and water checked, March pointed out to Anj the distinctive peak towards which they were to hike and let her lead the way and set her own pace. Thoughtful silence soon wrapped around the walkers. As serious hikers, there wasn't much chatter as they stepped along, and this day they had so much to think about, not the least of which was whether they were being watched.

Two-and-a-half hours out, not long after a slow rising of Proxima and the welcome beginnings of warmth, they topped a ridge from which they could catch the first view of the valley. March took his gloves off to take a picture. Browning and the team would be interested, but wasting no time, they quickly strode ahead, all the more eager to see what this lovely green bowl held for them. They had not seen any other people and had begun to relax, especially as they thought further about the calm, unafraid, and friendly reception that they had both experienced with the boy.

In two more hours, reaching the edge of the valley, they were squatted in the shade of a spreading tree overlooking the fertile-looking dell, maybe less than one km long and half of that in width. Open and treeless with high grass, fairly level, but sloping down in the direction of the sea, there was probably a stream running down its middle, they surmised. They would explore after a quick reconnoiter of the area. "No sign of any habitation that I can see," Anj offered.

"Nope," from behind the monocular scanning the tree line on the other side. March spent a long time glassing the whole length of the valley. "You know those droppings and tracks we saw on the way up here; I thought we would see the deer or whatever left that sign. There has to be some large game somewhere in this valley I think."

By this time they had seen several more large high-flying birds, and had their first sighting of a small furry creature, very tame-acting, staring at them wide-eyed, the way a rabbit will stare at someone who is inside the house looking out the window; feeling no immediate threat. Smaller birds fluttered and called to one another, making the two alien humans feel almost at home.

Anj was peeling off her outer pullover, the jacket already folded in the pack as the day warmed. Having been able to make the hike without a trace of a headache, and carried away by the beauty of her surroundings, she was praising God.

On Earth, praising God, for Anj, had often been only through conscious intentional effort, and sometimes it just seemed like an obligation, or like carrying sandbags from one place to another. It was not always the easy flow of admiration. It was work, to which she devoted herself because she knew and had been taught how central praise was to any kind of fruitful life with God. Her Pastor had taught, "It is not phony to praise God when you don't feel like it, because He is always worthy. In fact, it is a lack of authenticity as a believer if you *don't* praise Him just because you don't feel like it."

Here, it was consistently the most natural and sensible joy and pleasure to praise God. She had noticed it from the earliest moments of being on the ground on ΔT. Upon landing safely, she was praising God because she was thankful they had arrived in one piece. He had carried and protected and guided them. She was thankful and was praising Him, and she wasn't praising Him out of obligation. Nothing was ever in the way of that marvelous freedom to declare His wonders. Nothing was obstructing the flow of awe and wonder about her Eternal Father. She asked God about it after such joyful freedom to express praise had persisted for the first couple of days because she was afraid that this was some kind of magical moment that would disappear, or that she would mess it up somehow. His reply was, "I have never had a struggle trying to be one with you, but I recognize that your sense of being one with Me has always been difficult. It has been a poorly defined mystery to you. You will continue to find it different here."

She was indeed finding that so. March's low whistle through his teeth lifted her out of her reverie. Still behind the monocular, looking directly across the grassy lowlands in front of them, he said in almost a whisper, "There they are."

His tone was so relaxed, she assumed he meant the deer, and asked, "What? Deer?"

"Nope, men; three of them. You can see them moving through the trees parallel to the edge of the grass; take a look." Without any sudden motions, he handed the glass over to her. "I don't think they have seen us, and probably have not even heard about us yet."

Anj looked into the eyepiece, finding her heartbeat racing, "Which way are they moving; I don't see them yet."

"Heading downhill, to the right."

"Okay, got 'em." Trying to sound as matter-of-fact as March as she found them in the scope, "Isn't that interesting; maybe they are hunting. What should we do?"

"I think we sit tight and wait for tomorrow's meeting with the boy and his friends. They will come knowing something about what they are getting into with us aliens, or whatever they perceive us to be. I don't want to surprise these three guys. Too much of an unknown quantity."

"Sounds very sensible. Right now we are in deep shade and not silhouetted against the skyline; if we stay still they won't see us. Hopefully, none of them have binoculars."

"That would be a long-shot, given what we saw of the boy yesterday. He did not strike me as a person who had ever seen anything made of steel or glass, although I don't know what that rod he carries is made of. It looked like a pretty refined tool. Basically, I think we are dealing with primitive people."

After allowing the men to get far down past the end of the valley and out of sight, March and Anj ventured into the knee-high grass to look for the stream, and indeed, a clear quiet creek had cut a path through the grass. At the upper end of the green bowl, a small waterfall over a rocky cliff was the entrance point for the stream. "That's the place for the cabin," March spoke softly, partly not to call any attention to their whereabouts, and partly because the dream of it had immediately captured him. "Plenty of building materials, fresh water, possibly even power-generating capability with a small water-wheel." His dream was kicking into high gear, but he checked himself. "But we need to know a lot more about how we can live with these people before we can plan anything. Hopefully, tomorrow's meeting will yield some kind of understanding."

"What if they want us to come with them, March?"

"Why would they want to do that?"

"Maybe they want us to see their homes. I don't know. Maybe they feel threatened. I'm not sure we will be welcomed as allies."

"You are the one who got the assurance there was not a malicious plot here. I think it is time to put all our eggs in that basket."

"I know; I keep dropping back into suspicion and fear, sorry."

"No worries, dove. Discovering people here is the biggest, most unlikely development we could ever face. Lots of adjustment." Then looking up at Proxima approaching her zenith, "It is time to head back if we don't want to walk the last few miles in hundred-degree heat."

"Copy, Cap'n," Anj smiled and slung her pack.

Four hours later, grateful that it's always quicker going home, especially if it's downhill, sweaty, and ready to cool off, they took a brief swim in the still semi-cool Browning Sea. The top foot of water was comfortably warm, but down at their feet, it was much colder. Refreshed, they climbed into the air-conditioned ship to review the discoveries of the day, get some dinner, and try to get a good 'night' of sleep while the temperature continued to climb outside. "How are we going to manage this in a log cabin, pioneer partner?" Anj asked.

"Oh, we are pretty clever, we pioneers," he replied, not particularly wanting to get into what he had studied about the temperature-stabilizing effect of thick log cabin walls and what could be done for insulation, heat production, and cooling.

Both hikers slept the dead-away sleep that physically taxed bodies demand, despite simmering heat and broad daylight outside.

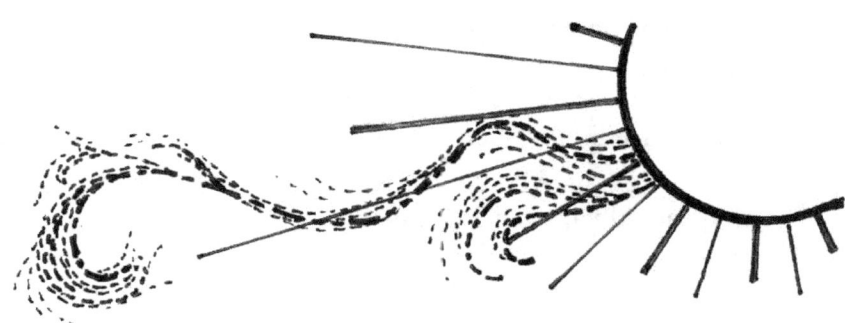

Chapter Sixteen: Launch Central

"Today is Wednesday, a dusk-day on ΔT. We slept well, thanks to Air Conditioning; God bless the man that invented it and bless you guys on the equipment team who retro-fitted it to be light enough to come with us. We would literally be toast without it, trying to sleep through the hottest part of the day. One thing we could not accomplish when we picked a landing spot was to have a place in the shade, so this ship sits out in the sun. It's so hot at mid-day, we have to wear gloves to climb up the ladder, but inside it's nice and cool. Someday, this cold fusion generator is going to run out, and there will be no more AC. Hopefully, by then we will have figured out a way to moderate the temps, or we will have gotten used to it.

"Yesterday's hike was great fun and I did not experience any edema, thank God. I seem to have adapted to the low oxygen here. We saw more people yesterday; three men walking through the woods, far away, and they did not see us, as far as we know. Having little data upon which to gauge what their reaction to us would be, we elected to let them go without seeing us. We were thankful that we had the friendly encounter with the boy first. These men, for all we know, could be from a different tribe, a hostile group that would not turn out so well.

"We are anticipating today's meeting with the boy, hoping that we have accurately understood him and that we will see him again. We presume he will bring some others. Our hope also is that we can communicate well enough to reach some kind of understanding between us. If you do not get one of these reports from us tomorrow, or even for a few days, don't panic. We may wind up needing to spend some time with this group of people.

"(Well, how could you panic, when you know the news is four years old anyway?) It must be strange to know that anything you might react to is already such old news that your reaction is immaterial. It is weird enough sending these reports out into space, knowing that we will be in an entirely different situation by the time you hear today's news.

"Allow me to attempt to help you with your fears of what might have happened to us four years ago as you read this. I'm trying to be funny to lighten this serious situation up a bit, but here is the assurance that I offer to you: I think I heard God tell me, just in my spirit, that there is no potential attack waiting for us on this planet. I received an understanding that being on this planet is not a dangerous situation, and it gave me great peace. I hope you too can receive my words, 'don't panic' and just wait and see what interesting thing is going to happen. It is not going to be bad. I have become comfortable with the prospect of going to meet some kind of delegation with the boy.

"I don't know what to anticipate at this meeting, but I had a premonition yesterday that they may want us to come to where they live, which frightened me at first. Then I had a dream last night about being in their dwellings with lots of people, a big-family sort of atmosphere and lots of food, and that calmed me a good deal. For you guys, I know that premonitions and dreams are just spooky stuff, not what scientists like to work with. I usually like concrete data too, but a couple of impressions are all we've got to go on right now.

"Yesterday we hiked up to March's valley, maybe fifteen or eighteen kilometers up into the foothills. It is idyllic. A stream runs through it from a little waterfall at the head of the valley, grassy slopes, plenty of timber. He is getting a little excited but is fixedly postponing dreaming big about the log cabin until we know more about whether we will be able to peacefully coexist with these ΔT people. I think if we did not know they were here, he would already be on a roll to get this project started. It is what he has had on his mind since before we finalized our ship's cabin-design so that it would serve also as a temporary dwelling for pioneers on an uninhabited planet. 'Temporary dwelling' he knows must be replaced by a 'permanent dwelling,' and that's his job!

"So we are in the process of morphing our thinking from 'desolate, hostile environment,' which we quite realistically expected, to, 'what a find!' We are still reeling from the discovery of what a great habitat this planet seems to be. Adding to that stunning discovery, we now have found that there are indigenous people here who seem to be friendly, at least the one we met in person. All of this has to be challenging your thinking as well. We are keeping in mind that CSE's philosophy about Proxima One as a colony was that they would wait for two years of reports from us on Deep ΔT before sending Proxima Two, if at all. The idea was that whatever was learned from our first two years of life here would advise what sort of mission, if any, would be sent to join us here. Following that plan, Proxima Two would be here, at the earliest, somewhere around eleven years after our arrival.

"I am reviewing all of that to say that I think it is still valid thinking, even though you have heard surprisingly favorable news so far from ΔT. Because our early reports paint a picture of an Earth-like eco-system, it will be tempting for CSE to advance the schedule and forego the two years of learning from our experiences. We still think any decision about Proxima Two should wait two years as was originally planned. As you well know, there is much to be learned and explored here first. I know I probably don't need to say that. My own worst fears were that our first impressions here would lead us to make choices that would be disastrous in the future.

"So far, God has been faithful to direct our paths and our thinking to be in harmony with what is here. We trust that He will be working on your behalf as well.

"Thanks for listening; I will sign off for now, Anj."

C.S. and Zam were the only ones who read that report live. Browning was out at a meeting about the upcoming launch of the next contingent of astronauts going to the Mars settlement. Cooper, ever the realist, spoke out loud. "I think they'll go," he predicted to her as if Anj was in the room, "I would put money on it, Anj. CSE will send them before you are feeling ready for them."

Zam countered, "What if those people on the planet turn out to be hostile? It is entirely normal for indigenous people to fight tooth and nail against intruders who bring change. We could get there with Proxima Two and find out that our dear friends had been massacred long before we even launched."

"It could happen alright, but they'll go, I think," Cooper said. "It is too tantalizing. They will probably go even if they find out the ΔT people are indeed hostile. There is so much world-wide enthusiasm about a human colony on another planet. The whole world wants to vicariously join March and Anj there, and the only way to do that is to send another set of Earthlings to the New World."

Zam, coming from the other end of the spectrum of caution, said, "Oh I hope not. I hope cooler thinking prevails. We at least need to know more about these people, to say nothing of all we don't know yet about that environment."

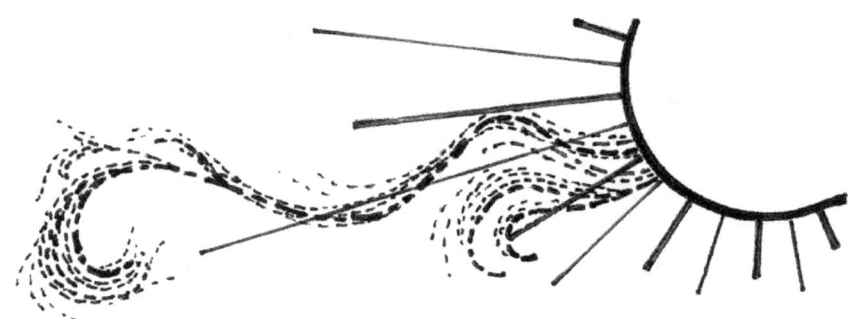

Chapter Seventeen

Even though it was a typical sweltering afternoon on ΔT, they packed outer layers: coats, hats, gloves, and head-lamps into the backpacks, not knowing what contingencies they might run into, and knowing there was a long cold night ahead. March was reminded of packing for high country backpacking in the Rockies. It is warm when putting on the pack, but, even in August, it could be snowing up on top. There were plenty of variables that could change everything. He packed two days' worth of food and four liters of water each. Anj had told him about the dream she had, a dream of being in the dwelling of the people of the boy, and even though it calmed her, it made him nervous, nervous enough to prepare for radical changes of plans. This might not be a short, predictable rendezvous with 'friendlies.' And even if hospitable as they hoped, he wondered what the expectations of these people were, expectations with which he and Anj might have to comply.

Anj was looking remarkably optimistic as she loaded food and water bottles into her pack. 'She must have received peace from that dream,' March thought, 'I hope it was God, and not just a random dream.'

"I wonder what they eat?" she said, not expecting a reply. "Maybe they are vegetarians. ΔT boy liked that pear you gave him. Do they have cows and milk and cheese? Is this the land of milk and honey?" she joked.

March interrupted as if he had not heard her propositions, "How is the weight of your pack; are you going to be okay, or shall I carry some of that water?"

"Hey pilot man, I'm fine," she said grinning, "This pack is still half of what we carry when we go hunting. I'm good, thank you."

They climbed down from the ship in t-shirts and shorts, carrying medium-sized packs bearing the rest of their gear. With a single look back at their home, they wordlessly set out for the point up the coast where they would turn right, up into the forest to find ΔT people.

It had all been discussed, but, with so many unknown possibilities, they had not come up with a concrete strategy of how to respond to the situations that might arise. They had agreed again, reminded themselves again, that it was becoming clear that God had brought them here for this engagement with people of another of His creations, and that they need not fear any attack or viciousness from them. Beyond that, God was remaining silent. Buried in their own thoughts and prayers, they soon reached the right turn from the beach and directed their steps up into the trees. Anj recognized the very spot where she had first seen the boy as they passed further up into the trees.

A few minutes up into the forest, they slowed to a cautious walk, scanning the forest ahead of them until Anj saw the first person. "There is a woman with long white hair squatting right up there," pointing to a spot where the female figure was still screened from full view by low-hanging branches.

Going a little further, March and Anj came into the woman's peripheral vision, at which she turned and visually took them in for a moment before turning back to speak quietly to whoever was with her, still out of sight to March and Anj. She held out her hand, palm up, in their direction, seeming to indicate to the others, "They're here." Other speakers could be heard, and the familiar boy stepped into view, peering below the branches. March and Anj kept walking slowly towards them until they could see two men and another woman along with the boy, who was smiling broadly, perhaps relieved that March and Anj had come, redeeming what must have seemed like a tall tale to the adults.

March smoothly unslung his pack and put it down softly, still five meters away from the group. Anj followed suit, and they both stepped up the final slope to where the small assembly was squatting on a level spot. Instinctively, they squatted too, completing a circle about two meters in diameter. No one spoke. March and Anj had agreed to let the others take the lead, so they waited patiently. All were quiet for a full five minutes, looking at one another. The silence felt peaceful rather than tense. The group was clearly sizing up the two strangers, and listening to the creation around them, maybe to God Himself, to find out what sort of beings they might be. The boy had done a similar thing himself in the previous meeting. Neither March nor Anj attempted any speech, knowing the futility of being understood using the language of another planet. As she sat among the group, Anj noticed what March had told her about, namely the boy's incredible green eyes and flawless features. He was indeed other-worldly, remarkable in many ways. She was also looking closely at the others, assessing their appearance in comparison to Earth's humans. She was struck by a notable lack of any nervous mannerisms. No one was drumming fingers, fiddling with a twig, or avoiding eye contact. Neither was their gaze intimidating or even suspicious, just looking.

March got uncomfortable squatting, not a normal position for him, so he easily transitioned to cross-legged. Anj remained with her arms wrapped around her knees, as the rest were, wanting to identify with their culture as much as she could to avoid the risk of being offensive, or even too different. She knew she only had one opportunity to make a first impression on this group and was sorry that the impression she had left with the boy on the previous meeting was probably not good.

Both women had long hair down well below their shoulders. All wore the wrap around the hips down to the knees, and the women had the soft material extending up over one shoulder, reminding Anj of an Indian Sari. Anj could tell it was not woven cloth, but some kind of fibrous sheet of material generously gathered around them. The first one had white hair, the other, shiny black. Of the two men, one was older and graying, one younger and black-haired. Both had shorter hair, just below their ears. Their eyes, looking over the two people before them, were calmly assessing. The older man's at-rest face wore an easy smile, and the creases in his face indicated that it often was graced with unbridled laughter. No one carried any kind of weapons.

Finally, the older man began to smile openly and speak conversationally to his group. He apparently had made up his mind about the two new people and was discussing it with his delegation. Agreement worked its way around the circle in a discussion among them, evidently, everyone affirming the conclusion he had come to. After a pause, he held his hand in front of him and waved it slowly across, as the boy had done, apparently signifying, "We are open to communicating with you." The other four then also gave this hand-motion. The astronauts from Earth mimicked it, somewhat familiar with it as a formality.

The older man turned to March and Anj and spoke a long sentence of words unknown to the pioneers. His gestures as he spoke acknowledged the boy, evidently signifying that they had come to this place to meet the people the boy had told them about.

March and Anj's acquaintance, the young boy, was visibly enjoying this opportunity to see the strangers again in the company of his elders but was not taking any kind of role in this second encounter.

March spoke, "Yes we have come here because of our young friend." He paused to also acknowledge the boy with a hand held palm-up towards him. "He invited us to meet again in this place." He spoke further, pointing back towards the ship and signaling, "We walked here to meet with you."

ΔT man's face revealed some confusion. He stared steadily first at March, then at Anj, then back again. Finally, he spoke calmly once more, making direct eye contact with March. His words were not accompanied by any clarifying hand movement this time, and his speech was several sentences. It seemed to be a question, and it seemed to be offered in total disregard that his language would not be understood.

March shrugged his shoulders with his palms up in a quizzical pose, trying to indicate with his body language the obvious, that verbal communication was not happening. He said, as quietly as the man had spoken to him, "I'm so sorry; I do not understand your language."

A look of unknowing disbelief was on every ΔT face. They seemed to be taken completely off guard that this person really could not talk, but only make meaningless sounds. After a minute of considering this unbelievable situation, the older ring-leader man did resort to hand motions. Putting his hands together beside his head tilted to the side, he pointed to the astronauts. "I think he wants to know where we sleep," Anj whispered to March.

March, in doubt about how to hand signal a reply, other than by pointing in the direction of the ship, turned to Anj hopefully. She picked up a stick and drew a profile of the ship in the dirt, right-side-up for them to see, and then pointed in that direction, signing the same 'sleep' hand-motions that ring-leader had used, and pointing to the drawing. "This is where we sleep," she couldn't resist stating out loud as if it would help.

The conical top profile of their vehicle would have been memorable, but none of their faces registered recognition. Either they did not understand the drawing, or no one had come across their ship parked by the sea. Looking around at one another, consulting in quiet conversation and pointing at the sketch, the ΔT people seemed to be confounded about how that could represent a place to sleep.

Willing to make another attempt to get past the newcomer's inability to talk, the white-haired woman, who was closest to Anj, tried taking another direction in this encounter. Curious, she pointed to Anj's feet, shod with ankle-high walking shoes, took off her own thick-soled sandal of woven grasses, and waved it around chatting the whole time, then pointed to Anj's feet again, inviting a reply from her.

Anj, in a bold moment, unfastened the laces at the top of her right shoe, took it off, and held it out to the woman who was overflowing with curiosity. ΔT woman held out both hands as if to receive something fragile, and once it was in her hands, examined it closely with murmurs of amazement, telling her friends what she was learning, maybe, "smooth inside, smells funny, flexible, it must be very tough." Her uncommonly lovely features were quite animated, genuinely fascinated, as she held the shoe from the alien woman.

Finally, she dangled it from its laces, grinning, and passed it back to the alien. Anj slipped her foot back into her shoe and motioned to the woman that she was curious about her sandal. The woman happily offered it to her. "Made of grass," Anj imitated the same style with which the woman had examined her shoe, "well made, very smooth inside, interesting straps, these must be very strong grass fibers," and having satisfied her genuine curiosity, passed it back, taking in with interest, how a woman so aged could remain so becoming.

That left the group at a loss what to do next for a minute. March landed upon an idea, and asked, 'Where do *you* sleep?' with the same hand-signals, pointing to them.

They understood his question immediately. Eyes brightened, smiles showed on the faces that had been so far uncomprehending, and simultaneously, they all stood, giving body language that was saying more clearly than words, "Oh, we would love to show you where we sleep. Please come along with us."

March and Anj, not confident that they were 'hearing' correctly, or understanding the invitation, did not move until ring-leader man and the boy made clear invitations with hand gestures, 'come along now, come, come.' March appealed to Anj silently, 'You feel okay about this?' He wanted to make sure that they were in agreement. Her wordless response was affirmative.

When March and Anj stepped down the hill to where the backpacks were, a flurry of curious conversation came from the group, and they watched with fascination as the two aliens settled into shoulder straps, the bundles on their backs. Each of the ΔT people had a small bag similar to what the boy carried on his hip.

Leader man started off, the boy close behind, setting a course to the northeast across the hillside through the trees. Everyone else motioned the guests to follow the man and the boy, signaling that they would come behind. The two women and the other younger man fell in line following the strangers. The three behind sometimes engaged in short conversations among themselves. Leader man and the boy set quite an energetic pace, putting distance behind them easily. "These people are serious walkers," March commented, "are you keeping up okay?"

"No problem, Cap'n, praise God."

Relieved to hear Anj feeling so relaxed and strong, March kept up fairly close behind the boy, all the while wondering how they could be feeling such peace when they were being led by unknown people with unknown motives into an unknown place on an unknown planet. But there it was; no fear. Questions lingered in the moment however as to just how far they had to go, and what was ahead for the night. Soon, miles had slipped away and only half of the red disc of Proxima was showing through Browning Sea haze as she quietly revealed that there were indeed mountains over there, their jagged profile held like a cardboard cut-out against the red orb of the setting sun.

Leader man's route eventually joined a well-traveled path, wide enough for the two pioneers to walk side by side, and they were able to talk quietly. Anj commented on the distinct increase in the variety of trees and their greenness in this area of the hills. Everything that was growing here looked bigger and more lush. March pointed out different kinds of trees they had not seen before, laden with ripe, hanging fruit.

Without warning, with a skidding sound and a thump, a man jumped from the uphill-side of the trail onto the path right behind the last three, greeting them with a loud voice. Apparently familiar, he fell in with the troop. Startled, Anj grabbed March's wrist at the sound, but continued walking, looking warily over her shoulder at the new man. His openly curious stare and grinning face eventually set her at ease. As he engaged the three others in conversation, Anj could only guess what kinds of questions and answers were being exchanged about the two strangers.

Soon, from another side trail that joined their path, three young girls in their late teens merged into the walking cluster, joining in right alongside Anj, beaming at the opportunity to be so close to the new people, as the trail was wide enough now and level enough for a large group to move along easily. One of the girls said something to Anj with her expression posing a question. Anj replied as conversationally as she could, "I'm from another solar system, so I do not understand your language." That same perplexed surprise, registering wonder that this person really couldn't talk, was what Anj received in reply. The three girls discussed this among themselves for a minute, then another one of them spoke up again, a little louder and enunciating very clearly with eyebrows up. Anj longed with every neuron of her language capabilities to be able to understand, but could only say, "I am so sorry that I do not understand your language. It will be my great joy to learn your language, starting today." All three stared blankly at Anj and giggled openly, but the boldest one took Anj by the hand and fell into stride with her in a show of camaraderie, despite the language malfunction. Anj hoped it was a camaraderie that would also help her learn this language; it was evidently going to be a necessity on ΔT.

Next, a group of young men came from the left to walk along with the youngster and the leader in front, casting long looks back at the two interesting strangers. The younger boy had apparently gained some status with them through his role in all of this. One of them, about sixteen or seventeen, dropped back and walked beside March, looking him over carefully. They too then had an exchange that Anj could not hear, but the boy continued walking alongside March, talking as if he knew he was being understood, pointing at the various fruit-laden trees, and gesturing about something up ahead that excited him. March played along, getting as much as he could from the body language and tone of voice.

In the deepening evening light, they could see they had come alongside a continuous high cliff on the right, their path running parallel to the base of it. Up ahead, they were approaching another set of cliffs that intersected at a right angle with this one. March and Anj assumed this was their destination. Unless there was a way up those cliffs, they would be able to go no further. They began to see lights up ahead in the dusk through the thick trees and could hear soft music and the sound of many voices. Finally, the trees opened, and they could see that, where the two cliffs met, there was a huge open grotto underneath the cliffs, a high, well-lit open space. Whether it was carved out, or a natural formation, they could not tell.

It was a warm and inviting scene, even festive, with good smells of hot food. All along the opening, under its shelf, were large low tables with gatherings of people sitting on rugs, cross-legged, or squatting around them. Children ran around playing freely, although a few stood staring open-mouthed at the approaching group with the two oddly-dressed new-comers. Mothers or fathers held babies; young people were in animated conversations, and the people who were cooking had the characteristic hurried movements of any chef about to have everything hot and ready to eat. One of the table-groups was making music with a variety of instruments and several singers.

The tantalizing melodies and rhythms they were using touched the astronauts with welcome like a fragrance, fresh and new, different from anything on Earth. Exquisite, quite distinctive to the pioneer's ears, it was music filled with both longing and rejoicing. As the cluster of walkers approached close enough to hear the music, something surged up from inside Anj's spirit compelling her to listen, as if driven by thirst. Coming under its influence, she began to feel liberated, free in ways that she didn't know she was chained. Unexplainably, Anj had the impulse, only overruled by her natural self-control, to immediately sit down near the musicians and soak in the transport of that music. It seemed to be the loveliest sound she had ever heard. So strong was its attraction that she had the fleeting thought that maybe God had brought her here for one purpose, just for this sound, this one soothing, peace-filled source of blessing. She felt her heart filling up with something satisfying and as necessary to her soul as water for thirst.

Even though the sun was down, which usually brought about a fairly rapid cool-down, the huge dark cliffs had been soaking up Proxima's rays all afternoon and were now radiating soothing warmth to the entire gathering. Anj, who had been thinking it was time to search her pack for a pullover and some long pants, realized that it would not be necessary after all. The three girls had firmly attached themselves to the alien arrivals' group, the strong one still holding Anj's hand like best friends. Those who had accompanied the boy out in the hills to find the mysterious strangers made no effort to shield their prize, if that is what Anj and March were, from encountering others. The group of boys also came along, clearly supporting the first boy concerning his discovery of these aliens. March's new friend kept talking with his hands and his words to March, sometimes laughing at his own jokes, and looking to March for his response in facial expression or body language. March thought he must be the most genuinely gregarious person he had ever met. The one who had suddenly joined them back on the trail, Anj thought must be a son of one of the women, the way he fit into that part of the group so comfortably.

Just as Anj was expecting Leader man to take a podium and make some kind of public announcement about them, he instead directed their group to a large empty table, and they all sat down as if they were a normal part of the daily life of ΔT people. March and Anj exchanged glances, each checking with the other. The glance turned into an exchanged smile as they shared this fascinating unfolding scene. March could tell Anj was at ease with it all.

Not sure what was to happen next, but feeling comfortable with the three girls, Anj turned to the nearest one, locked eyes with her, patted her own heart, and said "Anj."

Strong girl was puzzled at first, but then comprehension cleared her expression, and she smiled, "Anch," she tried, then pointed to her new alien friend and said to her companions, with some conviction, "Anch!"

"Close enough," Anj said, nodding and smiling. "I'm Anj, what is your name? I assume you have names here?" She raised their still-clasped hands and pressed into the girl's heart with the back of her hand so that strong girl's hand was also near her heart. "What can I call you?"

Anj was feeling uncharacteristically amiable with this girl and was genuinely eager to get to know at least her name. The girl looked a little hesitant, turned to her friends, had a short consultation, glancing back at the stranger, then brightened, and sat up straight. She put her free hand on her chest and said, "Maela."

"Oh, that's pretty... Mella."

Clearly not satisfied with the pronunciation, the girl said more slowly, "Maa-ella."

Anj was careful this time, "Maa-eh-la."

Maela smiled broadly at Anj and then towards her friends, clearly delighted with this development. It turned out that the other two girls were "Laena" and "Fantalo." and Anj repeated the names to herself, pledging to get good at remembering these unfamiliar names in the days ahead. She rummaged in her pack and found her digital electronic tablet and typed in the three names, filing them under, 'ΔT girlfriends.'

Bringing out the tablet inspired a great deal of interest from the whole group, and Anj put it on the table, showing them how it could generate pictures, things to read, and be a place to write things down. She showed the girls their names, resulting in wide eyes and exclamations. Maela pointed to her name on the tablet and said with disbelief, "Maela?"

Anj nodded and smiled. Maela turned and wrote in the fine dust on the floor beside her rug. It was unfamiliar scribbling to Anj, reminding her of Arabic calligraphy. Maela pointed to it and said, "Maela."

Anj went to the drawing option on the tablet and showed her new friends how to draw figures and erase them. Then she pointed to the symbols in the floor dust and handed the tablet to Maela, who unhesitatingly redrew her name with her finger, just the way she had on the floor. Anj saved it with the subtitle of 'Maela' in English, then smiled and offered it to the other two to do the same, which they did with a good deal of fuss and giggling.

While the name-game was going on, Leader man stood up and took the boy with him deeper into the grotto by the cooking fires. March watched the whole procedure, and his new friend narrated animatedly, explaining what was happening. It was obviously time to eat, as two people from each table went to the serving areas and picked up huge trays piled with colorful steaming foods and several kinds of fruit cut into pieces. The boy and the man returned with trays and set food before the group. Everyone sat back, waiting for something before eating, and the Leader raised his eyes to the ceiling and said, "Omeda kalitana kalimana," and continued with a few more short sentences. Everyone was looking alternately at the leader and at the food, and at March and Anj, as he spoke. As soon as he finished, they all began to take food and eat.

March whispered to Anj, "I've heard that before; I think it is a prayer over the food, 'Omeda kali something-something.' The boy spoke that before we ate pears together."

"It does seem to be a blessing or something over the food," Anj commented. "So I wonder who they are praying to?"

"It would be easy to jump to the conclusion that they know God, but that would also be what we would most like to discover," March answered. "Nevertheless, it sure feels the same in my spirit,"

March and Anj set aside all thoughts of caution as they first tasted and then gratefully ate generous portions of all the dishes. It was mostly finger-food and anything which was drippy, as they watched and learned, was eaten using flatbreads to scoop or dip, similar to many Asian cultures on Earth. Each bite introduced them to flavors that were spectacular. The new arrivals ate and exchanged glances and nods of amazement, unable to resist telling their new friends, even though they knew the words would not make sense, "This food is so good, so tasty, how do you do this?" and "What is this anyway?" New friends responded generously waving over the foods, encouraging the new people to try everything.

As the meal was enjoyed over much conversation and laughter, it began to rain softly, as it had every evening so far, and out beyond the edge of the overhang the open area became shiny with wet, little rivulets running out to water the trees beyond. Listening to the rain and watching it wet the hard-packed court, Anj could not remember that she had ever before enjoyed such a peaceful, at-ease, warm, loving experience with a crowd over a meal. She felt like she was glowing with the warmth, and she leaned into March cozily with a full stomach, satisfied with the most delightful food she had ever tasted. He felt warm too.

As the trays were cleared away, conversations picked up around the table. Everyone participated. The children and young boys and girls contributed and were being listened to as attentively as the adults. This was happening at all of the tables, until the Leader man who had brought Anj and March, stood, and waited for silence. It took less than a minute to collect everyone's respectful attention, and he began to speak. A couple of minutes into his talk, he did wave his hand towards March and Anj once, which was the only clue they had about what he was saying.

Anj leaned over to Maela, pointed to Maela, and whispered, "Maela," then pointed to the Leader man and raised her eyebrows. Maela, immediately understanding her curiosity, said, "Makkana," and nodded impressively.

Anj tried it, "Makana," but was corrected on her pronunciation because the 'k' sound was double as if it were two words, as in 'thank Kurt.' Again, she tried it, "Mak-kana," and was met with a smile of approval.

Makkana spoke for about ten minutes and sat down quietly to a low hum in the crowd as people turned to one another with comments of affirmation. Then another man stood and spoke for ten more minutes, followed by the white-haired woman at their table, who also waved her hand once towards the visitors during her monologue, casually referring to them in some way. March looked at Anj, and they continued to wonder in unison what this was all about. After she sat down, the musicians began a refrain, and everyone joined in with what was a familiar song to the assembled crowd. Some stood, most of the people closed their eyes or looked upwards, and some raised their hands in a manner that looked to March and Anj like a church congregation on Earth. This music and singing continued for at least an hour with everyone fully engaged. Anj was fascinated to see the children also quite absorbed in the experience, lost in the musical atmosphere, like going to another world.

When the community singing time ended on a soft romantic sounding song, it was followed by a full five minutes of silence, during which time many put their faces in their hands and others sat in reverent silence. No one spoke or moved until Makkana chanted some sort of incantation over the whole group. Then gradually conversation resumed at the tables and a few got up to leave, particularly the families with small children. March and Anj looked at one another, and Anj ventured, "That was their religion, don't you think?"

"Either religion or an extremely harmonious and musical community," March answered. "It felt like home, but a home better than I've ever been to. This place reveals one mysterious feature after another. First, we find out there are real people here, then we see that, though they are very simple people, they have universal practices of religion or music that feel both distinctly different and oh-so-familiar."

The white-haired woman, whom Anj found out was named 'Saala,' had her face in her hands during the entire silence after the music ended, and now she was smiling and had tears streaming down her face, completely unashamed. She began to speak to Laena and Fantalo, holding their hands and laughing softly as the tears continued to drip onto the table from her chin. The young girls also, drawn fully into whatever Saala was saying, began to laugh and cry at the same time, and Anj, trying not to stare, could not help but conclude that Saala was imparting wisdom or instruction to them as an elder. A sudden longing rose up in her to be able to understand this language, and for Saala to be able to speak to her too, about doing life in this place. Anj wanted to know how to live here, somehow, like this. It was beckoning to her.

Concluding her time with the two girls, Saala finally said something quietly towards each person at the table group, including directly to Anj and March, and it looked as if she were excusing herself and bidding 'good night' to each one. She left the table, going over to several other tables, evidently to greet many of the people in the general gathering. The other man from the original search group also left, with the man who had unexpectedly jumped down onto the trail.

Makkana stood as if to leave, and spoke to March and Anj, motioning for them to come with him. He nodded to Maela, Laena, and Fantalo, and spoke to them, apparently letting them know what was happening. Maela reluctantly released her grasp on Anj's hand and said something to her as they stood up. Anj thought, "That probably means 'good night,' or 'see you tomorrow,' I am going to try to remember the sounds of what she said," but in the commotion of getting her pack and hurrying along after March and Makkana, the unfamiliar words slipped away from her short-term memory. She determined to begin a language notebook right away. Makkana, carrying an oil lamp, walked on ahead, lighting the way.

They were led far back into the grotto, past huge stone pillars, and past openings to other large rooms, reminding Anj of a hotel with convention rooms. Eventually, the space narrowed to a wide hallway with several oval-topped wood-plank doors, through one of which they were escorted. They were met by a clean spacious room furnished with what was a simple hand-made bed, a stand with a large pitcher full of water, two cups, and a basin. A lamp with a bright steady flame lit the room quite adequately.

Makkana showed them across the hall to what they recognized as a toilet facility, and they indicated that they understood about that. March desperately wanted to ask if they were expected to sleep for twenty-some hours, or what time they were to be awake, but that was not going to be possible, so they thanked him and said 'good night' as best they could. He strode back down the hall, his lighted profile diminishing gradually until he turned a corner and they were alone, maybe. They did not know if other people were behind some of the other doors. But now, isolated in this huge complex, in this alien culture, the profound reality of their situation noiselessly settled in upon them.

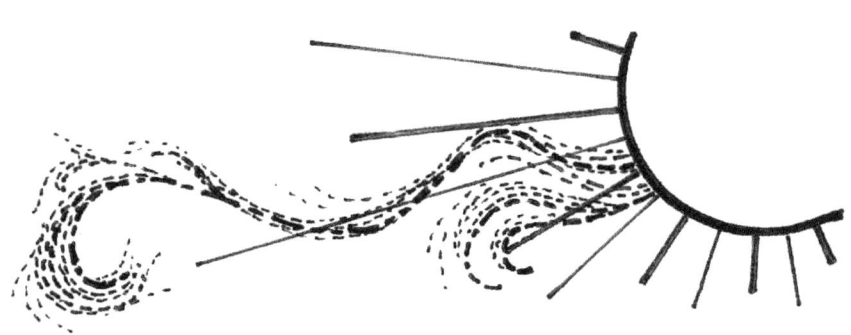

Chapter Eighteen

"What *is* this place?" Anj exclaimed, wrapping all of their experiences into a single question. Since meeting the little reception group in the woods, so much new information had come to them that they felt the need to once again redefine 'this place,' yet there were so many things they still did not know. The language problem remained a significant block to discovering more information about this culture and these fascinating people.

March confessed that he had an inner conflict. There was a part of him that still wanted to exercise caution going forward, but another part of him that wanted to believe that fear in any form was completely un-called-for. Anj agreed that she was also finding it quite unnatural to release all wariness, even in the face of the consistent message they had been picking up from this environment: the message of safety and freedom from threat. Anj drew herself up to her full five-feet, five-inches and said, "God is telling us to shove aside all our need for vigilance. It is clear, and we need to just get used to it."

March sat down cautiously on the low sleeping arrangement, a wooden frame of branches lashed together, with some kind of mattress on it. He spread his hands out on it and gave it a trial push absentmindedly. He did not comment on the quality of the bed; he replied to Anj's statement, "Yeah, this unbelievable peace: I think it is the real deal, and any fear or need for vigilance is just a left-over from our Earth life. I have started thinking of this place almost like being born again. Everything is new, and it is good, lovely, abundant, and peaceful. Nothing from our previous world applies."

Anj smiled, "I like that idea. I think it's true. It feels like truth. Nothing from our world compares to this; from the astronomy to the gastronomy (can you believe that meal we had tonight?), even the music, nothing compares, so why shouldn't relating to its people be an entirely different experience too?" She stepped over to the lamp on the wall, looking at it closely, "And the artwork; look at this beautiful vessel; never seen anything like it, and what a nice light it gives off, not that yellowish glow I've seen from antique oil lamps at home. All is new."

March said, "What I have noticed that is most striking, is the demeanor of the people, each one. They are different as individuals, of course, but they are the same in that none of them are hurting. Know what I mean?"

"Not really, please explain."

"When you meet someone on Earth, they present themselves in whatever way they believe is to their best advantage, maybe with a lot of bravado, maybe aloof and confident, maybe snooty, maybe even shy, but I usually find myself coming away from my first meeting of people with a deep impression that, inside, there is a bundle of pain. So many people live lives that are quite tormented, which of course they would prefer you do not see, at least at first. But here, I have not met anyone who is bearing a load of past hurts and failures."

"Whoa, that is a big thing to say without understanding the language, don't you think?" Anj asked.

"On Earth, when I see that pain, I rarely hear the pain in their words. I discern it in mannerisms and bearing, and it is obvious to me, probably because I am so worried that they will see where I am hurting," and he laughed aloud because Anj knew about all his scars.

Anj thought on that a minute, smiling at him, enjoying his transparency and his deeply perceptive way with people. She saw the safety he was feeling here already beginning to spill over into his own liberty and freedom. "I think I know what you mean. I feel it differently, in that, I unhesitatingly felt at ease with these people. When that guy jumped down onto the trail, it startled me, and I was nervous at first, but looking at him for just a short time, I completely felt okay with him, and by the time Maela took my hand, which I would normally have pulled away from, it felt as normal as saying 'hello.' Yeah, maybe that is her own freedom from pain, and I know she is not going to hurt me."

"Nice. The word is 'nice.' People here are authentically nice."

Beside the lamp, a large round hole in the wall, like a window, emanated a faint glow of light and a soft flow of fresh air. Leaning out the 'window' and looking up, Anj could see a small portion of the night sky, including the unmistakable Alpha Centauri A and B, shining down the shaft. "Ah! A light shaft," she said, delighted and impressed that this was not just a cave, but it would be a well-lit room in the day-time with plenty of ventilation.

Wondering what they were going to do until it was time to sleep, she asked, "Did you bring a book?"

"I did; I brought my thousand-page novel, *Interplanetary War*," he said grinning. Weight restrictions had made such a possibility prohibitive. "But seriously, you brought your tablet, why don't you read something to me?" They sat on the bed with their backs against the wall and noticed that this habitat required no supplemental heating even though they knew it was getting predictably cold outside. The stone wall against which they were resting was comfortably warm.

They agreed to stick to their agreed-upon schedule and put off sleep until about nine hours after the sunset, which meant staying awake another five hours, against a full stomach and a long hike. Both knew that would be a challenge. They took turns reading from her tablet, a book of research on the notoriously large star, Betelgeuse. Data from astronomical research filled the book, of interest to both of them, focusing on the author's predictions that the star was nearing its transition into a supernova, based on radiation signals they were receiving. The book and the research it contained was ten years old before they left Earth, but Betelgeuse was still shining, the bright star on Orion's left shoulder in ΔT's night sky.

Re-igniting his interest in that star, March maintained enough fascination to stay awake. Since that massive star was still over six-hundred light-years away, such an explosion did not represent any danger, but, should it explode, it would be very interesting to watch, probably brighter than the binary Alpha Centauri which was so close. March wondered what these non-scientific people would think about such an event in their night sky. It would be spectacular. Anj wondered out loud if any inhabited planets were orbiting that star. "I hope not," she said quietly.

Just before they went to sleep, Anj read from the Bible as she did every morning and evening, finding delight in how it still spoke to them in this very different place in the universe. This night she read Psalm Ninety-one out loud to put to rest any lingering fears that might generate bad dreams or distress during the next eight hours of much-needed rest. "You have made the Lord, my refuge, Even the Most High, your dwelling place." They blew out the lamp, which left a sweet fragrance lingering in the near-darkness, a bluish glow still coming down the light shaft from Alpha Centauri.

Even before March's watch-alarm went off, they both awakened to voices talking in the hall. Re-lighting the lamp, March went to the door and put his ear close. He could tell that, whoever it was, they were right outside. He signaled to Anj, "Should I open it?" She said, "Sure, why not, we are awake anyway."

Opening the door, March recognized the younger man who was with the group yesterday along with another he did not know, and the familiar young boy, who gave March a friendly smile.

The men signaled to March to follow them back down the hall. Stepping back inside the room, March said, "It's the boy, Anj, and two men, one we know, one we don't. They want us to come with them."

"That is a surprise, since we thought they would sleep longer. I guess we will find out what's up. Let's take our gear with us? I would like to go home today if we can."

March agreed, "Yes, me too, I think that is a good idea to keep our packs with us so we can depart simply if we may."

Leaving the men waiting for a few minutes, they washed up, used the facilities across the hall, and gathered their gear, finally appearing at the door, ready to go. Retracing last night's steps, they heard much activity ahead, signaling to them that everyone was up; they weren't the only ones. Out into the open area, amid much milling about and the smells of cooking again, their guides led them to the same table as the previous night, and, much to Anj's delight, Maela and her friends were already there, obviously anticipating their arrival.

March's talkative young friend, also greeted him loudly, so glad to see him. He put his arm around March's shoulders, and his hand on March's heart speaking very seriously to him face to face. The boy's behavior was that of a friend pledging undying allegiance, and March was getting the message of friendship, though nervous about having the young man so boldly entering into his personal space. He patted the boy on the back agreeably and tried to assure himself that he was safe to release himself to the level of closeness that the young man seemed to want. Makkana was there too, with his signature smile, greeting each one personally and warmly.

Was it time for breakfast, they wondered. March was hungry, his body already adjusting to the schedule they had adopted just two days ago. Both of them were wondering why everyone was up even though it was at least six hours before daylight. It seemed to Anj that these people must be on a schedule similar to what they had contrived, dawn days and dusk days, but there was no way to know for sure. They had to resign themselves to the process of learning as they went. The boy and the man appeared soon at the table with trays and food. This time, one of the other people at the table said the "Omeda kalitana kalimana" grace-like incantation. Anj reached for some good-looking bright orange fruit pieces in the center bowl, but Maela caught her arm, gently holding her back, and pointed her to any other food, but not that one. No one else was eating that one either. Puzzled and curious, Anj complied and enjoyed a variety of other fruits, nuts, and breads again, along with such happy conversation that it almost did not matter that they could not understand the words. Everyone was having a good time being together.

Finally, as the other bowls were removed, and the meal was drawing to a close, each person took a piece of the orange fruit; there was one for each, with none left over, and each one held the fruit up ceremonially with both hands. March and Anj were watching and followed along. After a brief silence, observed by every table in the place, the same phrase was spoken again by one person at each table, this time followed by a couple of other long sentences. It was a comforting soft hum that felt like a prayer gathering to Anj. Then everyone lowered the piece of fruit and took a bite. An indescribable flavor that nothing on Earth could approximate met Anj's mouth, and turning to look at March she found him turning to look at her with the same amazed and delighted expression she was feeling. Everyone seemed to be eating in reverence, slowly and quietly. 'No wonder,' Anj thought, 'something this good *should* be eaten with reverence.'

She also began to notice that something like energy or regeneration was coursing through her body as she finished her portion. Adrenaline provides an exciting availability of energy (fighter pilots get accused of being adrenaline junkies), but this was something quite different, entirely pleasant, with none of the trembling associated with too much adrenaline, and it was more than a physical effect. Spiritual, emotional, she could not quite put her finger on it. Everyone around the table was awash in the pleasant benefits of this marvelous fruit, or whatever it was.

A clear melody carried by some kind of flute began to reach over the gathering. Soon it was joined by another instrument in harmony, then another, and then by singers. The combined sound transported March and Anj to a place of perfect peace in their hearts. Sometimes all of the people sang with the music, sometimes it simplified down to just one instrument again for a while. The music continued for over an hour-and-a-half, exquisitely tender in the way it drew everyone into itself, never growing tiresome, cycling through moods from joy to deep reverence, from celebration to strident declaration. March, who thought the incantation over the meal was a true prayer of blessing, was also becoming convinced that this was genuine worship of the God of the universe, and he was fascinated. He mouthed the word, "real worship" silently to Anj. And she nodded slowly with affirmation.

When the music finally came to a close, there was a brief silence, then Maela sat up real straight and recited something for about five minutes, it seemed to be a memorized piece as she went through it with her eyes closed. At its conclusion, each person at the table spoke softly into his or her hands for a few minutes. March thought, "They are praying." Next, March's young friend, similarly, sat up and recited for several minutes, followed by people speaking into their hands again. Watching and listening to all this with interest, March thought that he was discerning the same Spirit of God present with Whom he was familiar. He decided that the next time they were speaking into their hands, he would join in prayer to God. He leaned over and whispered the idea to Anj, and she nodded.

Fantalo was the next to recite, a long, almost musical soliloquy that reminded March and Anj of when they had been in a Church service in Germany, and although they could understand but a few words of German, they felt the joy of God's presence and His encouragement. When Fantalo concluded, almost with a whisper, a silence pervaded, accompanied in the background by the recitations being made at other tables. Only after a full two minutes did the people at their table begin to speak into their hands again. March too, spoke quietly into his hands, "Father, thank You for bringing us to this amazing place and these amazing people. Your blessing, God, be upon these people, Your strength and revelation to these precious creations of Yours. God, we speak joy, we speak purity and holiness, we speak favor and protection on these, our new friends You have given us. Help us God with this language; help us understand these people, and help us to come to know what message they have for us and what message we have for them. We need this language, God, help us learn this language, Lord. I want to understand my young friend here, and all of these sweet people."

Quite transported in the Spirit, flooded by his recognition of the deep and comfortable holiness invading him, his eyes remained closed through the entire next recitation, meditating in the sweet unmistakable Presence of God, and, when the others began to pray again, he began praying in his spiritual language as his heart rejoined in a longing to make the very best of these friendships and to participate fully in cooperation with the reason why God had brought them here. His spirit was recklessly abandoned to the refreshing turmoil inside. "Whatever You want God, it is all for You."

He did not know how long he shared this oneness of the Spirit with the people of ΔT; it was so sweet, they all lost track of time. When March finally opened his eyes because it got quiet around him, he saw that they were the last table still occupied and that it was just beginning to get light outside. Anj was there. All of them were; no one had left, and they were all looking at him as if expecting him to lead them further. Anj ventured, "When you prayed in tongues, you sounded just like them. It appears that you were speaking their language. I believe they understood you, so they are quite amazed and somewhat confused I think."

"I hope it was all good," he joked, but then returned to the importance of the moment. "Yeah, I just was swept up with such a heart for these people. The Holy Spirit was all over this time of worship and prayer like nothing I ever experienced before; how about you?"

"Yes, I was glad you were praying along with them. It felt easy to fit in, comfortable in the Spirit, no fog of confusion, no interruption of lies, no fight against distraction. It was amazing. I feel like we were born for this." She glanced around, breaking away momentarily from her connection with him. "They are still staring at you, March."

March turned to his wide-eyed young friend and spoke to him in the only language he knew in the natural. "If I prayed in your language, I don't know what I said. Those words came from the Holy Spirit." He put his hand on the boy's shoulder, "I hope I did not alarm you or confuse you. I do not speak your language, but I want to learn it; I hope you will help me." He spoke as if the boy understood every word, just like the young man had been doing to him. As he spoke, the amazement on the boy's face gradually eased, and he broke into a big smile, beginning to speak again to March in that peculiar familiar manner, which only increased March's desire to be able to understand.

March asked Anj to find out the young man's name, and through a brief exchange with Maela, she found the boy's name to be 'Bendota.' Maela got March's name from Anj and told the young man the name of his new alien friend. He tried it, saying, "Mach."

March nodded and said "Bendota." After a pregnant hesitation, Bendota grabbed March in an impulsive embrace and clung to him like a drowning man for a full minute, March was also holding the boy like a long-lost son. Something quite new to March was beginning to take place.

After Bendota released March, Makkana took advantage of the uncomfortable silence that followed, interrupting to indicate that he wanted them to follow him. He took them on a tour, starting with the interior of the grotto. They walked through much of the underground village: family homes, meeting halls, cooking and food preparation areas, and food storage. Going outside in the cold morning air, they walked through cultivated fields to the north, some being freshly plowed by men with teams of oxen-like beasts. Between long rows of trees in huge orchards, March and Anj marveled at various kinds of fruits and nuts. There were also plots of cultivated fungi, mushrooms, and other edible plants. It was an impressive display to the pioneers, who had previously only hoped they would be able to eke out enough to survive by farming on their new planet. People here had worked out all the science of agriculture already. "What is this place?" again came from their lips as they observed the bounty, and the organization, and the joyful spirit of cooperation among all of the workers.

On the way back to the grotto from the gardens, March proposed that they somehow let Makkana know that they wished to return to their ship, to which Anj agreed. Apart from anything else, she didn't want the team at Launch Central to fear for them. She was already very late on the next daily report. With Maela's help, and Anj's sketch of the ship in the dirt again, Makkana understood. Immediately, Maela, Bendota, and the young boy spoke at length to Makkana, and Anj was first to read the behavior and discern that they were asking permission to come along with March and Anj. "Well, that will be interesting," March commented, wondering what kind of mystery a shiny, titanium-clad space ship would be to these people.

After finding out that there were people already living here, but before this visit to the ΔT village, he had been wrestling with defining exactly what living on the planet along with an indigenous people was going to mean. Now, from the rich experiences of being with these innocent, beautiful, loving people, he had come to believe that living on ΔT would necessarily entail complete engagement with this people, not just some kind of a treaty, defining, "This territory is yours, and that area is ours." His natural protective stance had completely dissolved, and he felt ready to set a course to merge with the existing society in their new world. As a next step, it certainly was 'going to be interesting' how it would eventually be perceived that March and Anj had come here from another solar system. How would they be able to explain that to these young friends?

God had brought the astronauts here, and He had a plan. That comprehension was changing everything. It seemed essential to March that they should all be in alignment with His purposes, alien and Native alike. God had supernaturally given March the language to pray with them, and probably for them. They had evidently all heard him; God knows what he prayed. He knew in his heart, that he only wanted to be in full cooperation with what God was doing. Whatever he had prayed had knitted his soul to these people in love. He had a sense that what was happening was something significant beyond his ability to comprehend.

Makkana bade March and Anj to be seated by one of the fruit trees while the young people hurried off in different directions. "Ah, they are going to get their satchels to go with us," Anj guessed. The sun was not yet up, and it was still very cold. They had worn jackets and sweaters for the tour of the fields and orchard. The ΔT people all had an extra layer of their fibrous material wrapped around them.

March took a seat, leaning against the same huge ancient tree trunk as Anj, and began sharing enthusiastically what was emerging in his mind; his newly-formed inclination to merge with the people here, abandoning the Consortium's plan to forge out a colony of earthlings. "Anj, my dove, I am being flooded with a new way of thinking about what we are doing on this planet. We had a plan which we had formed together with CSE. But finding people here, for starters, totally changed everything about how I imagined that would look. And then, really meeting them, spending time with them as we have for the last thirty hours or so, this entire village of loving people...." He shook his head slowly, mouth open as if unable to speak, his hand frozen out in front of him in the middle of a gesture. Eyes locked with Anj, he collected himself and resumed, "spending time with them was like heaven. I don't have another way to describe it. Who are these people? How do they live like this, in such beauty of spirit? I could spend the rest of my life learning how to be what they are, how to live like this."

Anj was smiling at him with that smile he loved so much, "I agree. I totally agree, and I could not have put it any better. I'm obviously not fully clear on how that will look, but I am at peace to move in the same direction as you are. We must be in harmony with this tribe."

Turning serious, his 'worry wrinkle' appeared and cut into his brow, "CSE is going to be challenged by this. It seems like it will throw a wrench into all their plans and dreams."

"Yeah, well, it tossed everything in the air for us too. Yet we are the ones who are here, experiencing this marvelous discovery, and it is incumbent upon us, first of all, to do the right thing, and then to make it clear to CSE what has to change in their thinking and planning because of what is actually here in terms of existing human civilization."

March and Anj left off their discussion when the three young people returned, each with a bag strapped over one shoulder. There was a brief conversation with Makkana, some words of instruction from the elder, then Bendota pointed to March with one hand, and up the path with the other, indicating, "Time for you to lead on," which he did without hesitation. Back down the wide pathway upon which they had first approached the grotto, following unerringly the trail they had come in on, and eventually breaking out into the forest, March had a good sense of direction, confident to find the way home. Bendota persevered in his habit of talking to March as if he were already fluent in ∆T's language, and the younger boy followed along closely.

Maela and Anj were hand-in-hand again, and Maela too had begun to chatter with Anj as if she understood everything. Spontaneously, Anj called out to March to stop for a minute. "I just realized we still don't know this young boy's name," she said, smiling at the boy. She pointed to Maela, and said, "Maela," and to Bendota and said, "Bendota," then pointed to the boy, looking at him, "Hmm?" eyes wide open. He seemed hesitant as Anj waited for his response, and he glanced at the others quickly. Maela said something to him softly with an encouraging wave of her hand that said, "Go on; tell them."

"Lalo," he said, clear-eyed, though plainly quiet by nature. Then he said, "Mach," with eye contact, and "Anch," completely guileless; he already knew their names.

Anj bowed deeply, hoping he would understand it as a gesture of honor. She said, "Lalo." His eyes told her he was happy with her pronunciation. "Lalo, what were you doing way out here in the woods all by yourself when you first saw me?"

He looked blankly back at her and looked to his friends for help, but the Earth-to-ΔT language barrier remained unmoved. Anj thought of launching into a complicated pantomime of what she was asking, but rejected the idea, considering that it was not an important question at this time, but she remained curious. Did God send him out there to find her? It might have been months before they discovered the village otherwise, or traveled in that direction far enough. It seemed like a God-ordained arrangement that they had met at that time, and had met him, an innocent boy who would bring elders to help him with the mysterious strangers. Now here they were, rapidly becoming involved in the lives of the people on ΔT, all because Lalo had been at the right place at the right time. She bowed again and smiled at him, putting a hand on his shoulder, reassuring him.

Resuming the trek, on they went, to the meeting place of the previous day, and then down to the beach. They all simultaneously stopped when they stepped clear of the trees at the sight of Browning Sea, wide, deep blue, and immediate, with scattered white-caps and the sound of shallow waves breaking into the gravel beach. Bendota had something to say about the scene; he was excited to be by the sea. Proxima had broken free of the horizon for some time now and was warming things nicely. Coats and the young people's extra layer came off. Anj was impressed by how well all that extra material compressed into their small bags.

March waved his hand south-westward down the beach several times indicating it was still a long walk to their destination. Even though trudging along on the gravel was more difficult walking, March chose to stay in the sunlight which felt wonderfully warm, instead of in the forest, and everyone was enjoying the sea air along the coastline. Some time and kilometers later, with some giggling, Maela and Anj crossed the river delta when they reached that point, hopping from rock to rock, following March and the boys, but Maela's right foot and sandal slipped into the stream, resulting in peals of gleeful laughter as she shook the sand and gravel off her sandal and washed her foot in the frigid water.

Nearing the ship, Anj pointed through the trees, anticipating its coming into sight. Maela started looking and was the first to spot it, a massive shiny metal interruption, completely foreign to ΔT. A startled cry from her alerted the rest. Staring at the completely alien object, Maela, Lalo and Bendota stepped up the embankment above the beach, but stopped there, unsure about venturing closer. March approached the ship and leaned his hand on it speaking to them reassuringly, then stepped up the ladder and opened the hatch, disappearing into it, and then reappearing head and shoulders, waving for them to come on.

Anj led the party up the slope to the ship. Lalo was the first to put his hand on the ladder, fascinated by the odd feeling of the shiny metal, and finally climbed up to peer inside. Exclaiming something to the others, he stepped into the cabin. Maela and Bendota followed. Inside they stood like persons who had been placed inside Carlsbad Caverns, gawking awestruck at the incredible formations all around them. March and Anj gave them time to take it in, trying to imagine what these non-technical people would be thinking in this situation. Eventually, Bendota's gaze fell on the reclining seats. He pointed and asked with sleeping gestures if that was where they slept. March obliged and lay down in his, pantomiming sleep. Lalo was looking out the portal, and he tapped on the glass with his index finger, fascinated by impregnable material that he could see through. Maela placed her open hand gently on a keyboard in front of one of the monitors as if she could soak up something from it to help her understand the mysteries of this other world, the world from which her new friends had come.

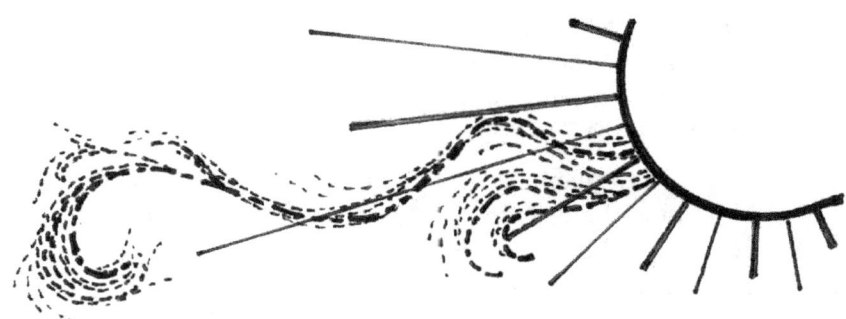

Chapter Nineteen: Launch Central

"11/01/00. Team; greetings, sorry for the delay. I know you must have been waiting with great anticipation for news from us. We spent the night in the village of the ΔT people, which is what I thought might happen. We are well, and back at the ship, obviously. We have company. Three young people wanted to accompany us back here. They are watching with fascination as I speak to you, and my words show up as text on the monitor as they are being sent out to you. So picture that, if you can. Three people completely devoid of technical knowledge, from another planet, are watching these words appear here, as its digitized form begins its long journey to you.

"These are lovely people; truly kind and without any hostility. We are beginning to see that we are going to be very involved with them co-dwelling on this planet. We now see that there is no way for us to move forward here outside of cooperation and harmony with the people of ΔT. We are redefining our purpose here as we adjust to this completely remarkable discovery. Our purpose here is manifestly not to exert our control over this tribe, or to establish our society as superior to theirs, or even separate from theirs. At least that is the way we see it now. What they have established here is quite impressive, from what we have experienced. They live, a hundred or more, in a huge cave which warms them at night and cools them by day. It is a peaceful and cooperative society, full of love and mutual respect. We are treated with the same respect as anyone else, in spite of our foreign dress and inability to speak a language they understand. Worship of their Creator, apparently the One Creator with Whom we are familiar, is a normal and wonderful part of daily life for ΔT people.

"They sleep in a cycle similar to what we have already been led to adopt here. After dinner with them last night, and a long social time, we slept in a room they led us to, far back inside the cave. After about eight hours of sleep, we were awakened for what would be called breakfast, even though it was still dark outside. We had a meal, and they led us on a tour of the whole village complex of dwellings and social areas underground. After daylight then, we spent the morning touring the fields and orchards in their community. We wanted to return to the ship and had a long hike back here with our three new friends. Now, the group of us are about to take our heat-of-the-day siesta. They have indicated by sign language their interest in sleeping. They are assuming we also will sleep at this time of day; after all, it has been about twenty hours since we woke up. March has turned on the AC, and we will find enough pads for the floor for our young friends, who will be a little cramped, but I'm sure we can make it work. It is getting too hot outside for any other sleeping options. Even these indigenous people do not try to do anything outside through the heat of the mid-day.

"These three young ΔT people are the most peaceful, gentle, and unblemished persons I have ever met. For these young people, it seems to be the most natural thing to live free and unafraid. In comparison, March and I have to make a conscious effort to rid ourselves of fear and apprehension. As we see it now, our priority is to come into harmony with this remarkably healthy and well-established society. We know alignment with these people will be essential, not only to our personal survival but also to establishing any vigorous, long term community of people who have originated from Earth.

"My whole construct of the word 'colony' is undergoing a radical revision in my thinking. 'Colony' was the old-fashioned term I used back with you guys, brainstorming this venture before we had any concept of what actually existed here. We were only thinking 'uninhabited planet,' and we only hoped for a habitat that would not eventually kill us. Indeed, a friendly environment is what we have found, and furthermore, the planet is not uninhabited, rather, is populated by a people in many ways more civilized than anything ever experienced on Earth, even though they haven't even invented the wheel. The outright kindness to one another is one of the most distinctive features among the gatherings of these people. There is a tangible harmony with all. We could feel it a little, even when we met the boy, but more clearly when we met with the first group out in the forest, and then it washed over us like a nourishing tide in the large gathering. It feels good. It feels supremely human; like I just stepped into my true destiny.

"In my worst fears, I imagined a planet in which there were aliens such as we have seen in the movies; aliens who would kill or imprison us, either out of raw fear, or because they have a murderous nature. I know that possibility had been a concern to many of you as well. You may lay that fear to rest. These people are of a loving nature, gentle and generous. They seem to know no malice. All we have experienced has been honest, kind, and understanding in a way that is clear despite our language limitations. For me, the most intriguing thing is that they trust us. There was no suspicion, caution, or fear in their approach. They carried no weapons out into the woods to meet with strange-looking unidentified people wandering their planet.

"Who knows what tomorrow holds? I have an assurance that it will be good, even though I do not know much about what will happen when we all wake up to tomorrow, which will be a dusk day, with the rest of our lives ahead of us.

"Very tired. Signing off for now, Anj."

Browning leaned back in his well-worn leather office chair, pushing away from the desk, letting C.S. and Carla crowd in a little closer to re-read Anj's report. "Remarkable! Just amazing," he said. "This is quite a shift. She and March seem to have abruptly abandoned all colonial aspirations, all the prescribed plans for them to forge out an independent existence on a new planet, as a new frontier. This is probably not going to sit well with the rest of CSE."

Elbows on the arms of his big chair, Browning held his right fist in his other hand and thumped his thumbs against his chin, a mannerism C.S. and Carla recognized. It meant he was stumped. Looking up at them now, he said, "They are quite captivated by these ΔT people. I mean, not like prisoners, but held fast in some kind of magnetic attraction to them. It seems out of character."

Cooper pulled up a folding chair, offered it to Carla, and seated himself on the edge of Frank's desk. He reflected, "I can see how you would think of it as out of character for them. It would be, in any kind of normal circumstances, but I have to believe these indigenous people present some sort of very distinct contrast, humanly, to anything March and Anj have ever experienced. 'Captivated' is a good word for it. The idea of joining in with these new people seems to have become irresistible to them."

"Listen to the way Anj talks about them," Carla added, "she says they are 'the most peaceful, gentle and unblemished persons I have ever met.' Wow, that says a lot! How would I respond to such a people who owned a planet that I just arrived on? I'm not finding it surprising that March and Anj would jettison all previous plans in place of what appears to be a vastly superior way of living. I think their new direction makes all kinds of sense."

Browning raised one eyebrow, his way of signifying that he was about to question what was just said, but it also meant he was taking Carla seriously. "Really, Carla? Our astronauts would toss out several years of planning put together by this global space exploration organization based on a few hours of experience with some new people? No matter how special, I'm baffled by that."

Carla had her hands folded in her lap, and she leaned forward, looking right into Browning's eyes, "Frank, you know how personable those two are. They love so genuinely that it takes new people they have just met by surprise. It is their priority to love. You have seen them make the whole crew of technicians wait five minutes for a simulator run just because the guy on the vital-signs monitor mentioned his wife was having a baby! Oh yeah, for the love of people they would toss out plans. And nobody, *nobody* saw this coming; a population of humans, *wonderful* humans. They are the only ones who can respond appropriately to their new world and its people."

Browning had his thumbs up against his chin again. He directed his expectant look over to C.S., hoping for some support in his reluctance to accept at face value March and Anj's capitulation from the plan envisioned and agreed upon by so many for so long.

C.S. was thinking out loud, more than posing a question as he spoke, "I wonder what kind of weight March and Anj's ideas will have in suggesting such a departure from what CSE has in mind. There is so much inertia behind the idea of a colony of Earthlings on another planet; I wonder if even this eventuality can change the direction that has been a source of great enthusiasm worldwide."

He turned to Carla, "I see your point, in that our intrepid pioneers are the only ones who can decide how they want to live the rest of their lives on ΔT. A different set of individuals, sent by CSE in the future might make an entirely different choice, however, and follow through with the plan for an independent colony."

Turning his gaze to Browning, "You know, colonies never did very well long-term on this planet. I'm tending towards agreement with March and Anj, even though I'm not sure their decision will change anything for the CSE board of directors. The assumption was that follow-up missions would be sent if the first colonists' experience indicated a habitable planet. Well, that seems to be a 'yes.' And the assumption was also that it would take two years to have a real assurance of such conditions. Fair enough, we still have a lot to learn about this place. And the assumption was that humans from Earth would have complete liberty to do whatever they wanted there. That assumption is now nullified or thrown into question by what March and Anj have discovered. What they have decided upon as the right course of action is a personal choice, but probably will not deter CSE. My personal concern is for them and their well-being there in the future."

Browning was thoughtfully digesting Cooper's assessment of the situation. He was not a man of prayer. He had decided a long time ago against the possibility of God, but he had allowed himself to hope that March and Anj were right; that they were going to get God's help. He now ventured, "How much do you think their discovery of worship to God among these people, at least from what they have observed so far; how much do you think that plays into the direction they have decided to take? I'm asking you and Carla because I know your outlook on religion is quite similar to March and Anj's view."

Carla chimed in eagerly, "If they have discovered that these people worship the God of the universe as we do, it would indeed be a huge factor in setting their direction. And why shouldn't that be the case, that the people of the planet know God? They obviously have the same Creator. Time plus chance evolution did not randomly come up with the exact same human form trillions of miles from here. They were created by God who created us. So, if the ΔT people have come to know God, and have a solid society based on that worship, yes, in answer to your question, that would be a very heavy influence on March and Anj. They would want to be cooperative with what God has established in that community. If it comes down to a question of either being in alignment with the purposes of God or living contrary to His purposes, following the constructs of CSE, March and Anj will choose alignment with God."

"Cooper?" Browning invited his thoughts on this suddenly bewildering situation, which had the obvious potential of becoming a real problem for him as liaison with CSE.

"I am not there, so it is impossible to say what I would do in that setting. Nevertheless, I trust our pioneers, and they do have a genuine and meaningful relationship with God. I am not surprised that they have decided to live in complete harmony with the indigenous people, based on what they have seen so far. I would definitely suggest giving them the two years they have requested, that were part of the original plan, because we do not know what other variables could crop up, and it is quite possible that they will change their thinking sometime in the next two years."

Squeezing the bridge of his nose, his eyes squinting shut, Browning asked, "Would you two be willing to contribute to CSE's considerations of these recent developments sometime?" Opening his eyes, "As challenging as this discovery is to me, I am not qualified to help the board reach a realistic understanding of what March and Anj are up to, particularly regarding the spiritual or religious aspects of the situation, which are of such great importance to our pioneers."

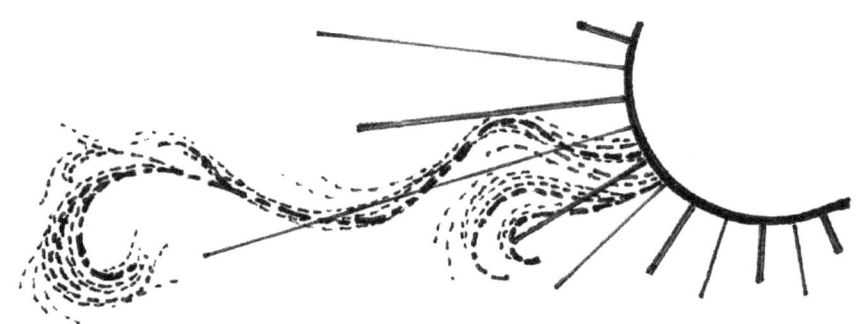

Chapter Twenty

Anj and March awakened simultaneously, facing one another. Anj's bright alert face was smiling at March, welcoming him to consciousness. She was clearly happy, at peace, and anticipating the day ahead, but also knowing that he was going to need a few minutes to become fully alert. He leaned his still groggy head over the edge of his memory-foam-covered gravity chair and peered down at their young guests still sleeping on the floor. He met Anj's eyes and understood, 'let's be quiet and still for a while longer,' and he nodded agreement, easing back for a little more sleep himself.

Air conditioner noise as the compressor cycled on and off, though relatively quiet, seemed to be what eventually alerted the young people that they were in an unfamiliar place. They woke up and were quickly engaged in excited conversation. Anj said to March, "I *so* want to know what they are saying. Let's see if we can learn some words."

She got down from her astronaut chair, and with a good deal of hand motions and pantomiming, she learned the word for 'sleep,' and for 'awake,' or maybe it was 'wake up,' she was not sure. Then she asked, "Do you want to eat some food?" and mimed her way through learning the words for 'eat' and 'food,' doing her best to sort out 'meal,' 'breakfast,' noting them in her tablet. She wanted to learn the language as quickly as possible, eager to find out about the life of these people who were so free and unafraid. March was quickly on board with the effort, and they began to consistently listen and catch phrases that were repeated so that they could find out the meanings.

It was time to have some breakfast, so March got out some MRE's. They prepared portions of instant hot oatmeal, reconstituted fruit, and juice from powdered concentrate, all the while practicing their new words and being alert to opportunities to learn others. When the meal was ready, they thought of saying grace, and with a gesture, invited one of the guests to say the ΔT blessing. Bendota stilled himself and closed his eyes, then said, "Omeda kalitana kalimana," the incantation that March and Anj had heard before.

Wanting to learn the translation, March asked, "Omeda?" The ΔT young people were getting used to this idea of helping March and Anj learn how to speak. The boys looked to Maela to help this time.

Maela said, "Omeda," with a dramatic tone of voice, and looking upward, put her palms together and extended her arms straight up, pointing. Then she parted her fingers and her palms like the opening of the petals of a flower, then her wrists, bringing her arms down widely in a grand gesture, swinging them around to include the whole world, and said again, "Omeda!"

March and Anj not only understood, but they also *felt* the Spirit of God revealing Himself to them in that short worshipful dramatization. "Of course, 'Omeda' means 'God!' They reverence Him, and He is all around us. Indeed, 'in Him we live and move and exist.' She just told us all of that."

The MRE breakfast was enjoyed by all, with much curiosity and discussion among the young people about the wrappers, the textures, and the flavors. They showed no interest in learning English words. As far as they could see, March and Anj were the ones who were ignorant and in need of learning how to speak. March brought out some Δ Pears to share also, which were of course familiar to the guests, and March and Anj memorized the name of that fruit.

Outside it was the hottest part of the long ΔT day, and no one showed any immediate eagerness to go out in it. March and Anj discussed what was next, while the youth looked around the ship and talked among themselves. March proposed that they return to the village with the three ΔT Natives, and carefully assess their new resolve to be absorbed into the community. As far as they could tell, the people expected that the new arrivals would move right in and become like them. Even after sleeping on it, Anj, too, still believed that was the clear direction that they should take. They put together a list of things that needed to be done to prepare the ship to be left for several days, not knowing how long it would be before they returned. One of the items was to notify Launch Central not to expect a report for several days and the reason why.

Anj asked March to try to clarify for the team back on Earth the reasoning behind the pioneers' change of plan. They were concerned that, to CSE, it must look like a sudden and perhaps nonsensical shift in direction that the astronauts were taking. He sat down at the keyboard to gather his thoughts, while Anj put things in order and checked the systems that would need to continue to function in their absence; the cold fusion power supply, the air conditioning to keep the ship's electronics reasonably cool, and weather recording instruments. Computers could be slumbering. She also packed some clothes that they might need for an extended stay, reorganizing their backpacks. The guests were fascinated by the interesting items of clothing, mostly synthetic fabrics, completely unlike their soft natural fiber material.

When everything was set in order and March had completed his transmission, radio communications were shut down, and together they stepped out of the hatch into the hot afternoon. As the little group stepped away from the ship, their faces set towards the village, March spoke to Anj, "I feel like we truly are walking away from something; like a big transition has taken place. I feel the impact of our decision to join with these people. It is a profoundly significant step, and I am excited about what it could mean, although I have no real picture of how that is going to look in the long run. I know we will have to keep coming back here to the ship to report home, but I feel my heart exchanging its allegiance on a very serious level, away from the ship and all it represents, which has absorbed our whole life up to this point, and towards this lovely people whom I hardly know yet, but already deeply desire to get to know. At this moment, I feel that I was born to live here. This is what I was made for. We are leaving everything else behind."

"I feel it too, darlin'," Anj said, "We thought our destiny was to explore outer space, but I'm realizing really that it was all about getting us here. *This* is our destiny. And as yet, we do not really know what awaits us here, but it will be defined as we go along with God. I sense that it's immense. We know that it is good, beyond anything that we could imagine. You are correct in noting it as a transition, a shift of grand proportions."

He said, "From the moment I landed that ship back there eleven days ago, I knew I would never fly again, and had resigned myself to that, but I had no real concept of how I could ever be excited about life again. Being a pilot had been my life. What could ever replace that? Yet something quite thrilling is here, something much bigger than us, bigger than CSE, bigger than just Earth. I can sense it sort of prophetically, but as yet it is hidden from view, quite undefined."

Anj asked, "What did you tell Launch Central about our choice to deviate from the original plan of setting up an Earth-directed colony?"

"I kept it very simple. I said that finding out that there were people here who had figured out how to live in this extreme environment caused a change in our thinking. We do not need to re-invent how to grow crops here; they already do it very well. We do not need to figure out how to survive stellar flares, one of our most serious concerns; they have survived for centuries without being toasted, so we can learn from them about that. We do not need to build a log cabin here, not knowing whether it would actually be sufficient shelter for us because they already have a sophisticated living arrangement that is safe and stabilizes the extreme temperatures. So we are throwing in with them. They are very welcoming and outwardly already assume that we will join their community.

"I did not touch on the issue of how colonization on Earth has always been destructive to the indigenous peoples. I didn't want to even open up the discussion yet about how badly the introduction of a high-tech Earth-based culture would fit on this planet. It seems starkly apparent to me that the stable and quiet culture of the ΔT people would be interrupted, at best, and perhaps destroyed, at worst, by what Earthlings would have to offer. It remains beyond question that this people group is in a category of its own. The thought of ever coming into competition with them, as colonists, for territory or resources seems unthinkable to me."

Anj was thoughtfully silent; then she repeated, "Unthinkable. Yes, that is a non-starter. All I need to do is think about the Native Americans, and I know we want to avoid, at all costs, any resemblance of what happened to them."

They had been walking a little separate and behind the other three, and moved to catch up. As soon as they did, Bendota started his running narrative about everything they were seeing along the way. He called out the names of trees, boulders, mountains, sky, and sun, in a continuous monologue, checking to see if Anj was getting the words typed out. Anj could not keep up with putting the new words in the tablet, mostly because the pronunciations were too unfamiliar to be able to write them down phonetically. He seemed to have an intuitive knowledge that the language learners were going to need words repeated many times before they could understand them and speak them. The words that he repeated several times Anj was able to get into the tablet.

Kilometers slipped away as Bendota led them back towards the village, which they found out was called 'Lendkon.' The sun was becoming that muted red as it drew gradually closer to the horizon before they arrived home. March and Anj did not know whether 'Lendkon' meant 'village,' or if it was actually the name of the place, but when the grotto first came into sight, Bendota repeated, pointing enthusiastically, "Lendkon!" And the language learners dutifully repeated it aloud for pronunciation check. Nods and smiles of approval from the three Natives encouraged the two new people in the tribe.

A young lad about Lalo's age ran quickly out to meet the travelers. He had some kind of urgent message. He pointed at the sun, radiating concern from his small boy frame, and all eyes turned to look at the setting orange ball. When the sun was low into the haze this time of day, one could look directly at it and see its shape, a perfect disc, but this evening it had a bright extension on the bottom, like a piece of burning yarn dangling from it. March distinguished right away that this was a stellar flare when the unusual bright extension was pointed out to him. It was a tongue of flame, actually, an ejection of plasma from the corona, the surface of the star, shooting out, potentially millions of miles into space. So this was the real thing.

"What do you think we should do?" Anj asked, her stomach knotting up with involuntary fear.

"Well nobody seems to be in any panic or hurry," March spoke as the calm professional astronomer. "It is just beginning, but if it extends out far enough in that direction, the planet will orbit directly into the flame itself in about sixty hours, unless it subsides before we get there. About this time tomorrow, we will be in the middle of it, if it is sustained."

Bendota, wanting to explain this situation to them, came over and put his arm around March's shoulders, facing the setting sun, pointing. He began to explain with a good deal of arm-waving what this could mean. March nodded affirmation, knowing full well what that little hanging string of fire on the edge of the setting sun could mean.

There was an almost excited buzz as they entered the grotto and encountered many of Lendkon's populace. Makkana welcomed them back with his usual happy countenance, no trace of fear, his mood convincing March and Anj that they were making the right move to associate fully with these people. He did not project any worry to the returning aliens, about a stellar flare, but helped them find their room again so they could deposit their packs and get freshened up.

Gathering with the community just after sundown, with the same table-group that they had met with before, the mood of the music seemed, if anything, to be a little more peaceful and calm. The meal progressed very similarly, and when one of the men stood to speak, Anj was carefully reading his body language. From that, she could almost hear him speaking calmly, "As you know, a flare was sighted this evening, and it looks like we will be moving into it tomorrow, about sunset…" Beyond that, she could not imagine what he might be saying, but he continued in a most in-control sort of tone, and it seemed to her that the possibility of the world burning up in a flame of nuclear fire from the sun was not part of the picture in his mind tonight. The spirit of this people was causing the distressing fear that had begun to well up in Anj to evaporate.

Music and singing then proceeded as it had in their previous experience, with perhaps less celebration and more peace-generating songs, but it was hard for the newcomers to tell if it was different in response to the flare. After the music stopped, there was some quiet conversation around the tables. Everyone retired to their quarters as the evening grew late, March and Anj too. There they reviewed the vocabulary words they had learned today, excited about being able to put some sentences together soon. They felt some of the familiar constancy of peace that was theirs in this place, however, in her stomach, Anj still retained some stubborn fear about that tongue of searing hot fire reaching out through space towards their new little planet. How was that going to look tomorrow? Would it be a fierce and frightening spectacle as a river of orange, glowing, nuclear detritus swirled around the planet? As March prayed for peace to rule in her heart, she finally received a calming influence on her mind to be able to sleep, and she resigned herself to not knowing.

In the morning, the prayer time after the meal was notably extended and serious, but it was distinctly not a weeping pleading type of prayer, asking Omeda to save them as if He had maybe forgotten them. March and Anj got the feeling that there was rather a declaration of His faithfulness and protection along with celebration that He is always good in every circumstance. Within their spirits, where there is no language barrier, they received a clear assurance that His love is strong, and His favor is sure. His protection is unquestioned; He is the Master of the universe. Anj concluded, from watching and sensing all she could, "These people entrust themselves and this planet confidently into His hands and under His watchful eye, even though they live close to a star that sends out these scorching flares occasionally."

It was all done as a village collectively in the most quiet spirit of rest and peace. There was notable freedom from fear. March told Anj, "I am looking forward to getting to know Omeda as they do. I feel the peace, but, like you, I don't rest in it with the same depth as they apparently are able to."

Later in the morning, when the sun was fully risen and bright, Bendota brought a young man to March, wanting to show him something. This man had a flat sheet of their hand-made paper in one hand, and a slab of smooth black slate in the other. He took the newcomers out into the bright sunlight. Bendota narrated all along, somehow sure that if he just kept talking they would be able to understand the science. The man propped his slate up against a boulder so that the sun shone directly onto the flat surface. Then he stood about two meters away and held up the paper so that it shaded the slate. "Ah!" March exclaimed as he recognized the pin-hole camera principle at work. A tiny hole in the paper allowed a beam of light to project onto the slate. March could hardly contain his excitement, "Genius!" He squatted close to the slate and inspected the image projected there. The disc of the sun still had that long bright strand reaching out from the disc, much longer now, ever-widening, until it spread out, too faint to see on the slate surface.

Bendota was still explaining, and March said, more to Anj than anyone else, "I wish I could ask him some questions. This shows me that the flare is still there, but I cannot tell if it is long enough that we will orbit through it." Bendota pointed at Proxima and then swung his arm overhead and down to point where it would be by late afternoon, in about twenty hours. Then he made an intense sound effect, like "paaaahh!" with his raised hands and outspread fingers wiggling in the air, indicating that was the time when it could get bad. Although his eyes were wide, he still wore a smile. It seemed to be amusing to him to talk about this pending threat.

He then took them inside to one of the large rooms deeper inside the cave, and there, about half of the population was gathered, clearly praying. The only sounds were the voices of prayer and a few musicians playing softly as the praying people squatted and rocked, or stood with their hands raised, or lay face-down on the floor. The spiritual atmosphere was thick with the Presence of God; it was intense, even overwhelming, yet peaceful. March and Anj had seen enough that they knew it was time to intercede.

Apart from a couple of hours of sleep in the middle of the day, Anj placed herself before the throne of God the best she knew how, resisting fear and trying to apprehend the level of peace she felt all around her, joining with the spirit of those in the room. During those hours she felt the longing of God Omeda for her to draw near to Him in confidence, like a Father drawing her close to His side. The sense of invitation from Him became stronger until all she wanted was to spend more time with that Presence, that Personality. No riches and no applause of man could ever replace or even compare to the place she felt she found with Omeda that afternoon. She had a picture that these collective prayers were constructing the place of protection for Lendkon, no matter what was raging out in space. She knew in her spirit that her prayers were contributing to the building of the place of safety that Omeda had for them. It was a tangible partnership between herself and the rest of the people in the room. She felt few distractions or interruptions in her prayer time with this community, and she gained a gathering confidence that Omeda God would spare His beloved people. She heard in her spirit, "Because she has loved Me, therefore I will deliver her; I will set her securely on high because she has known My name."

Sometime after the middle of the day, Bendota slipped out and March followed him. Out in the fields, a hasty harvest was going on, and help was needed to bring in a large quantity of vegetables and grains to protect them from the possibility of being burned. March spent hours carrying bundles of produce inside until Bendota indicated it was time to take shelter. Everyone then went in to join the gathering inside, and there arose a spontaneous happy-sounding song that all sang together continuously for the next several hours. It engaged all the children to be making a joyful sound. Anj was alarmed at one point to notice the faint but distinct smell of burning leaves visiting the gathered population inside. March could hardly contain his curiosity. The astronomer wanted to step out where he could see this flare, up close and personal, but Bendota remained steadily in prayer, so March yielded his natural interests, and aligned himself with the spirit of the community given over to trusting God.

As it finally began to grow dark outside, there was a sense of release in the spirit of the gathered citizens of Lendkon, with notable sighs of relief, and a shift to a song of praise. Smiles began to crease countenances that had spent most of the day in the most serious interaction with Omeda. Not knowing at all what to expect, March and Anj followed Bendota back out to the opening of the grotto. A lingering sunset remained, accompanied by an insidious swirling orange band of fire far out to the horizon. Apparently, the flare was still touching the planet far to the west.

The lingering smell of smoke was distinct but not strong. It was clear that the orchard had somehow been mostly spared.

That night at the communal gathering, the worship was celebratory, the speakers were energized in praise, and many hands were raised in thanks and adoration of Omeda who had once again intervened on their behalf. March felt Anj's gaze and turned to meet hers. Wordless, she was in stunned adoration of the lovingkindness of Omeda. March drew her close and said, "Yes, it is a very different world here. This place is under the tangible touch of God when there is a cry from His children."

She was still unable to respond with words, her heart, and her eyelashes overflowing with the revelation of a new level of God's willingness to hear the prayers of His people.

In the morning, stepping outside, they were able to see that just the very tops of the branches of the trees had been burned, but that was where the heat of the flame was miraculously stopped. Thanksgiving was clearly in the mood of the population during the morning gathering with a great deal of joyful singing and gladness. People went out to work in the fields, the gardens, and the orchard with a renewed sense of gratefulness.

A few hours into the day, March realized that their identification with the Lendkon community had been so complete during the crisis that he had not thought about how their parked space-ship might have fared through this encounter with a stellar flare. "Hey hon, did you give a thought about what might have happened to our ship?"

"Oh, my Gosh; isn't that interesting? I was so concerned about our new friends and their community that I did not think of it until just now when you mentioned it. I guess we did definitely walk away from our former life. This crisis has been quite an indoctrination into a new set of priorities in our new community."

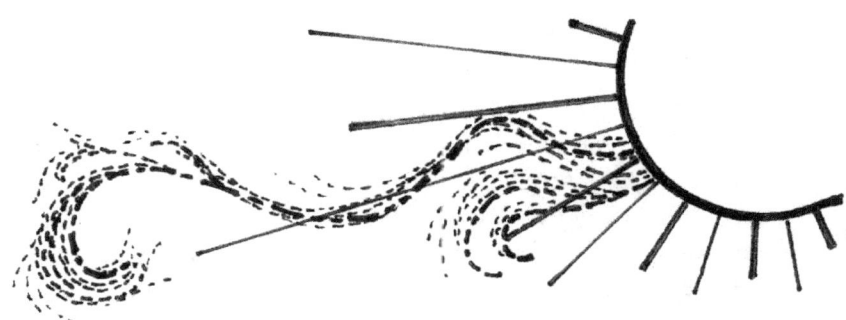

Chapter Twenty-One: Launch Central

"Greetings, Team. Thank you for your patience, and I trust that you were able to be at rest with our expectation that we would be safe spending time with the people we have discovered here. Indeed we have been safe with them, and we have discovered how they protect themselves from the stellar flares that have been one of our main concerns of our being so close to this Red Dwarf.

"Immediately after filing our last report, we hiked back to the cave where this community of people lives, about a three-hour walk. On arrival at about sunset, we found out that a flare was going to be an approaching danger before the following day's sunset. They have an ingenious early warning system, and they are protected by living in a cave, but the concern was their food source, their extensive orchards, and farms, which are exposed.

"It may sound preposterous to you, but we saw this: they protect the agricultural areas by praying. We sat through the whole thing, deep in the cave, in a huge room full of the people praying. We smelled wisps of smoke drifting into the cave near the end and were afraid maybe the praying didn't work. When it had passed, and we went out, the tops of the trees were scorched, but the rest of the trees were untouched. Even fruit hanging on the branches was unharmed. My scientific reason does not compute this phenomenon, but my natural eyes saw it. Even the wild trees out in the distant woods did not become the forest fire that my worst fears pictured. We have just hiked back through the forest to come here to the ship and file this report, and all along the way, it is the same, only scorched tree-tops.

"We were concerned about how the ship fared during this event, but, arriving here, we have just seen that all seems to be in order. The only evidence of the stellar flare was the rather shocking observation that the anemometer on the very top of the weather monitoring probe had melted. Yes, melted. We will have no more wind-speed measurements. I don't know how steel melted and sagged at the highest point, and nothing else was damaged. Again, I'm just reporting what we experienced.

"We spent the next three days after the flare, that is, ΔT days, three sunrises – more like a week to you - with the people, living in the cave, and accompanying our friends through what are their daily duties. Everyone is very industrious. Everyone seems to have definite jobs that are his or her responsibility. For instance, the young man who warned us about the anticipated flare; that seems to be his job. We see him all day with his instrument, a simple pin-hole affair, checking and re-checking every day, all day. One of the young men who has adopted March as his buddy works in the fields harvesting. From sun-up until the mid-day sleeping time - we have been calling it their 'siesta,' - he cuts and stacks grain. At least right now that is what his employment is. Then after his siesta, although it is still very hot out, the sun is on the way down and the air is slowly cooling. He is out there, along with his crew of guys, cutting and stacking grain.

"We were looking at this and thinking, "So we are to labor as farmers if we join this community?" Then we realized, "Well, that is what we were destined to do as pioneers in a new land anyway, wasn't it?" We brought all those seeds and had every intention of growing and farming everything we needed. I guess we didn't have a very realistic understanding of how that was going to look. We are beginning to understand now what the future holds and how simply we will be able to slip into it as a lifestyle.

"Since we do not understand their language, there are many unknowns; however there seems to be an expectation from the community as a whole that we will join in with them. They are very welcoming. The three young people that came to the ship with us last time are our constant companions. We are starting to pick up some of the vocabulary such as greetings, how to ask for things, names of foods, and such essentials. We learned that their flatbread is called 'polon.' It is very good, a little like naan in Indian food.

"By the way, all those seeds I planted to see how they would do in this climate? None of them germinated. Something in the soil? Something in the water? I don't know, but Earth seeds do not seem to work here. Fortunately, that is not a major problem since so many other food crops do grow here and have been planted and harvested for generations.

"Our plan is to send a report out to you every Monday (our Monday), a dusk day for us. We will hike down here and let you know what has transpired over the last week, what we have learned, and how we are doing. The strange thing of course is that, by the time you read this, we will have been here for four years and will be well into our lifestyle. We may have children by then, which is certainly something we hope for and will have pretty fully adapted to ΔT as our home.

"We trust that this finds you well, encouraged, and hopeful. We trust that CSE and Launch Central will be able to catch from our reports the information necessary to inform any future exploration to ΔT that might be initiated. It is our fervent hope that we can all remain 'on the same page,' so to speak, regarding an adjustment from a colonizing mentality to a philosophy of working in harmony with what has been discovered as existent here.

"Until next week, Anj."

Carla looked worried as she asked Browning, "How do you think it will go, this business of 'staying on the same page?' Anj and March have swiftly become quite committed to these people, and they hope that CSE will adopt their idea of cooperating and integrating fully with them. Do you think CSE will buy into their enthusiasm?"

Frank Browning, who met monthly with the board of directors of the Consortium for Space Exploration (CSE), put the tips of his fingers and thumbs together and looked through them thoughtfully, not wanting to try to predict the direction that would be taken by CSE in the future of Proxima Missions, but open to the opportunity to talk more about this dilemma with his peers. "Anj and March were chosen for this mission, partly in *spite* of their strong Christian position, and partly *because* of it. We all recognized that their faith imparted to them a steadfastness, strength, and hopefulness that would be essential to them as they faced the rigors of an entirely new and mostly unknown environment. They would be alone, except for their God. We saw that as positive. The manner in which they lived out their faith within the confines of Launch Central during training was entirely acceptable. They made it clear as to the truths they believed they could stand on, and those values in no way interfered with the priorities of CSE which are, as you know, the advancement of science, advancement of space exploration, and advancement of the possibilities for colonization in the universe.

He continued, "That all worked marvelously well up to this point. Now they believe they have discovered a people who hold to the same faith in God as they do, and have a culture and society very distinctly different from anything on Earth. This raises the risk that our pioneers will take a stance that does not, in fact, remain in harmony with CSE, especially regarding one of our central priorities: advancing possibilities for colonization of the universe. That seems to be what is developing at this point. It appears that March and Anj might now be opposed to the sort of colony which they were originally supposed to establish on their new planet."

C.S. asked, "Do you think they are disallowing any additional introduction of new personnel to ΔT? Is that the concern?"

Frank rubbed his palms on his pant legs. They were getting a little sweaty, as he was not too sure he wanted this discussion to go too deep. He was caught three ways: between his colleagues, the CSE board, and his own indecision on the issue. "I think that is what several of the members of the board at CSE are concerned about. Unfortunately, we cannot converse with March and Anj to clarify what they are thinking, and it is too early for them to have formed a complete concept yet of how they will proceed in the long run, but our concern is that they will abandon the introduction of science and technology to ΔT in the interest of avoiding any interference with the existent culture. They have not stated that intention, but that is the fear at CSE because it would challenge the possibility of moving ahead with the original Proxima vision."

C.S. was not getting sweaty palms. He was delighted that Frank was talking. He said, "Frank, you know March and Anj. You know them as scientists, and you know them as friends, close friends, and you once told me that you hoped they were right, that God would help them even though you have never really embraced their faith in God. I have two questions to pose to you. First, do you think that as scientists, people who value and are conversant with incredibly high-tech means; do you think they would prohibit the use of any of that on an entire planet, to protect a very simple non-scientific culture? And, the second question, as friends, how is your level of trust right now, that they will see clearly what would truly be the best strategy going forward?"

"In answer to your first question, if they did attempt to prohibit the introduction of civilized high tech culture into ΔT, that would confuse me. It would seem out of character. But it seems to me that faith in a powerful invisible being is not exactly congruent with the scientific mind either, so the fear at CSE is that they going to slip into an irrational religious position quite contrary to the science-driven philosophy which carried them there.

"To your second question, I do trust them both and I am relying heavily on them to be the ones who sort out the confusion that has broken into the plans of this world-wide cooperative effort, of which they are a key part."

Carla and C.S. exchanged a knowing look. Yes, they too trusted March and Anj. Yes, they did believe that prayer could protect an orchard. Yes, they would continue to pray over all the decisions of CSE, and they would continue to support and be available to Browning, who was caught in the tension between CSE and his pioneers on ΔT.

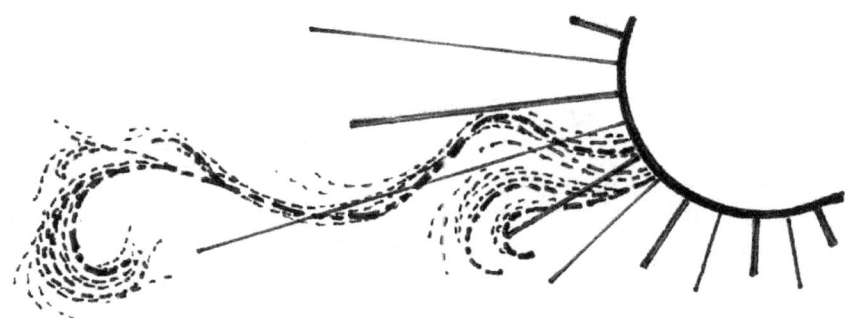

Chapter Twenty-Two

Anj wrote down the date from her hand-made paper calendar, recording the date of her report to Launch Central. It was now the seventh day, of the fourth month on ΔT, a Monday, which was only of interest to her and March and to the Earth team who expected to receive a regularly scheduled report. She closed the book and stood up, getting ready to leave. Looking around the ship, she checked for anything left undone before starting the hike home. Maela had walked to the ship with her today, accompanying Anj while she made her weekly report to Launch Central. Maela and Anj had become inseparable in the months that had intervened since she first held Anj's hand on that first day in the village. Anj, every bit the professional female astronaut was not usually given to swiftly making deep friendships, with men *or* women, but Maela had changed all that. From that first meeting, a softness had gradually replaced the hard place in Anj's heart regarding feeling safe with practicing trust and love.

Maela's authenticity, her transparent depth of caring, and her persistence in being a faithful friend had worked a transformation in Anj. Even March noticed it. He and Anj were sitting outside together one evening, soon after the friendship began, watching the spreading night sky as the heat of the day slipped away, and he commented to her, "I see you coming out of your shell and becoming a more warm, friendly, approachable person than I ever thought possible." Anj had merely snuggled in a little closer under his arm in response to that observation, much to his delight. She was aware of the deep work that Maela and Omeda God were doing in her, and it felt good.

While Anj was sending her report to Launch Central, Maela had fallen asleep on the soft reclining co-pilot seat that originally carried Anj here. Sleeping children are such a picture of vulnerability and complete trust. Maela was not a child, probably around nineteen, but the simple trust illustrated in her peaceful sleeping countenance was unmistakably child-like, and Anj's heart was once again warmed for her new friend and the love that she carried.

Anj gently lifted Maela's hand hanging from the astronaut chair. "Time to walk back home Maela," she spoke softly. Lendkon, which translated from the language, meant 'origins,' was 'home' now to the pioneers from Earth who had once anticipated building a log cabin. It had been the unquestioned assumption on the part of the people of Lendkon, the 'Similia,' that the newcomers would become a part of their community. Gradually spending an increasing proportion of their time in the village instead of at the ship was a most natural progression for the astronauts, until they were living in the village full-time. There was no means of filing a report remotely from Lendkon, so Anj or March would make the hike to the ship once a week to send a news update to Central, but they had not slept in the parked spaceship for over two months.

Feeling Anj's hand holding hers, Maela awakened easily, glanced around remembering where she was and smiled at her friend who had traveled here in this strange container. She had never asked Anj about what kind of life she had lived where this space vehicle came from. Her focus seemed to be fully on helping her friend from another star learn how to live here. There was much for her to learn to become Similia; that was the focus, and Anj was making good progress. She could converse fairly well now and was quick to learn new things every day that she could talk about.

"Your bed here is very soft. I go to sleep whenever I lie down on it," Maela observed. A few minutes later, when they climbed down the ladder, and Anj closed the hatch, Maela said, "Let us take the upper path to Lendkon, it will be a little cooler."

Anj was thrilled to notice that she immediately understood what Maela said without translating it into English first in her head. And she was able to reply without first mentally forming the answer in English and then translating it into Similia. Learning the language of the Similia had been a fascinating journey thus far, and now she was transitioning into actually thinking in this new language, a key to true fluency. Maela was a natural teacher, which was peculiar, given that the very idea of language learning was completely foreign to her. She had never heard of anyone speaking a language other than Similia. Everyone on the planet, as far as anyone knew, spoke the same language.

Anj believed that if it had been the other way around, and she was teaching Maela English, it might not have gone so well. March was doing even better with the language, and she thought it was because his friend Bendota spoke all the time about everything that was happening around them, whether March understood him or not. March was therefore completely immersed in the language of ΔT, and quickly picked up vocabulary and sentence structure just through exposure and repetition.

After these months of hiking back to the ship every week, two paths had naturally formed that were equally quick. The lower, mostly along the beach, was good in the mornings, and the upper path which offered views of the sea to the west and at times, vistas of the sharp mountains to the east. This higher trail was more shaded and better for these sunset walks back home because of the heat. They walked single file, Maela leading, occasionally pointing and commenting on something she had noticed: a bird, or one of the ΔT deer that were common up here, or a snow-capped peak in the distance.

They stopped for a rest after about an hour. Sitting on a huge flat-topped stone, looking down into the dense forest, Anj, encouraged by her progress with the language, decided she would be able to ask a question that had been on her mind. "What did Lendkon elders think when Lalo brought back his story of finding strange people walking in the woods?"

"We had been expecting you for a long time. The seers had seen you coming over a lifetime ago."

"Ha!" Anj was surprised, but it also made sense to her because of the way they were received so easily. She was thinking, 'That would explain why there was no sense of alarm among the group that came out to meet with us the first time,' but she had to ask about one of the words Maela used. "What are seers?" Anj asked, not familiar with the word in Similia.

"They are people who have dreams or visions, or sometimes hear the voice of Omeda giving them wisdom or telling them something that is going to happen in the future. One of the seers had a vision of some very different people coming to us from a distant star. The seer said that these people would come in a palopalo shell, and they were sent by Omeda."

Anj was fascinated by this narrative but had to stop and ask what a 'palopalo' shell was, another new word.

"Palopalo is a large fruit, almost as big as your head, which has a very hard shell. When the fruit has been scooped out of a hole in the top, we use the shells for carrying water."

"Oh those," Anj recognized that she had seen them in the kitchen, yes, palopalo shells filled with water, similar to Earth's coconuts. "Something like our ship then, a big hard vessel. We came here in a palopalo shell. March will love that!"

"Omeda did not tell the seer why you were coming, but He said it was He that was sending you, so we knew that Omeda was doing something new and amazing because everything He does is wonderful. When Lalo told us about you - two strange-looking people who could not speak - Makkana was quite interested to lead a group out to meet you. He and Saala were able to hear from Omeda as soon as they met you that you were the ones sent by Him."

Fascinated, Anj asked, "What else did the seer know about us?"

"He heard that you would arrive without knowledge of many of our ways because our world is so different from your previous world. I was very excited when Omeda asked me to be your friend because I thought I could help you learn the ways of we Similia. I knew I was capable of it. I have been loved and given much wisdom by Omeda. He tells me often that He is very pleased with me. Saala also encouraged me to be your assistant and teacher. She said, most importantly, that it would take great love for you to be able to learn and adapt to all the changes you will have to make here. She said I would do well loving you in-depth, the way that would be necessary."

"Ella," - the nickname that Anj used for her, "you are the best thing that ever happened to me."

Maela did not blush, but continued, "I have learned how to love. My family members are the substance of my Omeda because I am a part of the family."

Anj interrupted her, to clarify something. "Hold on, you just said something about 'my Omeda.' What do you mean by that?"

"Omeda is not just the name of our Creator. His full name is 'Omeda Topoliana,' and His name has meaning. Omeda means 'existence,' and Topoliana means 'everlasting.' So we often say 'my Omeda,' meaning how I am, or how much I am becoming like Him and will be with Him for eternity. It is the life goal for all Similia to become completely full of Omeda Topoliana's ways, His motivations, and His loves. So when I said my family is the substance of my Omeda, I mean that the things they have taught me, and the way they have loved me *are* what I am becoming. And I am becoming like Omeda."

"Profound," Anj said in English to herself. Then, in Similia, "Being part of a family makes you like Omeda," she wanted to add, "automatically," but she did not know the word if there was one. She was fascinated by the idea that just being in a family builds one's character to be Godly.

"Yes, Mama Anch, They are the ones who make me to know all of the ways of life. All I know about living is through them, watching them, and being part of them. Living includes all of us in agreement with Omeda and keeping our steps fast to His paths. We all contribute to the community by being generous in loving, by working among our people, and by helping Lendkon prosper. My father is a plowman in the fields. Crops grow well because he is one of the ones who prepare the soil for planting. He always has plowing to do because the harvesters bring in the grain or the vegetables, and then the field must be plowed for the next planting. He has to plow differently depending on what is going to be planted. He is an expert with soil, the plows, and with the oxen that pull the plows."

"You are very pleased to be his daughter," Anj observed.

"Is not every girl pleased to be her father's daughter?"

In contemplating that question, Anj could only reply, "Maela, you are right; my world is very different from this world." She did not think it would be helpful to explain her own broken relationship with her father. She, too, wanted to keep the focus on learning *this* world, its people, and on knowing Omeda more deeply. This girl was her main family here, and she was deeply thankful for such a one.

Maela continued, "We all know that our life here is to love Omeda Topoliana and worship Him forever. We become abundant in love for one another the more we draw close to Omeda. We learn His Presence and are able to grow in holiness the more we spend time with Him. Each person's destiny is to be with Him forever, and while we are here, every person is essential for the well being of the community. All that we do is important to all of us forever. My children will grow up in the world created by the work of your lives. You also, my friend from another world, will be important to my children and grandchildren, not because you are special, but because you are here among us now. Are you understanding me?"

"I think so, mostly. This world is certainly not the world I grew up in, and you are right, I'm here now, learning how to be here. I may need to ask you to help me when I try to explain to March about 'the substance of my Omeda.'"

"That will be enjoyable." Glancing towards the sun getting low, Maela asked, "Shall we continue now, the sunset meal will be being served soon."

Distance was covered quickly back to Lendkon, and the grotto was full of the bustle of preparing for the big communal evening meal. Musicians were already beginning the strains of a theme. As the musicians instrumentally explored the new strains, they carried on with casual conversation, encouraging one another to play it out; play out of the creative inspiration of the moment. Anj found March standing near the musicians with his hands clasped behind his back, observing and listening. He saw her coming up beside him and reached out an arm over her shoulders, his eyes still fixed on the music makers. "I love these guys. I admire them. What they do is other-worldly."

Anj knew about his fascination with people who could play music. He thought they were magical, and he had a very deep appreciation for what they could do to his soul. He and Anj walked together over to their regular table where Bendota, Maela, Lalo, Makkana, and Saala usually joined them. Sometimes others would come to share the meal there, and a few times March and Anj had been invited to Maela's family table with her Mother, Father, younger brother, and grandparents. Similarly, on other nights, they had spent time with Bendota's family. Tonight, Anj was particularly attentive to the conversational exchanges at the table. She was tracking how her new family was potentially becoming the 'substance of her Omeda,' as Maela had talked about. She now recognized that this group of people was hand-picked by God to magnetically draw her and March into the riches necessary to become fully human. Her thoughts reminded her, 'My being, my existence, my Omeda, are being formed here like clay in the potter's hands. I am free to become healthy and whole.'

"March, how did your day go?" She knew he had worked with Bendota in the fields.

"It was toasty out there, but we got a ton of grain cut, hauled, and stacked for the threshers. I love the work. I never thought I could be a contented farmer, but it gives me great joy here, and we have a unified team. We have a lot of fun out there. Today, it was so hot that Bendota thought it was funny to go around pouring water on each of us out of a coconut-like thing we usually use for drinking water."

"A palopalo shell! I heard about those today. I learned a lot today. I'll tell you about it tonight. We came here in a palopalo shell," she said, tripping his curiosity.

"What?"

"I'll tell you later." It was time for the blessing on the food, and she took his hand and Maela's hand as Bendota gave thanks to Omeda Topoliana, God Everlasting, for good food, abundant food, and the strength He gave to their bodies. March and Anj had come to joyfully anticipate these communal meals just after each sunset. As the newcomers had gained fluency in the language along with the understanding of the society and the spiritual center of it all, these evening meals and the morning gatherings for breakfast had become formational to their incorporation into the village. They had begun to feel like Similia.

March liked to sit next to Makkana and ask him during dinner what he was going to talk about that night because he usually was one of the speakers. He started doing that early-on to help with understanding when they were just beginning with the language, and Makkana was always generous to help March and Anj to be able to understand.

"Makkana, what is on your heart tonight?" he asked.

Makkana turned to March with his typically beaming joy-filled countenance. He always came across to March as if March was the one person he was most eager to talk to today. Everyone loved to be around Makkana because he gave that away to everyone all the time. "Ah, Mach, my lovely man, you are going to hear about how Omeda rejoices over you."

"Over me?" March pointed to himself, somewhat dubious. "He rejoices over you, Makkana; that I know. I rejoice over you too. You are a great person."

The elder looked surprised, but he was beginning to realize that March and Anj had arrived with significant deficits in their knowledge of Omeda. "Ah, my friend Mach, you disqualify yourself? But of course, He rejoices over you, and Anj, and Bendota, over each of us. He is as excited to talk to us as I am to talk to you. I always look forward to seeing you because I value who you are and what you are becoming. That is a part of my character, which I know comes directly from Omeda. He made me like Him, and in that particular way, I am very much like Him. He sees each one of us as though we were His only child. He rejoices not because you did something big, like the grain you harvested today. That was big, but He loves you because He *is* love; He is creator. He has so much richness to give us, that when we draw near, He gets excited that maybe He is going to be able to give us one of His special gifts of counsel or strength." He gave March another of his winning smiles. "You will see," he said.

Makkana stood up after the dinner was cleared away and spoke to the assembled village. He began by saying, "You are Omeda's only child," and went on to explain how each person is seen by God individually and fully, with eternal hope for each person's wholeness and growth. "Omeda only sees what each of His beloved ones is destined to become. And He is excited about it because it will happen. He will ensure that each one will be blessed, will go from strength to strength, and will appear before Him complete."

On the way to their room, March mused aloud to Anj, "I think I am beginning to believe it; that I can be complete; that God will accomplish what He set out to do in me. I can believe it here in this place with these people. It seemed impossible before, back home."

"Back home," Anj replied, "things were different in every respect. There was not the purity of heart surrounding us in every person. When Makkana says something, I have decided I have to believe it because he comes from such a profound place of truth."

She continued, "It came crystal clear to me today just how different this world is from ours. Maela was telling me on the way home that by being with her family growing up, she became like Omeda. How did she put it? She said that her family is the *substance of her Omeda*. She explained that Omeda, the name of God, means 'existence' or 'being' in Similia. I never thought about the meaning of the name of God here. Actually, she said that His full name is Omeda Topoliana, 'being everlasting.' It is kind of like 'I am' in the Bible; isn't that interesting? So it is common for someone to make a comment about her *being,* or about the way she is, the way she exists, but the way she says it is a play on words because Omeda means *being.* The act of *being* is the act of becoming like God, and that happens by growing up in a family. Her family is the *substance of her Omeda*."

March appreciated the way Anj thought about things. "That is absolutely amazing. I can't say that about my family, and I don't think you would say that about yours either."

Anj agreed, "Any *being* that I have, anything that bears resemblance to Omeda, is mostly *in spite of* the family I grew up with. For Maela, it is normal to belong to a fully loving family, and that is the key to becoming Godly, becoming a healthy and wholesome individual. That is undoubtedly the context from which everyone else understood Makkana's message tonight. He is speaking out of a world in which families work perfectly to instill the purity, the good sense, and the image of God in their children."

March asked, for the hundredth time since they had been among the Similia, "What is this place? How does such a society come to be?"

"I still don't have an answer for you, hon," she replied. "But I also found out today that we have been expected for a long time. Their prophet sort of people, they call them 'seers,' had a vision of people arriving here from another star in a palopalo shell. That's how I found out about what they call those shells that are like coconuts, palopalos. So, months ago, when Lalo came home from the woods with a story about seeing us, they quickly surmised that we were the expected ones from another star."

He smiled, "Ooo, the 'expected ones!' Sort of sounds like the coming of the Messiah, but I don't think we were expected in that kind of way were we?"

"No, just that they knew it was something predicted by and arranged by, Omeda, and it would be a good thing. Even though - and this was an interesting point – even though they knew we would arrive completely ignorant about how to do life here and would need a lot of help to adjust. That is why Maela so aggressively became my friend. Omeda gave her the project of helping me learn how to be Similia, and I expect that Bendota had much the same assignment from Omeda for you."

"How interesting; does that cause you to question the authenticity of Maela's love for you?

"Not at all. When Omeda makes a deposit of love, it is the real thing, of that I am sure. I have experienced Him depositing love to me. Omeda gave me love for Saala, and it is very real. I remember when it dropped into my spirit. The first time she locked eyes with me and handed me her grass sandal out there in the woods, I felt my heart turn physically in my chest, and my spirit said to me, 'I *love* this woman,' before anything else ever happened between us. It's just *there* and it's real. Do you question if Bendota is being real with you?"

"No. I see every love we experience here as genuine and as an active part of how we are re-learning how to be. It is that 'substance of my Omeda' idea that Maela was talking about. We are experiencing transformation through being loved and accepted, just like family is supposed to work."

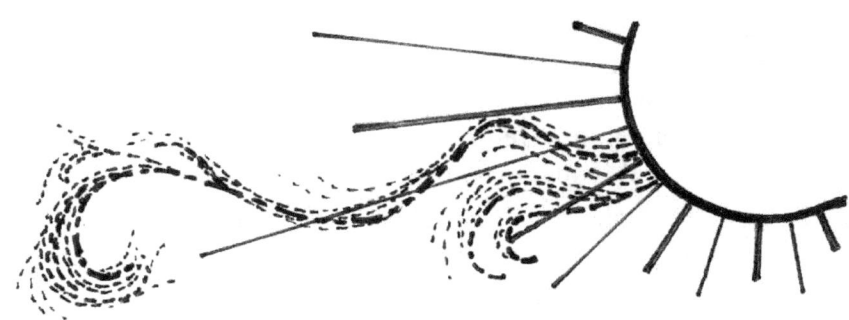

Chapter Twenty-Three

March had long since given up his watch alarm to awaken him in time to get ready to join the communal breakfast. His internal clock had become fully engaged with ΔT time. Inevitably though, by the time he awoke, Anj was already up, or at least awake. This morning, as he turned over to see where she was, she was sitting on the bed with her legs crossed, looking towards the light-shaft window. "I don't think the twin stars are out tonight," she spoke to his stirring, observing the paleness of the light coming in.

March engaged in his morning routine, more slowly coming to alertness than she, and put his feet on the floor. She got up and lit the lamp. She had learned by now the technique of striking a spark with the crystals hanging nearby to ignite the fluid on the wick. The sophistication of this culture in certain points always interested her, anthropology having been her minor in college.

March said, "Thanks, Babe." He was usually a man of few words early in the morning, but he added, "You're a doll. I think when you start the lamp, the light shuts down the production of melatonin in my brain, so I can begin to get over my sleepiness."

"Really? You never told me that before, and I know you didn't find that in a Google search here. What made you think of that?"

Silence from that side of the room was eventually interrupted with, "I think I like morning times here; waking up, getting up, getting going. I look forward to our 'family time' with breakfast. I'm going to call it family time from now on to remind me that my family is the substance of my Omeda. It is family time, worship time, and transformation time. It all has become very special to me, to us."

She came over and sat down with him on the edge of the sleeping frame, putting her arm up over his square shoulders. "You're a doll too, for bringing us here."

He sat up suddenly, looking at her to see if she was joking. Of course, he could see that she was, and he said, "No, you can't blame me for being stuck on a planet trillions of miles from Earth," and he poked her in the ribs. "It was your idea, if I remember correctly, that we could come here without a means to return, and it was you who sold the whole idea to CSE."

"And it was you who were the first to agree that was a grand idea. Well, wasn't it? In the long run?"

Holding her snugly up against his ribs, he admitted, "Indeed, it has been the grandest idea of all."

As they dressed and washed up, March was humming one of the tunes he hoped to hear during this morning's worship time. He even thought of asking his musical friend to include it, but rejected the idea on the basis that he could trust the musicians to hear from Omeda what to lead with today.

When he and Anj got to their table and saw their familiar companions there, he found that he had an amplified heart-response to seeing his new 'family' now, and was filled with anticipation about what might be deposited in his being today that would make him more like the One they all worshiped.

Breakfast was sumptuous as usual, and worship carried March off to a spiritual place of joyful expectation without fear. Suspicion, fear and foreboding had been disappearing from his experience little by little here, and this morning, he completely lost sight of those features of his life as he placed himself fully in the trustworthy hands of Omeda Topoliana, even though they did not play the tune that he was hoping for. In his thoughts towards Omeda he concluded, "What You want to do, and how that will look between You and me is all Yours."

As the music quieted, He and Anj were eager to hear what would be declared by the younger members of the family. Each morning, several of the young men and women recited long passages after the music. This was their time to lead. Anj had asked Maela, a few weeks ago, if she wrote the things that she spoke in the mornings. Maela said, "No, I am not the source of what I speak, although some of the young people do compose beautifully worded things that they memorize and recite. These that I recite are passages from the ancient writings of our forefathers, and sometimes I will also tell about how the written words have influenced and enriched my own life."

Interested, Anj asked, "Ancient writings? Tell me more about those." She had been aware that there was a written language but had never seen anything like a book or even a written paragraph. She had concluded that it must be only by oral tradition that the important teachings were carried from one generation to the next.

Maela was delighted that Anj was interested in a favorite subject of hers. "Lendkon has been here many lifetimes. Long ago some of the earliest people wrote down wisdom from their experiences; what they had learned from Omeda for the benefit of the following lifetimes. Hearing this wisdom often is important to staying close to Omeda and seeking His holiness. It is the ancient writings that are the source of most of what is taught here."

"Where are the writings?" Anj asked.

"We have a room Makkana will show you someday, that contains all of the wisdom of the ancient times written down for us."

On this morning, as the music quieted, and a waiting silence pervaded, Bendota stirred himself first. He raised both hands in the air as if a very large object was coming down from heaven for him to receive. He waited, motionless until his lips began to move, but without a sound, until he began, "All the stars of the night sky tell of the beauty of Omeda; Strewn across the whole sky, they declare His creative power. Day after day, we hear what they say, night after night, we come to know wisdom. There is no speech, nor are there any words we hear, but what they say goes to every ear, the silent sound to the end of the world. Among the stars, He has placed the sun which is radiant like a young man about to get married. It appears strong and able to endure anything. It rises upon the eastern horizon and courses across the sky until it meets the western horizon, and everything experiences its heat."

March almost could not believe his ears. As an astronomer captivated by the mysteries of the stars, he had memorized, Psalm 19 years ago, and here it was, in essence, not exactly word for word, but as if it had been read from one of those unusual translations. Once again, he was standing amazed that Omeda's very fingerprints were on everything that was happening here. With difficulty, he contained his curiosity through the rest of Bendota's message and through the communal time of prayer, until the final praises were spoken. Then he put his hand on Bendota's arm, "Did you write that passage you spoke out this morning? It was beautiful."

"Oh no Mach, that is from the sacred writings. We have known this passage for many lifetimes, and I am particularly moved by it. I knew you would like it because of your great interest in the stars. Did you know that Omeda speaks to us of His glory through the stars?"

March could not figure out a way to tell Bendota that he had read the very same thoughts in his own book of ancient writings, but he said, "Yes, my friend, I think that is why I chose to study the stars because they tell me mysteries about Omeda; I am constantly filled with praise when I look out into the night sky. There is no speech, nor are there words, but they are heard all over the world."

Bendota gave his big friend a deep brotherly embrace, and said, as he had said many times since they met, placing his hand on March's heart, "Omeda is uniting our hearts; my heart and your heart, He is creating something bigger than both of us that will help many see Omeda more clearly. Come, we have something to show you today that you have not yet seen."

Almost every day they saw new things about this well-organized and vibrant community that were amazing, but something about Bendota's demeanor stirred March's interest afresh. At dawn, as the day began to warm, Bendota and Maela led March and Anj out directly into the orchard, where they had recently been spending more and more time working among the many varieties of trees, pruning, harvesting, and even helping with the planting of new rows of tiny trees, just sticks with a few new leaves, but here they would grow.

March and Anj had come to love the orchards. They constantly marveled at the knowledge of botany and agriculture that had been passed down through the generations, dictating how far apart the different types of trees should be planted, how wide the branches of the mature trees should be allowed to grow, which branches to prune, and which to allow to bear fruit. Today as they walked between the rows it was like going there for the first time all over again.

It was a marvel, these acres and acres of food-producing man-made forest, all planted just so, trimmed, pruned, shaped, beautifully. They were like works of art, tree after tree, bearing produce similar to pears, melons, avocados, plums, and peaches, besides a number of things that have no comparison to earthly fruit, and all of it scandalously tasty. Makkana and Saala had observed how much the newcomers admired the way the orchards are managed, and March and Anj suspected that they had a hand in directing them into work in the orchards. The newcomers were aware that people who were their age would normally have been deep into their profession years before now, their placement recognized and valued in the community much earlier. March and

Anj felt like they were ready to settle into a regular work assignment.

No one was putting any pressure on the new arrivals to work and contribute, but they had basically 'gone native' by now, and knew that settling into a career was part of being Similia. Since they ate the food and lived in the village, it was only fitting that they would work like everyone else. Work was one of the ways to become a real part of this society. Work was viewed as one of the great joys that Omeda gives to the Similia. Around the table at mealtimes, they would say, "We eat and we drink, and we see the good of our work, it is a good thing from Omeda."

Maela and Bendota, faithful friends, constant companions, and teachers had introduced them to the people who were in the top tier of orchard workers, those who could show them the specific qualities of the different varieties of trees. These people and had begun to teach them the vast knowledge behind the food-growing operation. But today seemed to be a different sort of lesson. The two young friends guided March and Anj deeper than they had ever been before into the center of the wide orchard area until they came to a huge and ancient tree, very beautiful and laden with what looked like cantaloupes. The new orchard apprentices did not recognize the fruit, nor had they ever seen such a magnificent tree. The tree itself carried a presence that was as distinct as its fruit. It felt friendly to March. To Anj, it felt loving, safe, motherly, peaceful, and grand. Furthermore, it felt like forever. There was something of eternity about it, this tree.

All four of them gazed in silence, like visitors to Niagara Falls. What was to be said? Stupendous. Impressive. Finally, Maela held her hands out in front of her towards the tree with a twinkle in her eyes, like she was introducing them to a guest of great honor, or telling them something she had wanted to tell them for a long time, and she explained that this is the fruit which, when it is peeled, is the orange and especially excellent fruit that is served at the close of each morning meal, followed by closing prayers.

Anj said, "Ah, the one that tastes so marvelous and seems to energize us?" wanting to make sure she understood. She had often wondered what that fruit was, because it always appeared at the table with no peel or seeds, and in carefully cut segments.

Maela nodded, "Yes, this is Omeda's special gift to the Similia. All of the other trees grow wild in other places, and the animals may eat them too, but this one only grows in the garden, for us," she said, "Omeda calls it the 'Tree of Life.'"

Anj suddenly felt dizzy and her knees buckled. March reached out to catch her from dropping to the ground, but she recovered and regained her feet. She whispered to March in English, "She said it is the Tree of Life!"

He responded quietly, "That is what I heard too. The Similia eat from the Tree of Life!" Then, after a pregnant pause in which Maela, observing her friends' reaction, was not sure whether to continue with her explanation, March spoke to her in Similia, "Maela, we do understand something about how important this tree is to the whole community. It surprised us; we were unprepared to see it for the first time."

Maela was concerned for her friend who had unexplainably almost collapsed at the mention of this most-special of all trees. "Mama Anch, are you not feeling strong?"

"I'm feeling strong again now, Ella, I was overwhelmed when I found out this is the Tree of Life! Please, go ahead and tell us what you were going to say about this tree."

Maela picked up where she left off and went on to explain that this fruit, this special gift from Omeda, enables people to live out their full number of days with youthful energy and strength. As she spoke in glowing terms of Omeda's lovingkindness, Anj's mind was racing to remember the Genesis account, thinking of how the Garden of Eden compared to this amazing garden with Omeda's Tree of Life in it. This would explain so much about the Similia who were so uniquely innocent, so healthy and strong, and so devoted to Omeda Topoliana. They were able to still eat from this Tree. The obvious question to follow was about the other tree. She did not know if she should ask if there was another tree.

Before Anj could even complete her thoughts to form a question, Maela, having ended her remarks about the Tree of Life, pivoted on her feet to face one-hundred-thirty degrees to her left, revealing a little behind them, an even more beautiful tree that somehow they had not noticed as they wound through the orchard and approached the Tree of Life. She held her hands out in front of her again, but this time as if she was introducing them to someone she would rather not have to introduce. Anj and March's eyes were riveted upon this additional and even more spectacular arboreal wonder, with seductively lovely fruit offered among its lush leaves. Maela continued her uncomfortable introduction in a statement that was, to the people from Earth, predictable. "From this tree, Omeda says we must not eat, or life as we have known it will cease. He says this is the Tree of the Knowledge of Good and Evil."

Anj kept her knees locked but leaned into March a little as she stared, and thought, and felt, and unscrambled so many different levels of meaning and knowledge that were stirred up together in a whirlwind. Mysterious things about the ΔT people that had been puzzling to her quickly began to fall into place, given this startling disclosure. Now she was able to see how this unified, loving, perfect society could exist. She understood at once, why she found it so easy to pray and praise God in this place. This explained how she was able to effortlessly maintain a pure and faith-filled relationship with God: she was fed life from Omeda God daily. Furthermore, she was among a people who did not know evil. The environment did not include evil in any form. There was no static; everything came through loud and clear.

Anj felt strength return to her knees again, and said to Maela and Bendota, "We are very grateful that you showed us these trees today. Thank you. As you can tell, no doubt, this is astonishing new information to us, but it is very good. It is so good. It is unbelievably good. I look forward to learning more about the historical relationship between the Similia and these two trees. Another time, after March and I have been able to think this through, I want to hear more. Now may we leave before my knees get wobbly again?" she tried to inspire at least a little chuckle, but Maela and Bendota remained serious. They were intuitively aware of how weighty this new knowledge was to the people from Earth, although they had no understanding of why.

Feeling very much aware that they were members of a fallen race from Earth, rather than Natives of ΔT, March and Anj filed out of the orchard behind Bendota and Maela, past the trees that bore fruit similar to avocados, the trees that bore something like pears, and the trees that were laden with red apples, but there were only two trees occupying their minds. Excusing themselves from their friends, they climbed to their favorite spot on the top of the cliff above the grotto via a wide chimney they had found just to the north of the village. It was an easy ascent for the experienced free-climbers. It offered an amazing view over the whole area, and now they could just see, way over to the left on a rise, those two much larger trees, profiled against Browning Sea in the distance. They wondered why they had never noticed them before.

March began by saying, "From the very beginning we had heard a caution from God that we did not need to tell our new friends about the fallen world that we left behind. We were to focus on learning about this world. I think that has been appropriate, but today, not being able to tell them that we know about those two trees put me in a difficult spot. I felt like I was lying to them, or at least keeping a secret from them that they had a right to know."

"I know what you mean, but, seeing that tree of the Knowledge of Good and Evil, I realized today that there is no way they could even conceive of what we have come from. They have no concept of evil. And we would do them no service trying to explain it to them. I couldn't utter a word. What could I say to an innocent and undefiled people who have no concept of what evil is? Our young friends sensed how uncomfortable we were in the moment, although they could not have fathomed at all why."

March nodded thoughtfully, "People of ΔT, our friends Maela and Bendota, could never imagine the immense disaster that we have witnessed on Earth because that one directive from God was disobeyed. The Similia have obeyed; they have never eaten from that tree, and they continually benefit from the Tree of Life. From the context of ΔT, the chaos, hatred, murders, greed, and wars we have seen on Earth are *unimaginable*. I don't think I will never attempt to explain it to them. Omeda would have to give me very clear instructions and a direct order for me to do that to a people who have never been subjected to evil, who have no idea of human depravity."

Anj, still processing, said, "Not only do they not know evil; they don't know what 'good' is. Did you ever hear the philosopher's joke about the two young fish? They swim past an old fish who says, 'How you boys enjoying the water today?' and one young fish turns to the other and says 'What is water?' Haha, it's supposed to be funny that the young fish don't know they exist in water and depend on water. But in the same way, the Similia are swimming in 'good,' and they don't even know how good they have it. Good is as natural as water to a fish for them. Good is their environment, one another, and their God."

They sat in silence for a long time. March finally ventured to talk about how he was managing to fit it together. "At first, you know, involvement with this community and getting to know so many of the individuals here raised one difficult-to-understand question after another. Why are they so universally kind and accepting? Not one person has questioned us, feared us, or turned against us. Not one; not even a shadow of it. How does a society become so homogeneously righteous, helpful, and kind?

He continued, "Ah, then we discovered that they worship God; and we thought that must be the key, but still, we wondered how they all live so fully in harmony with Him? No one disdains

God; no one rolls his eyes when it is time to worship or pray; no one has to be forced to enter in, not even the children. No one has fallen away, but all live in unity. I had major questions about how a culture manages to live in such unblemished love, genuine kindness between every person, with innocence of wrong. There is no ruler forcing anyone to conform. There are no police to enforce laws. In fact, there are no laws; they know how to be the very best of what humanity can be, without law. The consistency of kindness was very unfamiliar at first, as I was surrounded by it, but it is becoming my soothing normal. No, much more than that, it is reshaping who I am.

"Today, I am able to see answers to those questions because we were shown those two trees. They never ate the forbidden fruit. They never fell out of perfect relationship with God. Down through the ages, for countless lifetimes, everyone stayed away from the wrong tree, and they are still able to eat from the Tree of Life. No one ever gets sick; it is unknown here. Everyone lives a love-filled vibrant and healthy life until they fulfill their days and go to be with Omeda. I see it all now. It's not a social construct of their own making. It's all Omeda and perfect harmony with Him.

"Staying in perfect relationship with Omeda has to be how they all become such wholesome human beings. These people's wonderful nature is in no way attributable to their efforts, or their striving to achieve a standard. They have become, only by staying close to Omeda, what He intended them to be when He created humans. We humans are an exquisite, beautifully crafted work. It is what was originally intended for Earth, but it all went wrong. It is the Similia's glorious freedom to live out the manifestation of the image that the Creator formed in them."

Anj was gazing beyond the spreading orchard, far out to sea, soaking it all in, along with March's soliloquy, trying to get used to the idea that she now lived in a world that was not fallen. 'How is that going to work?' her thoughts puzzled over whether she could successfully negotiate such a life.

Then she responded to March's long meditation, "Well put. You got that all sorted out pretty quickly. You are more of a theologian than I realized. But I know it will take us maybe a lifetime to become as unstained as the Similia."

With that daunting thought, she decided to change the subject, and said, "Hey, astronomer; 'the stars strewn across the sky are telling about the work of His hands.' Was that not amazing what Bendota recited today?"

"That completely took me by surprise when he essentially quoted from our Bible! What God is doing here is deep and complex, beyond what we can fathom. We are in the middle of something that God has set up, something the scope of which He is not telling us. We are walking out 'the days that were ordained for me, when as yet there was not one of them.'"

"Really?" she questioned, hoping to lift the weightiness of all this, "we're not here just by accident?"

He just smiled at his little wife, trying to be funny while they were trying to comprehend the most serious discovery since the first sighting of Lalo out there in the woods.

Eventually coming down off the cliff, they spent the rest of the day working with Bendota and Maela whom they found harvesting the avocado-like fruit. At the peak of the heat of the day, they all moved inside for the long 'siesta' in the cool of the cave. A light breakfast of nuts and fruit then armed them to continue where they left off out among the avocados. Though it continued to be very warm outside, the pioneers' hearts were warmed in a different way as they realized that they had been invited by their new family into understanding some of the most important aspects of daily life with Omeda and the Similia.

When they saw Makkana at that evening meal, he said, "I understand that you went to look at the Tree of Life today, and you saw Omeda's other tree also." Anj noticed his wise old eyes searching their faces carefully. She was not sure what he *hoped* to see, but she suspected that he hoped *not* to see any curiosity or eagerness in them to taste that fruit from the other tree. Then he said something that added yet another thing for them to consider. He said, "Our seers have said that you would know what the 'knowledge of good and evil' means. We have never had a full understanding of those words. It is Omeda's words about the tree. We understand clearly that we must not eat of it, and for all the lifetimes of the Twin Stars, we have followed that request from Omeda. Life as we know it is all from His generous hand, and we would never put at risk the continuation of His life and love."

March decided to tell him, "The seers are correct, Makkana; from our previous world we know what happens when the fruit on the Tree of the Knowledge of Good and Evil is eaten. It is no longer a beautiful place, our world. People there, who are made in the image of Omeda the same as here, are still capable of beauty and life but are also capable of the opposite of beauty and life, and that tends to become the predominant factor in our world. That is the evil. It influences everything." March hoped he did not have to explain any further, but it felt good to have been able to reveal that much. He did not feel like he was lying or keeping secrets any longer.

March's words had put the elder deep in thought. His eyes were directed up and to his right in the manner of one who is working on an arithmetic problem in his head. Holding one hand out in front of him, with one finger moving as if he were drawing something, he pondered, "Evil is the opposite of beauty and life," paraphrasing what he had just heard March say. He said it aloud to no one in particular. Still gazing into his own thoughts, he continued, "I can understand that the opposite of up is down, and the opposite of in is out, but I cannot understand the opposite of beauty and life." He was unable to conceive of it.

"And that is a great blessing," March encouraged, "A great blessing indeed. If you had only ever experienced light and had never seen darkness, you would not be able to imagine it. You live in the light of beauty and life from Omeda, and you have never seen its darkness, so darkness is unimaginable. May that always be so for you and for this world."

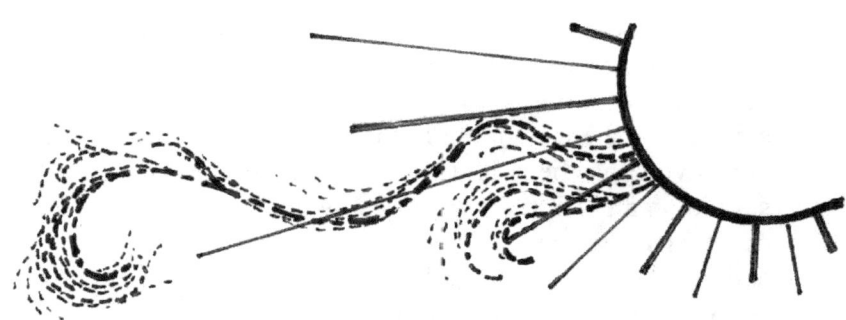

Chapter Twenty-Four: Launch Central

"Greetings faithful friends, Anj here. Another week has passed, and it has been an eventful one. I think I told you that we were being trained to work in the orchards, nothing real formal, like everything else here, no pressure. Maybe it is up to us to eventually enlist or something; I don't know. I just see that we are regularly given the opportunity to work in the orchards and that we are being taught some of the science of it by the experts. Learning new and useful things is always great fun.

"Last week, we were hit by a 'bolt from the blue,' when our friends showed us two huge ancient trees that we had never seen before in the center of the orchard. They said one is the Tree of Life, and it is the one from which we eat a portion at every dawn meal with the community. The other is the Tree of the Knowledge of Good and Evil, and nobody eats from that one. I am in no way joking with you. This is a planet where people were placed by God with the same scenario as the Biblical story of Adam and Eve, but they never ate the forbidden fruit. They have stayed in perfect harmony with the Creator because they never disobeyed Him.

"Whether you regard the Biblical story of the forbidden fruit as mythology or not, I present to you that here, it is historical reality, and the result of this people staying in right alignment with God is evident the very moment you come in contact with them.

"Most of the things that have puzzled us about the wonderful people of ∆T have now been resolved through the disclosure of those two crucial and unique trees. In the few days since I saw them standing in the center of the garden, my ∆T world view has been undergoing a fundamental redefinition. I started on arrival, thinking, 'I can view this world as a hospitable eco-system; we can survive.' To that simple view, soon was added my awareness of unheard-of freedom from fear, as I received the impression that we were safe from any malice whatsoever here. Then we met Lalo and his people; not hostile vicious aliens, but friendly, generous people of character. So my world-view had to adjust again, to include that this was a place where we would be in relationship with indigenous people. I had thought, of course, our colony was going to be March and I and our kids, but here we have a whole culture of other people to get used to, but what a people! Another big world-view shift.

"You have read my reports over the last four months about living among these good, peaceful, loving, helpful, understanding, patient, joyful, kind, and thoughtful people. At first, we were waiting for 'the other shoe to drop.' Where is the dark side of this tribe? When it became clear that there was no 'other shoe,' no dark side, we began to wonder, 'How do they do it? How can they be so consistently good?' But now we know: perfect communion with God Omeda all the time, no distractions, no guilt, and no shame. We have found that perfect communion with God Omeda is easy here, even for us Earthlings. Here, I have no greater pleasure than to turn all of my affection to Him and find Him near all the time. I take great delight in being in perfect alignment with God. I know what to do, and I am empowered in how to be, at any given time.

"God is not an add-on feature of life here, but central. He is the order, the reason, the beauty, the actual breath of life. Every evening after the meal, several of the elders will stand and speak, one at a time, about the love of Omeda, His pure light, His Joy in them, His good hand on them, providing all they need. After the set of short speeches, a significant amount of time is spent giving thanks to Him and praising Him for His supreme help, as we sing songs together. Joy easily emerges from the spirit of the gathering. There are no exhortations to follow or to obey, as a part of those evening speeches, no threat of punishment for disregarding Omeda. Being always in alignment with Omeda and His purposes is a given here.

"Maybe I got a little carried away there. I don't mean to preach; I just hope I am making sense. I am trying to convey to you on Earth what we are discovering here on ΔT, and I would be doing an injustice to keep exclusively to geology, botany, and the weather. Of much greater significance to any human population here, is this oh-so-different relationship, this fulfilled unity, between God and man. And, especially this week, I am able to present to you a very key factor of why that relationship works so well here. We have discovered why it is indeed so different.

"Hopefully March can be the one to file our report next week. He is always able to say things in a significantly different way than I, which I hope will be helpful as you all, believers and unbelievers alike, consider the facts of what we are finding here.

"Much love to all, Anj."

Browning had pushed his chair back from the desk while he read, as if to gain some insulation, to distance himself from the unusually Bible-focused tone Anj had taken, but he kept reading. C.S. was beside him, also riveted to the screen. Before this, they had been discussing the latest hyper-sleep experiments, but the notification of a report from Anj came on the monitor, and the topic was dropped until later, and they read together.

Cooper finished reading and scanned back over key portions of it, making sure he had read and understood it correctly. He folded his arms thoughtfully, and said to no one in particular, still staring at the screen, "Well I'll be."

Browning had been waiting, curious to see what kind of reaction C.S. would have to this. "So this is surprising to you also? Even though you believe in the story of the Tree of Good and Evil on this Earth?"

"Well, many of us who do believe that story also view it primarily as metaphorical rather than literal, so this is quite surprising; quite surprising indeed. It does explain a great deal about these people that March and Anj's reports have been telling us about. These too-good-to-be-true people have apparently been able to maintain a deep and flawless friendship with God for centuries, as illustrated by the literal presence of those trees. They aren't only symbolic."

"So, Cooper, you are telling me," - Browning was trying not to sound like he was challenging his friend's belief system, but he was having quite a struggle with this - "you are telling me that a big old fruit tree that no one ever ate from on that planet has made the difference between a culture like Anj talks about on ΔT and the culture we experience on the nightly news here?" He couldn't help the rich layer of cynicism in the tone of his question.

Cooper and Frank Browning had been friends and co-workers on this Proxima project for two decades with a lot of mutual respect, so the cynicism not only did not offend Cooper but also informed him just how deep this struggle was for his friend. "Frank, this is hard for you to logic your way through. Actually, it is not *hard*; it is *impossible* because the message of God is foolishness to those who approach it logically. There always has to be an element of faith – completely outside of logic - in order to receive it. The unseen realm, the cannot-weight-it, cannot-see-it, cannot-hear-it realm of the Kingdom of God, is only apprehended by faith. Even on ΔT, you notice that God is invisible. He is only known by faith, and yet those people do *know* He is there."

C.S. continued to bring his point, "You remember when we were right on the edge of success with the hyper-sleep project? I had an idea that I couldn't prove mathematically or medically. It was just an intuitive notion, a hunch. It was about a higher rate of temperature drop in the human body. Remember that?"

"Sure, you thought it could go much faster than the medical guys thought feasible, and the existing data from experimentation on cooling tissue quickly did not verify that it was possible without cell damage."

"And do you remember Frank, what your response was finally?"

"It was uncharted territory. Nobody had ever done it before. The medical guys could not predict with any certainty what would happen. We had no numbers to go on. I had you on one side, the genius saying, 'I think it will work,' and them on the other side saying 'no-can-do.'"

"As director of the project, what was your final decision?"

"You believed it could work, Coop, you really did, and I believed in you, aside from the dearth of information that science was able to offer, so, yes, I gave the go-ahead on it. We were only putting rats' lives at risk then, but it was eventually going to be human subjects, so it was a critical decision. I remember it well. And, that is ultimately what got March and Anj to Proxima."

"Okay then; that was a little bit like faith, Frank. You had no data to go on, just intuition, just your gut; in fact, not even your gut, just my gut, and you said 'yes.' And here we are, with astronauts on ΔT because of that 'yes.' So my point is just that it doesn't have to be logical to be true and important. We only need to say 'yes.'"

"What has that got to do with those trees?"

"Without any hard data to go on, Anj just hopes that you will be able to acknowledge the elements of what makes ΔT function the way it does. She sees it clear as day now. It is all about staying close to the heart of God."

Browning raised his eyebrows and gave his head a little shake, as if there were mosquitoes in the room, and said, "Pretty deep stuff Cooper. I do appreciate your trying to help. I know your heart is in the right place."

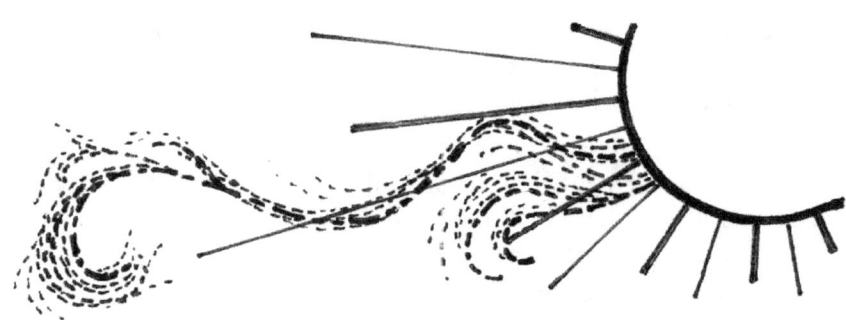

Chapter Twenty-Five

Four days after the discovery of ΔT's Tree of Life and the other Tree, and after a good deal of discussion about it, Anj told March that she was going to go back into the orchard to look at the Tree of the Knowledge of Good and Evil. "I have to be a person who has had the chance to pick that fruit with no one but God watching, and did not. I think I need that experience to be real Similia."

March looked at her with a knowing smile. "I can see how that would be important to you. Far be it from me to question you."

Anj believed that this would crystallize something deep in her being, something of identity with the people, the village, and with Omeda. On her walk up through the orchard, she began to feel the spiritual burden of what she was about to do and made sure to yield her heart to be open receive the input that God had for her in this experience. The orchard pathway granted her a view of the Tree of Life first, as it had on the first visit with Maela. Enthralled by its perfection and impacted by the Spirit that it projected, she spent a long time standing in its shadow, soaking in it and being thankful. She came to a depth of gratefulness beyond that which she had ever previously experienced. Wide vistas of beauty from the generosity of the Creator passed before her mind's eye. Gratitude took on a whole new meaning in the several minutes that she stood there sensing the divine of life all around her. She gave whispered thanks for the opportunity to stand in a place of being more deeply alive, with a pure connection with God.

Finally, she turned to view the Tree of the Knowledge of Good and Evil. Silent; beautiful beyond any painter's craft to capture, alluring but silent, offering nothing of the spiritual attractiveness of Omeda. Anj considered it carefully. It was distinctly desirable, but on a totally different basis than the Tree of Life. She was confident that she could deny its insidious temptation simply because she had witnessed and experienced the terrible results of man's giving in to that temptation on Earth. She would never want to go back to that.

She lingered there, and considered what was before her, and Omeda's word to not eat of it, and she thought she began to understand how the Similia must have managed to deny the attractive opportunity to try that fruit. They resist, but not because they understood the consequences, as she has known them. Rather, they come from the place of knowing Goodness and Love, personified in Omeda. And He has said, "Do not eat of that tree," so they don't, because the irrefutably good One has spoken to them in love, and they simply know they *must* remain in His goodness.

Where else would they go? They could not conceive of anything better. It occurred to her also that there apparently had never been a tempter to cause anyone to question the goodness of God. Or maybe there was, but he has been forgotten because his efforts came to nothing. She wondered if she would eventually learn more about that as she got more familiar with the history of ΔT.

With lightness in her step, she walked away from the Tree. Strolling easily out of the orchard, between the rows of bountiful provision, she extended her right hand out to allow the leaves to lightly caress her fingers as she passed by. Her stroll directed her feet over large areas covered with delicate, pink, flower-petal confetti on the ground. She began to feel a new freedom to receive Omeda's generosity, His favor, all that He had for her, no longer disqualifying herself on any basis of the past, or where she came from, or what her record had been before coming here. Passing between the rows of trees, she sighted Maela in the next row over, picking fruit, and something sprang out of her heart with an unaccustomed power, a cascade of love, and she ducked under the branches to go over to wrap her arms around her sister. Maela responded in kind, intuitively understanding that Anj must have just been spending time in the Presence of Omeda, and rejoiced with her.

March was loitering around the edge of the orchard, anticipating her emergence and wanting to hear a report. When she saw him loitering with an eager interest to see her, she had to ask herself, "Am I the most blessed person in the universe to have such people in my life? Surely I am." March listened attentively to her account of her experience. He did not feel a kindred need to also participate in such a venture, but he deeply appreciated the way Anj processed things and was fascinated to hear her account of it.

It was almost time for day-sleep, the siesta in the heat of the day, and Lalo happened along on his way back to the village. Dropping down in the shade with them, he lay propped up on one elbow, looking at them, waiting for one of them to start a conversation. Anj was gaining enough confidence in the language to talk about deeper things, so she asked him, "Lalo, my young friend, allow me to ask you; what were you doing on the day you first saw me? I am curious about the reason you were out by yourself such a long way from home."

He said, "Oh Anch, I was hunting for 'pattei.'"

"And what, do tell me, is that?" she asked.

"Pattei are large fungi, like a mushroom, but underground, and hard to find. It is a skill that I have, to be able to find them. They cannot be cultivated, but they may always be found out in the woods, among the tree roots, and the cooks like to include them in certain dishes. One of my older friends, a cook, asked me to find her some. I asked Omeda about doing that because I always seek His approval and guidance. Omeda said to me, 'I have put that request on her lips, and I have another important reason for you to go. Follow Me closely as you go,' and so I went out that very afternoon, looking for pattei and listening to Omeda all along the way.

"I saw you some time before you saw me, and by the time our eyes met, Omeda had told me, 'Here is your special assignment today. She is from another star. She does not know our world or our ways yet. You will be able to help her.' When we stood looking at one another, I saw that you did not expect to see me. When I spoke to you, I said, 'Omeda says that you are from another star, and I am here to help you.' But then you did something that confused me; talking, but not talking to me. I looked to Omeda, and He said, 'She is not talking to you, she is talking to another person up the hill.'

"I did not know why you would do such a thing. I asked Omeda what to do, and Omeda directed me to run up the hill towards the other person who He would show me. Immediately, I ran in that direction, knowing that Omeda was still entrusting me to carry out an important appointment that would be significant in His plan. I trusted Omeda when I met March, and Omeda told me how to arrange a meeting the next day so that Makkana and the others could come and meet you."

"So, Lalo, you knew that there was more than finding these mushroom things for you to do that day, but you did not understand very much about what Omeda was sending you out to do?"

"No, Anch, but I am a greatly loved son of Omeda, and I was happy to be chosen to go out, not knowing. I was then able to have that encounter with you and with Mach. There was much that I did not understand that day, but I trust Omeda in all things."

"Well, Lalo, you have become a dear friend of ours. We are very thankful that Omeda sent you to meet us, and that you so carefully listened to His instructions through the experience of meeting people from another star."

Lalo beamed, basking in the appreciation that they had for him, and then asked them, "In the cool of the next morning I am going to hunt for pattei again, would you like to come along? I can show you how to find and harvest them."

March and Anj, always up for an adventure, said "Yes," in unison, and March asked if there was something they should bring along.

"A little food and water will be sufficient. We will not return to Lendkon until day-sleep," he replied.

Lalo came to the next morning meal with his pouch slung over his shoulder and carrying the peculiar long rod which he had been carrying the first time they saw him. March and Anj also had packed a lunch and water and were prepared to set out right after morning prayer and worship.

Dressed for the early morning cold, they started off when it was beginning to get light, but well before the sun was above the horizon. Lalo had planned ahead the region to which he wanted to go and begin his search. March and Anj were eager for an adventure and interested to observe the process of finding this peculiar food.

Wandering quite far afield, Lalo led them up into the foothills as the day began to warm. They stopped to take off the outer layers of clothing as the reddish sun rose, its penetrating rays reaching through the leafy branches in tatters. They sat for a short rest and a drink, and March asked about the rod that Lalo carried.

"Ah, this is a gift from my father," Lalo said, holding it up so they could see it well. "You have met my father." Yes, they had. He was a big quiet man who usually worked with a few other men making the tools that were used daily, shovels, plows, pruning hooks, and so forth. "He made this from the same very hardwood that is used for plows. He put this twist on the end to hook the pattei and pull them from the ground. You will see how well it works."

March, smiling, recalled their first meeting, "I have seen how well it works to pick a pear and hand it to me."

Lalo smiled in remembrance of meeting the big stranger with hairy arms, under the pear trees, now his close friend. He added, "Although Father made this tool, he does not enjoy hunting for pattei as I do. Perhaps someday I will tire of it too, and give it to a son of mine."

"You hope for a son someday?" March asked.

"I trust what Omeda decides. Do you hope for a son, Mach?" Lalo asked, discerning a subtle longing in March's question.

March tossed a glance at Anj, knowing that she too was hoping children would come along soon. "Like you, I trust Omeda to decide. Most people our age already have children, but we had to wait in order to come here to your world."

"I believe that Omeda will honor you for waiting and will give you the desire of your hearts," Lalo offered gently.

With a look towards Proxima's warmth, Lalo picked up his bag and continued leading them along, traversing the hillsides. Soon, he began to slow and look carefully for the subtle signs of pattei between the roots of the young trees. Finding some, he was able to quickly demonstrate to them how his rod went deep into the soft organic-laden soil, and with a twist, he was able to snag the fruit and pull it to the surface. Soon their pouches were being filled with the odd-looking kiwi-sized whitish fungi.

"Lalo you will have to show us when these appear on the table at mealtime. From looking at these I cannot recognize that I have eaten them." Anj observed.

"Oh yes, they look very different sliced up in the dishes that my friend makes, and I think they are quite delicious, perhaps because I also feel happy to be able to provide them for everyone."

While they sat under a Δ Pear tree enjoying lunch of toasted polon and fruit slices, Lalo's countenance became very serious, and March sensed that Lalo had something important to bring up. Without any preamble or warm-up, Lalo launched into it; "Why do you think Omeda put a beautiful fruit-laden tree in the garden from which we may not eat?" It was an entirely honest question. He had obviously been pondering it for a while.

Anj's eyes were immediately glistening with salty tears. March looked down and poked in the dirt with a stick, not sure how to answer that without explaining a lot about the fallen world from which they had come. Anj was struck by Lalo's incredible innocence. He had no idea what her world had had to endure because her forefathers had eaten from that tree. Her shining tears didn't spill over and run down her cheeks, but she had to blink them away to be able to see Lalo.

Anj's tearful reaction was out of a deep cry from a hidden place within, something like, "Dear Jesus, this sweet boy has no idea that he is touching the fringe of what happens when we question the ways of God." She was not sure how to approach an answer, but Omeda spoke to her, "Just open your mouth and loose your tongue; you'll do fine."

She put the last bite of her toasted polon into her mouth so she could think for a while as she chewed. Swallowing, and taking a sip of water, she said, "Lalo, do you love Omeda?" March looked up at her and subtly nodded his affirmation that it was a good place to start.

"Oh yes, Anch, He is my first love, the source of all love. I spend time each day upon waking to tell Him how wonderful He is and how thankful I am to know Him more this day. He loves me first every morning. I wake up to Him, and my heart sings in response. The elders tell me that knowing Him and staying close to Him is an assignment given to all people for all our lives here in the world. And when we enter the life that goes on forever in

His eternal Presence, we will continue with revelation after revelation for eternity, even when we are in His visible Presence. I very much look forward to that. Each day He tells me many wonderful things about who He is, and about the way He has made me, about His delight in me, in everything I am. It is always wonderful to take time with Him. Everything reminds me of Him. That tree you are leaning against reminds me how much He loves me and you. In my spirit I say back to Him, 'Omeda You are the glorious one; I am thrilled that you love me.' Yes Anch, of course, I love Omeda. You know that I do; it is odd that you would ask such a question."

Anj was encouraged by his enthusiastic reply. "I am excited to hear you talk about how much you love Him, and how that affects your everyday life. Thank you for being willing to remind me of your first love. It is good to have that background in place as we talk because I think the answer to your question is that Omeda offers you a chance to do something other than to love him. That tree that we may not eat from offers you another option."

At this, she saw Lalo's eyes narrow, "What would I ever want to change about loving Omeda and being loved by Him?"

"So you love Omeda the way you do by your own choice, and you would not choose to change anything?"

"Yes, that is true, very true," he said, still a little puzzled by this line of questioning.

"Okay, Lalo, then you will keep on loving Omeda even though you have another option?"

"Yes, Mama Anch; what are you trying to show me?"

"Lalo, I am letting you see that Omeda gives you the choice to love Him or not, and since you have chosen to love Him, you have the wonderful life of love you now experience. If He did not give you another way of life besides loving Him, He would have created you as a person who could not do anything other than to love Him, and that would not be the same kind of love as that which you have now chosen to guard carefully, and to cherish."

Comprehension slowly materialized as he pondered this thought, cognition visible in the way tension on his young face gradually disappeared. She thought he was going to come up with another challenging question, but he said, "Thank you Mama Anch, I never have seen it in this way, that He has given me a choice. I would never choose to do anything but to love Him."

They were quiet in the shade of the pear trees for a while; then he did ask, "Eating from that tree would be choosing to not love Him?"

"Did He ask you not to eat of that tree?"

"Yes, Anch, I have stood and looked at it, thinking of this question, and He has asked me personally not to eat of that one tree."

"What would it mean if you did?"

He squeezed his lips together and wrinkled his nose, trying to imagine. Presently, he concluded, "Yes, He would see that as very unloving, I think." Then thinking some more, staring at the ground beside him like he could bore a hole in it, he added, quite seriously, lifting his face to Anj, "It would be a thing such as has never been done among Similia." Another pause, waiting for thoughts to fit together, then, "Not loving Omeda is a subject no one knows about. Loving Him is our life, our heartbeat, and our breath; what else could we do?"

Anj knew that was not a question that sought an answer, so she decided not to venture one. It was acutely revealing to her of the totality of Similia's world view entirely around Omeda. She and March gave him some time to be sure he had completed his thoughtful expedition into this uncharted territory. March added, "I hope you will also talk to Makkana or another elder, and tell them about your question and what Anj has told you, and ask them what they think. We don't want you to keep this just between us, because you have many wise people around you who will also be able to help. We know that you love us, that you trust us enough to ask us this question. It is out of Anj's love for you that she has offered an explanation."

He was finished talking about it, and he packed his bag and led them further on in the hunt for pattei. The young boy had become very dear to March and Anj. He was pure and undefiled like no boy they had ever met. He loved with a frankness and full trust that was almost intimidating in the fear that they might mess it up somehow, having come from a very imperfect planet.

The imperfection of their planet of origin was the center of the conversation that March and Anj had when they got home that day. Although tired from miles of hiking through the foothills all the long dawn-day, and ready for sleep, Anj wanted to confess to March a plaguing thought. "One of my great worries, after finding out that people of this planet never ate from the Tree of the Knowledge of Good and Evil, has been that I would somehow bring evil, introduce an 'infection.' I have been afraid that it would be me that would bring fallen behavior to these perfect people; that my selfishness, hatred, pride, or something like that would break the spell of God's goodness here."

March tagged onto that thought, reflecting his own concern, "Man's cruelty to man, and the rampant corruption that infiltrates every arena of human endeavor on Earth stands in such contrast to this place where corruption is not even a concept. Similia-man is good; Similia is not proud or selfish; he is kind to his fellow man; he loves Omeda and loves people, consistently, without interruption. I too have been living afraid that I would introduce evil into this world, and at the same time I have had the unexpected daily experience of being quite mysteriously free from selfish, disappointing, and hurtful attitudes and behaviors."

"Exactly. I find the same thing: I fear that I will be an awful human being here, yet I live in unexplainable freedom from that old nature. I fear that the magic will be broken, and I'll have a break with this new reality; that I will do something catastrophically ugly. You know that I could."

March was stretched out on the bed, still thinking, but also allowing relaxation to begin to settle in for sleep soon. "And you, dove, know as well, that my fears of doing something 'catastrophically ugly' are just as well-founded."

"So I should wave a red flag if I see you are about to do something ugly?"

"Great idea," he said smiling at her attempt to defuse the heavy topic before sleeping. They called it a siesta between themselves but it was not a siesta. It was a full night's sleep even though it was the hot ΔT noon outside. All was quiet outside their door as the entire village entered into rest for the next eight hours.

Coming out of deep sleep was usually a quick routine for Anj, and March was the one who took a while to emerge fully conscious. The room was fairly full of illumination from the light shaft as he sat up and looked around for her. She was standing outside of the 'window' to the light shaft, standing on the floor of the shaft gazing up at the circle of very blue sky, raptly, and with graceful motions she seemed to be washing, pouring something unseen over herself by the invisible handful.

He watched her for a while, sensing that she was in the middle of something between her and God. After some time, she became still, now with her hands crossed over her heart, looking up, with tracks of tears glittering on her face. He recognized that as her expression of thankfulness. It was not sadness. He waited quietly, knowing she would tell him about it in a few minutes. Sounds of some of the neighbors waking and heading out to work on this dusk-day began to intrude into their room with some shouts of encouragement and good humor in the hallway. The hubbub began to penetrate her consciousness, and she recovered herself. She stepped lithely back through the window and said, with her always-welcoming smile and her arms open for a hug, "You're up."

She was very still in his arms for a long time. Finally, he ventured, "You and Omeda keeping secrets?"

"I had a dream."

"Oh that is always exciting," he encouraged.

"It was an epic dream. Omeda showed me that when we were baptized, we actually did die. That was a portrayal of the real death that we experienced by faith when we accepted Jesus. You know that popular verse, Galatians 2:20, 'I have been crucified with Christ.' Yeah, well that was not symbolic. It is stating something that happened in His superior reality." They were sitting cross-legged on the bed, opposite one another, and he was listening attentively.

She continued, "You know how, when you go to sleep, you start dreaming about what you did all day? Well, I went to sleep worried about polluting the Similia society with my fallen nature. My body, however, was remembering all that walking we did yesterday. So in the dream, we were walking through the woods in the hills again, but this time Omeda – or Jesus, I couldn't tell for sure - was walking with us. It was just you and me and Him. Lalo was not there in the dream. As we walked along, Jesus began to explain things to me about our transfer from a fallen world to this one. He said, 'I allowed you and March to come here because I trusted you to leave behind all of your fallen man, to forget that you ever were degenerate. You always wanted to nullify your past, but you believed the deception that it is impossible, that you would never be able to satisfy that longing for holiness without the stain of past sin. I understand. Then the trillion-mile journey itself was a confirmation of your baptism by Me, a washing from the world you left behind. You both died in that baptism pool, and your traveling here was a demarcation. From this time forward you may walk in the truth of your crucifixion with Me by faith. A very real death of the old Anj took place, and now you are living as a resurrected human being, you are born anew. You are cleansed of all iniquity. I do not remember it, nor should you.

Anj continued, "Then it seemed to shift, and it was definitely Omeda saying, 'Here, you are fully entering into the newness of life that you had already been given by Jesus on the cross. The freedom to which Jesus ransomed humanity on Earth has been existent here without interruption since creation. That which was such a struggle to even partially succeed in back home, you find here to be effortless. You have marveled here at your freedom from your old fleshly impulses. It is because you are a new person. You were that new person stepping out of the baptism pool, but it was *extra*-ordinary on Earth. Here, it is ordinary to set your mind on the things of My kingdom. It is a normal and effortless response for you to take up My praise. Yield fully to it; fully live out the goodness; do not disqualify yourself from the abundant and sustained freedom you have experienced here.' And then He stood you and me side by side and smiling, said, 'Walk this planet as Natives. Give no thought to your past. To me it did not exist,' and then He was gone."

March sat gazing at her. She was still radiating from the presence of God. He observed, "You are still under the influence of that Presence and that revelation. Tell me again what it meant to you."

She reached out her hands and placed them on his knees, her eyes like shafts of light shining straight into his, "Nothing from the way we used to be, nothing that we have ever been ashamed of, no thing that we fear coming back to destroy the peace of this place is valid. That Anj is dead. That March is dead. Not symbolically dead, but really dead, without life. We have nothing to fear from our past."

"That is what I hoped you were saying," he whispered back down those light beams. "I want to have that assurance that I can see in you right now. I want to reach out to Him for that too. And what was happening in the light shaft a while ago?" he asked.

She pulled her hands from his knees and placed them over her heart, "After being so deeply in His Presence in the dream, I did not want to leave it. He was so real in the dream. He was *there*, and after He pronounced such good news over us, I just needed to linger, to soak it in, to immerse myself in the truth of truly being made new. I will never forget this. I believe it now, finally, this is our new life. No more fear that we will be poison here."

March's eyes were riveted on his wife and closest friend with the intention to receive from her whatever she was radiating. He wanted the same impartation that she had been given in the dream and from meditating on it in the light shaft. He and she were one. He could read her. This was real, and this was deep. After hearing the account, he nodded thoughtfully, stood, and walked over to the window. Stepping through into the light shaft, he raised his eyes to the blue circle above and began to drink in by faith, the truth of what he just heard and seen, and let it wash over him. Under the waterfall.

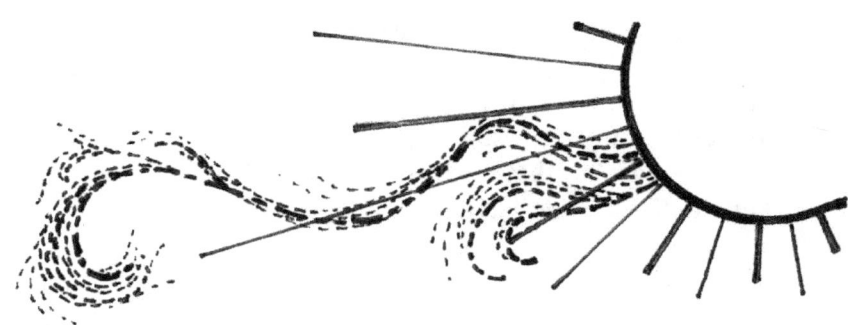

Chapter Twenty-Six: Launch Central

"Launch Central Close Team, greetings from ΔT. This is March writing the report for you today. Six more weeks and we will have been here one ΔT year by our calendar, the first year of the rest of our lives. As you know, there is no plan B. We came without a return plan, and we have no regrets. If one frames it as a move from a space-age culture to a stone-age culture, that sounds like a loss, a huge step backwards, but that is looking only at the material aspect of our lives here. Looking at the spiritual side of life, which is the most important aspect of the population here, we have experienced great gain. I know that we are expected to provide scientific information about our new planet in a different solar system, and we will continue to give you that, but allow me to explain a little today how life makes sense to us here from a spiritual viewpoint.

"The spiritual situation on Earth was vastly different. We knew God there because Jesus had come and opened our blind eyes. But instead of enjoying re-connection with Him, we got distracted by focusing on sin and hell. His love was right there to embrace us, but I can see now that we mostly missed it. Here, our great gain is to finally step into God's clear and superior intention to unite us fully with Himself in love, the relationship He always desired. Flawless love, that is the norm, the goal, for the Similia people, and Anj and I have grown into seeking Him like the Natives.

"We have discovered that we can actually become the 'new creation' that we became by faith in Jesus. He had paid for it all, but on Earth, there seemed to be too many distractions to be able to grasp it fully. Our starting point was so far away from a true likeness of Jesus that it seemed impossible, even heretical, to think that we could have His mind, or walk in His holiness and power.

"Part of our newness of life here is recovering from our own previously neglected spiritual life. A very wise person back home told me that we are primarily spiritual beings who also happen to have a body. On Earth, my body took center-stage and did all the talking. My spirit-being was mostly invisible to me. When I met Lalo and his friends, I began to see people who are centered on the spirit within. As a result, their lives are open to vastly expanded opportunities to connect with the heart of God. There are opportunities to love and be generous. There are ways one may spend time that would never occur to the body-centered person, like spending all morning watching a flower open or playing with a toddler. There are opportunities for creative expression that are wildly more unhindered and free compared to body-centered creativity.

"Allow me to tell you a little about the painters here. Paintings of scenes from ancient history fill the walls of some of the larger meeting rooms and hallways. We would call them impressionistic; just little dabs of color put together on a huge wall, quite expressive. There is a painting in one of the large meeting rooms that depicts creation. It is eerily reminiscent of Michelangelo's Sistine Chapel, in which God is reaching out to touch the finger of Adam. Lendkon's illustration however does not have Omeda's figure shown at all, like the bearded old man in the Sistine Chapel, nor does it have the pathos of the fall of man invisibly overlaid, which makes it in fact a tragic picture. The ΔT artist was not painting from the place of depraved man enslaved to all the wrong things. This illustration is incredibly inspiring. The breath of God is whispered into the clay and the clay becomes a living being full of the very life and Word of God. The painting cries out to my soul with a shout of affirmation for the eternal nobility and purity that was meant to be in the creation of man.

"Of course there are no paintings of the Christ or His crucifixion, so common in sacred paintings on the home planet. There is no need for a Savior, no need for God the Son to enter into the world, in all appearances as a normal man, posing as sinful flesh, but coming to be an offering for sin, to bring His own blood into the Holy place. It stands as the most impressive act of all of history; that God would come to Earth to do that. It is Earth's unique gift, beautiful to us, but unknown here, except in the Similia's recognition of the depth of love in the heart of God. Take Lalo, for example. What wouldn't He do to preserve the father-son relationship He has with that boy? To preserve us is why He came to Earth personally two thousand years ago.

"Another difference for us is in the idea of 'holiness.' Holiness is seen here as something that one grows into over a lifetime. Makkana told me recently, 'If you want to do well with holiness, you must allow Omeda to live through you. It is not something you can make up on your own.' Similia are born innocent, free from sinful nature, but they are not born holy in the way they define holiness. Holiness to these people is in the character of a person, not in outward behaviors. Holiness is the actual loving character of God that grows in a person over a lifetime, through that submission to Omeda. Holiness is not seen as a struggle against unholy behavior, but as maturity in faith and trust. It is the reward of a well-spent life. It is the purpose for which we were created, and it is preparation for eternity with Him.

"I can hear you asking, 'How then, does life remain interesting there on ΔT?' I know, the most exciting stories on the Earth are rich with the struggles of life. Love stories are not good unless there is some threat of loss, unfaithfulness, or flip-flops from love to hate or hate to love. A story is not interesting unless it has some 'action,' which means murder, theft, disaster, and the misdeeds of its flawed human characters. Overcoming all those contingencies of life is what we Earthlings believe makes life rich. On Earth, our favorite stories are about people who have overcome the most distressing circumstances.

"So you ask, 'Where is the action? What is happening in life that is exciting?' I can just picture a group of you trying to figure that out, sitting around Carla's desk over the second cup of morning coffee. 'What in the world are March and Anj doing for interest?' I know you are just trying to develop a clear picture of our life on ΔT. I love and respect all of you. I hope that you are all well. I know that the burning torch of space exploration is in good hands!

"Maybe without the actual context of this planet and the Similia, this will not communicate well, but let me try. Here, our delight and richness of life come from the beauty of Omeda. Glory and splendor are around Him, indescribable light, worthy of all our attention. There are those who abandon themselves to the pursuit of deeply knowing Omeda without distraction. Just like on Earth, it is easy to be busy about other things; craftsmanship, work, and friends, but our friend Saala, one of the elder women from our table, has sought the face of Omeda without distraction. The result is that she finds life to be meaningful. Into the Divine illumination of Omeda's Presence, she ventures daily. Sometimes we see Saala, and her face is shining like she just spent the weekend at Disneyland, so we ask her to tell us about her encounter with the Holy One. She recently told us, "All ignorance and unknowing bows to the light unimaginable in brilliance. I have just been bathed in light." For her, all other pleasures pale in comparison to the pleasure of being with Him. Our true life is hidden with Omeda in the eternal.

"On ΔT everyone is a child of Omeda. We are not pretending or trying to imagine what that means, as I did on Earth. Here it is easy to see Omeda as our spiritual Father, more real than our closest human relationship. The archetype of Father carries with it an idealism that no Earthly father is able to meet.

Father Omeda fulfills every expectation of us children for wisdom, provision, and protection. In raising us as children, He is sure to keep us from all harm. Think about it; children are not helped by adverse experiences like trauma, neglect, or horror - those 'action' things - which are actually quite damaging. Children are built up by consistent love and attentive care, and within that, we experience life as fun and exciting. There is plenty of 'action' in the loving relationships that surround us. As children of Omeda, we have a life that is in no way dull or lacking in interest.

"I have faith that I am a son of Omeda. My future, my destiny, is as a child of Omeda. I know I have forgotten a lot about how it is to live on Earth, but here we *really are* children of Omeda. The choice remains, even here, whether we allow that to become the most important fact of life, the number one thing we seek after. Once we make that choice, no other love, no other person, no other smile, no one else will do, only His Presence. No other light will do, no other brilliance. No other object receives our praise; there is no other to adore, no other covering, no other blessing, no other hope. No other music is attractive; no other sound draws us in. No other word is the word of life; there is no other glory, no other beauty, and no other set of colors, only Him.

"Well, I set out to tell you a little about what is going on here spiritually, since that is our priority, and I unloaded all that was on my mind. I hope it is helpful to anyone who reads these reports to gain an idea about life with God on ΔT.

"All for now, much love to all, March."

Browning was looking tired, as he and a few of the close team were reviewing the latest report. He started, "So they have been there just a month or so shy of a year. Seems like five years. There has been a lot going on. Everything in Proxima Mission has been shaken up ever since they found people there. Real people; I still haven't been able to get used to the idea."

Browning was with Carla, C.S., and a man named Duke who was Launch Central's IT supervisor. Everything that had a computer, radio, or phone associated with it was his territory, and he ran a small army of people who were the tech wizards for the whole Launch Central arm. His real name was Richard Ellington, and the office called him 'Duke,' thinking of the Jazz great, Duke Ellington, from so long ago, whose music he had playing in his office constantly.

"You find it hard to believe," Carla observed, in response to Browning's complaint, "that there is a Creator that would do a similar thing in another solar system, on another planet."

This had been a long-standing, on-going discussion in which everyone was careful to ensure that there was no animosity between the Christians and the agnostics or atheists in the team because March and Anj, the crucial personnel in the project, were believers, and they fully respected all those of other persuasions who were contributing so vitally to their success.

Browning gave Carla a knowing grin, "I don't find it *hard* to believe, Carla, I find it *impossible* to believe. But that stands in stark contradiction to what our astronaut pioneers have discovered. I don't want to *believe*; I want something to make sense. And March goes on and on in this report about how being a child of this God, Omeda, is all-important in his life. *That* doesn't make sense either. Where is the radical astronomer-nerd scientist we once knew?"

C.S. slowly spun around once in his desk chair, thinking, and decided to jump in. Leaning forward with his elbows on his knees, he stated, "I am really excited for March. I wish I could experience just one hour on ΔT, and sense the holy Presence he gets to live in all the time."

Nobody else ventured anything, so he continued, "What they have found there in spiritual reality, is tremendously encouraging to my own feeble attempts to have a meaningful life. Hearing from March and Anj, I have been gaining in my hope that I might have a life that somehow counts in the eyes of God, counts for eternity. I am hearing now that it is not in vain that I try to live in a way that serves God. I have renewed hope that I do fit into His purposes in the universe somehow. That used to be inconceivable to me. The big picture just got exponentially bigger with the possibility of God being active in other parts of the universe."

Browning was swinging his knees back and forth gently, listening. When C.S. finished his thought, Browning raised his face up to his right, looking to his fellow-agnostic, Duke, who was standing beside him. Duke noticed the look from his boss. He sensed that Frank was hoping for an escape from the direction that C.S. had taken, a focus on the reality of God.

Duke decided he could safely return the conversation to what was the real issue to him. "For those of us who find the spiritual discoveries on the new planet confusing, the main question has become, 'What happened to our mission?' We had a vision going forward, that could have served the future of space exploration, perhaps for generations, with the establishment of a 'mini-Earth' out there. Suddenly it seems to be seen by our people there - all due respect to March and Anj – that our vision is one that would be intrusive to a beautiful culture already existent. We get it, Cooper, that this development has profound ramifications for your faith, but does it also have to be destructive in its ramifications for the vision of CSE? It seems that there could be both somehow, not either-or. CSE, at this point, is leaning towards the establishment of another colony on ΔT that would stand separate from, but not in opposition to, the indigenous people with whom March and Anj have so seamlessly merged."

Browning, nodding silently in agreement turned to C.S. and Carla who were the leading Christians of the group, inviting further comment from them.

Carla looked to C.S. as he commented, "It is a big planet, and maybe that would be possible, but we don't have –by far, we don't have - a good grasp of how incredibly different this culture on ΔT must be. It is a society without any theft, lying, or murder, with only kind people, no wicked people. There is perfect cooperation within the community, and all of the families love one another for life. I guess the question I have is, 'How fragile are these people? How well would they withstand exposure to all the elements of a fully Earth-based culture somewhere near them?' We don't know, do we? And my question to you is whether it is worth it for the sake of raw space exploration to wreak destruction on an entire planet and an ancient culture that is far superior in many ways to ours?"

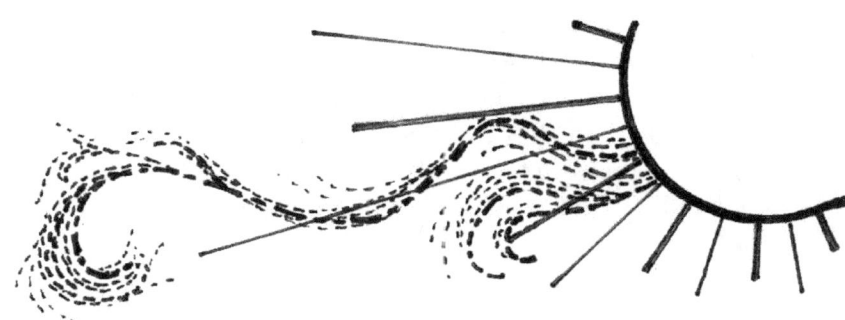

Chapter Twenty-Seven

Anj was working with Maela during the cool dawn of the day, carrying bundles of citrus-like fruit up to the grotto for the food handlers to distribute or store. One of the kitchen workers came over and told Maela something that Anj did not hear, so she asked what it was about. Maela said, "Do you know Lana?"

Anj did. "I don't know her well, but yes, she is one of the older women at Lalo's family table. We have spoken a few times; she's very sweet."

"My friend just informed me that she went to Omeda this morning."

That was something Anj had never heard spoken about in that way before. At first, she thought maybe it meant that Lana had died, but Maela had spoken of it so matter-of-factly that Anj thought it could also mean she had a mystical experience one-on-one with the Creator. She asked, "Please explain what that means."

Maela said, "Lana had lived out her lifetime and she had been expecting for some time now, to go be with Omeda."

Anj wanted to say, "So you mean she died?" but she realized she did not know the word for 'died' and had never heard of a word for 'death' in Similia, so she asked, "Lana has come to the end of her life?"

They had walked back to the citrus trees by that time, and Maela realized that Anj was not understanding, so they sat and shared a drink of water from a palopalo shell, while Maela explained. "Lana has fulfilled the number of her days in this world, and her life here with us at Lendkon is finished. She has gone to be with Omeda. Do you know about 'Osoto-ban-talia-da'?"

Anj had not heard that phrase before "No, what is that?"

"Osoto-ban-talia-da is life that goes on forever with Omeda. It is the place where we go when we fulfill our lifetime here in this world. That is where Lana is now."

Anj couldn't help but ask, "Is her body still here?"

"Oh yes, when one goes to Osoto-ban-talia-da, one does not need this body anymore, so it is left behind as a memorial of a lifetime."

Anj asked, "You are saying the word 'lifetime' as if it was a predetermined amount of time for Lana. You said she fulfilled the number of her days. Is a lifetime the same for everyone?"

"Yes, for most people, a lifetime is the number of days it takes for the Twin Stars to completely circle each other." Realizing that she needed to explain, Maela drew a narrow ellipse in the dirt with a twig. "This is the course of the Twin Stars. Right now, the stars are here, and here," she poked two holes in the extreme ends of the ellipse. "They are as far apart as they ever get, but they are beginning to move along these lines and will draw closer, pass each other, and go to the other end of the course, here, and here," poking new holes in the ends of the ellipse. "And then," she continued patiently, "they will begin to draw closer together again, pass going the other way, and they will be back where they started. It takes a lifetime for all that to happen." She looked up at Anj to check for comprehension.

"Fascinating!" Anj was thrilled to be learning this important marker of time for the Similia. "You are saying then, that Lana was born when the Twin Stars were far apart, then they made a full rotation around one another, and now the Twin Stars are back where they were when she was born, and her lifetime is fulfilled."

"Exactly," Maela smiled, enjoying her friend's interest. "You will notice that older people will ask one another, 'Has Omeda given you a full lifetime?' If the Twin Stars are coming close to where they were when that person was born, she will say, 'Very near,' meaning it is almost time to go to Osoto-ban-talia-da. But if it is still a long time, they will say, 'I have many more days to be fulfilled yet.'"

Anj said again, "Fascinating. I have noticed that it is hard to tell how old people are. The hair grows white, but everyone maintains perfect health. Lana, for example, was working yesterday; I saw her in the food store, stacking bags of dried fruit."

"Yes, everyone knows the station of the Twin Stars when they were born. This present station is called 'Champa-ki.' We have names for eight positions of the Twin Stars, and you may always ask what station a person was born in to know his or her age."

"So I need to learn the eight names," Anj observed.

"I will teach you at the evening meal, and you can write them down to memorize them."

"March will be so interested to learn this too. You are a wealth of education for us, Maela, thank you."

When Anj met March going back to the village at the end of the day, she was able to tell him all her new-found information, and let him know about Lana. They were curious about what would happen with her body. Would there be a funeral or anything? Maela had said that the body was a memorial of a lifetime. March knew that the Twin Stars make a complete rotation every seventy-nine of Earth's years, so it made sense that it would be the marker of a life's span.

At the following communal evening meal, after the food trays were cleared away, Lana's closest friends and family sang a song, long and lovely. It was the first musical offering after the meal, in which Lana's life was recounted, her investment into the community applauded, and her love for all was recognized.

Bendota told March that her family will bury her body tomorrow in the ground. "There is a high hill nearby that is the ancestral burial grounds," Bendota said, "Look at the leaves on the trees. One by one they fall after they have served the tree for their prescribed length of time. They fall when their assignment is completed, not all at once, and eventually, go into the ground again. Nature is patient, and everything gets accomplished. Although Omeda dwells in unapproachable light and in holiness that is beyond our limited ability to comprehend, He regards every person equally. Every leaf is celebrated, just as every person is, for his or her time here among us. Now Lana is living in the spirit in the presence of Omeda, and she will be with Him forever. All people go to Osoto-ban-talia-da and their bodies go into the ground, like the leaf."

March asked further, "I see tears among her friends and relatives. Is there sadness that she has gone to be with Omeda?"

Bendota explained, "They are not sad that she is with Omeda, but she will be missed. This is the sadness of a sister, a son, a daughter, or a close friend who received love and help from Lana, no longer with us. Of course, we miss her smiling face here, even though she is now bathed in glorious and uninterrupted Presence. There is joy for that."

March had to ask, "Is there another place to go rather than Osoto-ban-talia-da when one's life is over?"

The puzzled look on Bendota's face registered incomprehension of March's heaven or hell question. The thought that there would be any other destination after this life simply did not compute. "Where else would you go?" was written in his wrinkled forehead and parted lips. So March did not pursue it or try to explain one of the most troubling theological considerations of his previous world.

During the meal, Maela did teach Anj the eight names of the stations of the Twin Stars, which helped Anj know that there were about ten years between each one. Eager to test her new knowledge, she decided she would ask Saala at what station of the Twin Stars she was born.

Saala was the first older woman that Anj had met here. On that day Omeda had imparted to Anj a deep love for the elder lady, and from then on, she had been regularly sitting at the new arrivals' table for the morning and evening gatherings. At first, the two could only politely exchange smiles, but, as Anj gained fluency in the language, the relationship had deepened. Recognizing wisdom, Anj had developed great respect and grew in the depth of her love for this pillar of the community. Long before they were able to talk, she could tell that Saala wanted to reach out to her. She would hold Anj's hands and lock eyes with the new girl and speak. Anj could not tell if she was praying, prophesying, or imparting wisdom to her, but she felt her love and the depth of her life understanding, even without the help of language.

As it turned out, Anj found out that sometimes she was praying for Anj, sometimes prophesying, and sometimes giving her wisdom about life on ΔT with Omeda and His people. Saala had such depth in the spirit that Anj received almost as much spirit-to-spirit as she would have through language. Now, however, they could converse, and Saala was a fountain, a constant flow of pure, clear-eyed life for the young new arrivals.

That morning, with her new knowledge of the stations of the Twin Stars, Anj asked Saala when she was born. Saala gave the name 'Sandi,' which meant the station that was two stations before the present one, which would have made her only twenty years old. Confused, Anj said, "I certainly thought you were older than that."

Saala recognized the miss-communication and corrected it, saying, "I was born on the previous passage through Sandi, not the most recent one."

Anj said, "Then you have lived longer than a lifetime. Why did you not go to be with Omeda twenty years ago as your husband did, and, in fact, as most people would have?"

She gave a patient smile and said, "How blessed I have been. I am happy and it is well with me. I am a fruitful vine. As long as Omeda wants me to bear fruit here, I will do so. He has all my love, all my heart, all my soul; He has it all. I am also happy that I am still here at this time to be friends with you, the people from another star."

Anj's eyes widened. "Wow. That is a wonderful gift from Omeda to me. You have been a very important person in our lives here."

She was remembering when Saala had taken her hands after breakfast one morning recently and held her with her eyes the way she always did when she had something important to impart, and said, "I see that you will soon have children. You have been concerned that you do not know how to bring up children in this world, but your children will be born into this world, not in your past world. Omeda will make them to be fully Similia." Anj's eyes were filling with tears by this time. She had nursed a hope that her children would somehow be born free from the inheritance of Adam's disobedience. ΔT knows no other kind of children. What if her children were to be born with a fallen nature? These words from Saala relieved her of that terror. Immediately her concern shifted to how much she needed to know about what is involved in raising ΔT children. What do parents do who don't have to train children not to be selfish, not to tell lies, and not to hit people?

"How do parents bring up children here?" she asked. "I have no idea where to start."

Saala said, "Similia parents exalt the name of Omeda. They teach that name to their children. Although He is invisible and mysterious, the name itself is concrete enough to be the foundation for everything, even for a child. Worship the name; praise the name; give thanks to Him by name. Call on the name for provision, protection, wisdom, and strength. Children will begin to recognize His name in all they see and experience.

"His name is recognized as the One who possesses immortality and lives in such brilliant illumination that He is not physically approachable. Awe attends the recognition that such a One approaches mortal man with deep love and care. Who are we that such a One would take thought of us? It is a marvelous influence in our very existence that He does, and children can grow into an understanding of all of that, as they see your own awe of Him.

"He only is seen, touched, spoken to, spirit to spirit. Such experiences are recognized here as the most real and eternal, above everything; better than eating, better than making music, better than dawn on a frosty morning, better than all of life, and children can come to understand that early.

"Even little children and infants may experience Him spirit to spirit. Children are helped by their parents to know how to call on that name and move out of the confines of the mortal body, awakening the immortal soul to the spirit of Omeda. Children learn this delight very early. They find strength in Him. He becomes the fountain of their love, their perseverance in difficulty, their patience in waiting, in learning, and in growing."

Anj felt overloaded with too much instruction and asked, "Have you ever written this down in one place for all of us to learn from?"

"It was written many lifetimes ago by the forefathers," Saala said, "You will learn to read those writings, and you will receive so much other wisdom for your life here. You will raise a fine family here. In your children we will all see Omeda as the fountain of their joy. Happy fun-loving, peaceful children grace every part of life, as you know, here in Lendkon. Your children will be among them. Kind gentle parents who have been living in the flow of Omeda's stream inscribe that pattern on the minds and hearts of their children. They know no other influence."

"No other influence," Anj repeated. "Omeda has this amazing capability that I am beginning to recognize. He is able to intrude upon the simplest of us and exercise His powerful influence to bring us into harmony with who He is. We become increasingly like Him, not because we are trying hard, but because of the influential power that He has. We can begin to conform to His image. And you are saying that it begins in infancy, in childhood. You are saying that Moms and Dads, by being as much under that influence as possible, are able to bring it to the children."

"Yes," Saala agreed, "and we call that capability of His, 'mesonna.' That is the word for His general and generous influence. It is given freely to all, without anyone being able to earn more of that influence than others. Sometimes people ask for His mesonna because their souls long for Omeda, long to find and receive from Him, and sometimes He gives mesonna to those who were unsuspecting. He surprises those who did not know that they even needed His influence, and that invisible but unmistakable influence of Omeda intrudes upon them and changes how they understand everything."

"We need mesonna don't we?" Feeling like she was beginning to understand it, Anj asked. "Omeda's mesonna makes it possible for us to become what He intended for us to be?"

"Without mesonna, conformity to the image of Omeda would be entirely dependent upon each individual's ability to seek or to understand Him, but mesonna can make Lalo as marvelously full of the character of Omeda as Makkana is."

Something suddenly crystallized in Anj's mind, and the thought came to her, "This is grace! 'Mesonna' means grace. I can hardly wait to tell March. ΔT and the Similia are dependent upon grace. I am dependent upon mesonna to grow into the likeness of Omeda, and it is happening! That's the best part. I see it happening to me by grace."

That night when she had March's undivided attention, she excitedly told him of her discovery of the word 'mesonna.' She explained what Saala had said about this aspect of Omeda, and then proposed, "I think that it is the same as 'grace.' It is not earned; it is available to all; it is part of His character; it is not a human characteristic, and it lifts us out of our limited existence into the freedom of holiness. It is Omeda's ability to impart Himself to us."

"Wow," March was awed. "That is such an interesting discovery. Saala's explanation of it also lifts grace to a more comprehensive place in the work of God than just His being nice to us even when we don't deserve it. 'Mesonna;' I like it. I see it now every day in my life, irresistibly lifting me to a higher plane, a greater generosity, fuller freedom, and more comfortable confidence in Omeda's abundance."

March lifted his hands high, reverentially recognizing the Holy, "Thank You Omeda for unfolding this truth for us today. I worship You for Your mesonna. I don't mind saying, I need You. I welcome You with all Your generosity by mesonna. We were brought here by Your mesonna. By a mysterious act of mesonna, we chose a landing place just a handful of miles from Lendkon. That was a miracle, a complete gift."

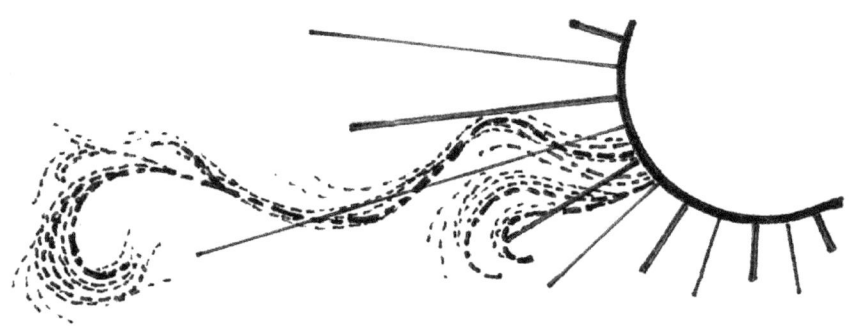

Chapter Twenty-Eight

One afternoon when Maela and Anj were working together setting up shelves in a food-garner, Anj asked about a painting she had seen many times in one of the major hallways. It showed a group of three men and two women, carrying bags much larger than the usual pouch over one shoulder. They were in a desert-looking area, very barren with no trees. They looked exhausted but focused, determined, on some kind of mission.

Maela explained, "This painting is a story from our history many lifetimes ago. It tells about a group of explorers who were led out from Lendkon by Omeda and sent on an assignment. They departed not knowing if they would return or be led to settle somewhere new. Omeda did not tell them what they were looking for; they only knew that He was sending them, and they trusted that He would provide for them. They were all young, strong, and single. There was a good deal of excitement about it in the village, and they were sent out with gifts of food, blankets, clothing, and new sandals for when theirs wore out. There were tears when they left because friends and family did not know if they would ever see them again. They departed on 'Champa-ana,' when the brighter Twin Star is one station to the left of fully right, and they did not return for so long that many assumed that they had found another place to live and would never be seen again. Seers however kept predicting that they would return, and families prayed to see their sons and daughters again."

Anj asked, "How long were they gone?"

Maela continued, "After two full stations of the Twin Stars had passed, on 'Champa-o,' they walked back into the village."

Anj figured that was about twenty years, and she said, "That's amazing. What a long journey!"

"The men and women of the expedition had remained celibate the whole time," Maela explained, "for the sake of the mission. They knew that they would not be able to continue if they had children to take care of. They are highly honored in the history of Lendkon for their sacrifices on behalf of everyone at home who would benefit from their discoveries."

"What did they discover?" Anj asked.

"Very many things," Maela praised. "Traveling northeast, they traveled to the end of our sea, then turned west. They discovered that the climate in the far north was much colder at night and cooler all day. There were none of the fruit trees there that we have. The sun was much lower in the sky all the time. Coming back south on the other side of the sea, they were surprised to discover two other communities similar to Lendkon and enjoyed the hospitality and generosity of those other communities. All spoke the same language and lived in huge caverns underneath the cliffs that Omeda had provided for them just as here in Lendkon. In the vicinity of each village, the explorers observed that the forests were filled with huge fruit trees that produced constantly. Because the Lendkon explorers had seen much sparse forest and few fruit-bearing trees in much of the world, they concluded that Omeda chose to bless the places of habitation of His people."

Anj wondered, "Where did the people of those other two villages come from?"

Maela said, "People from the other communities had recorded in their histories that it was a group of people from Lendkon who first established residence in their caverns. Omeda had sent them out in a manner similar to the explorers in the painting. Lendkon's history only had recorded other explorers going out, but since they did not return, it was not known that they had established new villages across the sea."

"Where did the explorers go next?"

The thrill of history was beginning to animate Maela as she warmed to the story. "This amazing team of explorers then walked further west, climbing through high snowy mountains. They survived the dangers of wind, blowing flakes of ice, and walked across rivers completely solid with ice. Descending the other side of the peaks, they discovered another sea. Following the coast of that sea to the south, they came into a dry and barren land, unimaginable to our people, as they recounted their journey. That painting shows how desolate it was. Crossing that wasteland, they discovered other seas and several other communities on the shores of the seas, all having their origins from Lendkon. Finally, they returned, bringing detailed descriptions of all they had seen, and history not previously known, of other communities of Similia. The picture was painted by one of the travelers to illustrate the extreme conditions in other parts of our world, reminding everyone to give thanks to Omeda for all He has provided for us in this place."

"So all this is written down somewhere?" Anj asked.

"It is all in the writings of the ancients. I will ask Makkana to take you to see them. I see that you are very interested to learn how to read."

Anj marveled, "This is amazing that the world has been so explored, and so much history has been uncovered. Similia have been quite busy on this planet"

It was on the next morning that Makkana asked March and Anj if they would like to visit the room where the ancient writings were kept. Makkana saw that they were serious about learning to read Similia's writing. He was thrilled that people from another star and another culture would have an interest in the poetic, historic, and wisdom literature of his world. Both of them were eager to have a look at this repository that they had been hearing about, and from which they had heard so many excerpts during the community gatherings.

Not far back in a major hallway, Makkana opened a door they had passed many times, not knowing that it held this library. March thought it must have been one of the earliest rooms to be carved out in the village. It was not a huge room, but the walls were lined with tall narrow shelves. Each shelf had a stack of papers stored carefully. There was the faint smell of straw or dry grass in the room, and it made March think of a library. There was a low table where one could sit and read late into the long nights if so inclined.

"Those must be the books," Anj wondered out loud.

"Not books like I expected, " March observed. "They are not bound together, but loose pages. I kind of thought they might be in scrolls, but they are just stacks. They must handle them very carefully. Some of these must be incredibly old."

"Yes," Makkana said. "The oldest was written almost one hundred lifetimes ago by our earliest forefather, Dama. Of course, we do make copies when the original becomes damaged or faded."

"Dama?" March was amused and fascinated. "Hmm, 'Adam' on earth and 'Dama' here; how interesting. And almost eight thousand years ago. Wow. More ΔT mysteries. There must be dozens of books here; assuming each stack of paper is a book. Look at them; some of them are almost ten centimeters thick."

Makkana said, "Some of the collections read like music, rhythmic to read aloud, expressing the inspired beauty of knowing Omeda. Some of them are histories, like the story of the extensive exploration of the world so long ago which is filled with recognition of Omeda's goodness and full of thanks for the obvious ways that He has reached down to touch the areas we live with rains from heaven and fruitful harvests, satisfying our hearts with food and gladness.

"One of the books, this one here," Makkana said, reaching up and taking down one of the compilations, "deals with a critical time when flares from our sun scorched the orchards and fields severely, causing a food shortage and rationing. It was a time of severe hunger, and not everyone kept giving thanks and worshiping the way they did during times of plenty, but sat sadly during public worship, saying they would be able to worship again when they had something to give thanks for. During that time, one of the seers had a personal encounter with Omeda, receiving inspired words of wisdom and encouragement to be written for future generations. It is this very composition. It has been read and recited through the lifetimes ever since, inspiring undivided worship and trust of Omeda, regardless of circumstances."

Makkana gently put it on the table and seated himself, motioning to the visitors to sit too, while he leafed through to find the portion he wanted. Aloud from that passage, with his clear speaking voice, he read, "Though the pear does not blossom, and the grain field is empty, though the leaves of the trees dry up and fall from the branches, and even the deer in the forest languish in hunger, I will still be glad in Omeda and declare the goodness of the Lord, for Omeda is my strength, the encouragement of my heart, and my joy."

Recognizing a clear similarity to a passage in Habakkuk, March and Anj leaned in to see more closely this inspired writing. Anj asked with her hands held out, if she could touch the book. Makkana slid it across the table to her and turned it right side up, putting his finger on the starting place.

"That is inspiring!" March spoke reverently, "just to see it. Can you make heads or tails of it, dove?"

"It looks sort of like Arabic or something. No, of course not. But I am going to learn. I am going back to first grade if I have to!"

Makkana stood and went over to another shelf, "One of Maela's favorites is this one," placing a hand gently on a thick sheaf of pages. "It is what the orchard keepers study. It was written by several of the keepers of the trees many lifetimes ago, people who developed such a personal love for the fruit trees as an extension of Omeda Himself, as an expression of His love, that they were inspired to write out of their joy over what Omeda has provided for man, a beautiful thing. Listed here are all the exquisite stages of blossoming, fruit development, ripening, picking, and they even wrote about the fruit falling to the ground when there is too much for all the people to eat or store. The fruit goes into the ground to come back as food another time."

"What an amazing treasure is kept here," Anj marveled. "Does everyone come here to read?"

"Most people depend on the recitations of selections from these writings that are given in the communal gatherings and do not come to read for themselves, but people like Saala, Bendota, and Maela, they do come and drink deeply of the inspired work of the ancients."

"May I be one of those people?" Anj inquired with hope.

"Of course you may," Makkana encouraged with his beaming fatherly face. "They are provided to us by Omeda, and all who desire to draw near to Him may read. One of the parents who have children learning to read will be happy to instruct you along with their children. In fact, Lalo's mother would be good. She has Lalo's little brother and sister to teach, and she herself is an avid reader, coming here often for a few quiet hours of inspiration."

At the very next evening gathering, Anj was over at Lalo's family table eagerly talking to Lenata, Lalo's mother, who was not only willing but thrilled to be the one who could teach the people from another star to read, people her son had found out in the forest. Instruction began the next morning in their home, Anj and March seated with the two children.

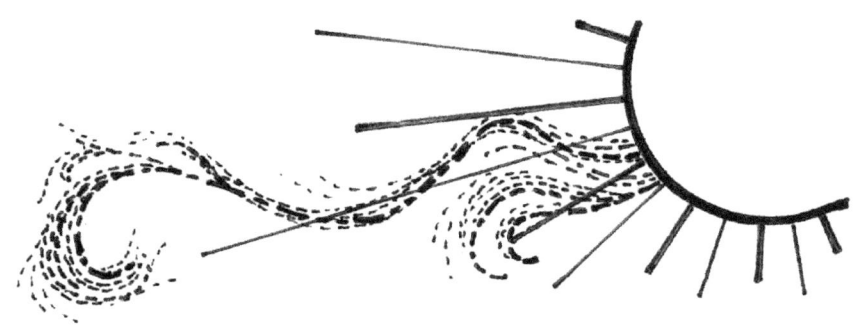

Chapter Twenty-Nine: Launch Central

"Hello, Close Team, Anj here with the weekly report from regions beyond.

"There is a written form of the language of Lendkon, but the primary way in which the knowledge and wisdom of Omeda are continued from generation to generation is by oral tradition. I have heard much of that wisdom recited from both the elders and the young people who memorize long passages that have been taken from the ancient writings. Makkana took us last week to see the library of those very old works for the first time.

"I am so interested to know how the history progressed all these generations without that central problem that fills the Bible, namely the problem of man's rebellion, disobedience, and the worshiping of all kinds of things that are not God. The Bible's story is about God's time-line to restore mankind to a reverent relationship with Himself. Here, the entire history has a different theme. Here the starting place is an unbroken relationship with the God of heaven, and the direction in which people move throughout a lifetime is into intimacy with God. The goal is an ever deeper connection with Him through the revelation of His infinite brilliance and eternal purpose.

"I want to read the wisdom of a culture living in the purity of a flawless connection with God. Perhaps that is one of the reasons God has sent us here, to give hope to our previous world, to give an account to you on Earth of the full riches that God originally intended for mankind, and that I believe Jesus came to make possible on Earth, even now, to those who will believe.

"The guiding framework upon which human life is built here is the unlimited opportunity to apprehend all of the life that exists within Omeda's love. We just move into that love. He is eager to reveal the ideal of life to anyone who seeks Him.

"There is no equivalent of a Sabbath in this society. Omeda is deeply worshiped, acknowledged, and thanked at dawn and in the evening every day. There are none who excuse themselves from listening to the evening speeches or skip out of the dawn times of worship and prayer. Everyone is truly present, drinking in the spiritual nourishment of being together, and immersed in the words and the music. Love is palpable in the experience. For the first months I was in those meetings, I could not understand much of what was being said, but it was still like warm liquid love being poured into my inner being. March and I easily began to melt into it every time, looking forward to the next one, feeling washed and purified and whole.

"There is no vocabulary here for drought. It is an unheard-of concept. Every night it rains softly as the intense heat of the day encounters the cooling night air. Rain irrigates the fields and orchards. I think the warm rain also minimizes the effect of the freezing frost that comes late in the long night. Crops grow, ripen and are harvested; then they plant again and repeat the cycle. There are no weeds, blight, or devouring bugs. It is a farmer's dream world, dream climate.

"It is all Omeda; it is all His creative wonder and provision in a place that is suited for mankind. Much thanks and appreciation goes up to Him daily from the mouths of these people for that favor. This huge cave which is our village compensates perfectly for the blazing heat of long days and freezing cold of twenty-eight-hour darkness. Furthermore, protection from the danger of stellar flares is provided here by the cave and by our early-warning people constantly on duty.

Because of their faithfulness and the shelter of our village, we can all survive even severe flares.

"I have learned to focus on all that Omeda has provided rather than on what He has not done, or what I would do differently if I were Omeda. If I were to ask, "Why did You create a world that is periodically subjected to stellar flares?" that would be to focus on what I think He has not done. It is to raise that question from the skeptics of Earth, "where is your God?" It is the voice of doubt and fear which comes from distrust. ΔT people trust in Omeda with all their hearts implicitly. The notions of "I have a better idea," or "I would do it differently if I were Omeda," are not here.

"I have often thought surely there must be some here who do not have that kind of trust in Omeda; those who live in fear or even anger that He would subject them to occasional searing stellar winds, but I have not found such persons. None of the speeches offered in the evenings, nor any of the recitations in the mornings include directives aimed to correct or influence any such doubters. No preaching seems to be targeting the faint-hearted or dragging the slothful up from complacency.

"My mind is being renewed as Omeda reveals to me daily His character, His nature, and the beauty He included in the creation of mankind as residents in His universe. His beauty is incredible, colors are beyond imagining, tastes are transporting in delight. The simplest experiences here, even watching water run over my hand in the river, are wonderful exchanges between me and God and His majesty. Meeting with people here, talking, holding hands, and laughing together, carry such delight that it becomes clear that what God intended for us is so much richer and laden with glory than I could ever have imagined back home. On Earth, we have been robbed.

"I realize that much of what I send in these reports makes the most sense to the believers among my readers. This ΔT community is a world of people who believe in Omeda; a world blessed by flawless following of the invisible God who made us all. There is nothing of more importance that we are involved in here to write home about, so forgive me Browning, Duke, and others; I respect you and value our history together of hearing one another out. Granted, this gets one-sided in these reports. I eagerly look forward to hearing from you all eventually. I can only imagine what you will have to say about what we have found here.

"Even though life here is so full of goodness for me, for each person here, life is not about me. Omeda is not here for me, but I am here for Him. That Psalm we all like so much, "He guides me in paths of righteousness for His name's sake," really does mean that it is all about Him. Being one who lives in harmony with Omeda is not about making me comfortable. It is always primarily about Him because He is so spectacular; He is so worthy of all our attention, all our adoration. Alignment with Omeda is the best possible thing for me, but my benefit is not the end goal. The end, the grand splendor of it, is that we get to be a part of who He is in the universe. We partner with what He is all about. If He is a diamond, we get to be one glittering facet of that spectacular glory. His light shines through us flawlessly and breaks into colors and unimaginable demonstrations of dancing, sparkling brilliance.

"Something of that must have been the joy of Jesus when He was on the cross. He saw what He was winning back for us. He saw this. He saw what I have described here about life's loveliness on ΔT as what He was reclaiming for His people on Earth. The principle of the spirit of life in Him was setting us free; free indeed. I see so much more clearly now, what was very unclear before. I had no idea how truly spectacular my inheritance was, as a believer in Jesus.

I think now that He had all of this for me on Earth too. I would not necessarily have had to come here, but I wasn't able to make it real on Earth because of all the static. It is unfortunate that coming to a realistic understanding of full reconciliation with God has only been done on Earth by a few. Through Jesus, darkness has been sent running, and the light of the knowledge of the glory of God is seen in the face of Jesus. That which Jesus has won for us is so deep and rich that it is almost impossible to imagine from Earth's perspective. For me, I had to see it from here. On Earth it must be seen from the perspective of heaven, which is available, seated with Jesus in the heavenlies. I pray for the fullness of Jesus' scandalously generous work to become known on Earth.

"With the most genuine love and respect for you all, Anj."

Browning had brought Duke over to read Anj's report because he wanted to talk with him specifically about it. "So, Duke, Does the word 'Utopia' come to your mind when you read Anj's reports from Deep ΔT?" Browning had been fascinated at times in his youth by the idea of Utopia, but adulthood, and his repeated discoveries of how fallible humanity can be, had fairly well quenched any on-going interest. How could he be interested in a concept that had no chance whatsoever of being fulfilled?

Duke checked his boss's demeanor to see if he was being funny. It wouldn't be unlike him to use a preposterous notion to spark a discussion. Seeing that it was a serious question, he spoke up, saying, "Frank, Utopia was a concept that I realized was just a dream a long time ago. It's a nice dream, but it won't work."

"I know Duke, but the way Anj and March describe their new culture, it sounds like everything there works the way it is theoretically supposed to work in a Utopia. Sure, it is an unrealistic idea here, maybe even a dangerous thing to attempt here, but what is not perfect about ΔT?"

Like the rest of the close team, Duke had given much thought to what March and Anj were reporting and had an immediate answer. "Stellar flares that fry the planet several times a year might be a place to start," there was a hardened edge to what Duke was saying. "How can that be perfect? And how is the difficulty of flares in the environment congruent with the implication that all of the beneficent Utopian qualities of Anj's world are the blessings of their God?"

Ignoring the challenging tone from his friend, Browning pressed on, "But everything else works perfectly; the peace in which they live and work together, the sharing of space and responsibilities, the way they raise their kids, the complete lack of violence or even anger among themselves; it's all astounding to me. I am beginning to be convinced of the reality of it. Anj and March are *really* happy. They don't talk about anything else. And they do accredit all of it to their Omeda God."

Duke was catching the seriousness of Browning's thinking about the possibilities of the new planet's existing culture. "You're quite right. They are smitten by their new home, no mistake. Are you beginning to believe that *God* is responsible for the good aspects of it?"

"Duke, I worked with March and Anj for almost six years, training for this mission, and they were always clear about their belief that, if this was going to work, they had to have help from God. They knew that, and they believed He would help. I hoped they were right, even though I had none of the confidence that they had, or faith, as they would call it. I just figured, if it worked for them, it couldn't hurt. Then within this last year, we started getting all these messages from ΔT reporting about God there: God this, and God that. But what they report, in terms of human society that is existent there, is so remarkably distinct from anything on Earth that I am trying to attribute it to something. Then that flare thing, burning the tops of the trees, melting the anemometer, but not touching anything else, and they say it is all because they prayed to God and had faith. My faith in no-god is beginning to weaken, I have to confess."

A little shaken by this sudden transparency from Browning, Duke decided it was not time to try to reinforce his friend's flagging convictions. In fact, he didn't think that Frank Browning was asking him to bring him back to center. So he said, "Frank, we all have to figure out for ourselves what we think about those people on ΔT and their God. And we all have to give March and Anj some time to adjust to where they want to settle in as cross-cultural implants in this unique society that they have discovered, and with which they have become so enamored. Let's give them and ourselves some time."

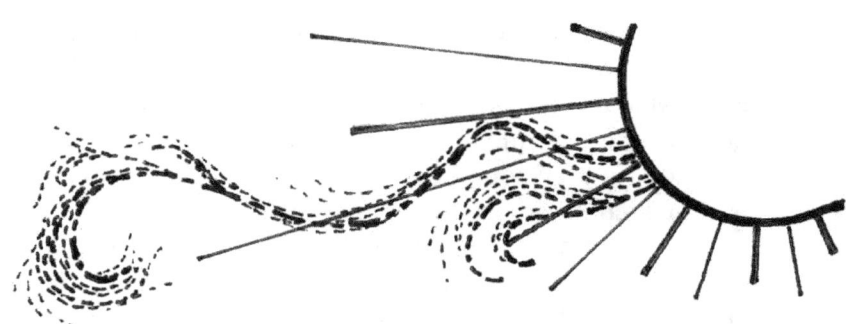

Chapter Thirty

Anj found learning to read to be the occasion for a lot of laughter, mostly because Lenata, her teacher, had such a joyful attitude. Lenata teased March because he did not seem to have the same eagerness about the alphabet, and accused him of being like Lalo's little brother, about six, who also was not an eager learner. March retaliated with a threat of teaching the little guy how to fly paper airplanes like the one they flew here on. Lenata pleaded with him not to do that, knowing it would be the end of learning phonetics for the boy for a long time.

ΔT phonetic rules were consistent, unlike in English. Once a symbol was memorized, it always indicated the same sound. "Thank You Omeda," was Anj's exclamation often as she worked, "thank You for making a written word that is easy to learn." The symbols themselves, although more complex than the English alphabet, were not as difficult to form on paper as Chinese characters, nor as numerous.

After a few weeks, she began to read simple children's stories, borrowed from Lenata's little son and daughter, and her eagerness to be able to delve into the writings in that library only increased. One evening at the sunset meal, she asked Bendota, who was something of a scholar in his own right, if he could recount to her a summary of history from the time of creation until now, from what he had read in the old writings.

"Oh Mama Anch," - she liked it when they called her that. Lalo had started it. All the women over about twenty-five were called 'Mama' because most of them are mothers, and it recognized their valued place in the community. - "Mama Anch, our history is very complicated," he said. "There is so much that has happened in almost a hundred lifetimes, but I will be happy to assist you." After dinner and the time of worship and prayer, He seated himself comfortably and invited some of the youngsters from nearby tables to also come and listen to the story. Anj and March sat right across from him in the circle of rapt listeners. The seven children who joined the group were thrilled to hear the account, although Anj knew they were already familiar with these stories.

Bendota began, "You know that in the beginning, Omeda created everything, using nothing but His spoken words. He started with speaking light into being, giving us night and day, the sun by day and the stars by night, even at night, small lights. Then He spoke again, and there was water; He spoke and there was land, and He spoke all the plants into being. Everything began to grow because it had life. He next created all the creatures of the sea and the land. Omeda finally said 'We will now make mankind,' and He took some of the clay He had made, and breathed into it. He made them male and female, and said, 'these shall be like Me, with My character, My creativity, My appreciation of beauty, and with My love.' Into them He breathed His own Spirit. Omeda Himself was life and the life was the light inside of every person. We are children, March and Anch, children of Omeda, and full of light. Do you understand?"

"Yes, Bendota, we have been made in the very likeness of Omeda; I understand your story very well so far. Please continue."

"Omeda said that the plants and seeds that grew were given for food for men and the creatures of the mountains and valleys. Along with all of the fruit trees, He had planted two very special trees, as you know, the Tree of Life and the Tree of the

Knowledge of Good and Evil. We are to eat joyfully from the Tree of Life and all of the other trees, but we are not to eat from the other beautiful tree. He said that life as we have known it would cease if we ate from that tree. Doing so would mean that we would not be able to live with him for Osoto-ban-talia-da when our life here is finished. To this day, no one has ever eaten from that tree, even though it is very desirable. Every person has the destiny to go to Osoto-ban-talia-da with Him. Being with Omeda is everything of value to us. Not one person has been able to believe that something could be gained by ignoring this one instruction that He gave, and to lose being with Him forever. Being apart from Omeda would be darkness I think. I cannot form a picture in my mind of how that could be, Anch."

"I can understand, from your experience of life, how beyond imagining the total absence of Omeda would be for you. It would be emptiness; empty inside and outside."

"Yes, Anch, Omeda is love, and love is joy. For me, every day that happens; it is my joy to know His love for me, and His love for me makes me want to love Him back, and then I feel His joy that I love Him. It is a circle, and every time I go around, it keeps on getting deeper and more enthralling. Something about love is joy, and something of joy is love. Life is not life without love and joy. I cannot imagine what it would be."

Bendota had a pained expression as he considered this possibility. Anj and March had never seen him look so troubled, as he tried to conceptualize what existence would be without Omeda, and without love, or without joy.

Shaking off the thought of that impossibility, he continued, "I will go on with the story for you, March and Anch, and for you, young ones. Many sons and daughters were born to the first man and woman, Dama and Ojenneh, the first husband and wife. All of these children were born into the light and the name of Omeda, loved by Him and experiencing His invisible Presence. Dama and Ojenneh taught the children the single instruction that Omeda had given, about the tree that was prohibited. As an adult person, one of the older sons, halfway into his lifetime, began to question Ojenneh about the Tree of the Knowledge of Good and Evil. He was drawn to its beauty and to its wonderful-looking fruit. He could almost taste it, it was so beautiful. It must be good. He asked his mother, 'What is 'evil?' Maybe it is a desirable thing that Omeda is not letting us have.' Ojenneh told him that we were given a choice: did we want to live obeying and loving Omeda forever, or try another way, by disobeying that one instruction. It was very good, I think, the way she saw it.

"This young man persisted in his questioning, and when his father, Dama, told him the same things that Ojenneh had told him, he began to accuse Dama of being in collusion with Omeda, keeping a secret about what it was that Omeda was not allowing him to have. He announced one morning that he was going up on the hill to eat the fruit from the prohibited Tree. All of his family, brothers, sisters, and Dama and Ojenneh gathered to pray, to re-confirm their deep love for Omeda, and to seek His help. Praying all together, they agreed in prayer that staying with Him forever was all they wanted, that they trusted Him and did not believe that He was keeping a secret delight from them in the Tree of the Knowledge of Good and Evil.

"No one else was at the Tree when this son went there, intending to eat its fruit, but everyone was praying with one voice. Omeda met the young man there. He came in spotless perfection and love, without accusation or command. In their conversation, it became clear to the young man that Omeda lived and existed as incomparable love for him, and that he was failing to respond as the devotee that he was created to be. He was being stingy with his love, and not trusting. He had a choice to respond to the love of Omeda because Omeda offered him love first. He also recognized, through the compassionate words of Omeda, that the ugly thing that had begun to grow inside of him was his responsibility, and he became frightened that if he allowed it to remain, it would wreak destruction for himself and his entire family because it would drive him to take the fruit and lose love and life forever.

"He left the orchard without taking any fruit, quite shaken and alarmed at what he had almost done. He never went back to that Tree, but, of the Tree of Life, he was able to eat with the rest of the family for his lifetime. He eventually wrote the second great collection of wisdom for us, the first being what Dama wrote about how Omeda created the heavens and this beautiful place and His people. What the young man wrote is the answer for anyone who has questions about the prohibited Tree. The young man's name is not known. He did not want his name to be important to anyone, only the name of Omeda, and only the love and trustworthiness of Omeda.

"This unknown son of Dama wrote, 'I recognized that it was possible for me to become a person who was not in right relationship with Omeda. I *could* persist in that direction; it was not at all impossible to do so, and it would put me in opposition to Him. He had given me the opportunity to make that choice. And yet it is established that splendor and majesty are only before Him; strength and joy are in His place. If I chose my own ways in spite of all that He is to us, I would have my own finite small life, but no longer the life that Omeda makes available to me. I have only a moment, one lifetime in all of eternity, to have His favor here, and beyond that is an incomparable eternity in Omeda's Presence.'"

March and Anj were impressed with the eloquence of this account. Anj said, "I am even more motivated to learn how to read now because I want to read the book of the nameless son of Dama and Ojenneh. There must be pages of an essential message to humanity in it."

Bendota interrupted his story at that point because it was time for the children to get to bed. The young story-teller said he had a great deal more to tell. March and Anj assured him that they were very interested to hear more whenever he could continue the narrative, and they had much on their hearts from his story to be thankful for.

Having lunch together under the fruit trees the next day, March brought up his interest in Bendota's story. "Wasn't it striking how similar the story of creation here is to Earth's creation story?"

"More than similar," Anj agreed, "I thought it was basically identical. And yes, it was quite fascinating; same Creator God. The departure comes with the story of the son who went up to pick the fruit but was met by Omeda. There was no serpent whispering in his ear."

"Maybe one of the other children of Ojenneh already crushed his head," March ventured. "Or maybe there just wasn't a serpent here. When you get into those books, you may learn more about the question of the serpent."

"You're not as interested in learning to read as I am?"

March grinned, "If there is an astronomy book, I'll learn to read that. You let me know. You know you will take the lead in this library project. I will always have an interested ear to listen to what you have learned. I very much enjoy what I get from the recitations of others from those books. I will work on learning the writing system with you, just for the usefulness of it, but I am not as committed as you are to the reading of that library."

At the following sunset meal with all of the families, Bendota alerted the children and his adult listeners that he would continue the story tonight. After a sumptuous meal and a sweet time of worship, the children scooted over close to Bendota's side and looked up at him like hungry baby birds. March and Anj, no less enthusiastic, were seated opposite him again in the circle.

Bendota began, "In the third lifetime after Dama and Ojenneh, there was an influential group of young women who began to express their wish to know about the appearance of Omeda since He is invisible. This was, at first, an entirely honorable desire to know Omeda better, but it grew into something else as they began to imagine how He looked and to request permission to paint pictures of Him on the walls. Omeda spoke at that time to the seers and to the elders that this would result in the people worshiping something else entirely, a false image of Omeda, and forgetting the living Omeda who had created them. By that time, these young women were eager to create a statue, a likeness of Omeda from their imaginations, that would attempt to make Him visible. Have you ever heard of such a thing Mama Anch?"

"Oh yes, I certainly have heard of that, Bendota. I agree that it would be a serious problem. What happened?"

"Elders approached this passionate group of young women and asked them what they expected to gain from having an image of Omeda since they already experienced Him continually in the spiritual realm in such a real way. They complained that their problem was precisely that they did *not* experience the presence of Omeda in any tangible way in the spiritual realm or in the visible realm. They wanted to see Him. The spiritual experience of Omeda's voice was not clear to them. Questioning them further, the elders discovered that the parents of these girls had never intentionally taught them how to open their spirits to the very real Presence and the living voice of the Creator.

"Subsequently then, the elders taught the girls how to recognize the Presence and how to listen to the voice of Omeda, which is an easy thing to do. They just hadn't known that it was a normal part of life, as normal as eating and breathing. Once the young girls began to hear from Omeda clearly and learned how much love and favor He had for them, and how strong His love was, the need to see Him disappeared. They had no more desire to know how He looked with their eyes because they saw, felt, and heard Him in their spirits, and they realized that He is beyond capturing in any sort of man-made image.

"These young people had not been instructed in the ways in which anyone may intentionally open the doors of their heart so that Omeda may enter and spend time with them. They had missed out on these most delightful experiences of life, and, as a result, were feeling quite empty. It became clear to the elders that merely bringing children into a place where they were watching adults in public worship and prayer times was sometimes not sufficient to inspire children to begin to do that for themselves. Watching others get lost in the presence of God was not enough for these girls to discover how to find a personal experience of Omeda.

"A third book of wisdom was then written, a collaboration of the elders and two of the leading figures among the girls. It was written as inspiration and instruction on how to open one's spirit to connect with Omeda, how to hear His voice. Parents learn from this book how to assist their children to move into a vital relationship with the Creator. Now we have portions of that book recited almost every day in our morning times of worship, and the elders speak about the intentional ways we all need to remember to find Omeda, not only in the public times of worship, but also every day all day, for that is where our love, our joy, our strength, and life itself comes from."

One of the children, a bright-eyed boy of about seven, piped up, "I know how to open the doors of my heart so that Omeda can come in. Daddy told me how."

"And just how do you go about that young man?" Bendota asked.

"I know about two doors in my heart so far," he began. "When the watchers tell us a flare is coming, instead of imagining what it would be like to get burned up, I imagine myself being cradled in the great big strong arms of Omeda, and I let myself feel how that would be. Daddy says that is my 'safety door.' I can step through it into the safety of His arms. The other door I know about is the door of pretty things. When I see colorful flowers or an amazing sky with round white clouds, I let myself feel Omeda forming those pretty things in His hands, just to bring beauty to our lives. That becomes a big love inside of me for Him. Daddy calls that my 'beauty door,' and I can step through it into His love any time.'"

"How do you think Omeda looks?" Bendota asked.

"Oh, He is too many different things to be seen. Sometimes I see colors; sometimes I hear music or a sound like a voice. Other times, the silence takes over everything with holy stillness."

Bendota looked up from the child's face and smiled his enthusiastic approval. Anj and March shook their heads in wonder. Anj put both hands on her expanding abdomen and quietly prayed for help to do that for her children.

Bendota took a long deep breath, looking around at the children in the group, and asked them if they wanted another story, which of course they all did, and called out to him for more. He met their hopes with a long account of the explorers who went out for a quarter of a lifetime trekking far across their world. He told of the perils in unknown lands and taught about the history and geography that had never been known before those explorers made their journey. Even though the children had no doubt heard this story many times, Bendota was able to bring new details of the seas and the difficulties of the mountains and the deserts from his own reading of the book that the explorers wrote. And children never tire of a great adventure.

Bendota told about an interesting discovery that the explorers made. "Lendkon is the only village that has the Tree of the Knowledge of Good and Evil. The explorers asked to see the Trees in each community, and they were always taken to the Tree of Life, but no other village had that Tree of the Knowledge of Good and Evil. Other communities knew very well that such a Tree was created by Omeda, and that its fruit was not to be eaten. They understood the importance of the decision made by our forefathers to obey Omeda and never eat from that tree. They have the *story* of that Tree; they do not actually have such a Tree.

"Whenever there was a group of people who set out from Lendkon to establish a new community, the pioneers would take a cutting of the Tree of Life with them and plant it in the center of the orchard when they found their new home. That Tree not only ensures physical and spiritual health throughout their lives, but also stands as the representation of Omeda's goodness, and is the foundation for teaching about who He is and what His plan is for eternity. The importance of the story of the other Tree is carried on from generation to generation. These two Trees are Omeda's unmistakable offer to give His life to all who want it enough to refuse any other choice. Omeda wants to give life eternally to those who choose to receive it and accept no other.

"Faithfulness to Omeda is carried on by these stories from the people of Lendkon. The truth has been a bright enough light to inspire every other village to the same life of devotion and the same rewards of His Presence. According to our history, a few people at a time journey occasionally from far-away villages to Lendkon, just to see the other Tree. They have not come, like the unnamed man in the second book of wisdom, who wanted to challenge the goodness of Omeda. They come rather to validate; perhaps they just have to see it and have the experience of choosing obedience to take home to their families. None of them have chosen to take a cutting from that Tree home. I believe that they are thinking there is no use having a tree around that we cannot eat from."

Makkana happened by at the right moment to hear the end of that story, and sitting down with them, joined the group in his magnetically warm way. "I got to talk to the leader of one of those visiting groups many years ago," he said.

"Ooh, what did he say?" the children asked out loud, while the adults looked intently at Makkana to hear more.

"This was interesting. He said that they had no desire to take a cutting from the Tree of the Knowledge of Good and Evil home. Their decision was not because the Tree would be of no use, as Bendota, you have guessed, and not because they were afraid someone would weaken and eat from it, but because their entire journey was one of worship. They came for Omeda, not just to see the other Tree; rather, they came sensing that He had something to teach them by seeing it there. And in seeing the two Trees side by side they indeed were further enlightened to see that

Omeda inspires us to love freely, by our own choice. He values that we grow to understand *loving Him* as the supreme choice of life." Makkana lifted his eyebrows, looking around the circle for comprehension. "There is no other choice we face in life that is of more importance than that: will I love Omeda with all that I am?

"The man from so far away told me that he would take home to his village affirmation to his people, about the very good way they have chosen, what a glorious and courageous way they have taken, and what a delight they are in the eyes of Omeda as His loving children. All of you are His children, and you get to live in that supreme choice too. It is the choice of our forefathers. It is why we have all this," he said extending his arm out and swinging it all around, indicating the home, the lifestyle, and the community.

Once again, it was bedtime for the children, and Makkana's weighty contribution was a lot to ponder. Thus ended the story, so the little ones could go home with their families.

March turned to Anj as the children disappeared into the throng, "What a grand thing mutual love is, and how precious it is to Omeda that we choose that daily; His love for us and our love for Him."

Anj was still lost in her fascination with the story and with what the smiling elder had brought at the end. "Makkana put it well. I think that is what I came to understand when I went back up to look at the Tree, but I could not have explained it like that."

"You are such a thinker," March commented. "I admire that about you and hope you will always share from your heart and mind. I like being challenged by your meditations."

Going to something else on his mind in the moment, he said, "That expedition was this world's equivalent of Marco Polo on Earth. I think he was gone for over twenty years on the Silk Road to China, wasn't he? This small band of walkers wandering over ΔT was phenomenal in what they accomplished. I, for one, am thankful to them for returning with so much knowledge about what is happening on a huge area of the planet. I wonder how far they traveled around the planet?"

Anj said, "I hope the written pages include some maps, or at least enough description so that we can map out their route on our photos of the planet. That will be very interesting."

Later that night, they stayed up studying the symbols of the Lendkon alphabet and practicing writing them. March was a little surprised by now to find that he had more interest and curiosity in learning to read and write than he originally thought he would. Perhaps part of his enjoyment was because he and Anj got to sit close huddled over a page together for hours, and he found her to be even more magically attractive as her pregnancy really began to show. He was overjoyed that this little pioneer family was going to happen. He had had his doubts, given the rigors of hypersleep for six years, even though the medical assessment was that none of the internal organs would suffer damage from sustained hypersleep.

Saala and the other women were encouraging and coaching Anj along in the process of making a baby. In fact, Saala believed she was carrying twins. "Maybe these children will be born already knowing the Lendkon alphabet," he proposed, smiling and putting his hand on her round tummy. She thought that would be a grand development, but was yawning too much to be able to join in much of a fun exchange about it, so they retired a little early.

After a satisfying night's sleep, they rose and lighted the lamp. There was only a glimmer of light from the light shaft, the Twin Stars being on the other side of the sun on this night. By now, they were quite used to rising six or eight hours before the dark eastern horizon began to light up with the dawn. They read one of Lenata's children's books twice just for practice and got ready to join the families for breakfast. March had a personal interest in the morning family gatherings because the portal of the grotto looked to the west, and the sky was still dark so he could observe his favorite constellations sinking slowly to the western horizon, the blackness where the stars winked out.

On this morning, as the black star-strewn sky began to gray and the stars disappeared one at a time, March's attention was divided. In the aftermath of being transported by his worship experience, He had noticed Orion's belt low in the sky, and Orion's shoulders, one of them marked by Betelgeuse, was up higher, almost too high to be seen from his position seated near the mouth of the grotto. March thought that Betelgeuse, still visible against the beginnings of dawn, looked brighter and larger. His astronomer-mind took note, and he remembered the research he had read that indicated a greater likelihood to the probability that it would go supernova. In his fascination, he excused himself from the table as soon as the prayer time was over, while the rest of the table was still deep in conversation over what Bendota had shared that morning.

He stepped out into the darkness away from the light of the grotto to be able to see better. Unmistakably, he could now see that the famous massive star was indeed expanding, perhaps twice the size it had been last time it had been in the sky, four nights ago. Excited, he mapped the star chart out in his mind and realized he was seeing this some years before Earth's astronomers would. But it would still take his message to Earth so long to arrive that he might not be able to give his colleagues on Earth any advance notice of the event. This was, however, a thrilling development. He went back to the mouth of the grotto and signaled to Lalo to come out and join him. He told the lad what he was seeing, and Lalo, also sharing a keen interest in the stars, was quite taken by the sight, agreeing with March that it was bigger than usual.

"Why has the star changed, Mack?"

"Stars do not last forever. Omeda is the only thing in the universe that is eternal. Stars run out of fuel, kind of like when a fire runs out of wood to burn. But when a star comes to the end of its fuel, it is very different. Instead of simply going out, it explodes and gives off a huge ball of light. Lalo, that star is probably going to grow to be bigger than the biggest Twin Star, but it might take a long time to do that. You might be married and have children before it does that."

"How do you know all this?" the boy asked.

"On the planet where I was born, there are people who have been watching stars for twenty lifetimes, and they have written down, as in your ancient writings, things that have happened. From their records, we know what has happened to many stars that have run out of fuel. Most of them become very large and bright for a short time. When they do that, they are called a 'supernova.'"

Lalo's gaze went from the star to March's profile in the dark. "Supaova," he repeated, rather mysteriously. Then he said, "Mach, I could be one in our world who begins to write down the history of stars for Lendkon."

"That is an amazing idea, Lalo! Then future generations will understand when something like this happens again, and they will not question what Omeda is doing."

"Yes, at first when you showed this to me, I felt something strange in my stomach," Lalo spoke quietly, "the way it feels when something big is going to change. But since you have told me what this is, it does not feel that way anymore. You and I can help many people feel better about this when it begins to be noticed."

As they resumed their gaze at the star, March put his hand on the slight boy's shoulder as they both tried to imagine how that bright speck was going to look before long. March's love for the boy was so piercing to him in the moment, he wondered if he could ever love a son of his own as much as he loved this young man.

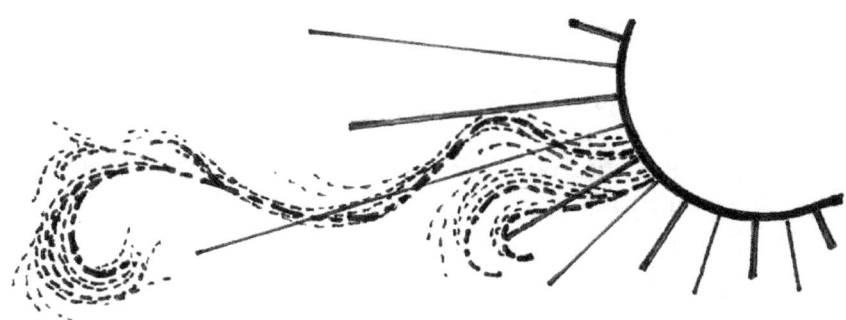

Chapter Thirty-One: Launch Central

"Greetings to Earth from March. Anj is feeling quite pregnant these days, so I will be the one hiking down here to send out your reports until the baby, or babies, are born. Did we tell you yet that one of the elder ladies thinks Anj will have twins? If that is true, our population of Earthlings will instantly double! Needless to say, we are very excited at the prospect of children, and all the more because we get to bring them up on Deep ΔT among the Similia. I trust you have some understanding by now of the significance of that development to us.

"I have some astronomical news for you, literally. I don't think you can see it yet, and probably won't for another three years as I make this report, but we can already see it. What we are seeing is the long-anticipated supernova from Betelgeuse. It is unmistakably expanding. I have hoped all my adult life that it would happen for me to see. Even from such a distance, I have wanted to see all I can of such a nuclear event, and it is happening before my eyes.

"Of course, by the time this message gets to you, so will the light from Betelgeuse. But, as they say, you heard it here first! Our young friend Lalo, about whom you have heard plenty, is very interested to become the first astronomer of Lendkon and wants to make a detailed written record of this star event for future generations. He did not think anyone in their history had kept a record of changes among the stars. That makes sense, I guess, since all their attention is on the stellar flares from their own nearest star. They have kept a record of the frequency and intensity of those flares throughout their written history. Those histories are studied by the up-and-coming young flare watchers whose job it is to provide early warning of a flare to the rest of the community.

"Isn't it interesting that a planet with such perfection in its society, the exemplary Similia people, was also created with this immense and scary danger that frequents its surface periodically? On earth we call hurricanes and tornadoes 'acts of God,' but the debate still rages whether God should get the blame, or they are just random products of nature, or maybe they are even demonically empowered somehow. Here on a planet obviously created for the residence of people, similar to Earth, it is something of a puzzle to me why stellar flares are included as part of the picture. Anj has a theory, from the Bible, that trials give us an opportunity to trust in God no matter what the circumstances. He is unchanged. So, since the flares are part of God's creation here, really an act of God, they are designed to increase our faith. I can't argue with that. To the Similia, the 'act of God' they see is that He protects them from harm as they trust Him.

"We know the love of Omeda newly every morning. We see Him in the sunrise, in the soft rain from the night before, in the life that springs up all around us as we wake to find one another and Omeda full of joy. We have been here for over a year-and-a-half now and it keeps getting more enthralling. Perhaps because of my background, I find myself so thankful every day for the life I have here, and I am never tempted to think about going back. I sometimes find it hard to believe that I used to live and thrive in a culture in which the presence of God is indistinct, where there is confusion about who He is, where I was surrounded by thick fog regarding who I am, and where there is pervasive lack, terror, greed, and avarice.

"As entrancing as the story of redemption through Christ is, how much more may we be spellbound with the idea of never having needed to be redeemed because an entire people have maintained a holy relationship with Omeda for two-hundred generations. On Earth, there is merit given to those who do the hard work necessary to maintain a holy relationship with God. Here, that work is also recognized, but the starting place is so different. On Earth, seeking holiness is started from a place of extreme need and brokenness, requiring great repentance, surrender, sacrifice, and an arduous journey of healing. There are rewards for those who seek Him which are handed out in joy by the Father Himself.

"Here, one begins to seek holiness from a place of rest; nothing is broken; nothing needs to be forgiven. It is not hard work here to spend time with Omeda. From rest, we go deeper into His rest. Grace is still grace. In our new language, it is 'mesonna.' One does not earn or achieve the phenomenon of becoming more holy like Him, it is by grace, or 'mesonna,' but it still must be sought after diligently.

"The long-range plan, even here, is that humankind will be able to live to the glory of Omeda in a dimension more spectacular than the stars. The heavens tell of the glory of God and their expanse declares the work of His hands, but, by comparison, what we will do emanates out of union with His very character. There will be a day, the writings of the seers say, when all things will be made new and this age will come to an end. All of creation will be transported into unimaginable heights at that time, and glorifying Him will be our on-going role. Giving glory to God is eternally our response because He is worthy.

"We don't talk about Him like He is not in the room. He has opened our eyes to His reality. He is why we are alive. I have concluded that human independence does not come from the fall. I believe we are created with it. It is part of the likeness of God in which we are made, and a facet of life that we value highly. That is why it is such a powerful factor when one relinquishes independence and chooses radical dependence on Omeda for everything. Only then may we live in true independence. I am always aware that I have a choice about how much I want to seek Him today. Whether I depend on Him for everything or not, He is always good; He will bless life with provision, protection, love, and acceptance. That is just the way He is, but moving deeper into connection with Him, that's the progress into holiness, the richness, the fun; that is where the 'action' is.

"How terribly bent I was on Earth, born fallen. My constant struggle on Earth was against the grip of sin, and my devotion to God was an uphill battle against continual distractions from the world, my appetites, and the accuser. By faith in Jesus, I knew my body of sin was dead, and I was resurrected to new life in freedom, which gave me great joy. But the accuser would bring up fears that my old life would come roaring back. My walk of faith required constant intentional reminders to myself of the superior reality of God.

"Here, slothfulness, inattention, and ignorance could still keep me from moving into the very best and most powerful realms of what Omeda is, but whenever I even just crack open the door to the spiritual realm a little bit, bright light streams in. Omeda is right there, attractive, and I am attuned with Him. We are able to boldly approach His indescribable light. His immediate availability is probably the most readily apparent fact of life here.

"Sin nature is not present, not in the people around us and not in us, Anj and me. Each person's spirit is alive, and righteousness comes without a law requiring it. Love is truly unconditional. Joy is a normal core value and strength. Peace surrounds. Hope abounds. Faith is still faith, but it stands without the constant challenges from the world, the flesh, and the oppressing enemy. Faith is still the currency, the flow of relationship with the invisible One who is still mysterious. Vision and hope for the future are not behind a foggy veil, but clear from God. He is a rewarder of faith. That is how big His love is for the people of ΔT, the lovely Similia, my friends, my new family.

"I spend time every day, on my own, apart from our collective times of worship and encouragement, intentionally opening myself to the presence of Omeda, right here, closer than my own heart. There is no condemnation, not even the slightest vestige of it. I am only aware that it is missing because it was so ever-present in my Earthly existence. Since coming here, it has vanished, by the grace of Omeda God. People here have never experienced condemnation. They only know His encouragement and the unchanging promise of the spirit of life in Omeda.

"I get enthusiastic when I begin telling about life here. It is so good. I trust I have been able to communicate something helpful to somebody.

"I love you all, more next week. Over and out, March."

C.S. finished reading March's report and looked to Browning. He was slumped in his big desk chair, a common posture for him when he was deep in thought. Cooper gave him some more time while he skimmed over the report again. They had stayed late, counting on getting the weekly report from the Proxima Colony. It was past ten PM.

Finally, Browning said, "Cooper..." still slouched in his chair. There was a long pause; then he shifted in his chair, not straightening up, his hands folded together in front of his chin. "Cooper, March is living a very different life there than he did here, according to his reports. Yet he seemed so happy here. I really can't grasp what it is that has made such a difference for him.

"Well it's all about God there," Cooper tried.

"Clearly. But what difference does an imaginary relationship with an invisible being make for a man like March who has so much going for him as a scientist-pilot and space-explorer? He is not delusional. I just don't get it."

Cooper was interested that Browning was opening these questions to him alone. Nobody else was around, so obviously

Browning wanted to pose this specifically to him. "You are asking me, one who also has an imaginary relationship with that invisible being, so I am assuming you want to know more about that perspective." He looked to Browning for comment.

Browning opened his hands as if he expected C.S. to hand him a cantaloupe, and waited patiently.

"Allow me to start with the obvious," Cooper began. "To those of us who believe, God being invisible is not a problem because He is not imaginary. We have experiences with Him. Different experiences than most in the world. Experiences that are mostly intangible to the five senses.

"As scientists, we like our experiences to be quantifiable, based on what we saw or heard or physically felt, weighed, or measured. As a believer, there is no instrument that will give me a number about God's love, or how near He is, or how good He is, except by faith. Faith is my only instrument of measure in relating to the invisible God. Faith informs me about what just happened, what I am to do, how I am to be, and what God thinks about it all.

"Look at it this way, Frank; you have your pilot's license, and I know you are qualified to fly by instruments."

Frank nodded, looking expectant.

"Flying by instruments is something like living by faith the way March and Anj are. You can't see the ground, you can't even see the sky, and your body will lie to you that you are dropping or rolling. But you, one who is used to relying on your body messages, must trust in what the instruments are telling you. March and Anj aren't concerned that it looks like they have lost their professional or career status. They know they are flying by faith, the most intriguing path ever navigated by an Earthling. Nothing will distract them from following the flight plan they have been given."

Frank was serious as he proposed, "Maybe I don't have any faith instruments. There is silence in my headphones, no faith-attitude indication on any screen, never a blip on faith radar."

Coop ventured to press in further, "You *do* have that instrument. It is put there in all of us, but like a radio, you have to be tuned to the right frequency, or the messages just flow right past you invisibly without being heard or recognized."

"So what is the frequency?" the scientist wanted to know. "Give me a number." He knew he was being facetious, but he was still serious about getting an answer.

Coop replied, "Maybe you just haven't ever turned it on." He waited for a moment while Frank stared at his folded hands again. "There was a person in history who turned it on simply by saying, 'Speak, God, I am listening.' Up to that point, this young man had been hearing things, but he had misunderstood it to be something else. When he began to listen for God, believing it was God who was speaking, he got the download. That is the frequency: believe it is God who is speaking, the One who talks to March and Anj. He will speak to you too."

Frank asked, "This young man you are telling me about believed there was a God, but he had never gotten a reading on his faith instrument?"

"Up until then, he did not have any experience of God. That was his first."

Frank said, "Coop, I have been hearing about God for decades and I see people, especially March and Anj, making critical decisions based on their experiences of Him. If I ask Him to speak to me just because I have heard about Him from them, do you think He would honor that with a reply?"

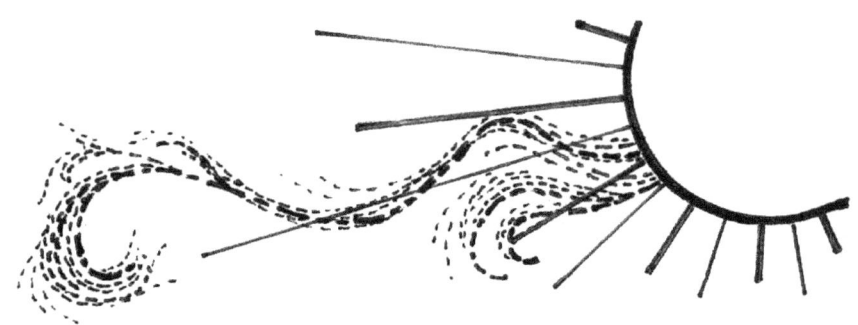

Chapter Thirty-Two

Anj was fascinated with the idea of seeing a supernova in their lifetime. She could not help but wonder if it was some kind of favorable sign about her babies. Four nights after March had first noticed it, when the constellation was again in the night sky, she, March and Lalo went out in the dark after dinner to have a look.

Pointing, Lalo practically shouted, "Look Mach, it is already much bigger!"

"No doubt about it," March agreed. "It looks like your future children will not be able to see this after all, because it is progressing much faster than I thought it would. It will be long over before they are ever born. In fact, our children probably will not see it either, unless it lasts an unusually long time. One of the biggest supernovae of the past was called Kepler's supernova about six lifetimes ago. When it got bright, everyone on our planet could see it, even in the daylight. It was visible to the naked eye for a very long time, and then it disappeared altogether."

Lalo asked, "How do I record this? What should I write down about it?"

March said, "Let's get a piece of paper when we go inside, and I will help you begin a daily log of what you see."

Lalo was thrilled to be doing a special project with March. "Mach, shall we tell everyone?"

"When we go in, we can tell Makkana, and let him decide when and how to tell the village about it." March knew it would not panic the people. Similia do not panic with fear, but the unknown does put a feeling into the stomach, as Lalo had spoken of earlier, and Makkana would have the wisdom to be able to help everyone understand that there was no danger. This was not like a flare in any way, but changes in the heavens can be unnerving because the stars are supposed to be constant unchanging facts of life.

Inside the grotto, when they told Makkana, he was most interested in this news. He said that unwritten stories had been passed through the generations about such things. March thought he had probably heard stories from long ago about the Kepler, even though it had been many lifetimes ago since it was so huge. Makkana slipped outside with Lalo to have a look for himself and he returned with questions for March about what to expect and when and how long. He said he would consult with the other elders about it and seek Omeda's wisdom before making any general announcement. He was thankful to have the information that March was able to offer.

Anj had begun to observe that certain people in Lendkon were called to become leaders, like Makkana, who loved everyone generously and inspired everyone around him to love Omeda even more fully. In turn, those he touched became more generous in every way to everyone around them. Makkana was loved for the way he led the community. Anj could see March becoming more like him all the time. He was being set free in ways he didn't even know he was bound up. This supernova thing was a great opportunity for March to work alongside Makkana in contributing something to the community.

As they talked back in their home about what a good opportunity this was for him, March said, "Life on ΔT is very meaningful to the Similia. Every activity and every job is viewed as essential for the prosperity of each individual life and for the corporate life of the community. Everyone feels significant by giving to the rest of us. I think that is part of the image of God in us: that we tend to find meaning and significance in our lives when we invest time and material in others' lives. Whenever we spend time serving another human being, we feel good about it, even if it is difficult, or costly. We feel good about it because our Maker gets great joy from being good to us. That character trait of His is reflected in our character. So, yeah, I am feeling good about being able to spend time with Lalo helping him write his report on the Betelgeuse supernova, and I feel good about being able to contribute some of my knowledge for the community's good."

Anj agreed, "Working in the orchard now is a place where I feel good about being able to contribute to the community. Sometimes I see something on the table at mealtime and wonder if I picked that one, but I do know that I picked a bunch like it yesterday, and everyone gets to eat what I picked. I get a simple, deep joy out of that."

She continued, "Just yesterday, some kitchen people gave Maela and I some food and fruit juice to take far back in the village to where new rooms are being carved out of the stone. I had never seen this work before, the continual expansion of the community. In Earth's setting, this would be considered brutally monotonous work. The cave cutters work completely in the dark except for lamp-light, with all the dust and the heavy labor. But even this job is carried out with the same laughter and twinkling eyes as the more obviously enjoyable work of harvesting or food preparation. Those guys back there were happy because they are recognized and valued. Each person is accomplishing with his or her own hands that which is good for everyone and is appreciated. We had a fun time blessing those men with their lunch."

March put his hand gently on Anj's tummy where new babies were being secretly woven by the skillful hand of Omeda God. "It is unbelievable that we get to bring up our children in this amazing society. I have friends on Earth who have told me they do not want to ever have children because they do not want to face the unfathomable difficulties of bringing up healthy human beings in the world with all of its ugliness. I don't think that would have stopped me if we had stayed on Earth, because I trust God, and who is going to bring wonderful new people into the world if not us? But by the leading of God, we were able to come here to this place to have our family. I wonder how our brood will look two stations of the Twin Stars from now."

"Twenty-year-old twins by then," she reflected. "I am concerned about how we shall teach them. Will they be bilingual? And will we teach them the Bible so that they can understand the world from which their parents came? If we do, they will find out there is such a thing as hatred and murder, idolatry and rebellion, coveting and stealing. None of their little Similia friends will know anything about those things."

March took both of her hands in his, "Omeda will guide us because He alone knows the purposes for which he has brought us here. We know He has a plan. I can't escape the occasional thought about the possibility that someday one of us might return to Earth, and if it is our children, it would be essential for them to understand that it is a fallen world, what that means, and the incredible sacrifice God has made to restore the possibility of love with His children."

She let the thought of her children someday traveling to Earth pass before her mind's eye. "What a stark contrast that would pose. A holy, innocent, undefiled person gets inserted into a place where the god of the world is the devil."

March went on, "The thought that I had was that one of our children might be called to visit Earth; that it might be part of Omeda's design from the beginning. It was out of the blue, and I am not confident it was prophetic, but it may have been. Either way, it is a real possibility if the capability is developed in future Proxima missions for a return journey to Earth."

She was silent for a while. "You are reminding me that we have been introduced into a plan much bigger than us, something that Omeda God put together long before we were born."

March agreed, quoting, "In Your books were all written the days that were ordained for me before there was yet one of them. How precious are Your thoughts to me, how vast is the sum of them. If I should count them they would outnumber the sand. When I awake, I am still with You."

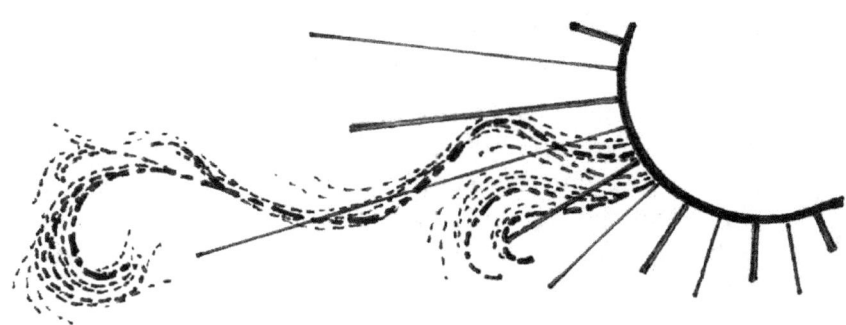

Chapter Thirty-Three

Betelgeuse was putting on quite a show. It had been four weeks on Anj's calendar since Lalo and March first began to log the phenomenon in the night sky. Every fourth or fifth evening, when the constellation was visible, quite a crowd would gather outside in the dark after the communal sunset worship. The supernova had expanded to become an irregular orange ball, still small enough to cover with the tip of a little finger, and not quite bright enough to be seen in the daytime unless March pointed it out. He always knew exactly where to look if it was in the sky, and with his help, Lalo and others could see it faintly, even in broad daylight. On the observation nights, it appeared different each time as the expanding gasses from the star's core moved at astronomical speeds.

Nothing like it had been seen by anyone alive at the time. Lalo's diligence to his self-appointed task was exemplary. On this particular evening, he was drawing pictures and even used Anj's calendar of weeks and months to create an accurate timeline of the event. Makkana assured him that his record would be kept in the library room with the writings of old when he completed his work. Betelgeuse would be remembered in history, long after it had disappeared.

Makkana spoke further to Lalo about his project, saying, "Lalo, you know that Omeda is eternal, and now you are seeing that the stars are not. They exist for a finite length of time. What do you think Lalo, are we Similia eternal?"

Lalo put down his drawing and stood up. He loved this kind of question, especially from his elders, because he knew it was going to give him more understanding of Omeda. He was not worried about whether he would get the answer right, so he ventured, "I know that Osoto Ban Talia Da is our experience of eternity. I know that our time here in this world is only for a lifetime, but that we learn, while we are here, how to live for eternity, for eternally experiencing the Presence of Omeda. But Makkana, I don't think we are eternal, because only Omeda is eternal."

The Elder enjoyed these talks as much as Lalo did because he was gifted at helping people to understand Omeda, to draw closer to Him, and to become, step by step, more like Him. "Ah-ha," he burst out, "Lalo you have been listening closely! Yes, eternity starts for us when we are born, but God is truly eternal because He never began; He has always been, hence His name, 'Being Everlasting.' This life prepares us for eternity. Our behaviors here adjust the more we come to understand eternity. It is not about time going on forever; it is about Omeda's eternity, His magnificence, His limitless revelation of Himself as present for us. In this life, we begin to see that He loves us out of His eternal heart; the largeness of that place is our project to learn for eternity. His beauty comes out of an eternal depth of creativity, only a taste of which we get to experience here, but what we do see is so inviting. And His holiness…" Here the Elder paused in a rare moment when he was at a loss for words, "His holiness, we only get glimpses of here, but they are so astounding that they propel me to draw continually closer to Him who personifies that eternal holiness."

Lalo stood there grinning like he was being handed an ice-cream-cone. "Thank you, Makkana; I am encouraged by your words to learn more of eternity. The length and width and height and depth of Omeda are eternal, but we are called to enter in. We must be prepared to enter into eternity."

As Makkana walked on to visit with other stargazers, Lalo sat back down with his lamp nearby to resume his drawing. Anj walked over to see what Lalo was drawing, and as she did so, she felt the unmistakable symptoms in her body, that these babies were making a bid to be born. She had been well taught by the midwives of Lendkon what to watch for, and she thought, "This is it." She left off her interest in Lalo's drawing, went straight to March to let him know, and then to her head-midwife.

Birthing babies is a family event in Lendkon, so March, Saala, and Maela were there in their room, as well as the two midwives. March had been coached as to what his role was, as a primary participant in this event, which mostly involved holding her hand and encouraging her through the experience. She was not in the pain typical of childbirth on Earth, but it was indeed a lot of work, requiring patience and coaching from the midwives.

March was watching closely as the first baby emerged. Since he was quite unfamiliar with infants, it seemed to be an unbelievably tiny person, a girl! His heart leaped. He had always believed that it takes a special man to raise a daughter, and he felt privileged to be entrusted with her. After the umbilical was tied off and cut, the midwife's assistant bathed her with a gentle deftness impressive to March. She dried the baby and handed her naked to him, helping him place her under his shirt, next to his heart, against his skin.

Holding her close with both of his big hands, he was gently flooded with multiple impressions which he knew were from Omeda: a welcome softening of his heart, a marked increase of his dedication to patience, an improved ability to listen and comprehend, and an overall willingness for his life to be spent for her well-being. And it all felt like blessing, not requirement. He knew at that moment that he would indeed be a good and wise daddy for her. He knew immediately that he could love her more than he even loved Lalo. Confidence and assurance filled him. He wanted to treasure these minutes in his heart. He leaned over close to Anj, so she too could look closely at her little girl.

Not long after, with a good deal more work from Anj, as Saala had predicted, the second baby began to appear, head first, and it was another girl! March's eyes overflowed with emotion. This was all so good. The second bathed and dried off infant was put against Anj's heart. As she held the baby close there, she and March exchanged a look that agreed, "We really are in this together." Something crystallized between them, the new Mom and Dad.

Twins are a lot of work, they discovered, every hour of the day. Suddenly the schedule that had been working so well for almost two years was null and void, and the feeding, changing, and cuddling needs of two new human beings in the family took over. Omeda's hand of grace was on the whole operation for them, and it went smoothly day by day. Community involvement helped tremendously, especially in the early days. People brought food, held a baby for a while to give the parents a break, and delivered messages. Lalo kept March up to date on the supernova, and he was able to break away and observe it briefly four nights after the girls were born.

'Nova' seemed an appropriate name for the oldest baby girl, born while the greatest astronomical event for centuries was taking place. The girls were not identical twins, and the second-born was named 'Ienna,' the Similia word for 'new,' so both girls had names that meant 'new' in vastly different languages, Latin and Similia. It seemed good that the twins had the same name because of the legendary inseparable relationship between such siblings.

March sent regular reports to Earth, announcing the birth, and weekly informing his audience, whether they liked it or not, about all the baby news. Carla had become more diligent to be present for the live arrival of reports from the pioneers as the birth of the twins had drawn near. One afternoon, she was all smiles, identifying with her surrogate family trillions of miles away, and excited for them to be finding so much richness in being a family, growing together. March and Anj had sent pictures of the twins which Carla had printed out, framed, and she was hanging them on the wall behind her desk.

Cooper teased her, "It sounds like your grand-daughters are doing well."

"I do have some Earthling grand-daughters, a little older, but Nova and Ienna are in a world of their own, so to speak," she chuckled at her own joke. "I have always felt very close to Anj. As they have undertaken this ordeal of travel to Proxima, and I have had a hand in helping them survive, yeah, it is like she's a daughter of mine, the daughter I never had. God blessed me with three sons." She stared at the two grainy pictures of the two babies as she tried to feel how being a Mom on ΔT would feel.

As the girls began to grow and flourish, and the months slipped by, the two-year mark of March and Anj's residence on ΔT was noted on Anj's calendar. Being a family was settling in on them comfortably, distancing them from the long-held identity of being a radically unique pair of individuals, astronauts and pioneers in outer space. All of that was becoming a distant memory, still distinct, but overshadowed by the new and powerful realities of being a real family, which was only something they could have imagined in their former existence.

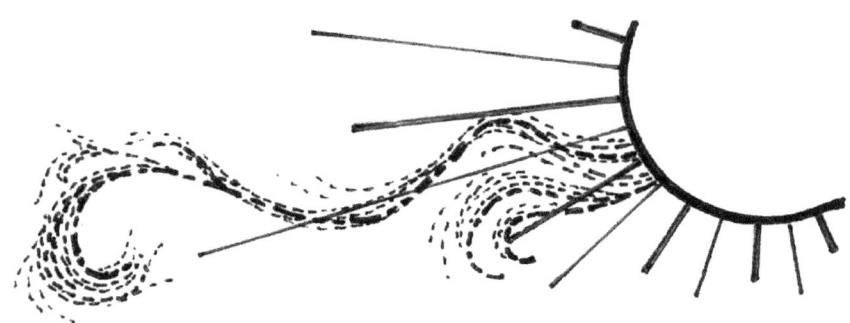

Chapter Thirty-Four: Launch Central

"Greetings Team, once again, March, of course, reporting to the home planet. At the risk of being a proud daddy, again, allow me to tell you the latest news on the girls. They are a little over two months old now and they have become grinners. The slightest stimulation will set one or both of them off and there are smiles! There is nothing like a baby's smile. It seems to come up from the very depths of their tiny beings, the most genuine, free expression of delight in the world.

"Okay, I will leave off there about my wonderful children. As you are well aware by now the supernova of the millennia is taking place. What a show for an astronomer! It is a show for all of our people here. There is a general interest in what is going on in the heavens because of this event. We meet out in the dark each night that it is visible, and stand in awe of what is taking place out there. The last thing I read about it did not state whether there were any habitable planets around Betelgeuse. This is very bad news for them if there are; which is a thought I never would have taken seriously until we came here. Having found out that God is in the business of populating other places in the universe with people, I got concerned that there might be planets within the influence of this supernova, but then I have to trust that God would not populate a planet only to see it get destroyed. I don't see that kind of careless sort of character in the way He relates to His creation.

"Returning our attention to our lives here on the planet Deep ΔT, here we are, and we are becoming a real family. This is far and away the most dramatic change of our lives, even greater than changing worlds was. We are becoming quite different people through this experience. I feel more human and more fulfilled in life than I ever have before. I have had what most people would call spectacular success in career and adventure. Nevertheless, our new reality with Nova and Ienna outstrips all of that with amazing discoveries every day about what God Omeda has given us, not only in this amazing community but also in the simple created beauty of what happens in a family.

"It helps me understand who I am, and you might be interested to know, it helps me understand the family-like structure of Lendkon, which is part of why it works so well. There are fathers in the community, like Makkana, and they are the ones who hold everything together by generating love among the rest of us. We stay in harmony primarily because we genuinely love one another under the love of our fathers for all of us. The mothers among the community, like Saala, are care-givers in the way that they give care deeply for everyone. They enrich and edify and make it fun. There is a lot of celebration here. Anything is an excuse for a celebration. Nova and Ienna's first smiles a week ago were great occasion for a song and lots of laughter for us and our friends.

"So that is life on this planet. If I go on longer, I fear that I will get repetitive, and I think you already got the message about how happy we are in our little family, in our bigger family. As I speak to you today, I am still well aware that our first messages to you are only halfway to Earth, and six years will have elapsed since our landing before you find out that we have succeeded in starting a little family of Earthlings here. At the time you are reading this, however, CSE will be making the crucial decisions about Proxima Two: whether there will be another mission sent here.

"I send our genuine love to you, and pray for you to have wisdom in all the plans for future Proxima missions, should that plan go forward. I have a theory that prayer is not limited to travel at the speed of light, but that when we pray for you, you *immediately* receive the benefit from our prayers because they go through the mind of God, not subject to the limitations of physics. I can only hazard a guess as to what the news of finding a human population here has done to the general thinking of CSE. When our girls are about six years old, we hopefully will begin to hear from you, your initial thoughts. Know that we are well, and we trust God in all things.

"All grace to you, my friends, March"

Browning laid his print of March's latest report on the table carefully before him and calmly looked around the conference table at the rest of the CSE board that was gathered for the quarterly meeting. Craning his neck forward to make sure he saw everyone on his side of the table, clear down at both ends, and counting, he saw that only one member was missing, the leading representative from India, and he had already heard from her, apologizing for missing this important meeting, but her assistant was present, and Browning gave him a nod. A copy of March's new report had been given to each representative as they entered since it was only hours since it had been received in Launch Central. Browning saw that several had taken the few minutes before the meeting to read it.

Browning himself was not the American rep. but was there as the link to Launch Central, the branch of the operation where the decisions that were made at this table were translated into training regimens that would ultimately launch another set of Earth's ambassadors out to the new planet. His branch also defined the limits of capability inherent in the ship and its systems. This group around the table tended to be dreamers. Even though they were mostly professionals in the fields related to space and its exploration, there was a definite leaning towards fantasy among these representatives, along with the populations of the nations they represented. Ideas were proposed sometimes to which Browning had to say, "At this point in the development of our technology, that is not possible."

At which time, they would invariably ask, "How long before we will be able to do that?"

Each nation that was represented had already begun, years ago, to train its team of astronauts, hoping that some of them at least, would be chosen for the proposed Proxima Two. The final selection would be made, first, based on capability and skill, but also with the intention to have a very international team. Furthermore, in keeping with the general vision of interplanetary colonization, sending couples was essential, since establishing a permanent population base was the priority. Four astronauts would be able to go this time, carrying a much more specific set of equipment, since they had good information about what kind of habitat they would be encountering.

He was glad to have Cooper Smith and Carla Peretti at his left, not usually a part of these meetings, but he had gained permission to include them in this discussion about the disposition of Proxima Two, which was almost certainly going to launch within the year. Browning had recruited Cooper and Carla to help him accurately represent March and Anj's views, and to explain the 'God factor' behind the choices that the original astronauts had made in relating to the indigenous population. As he saw it, in this meeting, the deck was heavily stacked against the thinking that March and Anj would have put forward if they had been present. Although he was in basic agreement with them, he knew that he would not be able to present the faith-based rationale for the way of life the pioneers had chosen on ΔT. He also knew that Cooper and Carla could paint a better picture of the Similia people existing on the planet, and the central importance of their worship.

CSE's chairman of the board for the last year-and-a-half had been Michail Vasiliev, the Russian lead representative, seated opposite to Frank Browning, in the center of the other side of the long conference table. He was not granted any power greater than the others by the charter, but, by the force of his personality, he had been wielding a fair amount of influence. Browning knew it would be an uphill battle to inform some of the other members about the validity of what March and Anj were advocating.

After opening remarks and attendance had been taken and the minutes read, Vasiliev launched directly into his perspective on what was to be the focus of this meeting. "Since our American astronauts have scuttled the original plan to establish a viable Earth Base on the new planet, we are to consider today what the goals of Proxima Two should be, in a second attempt to follow the vision of CSE for space exploration and colonization. We have in hand, as you all know, reports from our target planet for the first two years of their residence there. Our couple has found a surprisingly hospitable climate and an environment in which it is easy to grow crops and make a living. There seems to be every possibility that an alternate Earth Base could be established, even if the original American couple chooses to exclusively partner with the indigenous people. It is a huge planet and largely unpopulated; there is adequate room for a future Earth Base to co-exist with the Natives."

His bulldozer-like style of opening the meeting left most of the other participants momentarily without anything to say. It was quite clear that he would prefer that there be no further discussion so that he could launch directly into pushing for what shape he thought the new base should take.

Browning characteristically was the first to begin to grapple with Vasiliev's directive style. "Mr. Chairman, you seem to be disregarding a few key factors that need to be taken into consideration as we discuss the goals and direction that will be taken by the crew of Proxima Two, the next of earth's people to inhabit the planet Deep ΔT. Allow me to put them on the table for all of us to consider and discuss.

"Number one: stellar flares are not uncommon on the planet, and that one factor puts crops uniquely at risk. The only reported protection against these firestorms, according to our astronauts, is the prayers of the indigenous people, as you may have read in their reports. When they pray, their food crops are protected.

There were murmurs and some nervous titters around the table.

"Number two," Browning continued unhindered, "is the extreme heat and cold differentials for which the planet is named. Any colony to be established on that planet outside of the caves in which the Natives live will be severely dependent upon a major energy source for heating and cooling lest the environment should become insufferable for the immigrants from Earth. For the long term, that will be a problem that the personnel of Proxima Two will have to solve since the cold fusion unit they will take with them has a finite lifetime."

These well-thought-out reminders of the realities that colonists would face were creating a more somber mood among the gathered delegates, all of whom were scientific types on whom Browning's numbered contributions to the discussion were not lost.

"Number three, and probably the most difficult for us to consider, is that the Natives worship God there, and that one factor, that spiritual element of the environment, has a distinct influence on all of life for them. They have an exemplary lifestyle, a culture that is free from murder or even hatred, free from thievery or deceit, honest and loving in every respect. Our pioneers were so struck by these unique people that they abandoned every thought of forming an independent colony and resolved to learn from this tribe and live in harmony with them. Our reports from the two years so far offer no indication that our pioneers are wavering in any way from that decision. They have found that the ΔT people have effectively provided answers to factors One and Two that I have mentioned.

"What has been found existent on ΔT has been so far outside of any of the possibilities that any of us had anticipated, that it presents quite a mystery to a scientifically-based consideration of future involvement there. On the table today are significant sociological factors, and even more surprisingly, spiritual factors, besides the basic raw concerns about survival."

Vasiliev noisily placed his hands palm-down on top of the papers in front of him and leaned forward, his mouth open, ready to interrupt the direction that Frank Browning was taking, but Frank lifted one index finger up from the table, wordlessly saying, "Wait a minute please, I have more to say."

Frank, as an African American, was used to making sure he was not disregarded out-of-hand by those who would categorize him by race as less-than. He had everyone's attention with that single index finger held up. He continued, as the finger slowly relaxed back to the table, "The sociological concern lies in that the Natives are, on one hand, very primitive. They have no iron tools, not even the invention of the wheel, but on the other hand, they are more civilized than we are. They live in uninterrupted community harmony and peace. There is no history of war anywhere on the planet, and a lot of love is characteristic of the entire community. Within that, our pioneers have studiously avoided introducing sophisticated tools and technology, believing that no advantage would be gained to a society that is in so many ways far superior to anything on Earth.

"March and Anj were probably the perfect couple to have been planted there, since they easily came to understand the deeply spiritual society existing there, and, in fact, seem to have been adopted into it wholeheartedly. They recognized that their adoptive family possessed something far more important than iron tools or anything else that Earthlings would be tempted to offer. Sadly, we do not have March and Anj here to elaborate on their perspective, but it appears that they are opposed to the introduction of a secular colony into this deeply worshipful place and its people."

Vasiliev had leaned back into his chair with his arms folded across his chest, resigned to wait this out, his face unsuccessfully masking his irritation.

Frank continued, "I have asked two of my colleagues, Cooper Smith, and Carla Peretti to present to this esteemed body their thoughts about March and Anj's perspective. The view of our pioneers is a unique perspective, and it is so important to them that it has drawn them, two very loyal and intelligent scientist-astronauts, to abruptly and completely abandon the agreed-upon colonization strategy with which they landed on the soil of ΔT."

Frank turned to his left and introduced his trusted friend, "This is Carla Peretti, the personal trainer and psychological coach who works with all of our astronauts, preparing them to be able to adjust to the conditions they will be facing, both in flight and upon arrival. Carla, I look forward to your contribution to this discussion. Please," and he gestured to her to proceed.

Carla was not intimidated by 'big people,' since she held a PhD, and had decades of experience in physiology, psychology, and theology. She had a prepared statement and decided to stick fairly close to it considering the way Vasiliev had tried to ramrod the meeting and avoid hearing exactly what she wanted to present. "March and Anj are my friends. I know them very well. One thing we share is our faith in God, so I understand much of why they are so enthralled with the spiritual climate on ΔT. What they have found there is both the dream of every believer and the dream of God. Believers on Earth long to have an open line of communication with their Heavenly Father, and our colonists have found that dream in their new home. They report a completely clear relationship with God: no static on the line, no interference from the opinions of men, and no crushing or defeating messages from the liar, every believer's accuser, who is the devil.

"ΔT is also the dream of God, which may be a strange idea to you. What I mean is that, in creating mankind, He had marvelous intentions, a dream, to have an immeasurably wonderful loving relationship with us, so good that it is inconceivable from our present position. And on the planet where March and Anj live, God's intentions are fulfilled. He has an entire people there who love Him and recognize His spectacular generosity, trusting Him for everything, even protection from stellar flares as Frank has already mentioned. That depth of trust and love in relationship was His intention in creating mankind, both here and on ΔT. Here, things have gone terribly wrong, but there, God and man are united, of one mind, and one Spirit.

Allow me to draw upon a simple metaphor. Think of a perfect marriage. Few of us have anything very close to such a thing, but we have an idea of how that would be, and we wish it could be so. When we do see a couple who has a very good marriage, we wonder how they accomplished it. God has accomplished it on ΔT. It is portrayed in the Bible that God considers His people His bride. On ΔT, He relates to His people as a husband to his perfect bride, completely taken by her beauty, and committed to her well-being. He will do anything for her. And she, in turn, is thankful for such a One to be there for her no matter what, and she is faithful to Him.

"Maybe you have to be a believer to be able to relate to March and Anj's experience, but I think it is obvious that they have been magnetically drawn into this perfection of love, and that they do not want to leave it or ever see it put at risk. I believe their hope is simply to protect these beautiful people, their new family, the Similia, from whatever contrary influence might be brought by an Earth-based, secular population of the planet. They are only worried about the well-being of their new and precious friends, who have become so special to them. Thank you for hearing me out on this issue, so out of the ordinary in the scope of things usually discussed at this table."

Vasiliev leaned forward again, ready to pounce, but Frank ignored him and smoothly turned to C.S. and said, "This is Cooper Smith who designed and engineered most of the hyper-sleep technology that makes travel to distant planets possible. Coop, can you give us your input on this concern?"

Cooper put his folded hands on the table and leaned forward to be able to see all of the faces now turned towards him. "Assembled delegates, thank you for your kind attention for a few minutes. Thank you, Carla, for your input, very helpful. So the question on the table seems to be, 'Why would our colonists not follow through with the establishment of a proper viable base on ΔT? And since they have chosen another way, how shall we design Proxima Two?'

"I too believe that God created the heavens and the Earth, including ΔT, and He populated at least these two planets with people, in the mystery of love and beauty that is His heart, which is beyond fathoming completely, but not beyond experience. March and Anj had experienced some of that love and beauty in their faith journey while they were here among us on Earth, and were always quite committed to pursuing an ever-nearer touch from God. We had many enthralling late-night conversations about the splendor and glory of God that we all sought diligently, and I, for one, admired their steadfast gaze towards God in all things. Given that understanding of their hearts, I am not at all surprised to hear that they have abandoned all that 'makes sense' in order to be sure to remain in the fullness of His Presence as they have found it to be among the Similia.

"Now, whether the Similia can endure the intrusion of an Earth-based culture as their neighbors, we really do not know do we? What Chairman Vasiliev has proposed sounds good at face value, but how does that look a hundred years from now? It seems incredibly risky to me, just given the history of advanced cultures moving in upon more primitive ones on our planet. The simpler peoples get destroyed, and I am definitely in agreement with Anj and March. I am not willing to put what the Similia are - they are a gem in the universe - at risk to any degree. The importance of our grandiose notions of populating other planets fades in comparison to the potential of what would happen if the influence were reversed. What I mean is that ΔT may well be of more importance to Earth than we are to them.

"What if the influence of ΔT towards Earth could be the restoration of the relationship of mankind to God as it was originally intended? What if our contact with ΔT could result in a significant reduction of man's corruption? What if violence, war, and treachery could be somehow removed among us because Earth's population learned from ΔT how truly good God is, and discovered the faith and love required to draw close to God? What if we could learn how to step into the same level of clarity with God that is seen among those simple people? How that would look, I have only the vaguest and most tantalizing idea, but it might be the reason that God, in the first place, allowed some of us, interestingly enough, some of His best representatives, to go to ΔT and make this discovery." Cooper paused as if he was going to continue, directed his eyes around to make personal contact with each individual at the table, imparting, if he could, a fresh understanding to each one, and ending with a particularly intense few seconds on Vasiliev. Then he nodded to Frank.

Frank was more than pleased with his friends' statements, and leaned back in his chair, holding one hand out, palm up to Vasiliev.

Typically, the meeting from that point devolved into a confusing assemblage of overlapping and unrelated opinions, just what Vasiliev wanted to avoid, with a conclusion to put it to a vote in a month, after each delegate was able to report back and hear from his or her constituents. The vote was to be simply between two schools of thought: one prioritizing the preservation of the existing culture on ΔT and the other prioritizing the advancement of human exploration in outer space through colonization, without regard to the Similia.

Frank and Carla and C.S. decided to go out to dinner together to a place Frank wanted them to try. As they slid into the upholstered orange vinyl covered booth, Frank asked, "What do you think? About the meeting, I mean."

C.S. first commented, "This is the place that has breaded catfish, isn't it?" with an eager smile.

Browning said, "Oh, you've been here before?"

"Yeah, we come here for a treat now and then. Angie likes it." Then he turned his attention to Frank's question, offering his perspective, "Okay, then, about the meeting; ultimately of course we do not know what it is God will do with this situation. It is beyond complicated. I think we made the very best showing we could today. I loved the way you presented all the stuff the chairman wanted to gloss over, Frank. And Carla, you made it so personal and understandable, I thought. I trust God to bring a glorious result out of it, whether it looks exactly the way we want it to or not."

Carla, always the optimist, also expressed her trust in God's ultimate ability to do good things even when mankind makes a royal mess of things. "I trust Him; I just trust Him," she concluded. "He is so mighty to do good. It is going to be good."

Frank was in an uncommonly positive place, it seemed, to the other two. "What are you thinking Frank?" C.S. asked, "You seem to be in a good mood, especially for having just spent two-and-a-half hours in a meeting like that one."

Frank leaned back in the padded restaurant booth and stretched his arms out to place one hand on the near shoulder of each of his friends on either side of him, and said, "I do feel good. I feel good about a decision I have come to." He looked at the ceiling for a moment, composing his thoughts. "Thank you for your patience with me for so many years. You have listened to my agnostic arguments and tried to explain God to me, and I expect you have been praying for me." He turned to each of them and looked into their eyes. He saw love there, as a new thing that he had not recognized quite this way before. "I have come to the place where I am willing to put my trust in God as you guys do. I believe He exists; He really *is*; and that He is up to something incredible in all of this, beyond my imagining. And we get to be a part of it. I just realized that as you two beautiful people were speaking in the meeting. What you both said, in combination with all that Anj and March have reported to us over the years, finally got me across the line. I finally turned on the radio, and I can hear the music. It is beautiful." At this point Frank paused to collect himself, his eyes glistening, tears about to spill over. "Even though I can't yet see all I want to see, I will trust, just like you both just said. I trust Him too."